AVALON REVAMPED

AVALON REVAMPED

by O. M. Grey

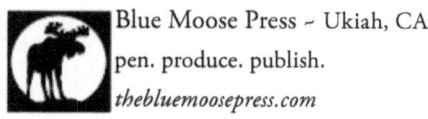
Blue Moose Press ~ Ukiah, CA
pen. produce. publish.
thebluemoosepress.com

ISBN-13: 978-1-936960-98-9
First Edition.

ATTENTION ORGANIZATIONS AND SCHOOLS:
Quantity discounts are available on bulk purchases of this book for educational purposes or fund raising.

For more information, go to
thebluemoosepress.com
omgrey.wordpress.com

Library of Congress Control Number: 2013951102
Grey, O. M., 1969 -
Avalon Revamped / by O. M. Grey
1. Steampunk Horror--Fiction. II. Title.
ISBN-13: 978-1-936960-98-9

Printed in the United States of America

for **Sean Ré**
whose light helped guide me
out of the darkness

Also by O. M. Grey

Avalon Revisited

The Zombies of Mesmer

Caught in the Cogs: An Eclectic Collection

The Ghosts of Southwark

...under the name Christine Rose:

Rowan of the Wood

Witch on the Water

Fire of the Fey

Power of the Zephyr

Spirit of the Otherworld

Publishing & Marketing Realities for the Emerging Author

AUTHOR'S NOTE

Trigger Warning: The following story contains depictions of sexualized and domestic violence, as well as other mature content.

When talking about this sequel to *Avalon Revisited*, I refer to it as a "sequel, of sorts." It does, indeed, pick up where *Avalon Revisited* left off; however, the tone and content of this novel is extremely different than that of its predecessor. This is what happens after the "happily ever after" of so many fairy tales once the princess discovers that Prince Charming is a sociopathic narcissist—his charm, just a part of a very convincing mask he shows the world. *Avalon Revamped* is a story of true horror, the kind so many women fall prey to, partially because sociopaths are continuously romanticized in fiction. Still, this story about vampires, succubi, and incubi, is also pure fantasy: unlike reality, the wicked herein receive true justice.

This book stands alone, so you needn't have read *Avalon Revisited* first (although I prefer you to read both). I've included some information from the first book that might prove helpful: Arthur Tudor has been a vampire for about 350 years and was the older brother of King Henry VIII of England. Arthur was born to be king and he married Catherine of Aragon first. After Arthur's early death, Catherine married Henry and became his queen. Arthur is extremely bitter about how Henry treated his beloved Catherine, tossing her aside for younger queen, so Arthur has spent the last few centuries in a debaucherous free-for-all: blood and sex, and then more blood. That's until he meets Avalon, who reminds him of Catherine. He puts Avalon on a pedestal and is determined to possess her. They solve a mystery together and fall in love, but Avalon's best friend, Victor, dies in the process. Avalon herself receives a fatal wound in the last fight, and the only way Arthur can save her is by turning her into a vampire.

I hope you enjoy it.

~Olivia

CHAPTER 1

CONSTANCE

I have been many women, played many parts. The demure virgin. The ignored wife. The experienced concubine. The lonely crone. So many others in between, and I continued to play these parts at my will.

My will.

Always, my will be done.

Forever and ever. Amen.

"Now that you've lured me back here, Lord Stanton. Whatever will you do with me?" I displayed my best look of innocent seduction, but I must not be too obvious or eager. It would give the game away too soon. After all, tonight I played Caroline, the demure virgin. This one liked virgins. Young and pure, so he could sully them, then discard them without a second thought.

Not tonight.

"Lured? Sweet girl, are you suggesting that I have devious intentions?" He scooted closer to me crowding me on the end of the Queen Anne sofa before he took my white-gloved hand and kissed the inside of my wrist. His blue eyes, intensely locked with mine, had shown such sincerity to so many, including me, seduced and deceived dozens, just in the last year alone.

Yes. I'd been watching.

I blushed and giggled. "Not at all, my lord. You wouldn't think of it, would you? After courting me for months, you've been a perfect gentleman."

To me, at least. All part of his act.

This was all part of mine. Tit, as it were, for tat.

"I intend to marry you, sweet Caroline, as you well know. Trust me, sweetheart. Never has there been a more beautiful and clever girl. How could I ever hurt such a gem? Never in my days has one touched my heart as you have. Yes, my dear, you are quite special."

"So there have been others? The rumors are true?" I snatched my hand back and turned away coldly.

Let the *seduction* begin.

Seduction. That word veiled so much violation. Coercion, more like. Some men liked to euphemize their mistreatment with pretty words like seduction. Nick was one of those men. Convincing a woman to do what she did not want to do, through words or force, didn't matter to men like Nick. To him, it was all "seduction."

Lord Nicholas Stanton had quite the reputation, as notorious as any I'd known in my long existence. Rich and privileged. They always thought they could do exactly what they wanted without repercussions or remorse or responsibility.

They were right. Under normal circumstances, they could.

I, however, was far from normal.

He was quiet for a long moment, and I began to think he felt I wasn't worth the effort. Perhaps one too many conquests in the past month had made him weary. Truly, after all these centuries, I should know better than to doubt the treachery and cruelty of man, not to mention the narcissistic entitlement of men like Nick.

I chanced a look back over my shoulder at him, and he still stared, blue eyes fixed on mine, full of tears. As one spilled over the rim and slid down his cheek, the one remaining spark of feminine humanity flickered deep within my heart. Something still inside me wanted to reach out to him, comfort him, trust him.

After all these centuries.

Women were built for compassion, but in a world full of predators, that compassion was too often our ruin. Of course, I had seen this show before. Many times. A grand performance, no doubt, and Lord Stanton was most certainly a skilled sod, more skilled than most. So convincing, indeed, that even I, in all my wisdom, wanted to believe him.

However, I did know better.

"What have you heard?" he started, tears falling. "It's Miss Daughety, isn't it? You've heard about Sarah Ann."

Among many others.

Upon seeing my nod of confirmation, he cried, "Oh God! Will this torment never end?"

Yes. He was the victim. Of course.

As I turned back to him, the sweet smell of his breath mixed with the feigned sadness made me rather faint, and I inwardly fought against my nature to nurture. This instinct helped my concerned aspect and my own performance, however. Young and so very handsome, along with his considerable skills of manipulation, he had the power to mesmerize his prey into submission.

Fortunately, my instinct to punish outweighed my instinct to coddle.

"Hush, Nicholas, it will be all right." I wiped the tears off of his cheeks, wetting my white gloves, so I took them off and cradled his duplicitous face in my hands as he continued to weep. "I'm here, my love. Please, talk to me. It will be all right. I'm here."

"We were to be married, Sarah Ann and I. That much is true, but the rest of the horrid rumors are not!" He sniffed loudly, pulling away from my embrace in mock shame. "She claims I ravished her, but I would never do such a thing. Not to any woman, but especially not her. Oh, I loved her. I loved her with all my heart, Caroline. We were intimate before the wedding, scandalous, indeed, but we were to be wed, after all. We did nothing wrong, for in our hearts, we were already one. We were so in love." He raised his sly eyes to me, seeking understanding and sympathy in my features, which he found.

I, too, was quite skilled at this particular ruse.

"Much like we are now, my love. My sweet Caroline. I didn't know it then, but I didn't know I could feel so vulnerable with a woman. I can be vulnerable with you, completely exposed."

A fresh tear fell between his lashes. The expression of transcendent love drained away into a distortion of confusion and pain as he continued with his story.

"Afterward, she changed. Somehow she went mad, or perhaps she was always mad and I was but blinded by love. I don't know anymore. All I do know is that Bedlam is her home now, and not a day goes by that I don't see her face and lament her fate. Lament our lost love. I bear her no ill will, despite what she and her family have said about me, sullying my reputation. For what else does a gentleman have but his reputation? Well," he continued with fresh sobs and new tears, "I had her and her love, but she is not the girl I loved. She's sick, poor thing. Poor, poor thing."

"It's all right, my dear. It'll be all right." I pulled his head to my breast and comforted him against my softness, where he continued to cry, but I felt the muscles in his face creep into a smile.

Yes. He was quite good.

"And since her, I have tried to love again. I have tried to move on, but"—sniff—"I just want her to be all right again. I have to go on or I will go mad myself. Do you understand? I had to love again, or it would've all been for naught. That I could not bear, dear Caroline. I'll never lie to you, sweetheart. There have been others with whom I tried to love, but no one has captured my heart since sweet Sarah Ann, except for you. You, my sweet Caroline. Now, I have you and your love, and it will be all right again, won't it?"

With those last words, he looked up at me, face once again properly morose, fresh tears gleaming in his bright blue eyes, wide with sincerity and vulnerability.

"You, sweetheart. You, my dear lady, my love." He brushed his thumb across my cheek, wiping my empathic tear away, and gazed into my eyes with such intensity it was as if he explored my very soul. After licking a drop from his lips, he pressed them against my own. I was about to speak, but he silenced my parted lips with one soft, tender kiss, gliding his bottom lip across mine as if he would pull back and let me go with sadness.

Then, aggression.

He pinned me against the back of the sofa and thrust his tongue inside my mouth. Probing. Poking. Prodding as I squirmed, trying to push him off, but he wouldn't relent.

Not so quite skilled after all. How terribly clumsy, and terribly stupid of him. The rumors were true. Not just exploitation, which was bad enough, but violence as well.

"Stop!" I cried, finally able to wrestle my mouth free. It was rather a challenge, feigning weakness with scarcely enough strength and determination to struggle free, when in actuality I could crush this lothario with a snap of my fingers.

"I'm so sorry." he pulled away and buried his head in his hands, weeping anew.

Back to the performance. This was getting pathetic.

"You're just so beautiful, and it feels so wonderful to be in love again. It's just, with the memory of poor Sarah Ann and her horrid fate, I know how important it is to seize the moment. To live for now. You look so lovely tonight, as always, my love, and we are to be married, after all. Perhaps you're right. We should wait until we are properly wed. I shan't wish anything unfortunate to happen to you, sweetheart. I couldn't bear it if you were to suffer like poor Sarah Ann."

"Yes, it is best," I said, standing with indignation. "I love you, too, dear Nicholas, and it distresses me to see you so, but I must protect my honor."

"But of course, you are a lady, through and through. How beastly of me to treat you thus. What you must think of me now. I must be contemptible in your eyes. What a dreadful thing to have done. Can you ever forgive me? No. Of course not. I'm not worthy to be your husband, after all."

"Nonsense, Nicholas. You're just distraught. I understand, but please, I should like to leave now, for propriety's sake. You understand, don't you? Please, Nicholas, don't feel rejected. I love you, and we shall still be married."

"I'll call my driver to take you home." Although he stood to pull the cord that would alert his driver, he kept his head bowed in shame, not looking at me. Yet, as he passed me, he brushed his arm against my breast, and I laid a sympathetic hand on his shoulder, which stopped him. He faced me again—those captivating eyes stunned me with a predatory stare.

"Just one kiss, sweet Caroline. Please, just one sweet kiss before you go. I couldn't bear if you left angry with me, for I meant no harm in it. Your beauty, sweetheart, I just got carried away, but I am once again in control of my urges. The past is the past, and you are my future, my love. My Caroline. I want everything with you to be perfect, for you are so perfect." He cradled my cheek with one hand, and I softened beneath his touch as a woman in love would do.

"I do love you, Nicholas."

"And I love you, Caroline. We will be married, and then we will be together and happy, sweetheart. I so feared I would never love again, but you have shown me what love is. It's madness! I've known you for such a short time, really, but you have captured my soul, sweet lady. It has never been this powerful for me, and look at me. Even with my unseemly blubbering tonight, you still love me. I am a lucky man, indeed! I feel as if I can be myself with you, truly myself. No pretense, just vulnerable and real. Thank you for that, my love. We shall be so happy together, won't we? May I kiss you, Caroline?"

"Yes, please."

While caressing my cheek, he touched his lips to mine with such tenderness, and I tasted the salt from his tears. As he pulled away, he caught his breath. A sharp intake, then a shudder throughout his body. "Oh, my love. The effect you have on me. The power of your kiss, just your simple, sweet kiss, sends a tingling through my entire being. Power, sweetheart, like that of a lightning bolt on a stormy night. You bring light and thrill into my broken soul. Only you, sweet Caroline." He breathed all those words into my mouth, for he hadn't moved but an inch away, his thumb swept a stray hair behind my ear while he spoke. "Thank you," he whispered, and then kissed me again. "Now, let's get you home."

He took me by the hand and started walking toward the door of his parlour, and I could see the golden cord to call his staff hanging next to it. "Although," he said, stopping, "it is rather scandalous for you to be in my home at such an hour, alone. I wouldn't want your reputation to be tarnished, my love. And I best not be alone tonight myself, not after reliving the heartbreak and disappointment of Miss Daughety. Yes, best not be alone."

"But," I started to protest. He hushed me with a single finger pushed against my lips.

So, here it was.

"My driver is quite the gossip, indeed. I've been meaning to replace him, and it is far too late for you to walk home alone. I fear for your safely. You can slip out at first light, and no one will be the wiser."

"You could accompany me."

"Not at this hour. What would people say? No, best stay out of sight. Besides, I just don't want to, and, well, I always get what I want." He stood between me and the door now with his hands on his hips, and he looked at me so coldly. Blank. Empty. Without affect or affection.

Nothing.

Those big blue eyes, full of such love and pain just moments ago, were now void, showing what truly crouched inside this beast. He sniffed, unlike that of his weeping performance, but rather a snuffle of derision. Of contempt. Of challenge. Daring me to try to argue or move past him.

"But…" I said again, knowing what was to follow. When the tears didn't work, he turned to violence. Knowing how terrified a virgin would be, even a lady of some experience would be at such a show of disregard for mercy. Knowing they couldn't do a thing to stop it. Knowing that fighting back would only make it worse. Knowing how many before he had treated thus. Yes, Miss Daughety, and so many others.

Lord Stanton was indeed a busy man.

"Shhhhh. You love me, don't you, Caroline? You wouldn't leave me alone tonight, would you? In such a state? We are to be married after all, sweetheart, and I do want you so. You can't just tease me and leave."

I backed up as he moved toward me. Back and back and back, until I hit the burgundy sofa and toppled onto it. My eyes were wide, full of fear, for it would be horrific. It always was, but it was part of the ritual, sadly. I would sacrifice myself again and again to be sure. Even though only one woman in over five centuries had been callous enough to lie, I would never again punish an innocent. Never again. For there were too many innocents hurt in this life, and I vowed to only punish the deserved. Since then, I'd perfected my procedure to ensure merit. Yes, only one in thousands of men, but it had been one too many for my conscience. There were far, far too few innocent, good men, so each one must be preserved.

This was my repeated sacrifice to that noble end.

He ripped open my gown, exposing my breasts, and I endured as he groped and grabbed and grappled. His mouth covered mine in angry, feverish slobbering, devouring my whimpers and screams.

And I endured.

He forced my legs apart, and I heard the thin cotton of my knickers rip before he clamped his hand over my mouth and had his violent way. Grunting and snorting and sweating.

And I endured.

Once finished, he shoved me aside, and I pulled my torn dress up, trying to cover myself.

Then, I wept.

I wished I could say it was part of my act, but it was indeed a devastating violation each time. A fresh trauma each time. Every assault, no matter how slight, strengthened my resolve. For even the slightest slight was too traumatizing, too horrible. Even when they used words to coerce or emotional blackmail to convince instead of physical force, it was too horrific. Each defilement, each exploitation, each instance of abuse reinforced my will and reminded me why I did this. Reminded me why I punished the guilty.

When I thought of the number of women he and men like him have destroyed, my heart burned in my chest, fueling my anger once again.

With the anger came the strength.

With the strength came the smooth satisfaction that I would be the last woman the miscreant would ever treat thus. I was far from the first, but I would indeed be the last.

"Well," he said, smoothing his hair back and buttoning his trousers. "About the wedding, Caroline." Another arrogant snuffle. "I'm afraid I couldn't bring myself to marry a tarnished woman. After all, I am a Stanton. You won't speak of this, of course. It will be our secret. No one would believe you, anyway, you odious harlot. No one. You would be shamed and shunned from society, as you well should, giving yourself like that to a man. As your betters have done before, you will endure or you, too, will end up in Bedlam with that crazy bitch, Sarah Ann. You may show yourself out, and you'll do well to keep your mouth shut. Otherwise, I should be quite happy to shut it for you."

"No."

Just one word.

"What did you say to me?"

"Yes, Nick. I suppose you don't hear that word often, do you? Well, many say it, but you don't hear it. Isn't that right?"

"You're already mad, you cheap tart. Get out!"

"No."

"Get out this instant, or did you like that so much you want to go again? I'm ready. I'm always ready for the delights of women, sweet Caroline. Perhaps I can shut your mouth for you tonight. I've just the thing to gag you good and deep. In fact, I think when I'm done with you, you might never speak again."

"It wasn't just Miss Daughety, was it, Nicholas? Those twins from the park that day in the rain a few months back, them too. I noticed they disappeared from society after that day. Oh yes, I've been watching you. Shattered, they were, weren't they? Their family hid them away in shame and even before they had come out in society. Barely sixteen, were they not? They had to cancel their debutante ball, if I recall. What horrors did you show them, Nick? What about Amelia Kensey and Lydia Flaharty? What about Nancy Howard? And those in just the past half year. How many before, *my love*?"

"You're daft, woman. I said, get out!"

Right before those big blue eyes, I shifted, changing out of this broken virgin's body into my own. Well, at least my preferred visage. My true self even I couldn't bear very often. Only when I needed my full power did I use that form. Humans were weak, especially cowards like this one, so I just shifted from the young, blonde virgin Caroline back to myself, Constance Saggese.

Now it was he who was frightened. Finally, something genuine showed in his eyes. Fear.

His fear was delicious.

 # CHAPTER 2

ARTHUR

Another morning alone.

There was something worse about being with someone and feeling so alone, so unfulfilled, than just being by one-self alone. The afternoon light peeked through the heavy curtains, creating just enough visibility in my bedchamber to see that Avalon was already up.

The only thing worse than waking up alone was waking up next to her.

Eternity would be impossible.

I thought back to when I was to be the King of England, all those centuries ago, and I watched a scene from my play. My wife, Catherine, had been perfection, but we were not meant to rule together in the end.

I died, or so everyone thought, and she married my brother. My fat, arrogant brother who became the most notorious king England had ever seen before or since. I was forgotten to antiquity, even by her.

None of it seemed real anymore. Too long a life. Perhaps, I was just bored with it all.

Avalon certainly bored me. Just like every woman before her. Every women since the perfection of Catherine. I had thought Avalon was special, different somehow. But, she's not. Same as any other warm body, really. I should know better by now, really. Still, at times, after lifetimes alone, it was nice to have the company.

Honestly, I didn't know if I would ever be satisfied.

Dragging myself out of bed, I donned my dressing gown and headed downstairs for tea.

"Arthur, did you see the news today?"

Avalon's voice reached me before I entered the room. Her supernatural senses were even stronger than mine, perhaps because they were so new. She had not yet learned to mute certain things. After a while, one must learn to filter or go insane, as there was far too much noise about the living. Still, it had only been a few months since I turned her, and mornings like this I regretted that decision. I wanted silence in the mornings, but it was continuous chatter and questions and noise.

Just some peace.

"Of course not, darling. I just woke up, as you well know." She sat at the small round table near the window, overlooking Kensington and Hyde Park. A white table cloth covered the table, and Thomas had already brought out tea for her. There was a brightness about Avalon that I sometimes resented. Today was one of those times. She gazed up at me with affection, eyes full of adoration, and when she spoke, her voice held the delight of a woman in love.

How very common and utterly dull.

"Look who got up on the wrong side of the bed this morning." She put the newspaper she had been reading down on the table. After brushing a stray sable lock off her face, she raised her teacup for another sip, her vibrant green eyes fixed on me over the porcelain cup.

"It's afternoon, Avalon." I plopped down in the chair beside her, and she leaned over to kiss me good morning, but I turned my cheek to her, which took some of her cheeriness away.

Good.

No place for such frivolity so early in the day.

"It's morning for us, Arthur. Really? Are we going to do this again today? You've been so impatient with me of late, and I just don't understand why. What's gotten into you? Weary of me already, my love?" She forced a cheerful tone, but a slight tremor of fear undercut it. "We do have an eternity together now, so I would appreciate some effort to be kind."

I cringed at the thought of eternity with her, but hid it well. I hoped. Else, I'd have more emotional nonsense to contend with, and I was not in the mood. "It just takes some time to adjust, as you well know, Avalon. Darling. I have been a bachelor for over three centuries, so just be patient with me, woman. All right?"

"Fine."

"I need a haircut," I said, running my fingers through the ruddy mop, smoothing down the night's sculpture. "Perhaps this afternoon before the festivities. I've heard talk of a new barber who's supposed to be very good. Near Fleet, I believe."

"I like it a little long, Arthur. It becomes you."

"I don't."

"I could cut it for you." She reached over and in an expression of loving kindness, brushed it back behind my ears. Any excuse to touch me. "I used to cut Victor's on occasion."

"Yes, and didn't he look fine?" I spoke with more than a hint of sarcasm, pulling out of her reach. Victor. I was so sick of hearing about her dear dead friend Victor. Would she ever stop bringing him up? So he died while we were hunting vampires. It happened. Dangerous work, that. Yet, she blamed me. I know she did. Besides, it'd been months now.

I scowled at her, and she turned back to her tea, cheeks flushed. Before I could say another word, Thomas entered with a pot of fresh tea. He was acting as both butler and driver for the time being. I had yet to find a new butler since Cecil's betrayal and subsequent demise.

Well-deserved and painful demise.

"One drop or two?" Thomas asked.

"Make it five, Thomas. Rough night."

"Of course, M'Lord." Thomas turned the spigot on the wrist contraption that fed directly into his vein. I had it installed on Thomas until I found a new butler, which would no doubt take some time. It was always such an ordeal to find good help, especially good, discreet help that would feed me his life blood if necessary and cover up any indiscretions or blunders. Although, my chance for carnal indiscretions had greatly diminished since Avalon and I had begun cohabiting. I hadn't really thought about what it would mean long term before I turned her, how it would infringe on my freedom and erotic desires. She had been dying in my arms, so what else could I have done? I loved her, so I had been thinking with my heart.

Never a wise guide.

Yes, rash action, that.

Five drops dripped into the cup of hot tea, making the brown water blissfully murky. The gauge strapped to Thomas's wrist bobbed as the blood left his veins, then steadied again when he closed the valve. The coppery scent opened my eyes and improved my mood ever so slightly, but it was a start.

"Lady Avalon?" Thomas turned to my immortal beloved and offered her his wrist.

"No, thank you, Thomas. I think I've had enough for now. Must watch so as not to encourage the hunger too much, lest it become insatiable. I truly wish to stay in control of those particular urges. You understand, don't you?"

That was her biggest problem. Control. She always had to be in control of everything. As for the blood lust, well, I had to keep a lid on that, didn't I? I had taken great pains to remain subtle about steering her away from her new natural urges, plucking the strings of her morality, convincing her of my innocence when it came to drinking people, and, especially, killing them. Too much power there. Couldn't have her becoming too strong too soon. No. That would indeed be a risk I wasn't quite willing to take just yet. Best to ease into this, keep her in check and all. Besides, had to stick with my original story, didn't I? Noble, tortured vampire, reformed by the love of the right woman, and all that nonsense. It was getting rather tiresome.

"Perfectly, mum. Will there be anything else, M'Lord?"

"Not at the moment, Thomas. There's a good man."

Thomas clicked his heels and bowed. His shoes, shined to perfection, left impressions in the plush carpet as he made his way across the room. His lanky frame disappeared through the door, and Avalon spoke to me once again, interrupting the lovely momentary silence.

"Did you see the news?"

"Didn't you already ask me that? And I already answered." I rubbed the sleep out of my eyes, tempted to plug my ears from the continued prattle, but instead ran my fingers through my hair, making it stand on end, hoping to get a chuckle out of Avalon.

Didn't work.

"Yes, love. Perhaps I should be clearer." Words slow and articulate, she tried to control her anger. Always control. "Would you like to see the news, Arthur? I think it would be of great interest to you."

"Read it to me."

"Very well." Avalon spread the paper out flat in front of her, smoothing out the wrinkles and made sure everything was just so before continuing. Maddening.

I craved whimsy. Spontaneity. Passion!

Then I caught a glimpse of that adorable tiny "o" just in the exact center of her mouth when her lips were set, and my heart leapt. There was my love! Oh! Sweet Avalon! The day brightened, and it had nothing to do with the sun outside, for it was another very cloudy day in London, as luck would have it. I did love those grey days. Leaning forward, I rested my chin on the palm of one hand while sipping my spiked tea with the other, gazing at Avalon with complete devotion.

She looked up and smiled when she noticed my change in aspect, shaking her head. "Well! Good morning, my change-ling," she said. "It's so nice to see you again."

Avalon had taken to calling me that because of how fast my mood shifted, or at least she claimed it shifted. From being cold and cruel, as she put it, to being warm and loving. She said I'd been like two different people.

Bah! A woman! Telling me about mood swings!

Daft.

Of course, I was cold and cruel. I was a vampire, after all. But I was also quite loving and kind. Complexity, thy name was Arthur Tudor. Ridiculous, this notion of person-ality shifts. I was who I was, and that was all there was to it. I didn't need her assessment of my behavior or bloody insight into my psyche. Still, even her judgments could not ruin my mood. "Just read the news, Avalon. What is so interesting?"

"This," she said pointing to the front page of *The Times*, "Young Aristocrat Goes Missing."

"Yes. So?"

Avalon gaped at me.

I was being difficult. I knew it, but I didn't care. It was my house after all. My tea nook. My window overlooking London. The room held but a faint remainder of what it was before she moved in. If I closed my eyes and focused my thoughts, I could remember the way it was before her. Quiet, except for the sound of the crackling fire and distant commotion of life outside. The clink of the teacup on the saucer, the slight hiss of the gaslight in the corner. Perfection.

After she sat back down, content to read the paper and drink her tea in silence to avoid any more of my blatant abuse, I spoke again, "Thomas really tries, you know, but he doesn't make a cup of tea like Cecil did. I must find a proper butler soon."

She didn't respond. Splendid. Now she was cross with me. For what reason? Because I had the audacity to be myself? Life was so much simpler when I was on my own, or with Catherine. It'd never been like it was with Catherine. A queen in every sense of the word. Perfection. Nearly four hundred years later, and I'd yet to meet her equal.

Avalon sniffed, and I noticed a crimson tear slip down her stone cheek.

So it began.

"Please, Avalon."

She wiped away the tear, smearing it into the white canvas of her cheek, and gazed out the window down to Kensington Road with her back to me. "I'm fine, Arthur. Finish your tea. It's Yule, after all. We have the ball tonight, just a few hours away."

"Of course. Tell me about the news story, darling. I'll behave."

"It's just about your friend, is all. I thought you would be interested. I mean, you two haven't been as close since he accosted you in the street, but he's still your friend."

"Ah! Good ol' Nick's gone missing, eh? He accused me of being a vampire."

"You are a vampire, my love."

"Indeed, but it is rather impolite to accuse one of being the undead in the street! With people about. Preposterous. Besides, that's not why we're no longer close, Avalon. I forgave him on the spot for that slight."

"Why, then?"

Because of you, I thought but didn't say it. I did know better than that.

Ol' Stanton and I would exchange stories of sexual conquest and prowess, and since Avalon, well, there wasn't much to tell. The same woman over and over. How altogether boring. I hadn't even bothered for a while, and that had started to get to me as well. Men must ejaculate, after all, mustn't they? It was how we were made, to spread our seed, and I was growing ever so weary of spreading it on my own.

"Never mind, Avalon. That's business of men, not women. What did the article say? He's gone missing, you say?"

"Yes. And under such strange circumstances. Just disappeared. He was with his fiancé, a Miss Caroline Weisenburg."

"Fiancé? Ha!" I slapped the table and barked laughter, startling Avalon. "A German one at that. What a laugh. Nick is not the marrying kind, my dove." I looked down on Avalon, so naive and innocent to the ways of men. How tiresome. "She must've been quite special indeed for him to put up such a show. Or quite difficult. He'd done so only once before, I recall. Sarah somebody, if memory serves.

Master, he is. Probably just saving himself from the prison of marriage. What does the lady have to say about his vanishing act?"

"Girl, more like. She was only seventeen, paper says, and she's gone, too."

"He does like them young, doesn't he? I miss the ol' chap." What times we had together. He understood me, and he almost surpassed me in debauchery, but I did have the advantage of my long existence. Still, in just a few years, he had given me quite the challenge to keep up. Renewed my own fervor, he did. Good ol' Nick.

"Perhaps they eloped?" Avalon offered, ever the hopeless romantic. Emphasis on hopeless.

"Nonsense. Let me see that." I snatched the paper from her to read the article myself. "Ah! Here's the rub, sweetheart. This is written by W. D. McFerret, London's ambitious journalist. Shameless," I said, slapping the newspaper with the back of my hand. "Aspiring author trying to make a name for himself in the papers first. American at that. This is sensationalized drivel, Avalon. Don't believe a word. I'm astounded at what passes for news."

"Aren't you even curious? Perhaps a new mystery is exactly what we need, Arthur, to get back our spark. Something to rekindle our love," she said, reaching out to touch my hand, but I turned the page, pulling it out of her reach, pretending I didn't see her trying to touch me, trying to bridge that ever-widening gap.

"Nonsense," I spat, shifting away from her ever further, and read more. The article was indeed intriguing. "Seems blood was found in Nick's parlour, along with upset furniture, which isn't too surprising. Nick did like it rough now and again. Looks like you're right, my darling. This is rather strange." I looked up from the paper, but Avalon was gone. "Perfect."

I found her up in our bedroom, weeping. "Avalon. You were right. That is interesting, and perhaps we could do a bit of investigating on our own. Would you like that?"

"I'm hungry all the time. I can't bear this constant ache, this insatiable need."

"Well. We could find some people to drink tonight, if we must. Just be careful about it. Make sure they don't remember and aren't hurt." I could hardly keep a straight face.

"No! I'm not hurting people for my own benefit." Excellent. Best to let her think it was her idea. "This…this is not natural, Arthur. How could you have lived like this for so long? How can you bear the constant ache, the constant thirst? Then the gala tonight. How can I be around all those people, hearing their blood pumping through their veins, knowing that relief from this anguish is just a prick away?"

"I've told you, Avalon, you will get used to it. I gave all that up for you, and it did hurt for a while, but it's better now. Even when I did drink humans, I fed from the willing when I could. And if they weren't willing, I altered their memory to a pleasant one. Like we did on your first night, for you needed that for your strength. To solidify the change. You almost didn't make it, remember? The problem with human blood is that it makes the thirst worse and worse and worse. Even when we just alter their memory, something inside them always knows what happened, and it's maddening for them." Just talking about it made me want to feed, to feel that rush of warmth spurting up into my mouth. Shackled. Huh. Infuriating, really, to have her and her bloody morals around. Having to keep up this bloody façade. That was the problem, not bloody enough. For me, at least. I did like keeping her away from human blood, else she would discover her true strength. Couldn't have that. Sneaking around to fulfill my desires just to keep her under control. I was beginning to think it wasn't worth the effort. That she wasn't. Besides. I longed for passion, yearning.

She had turned out to be a grave disappointment.

"You know how it has to be, Avalon," I lied. "We sustain on animal's blood from the butcher. There's plenty of that. I know it doesn't taste as good, but it's the only other option. I'll send Thomas out to get more. You learn to manage it."

"Yes, so you keep saying. It's been four months. Four agonizing months, and the only relief is a few drops of blood in tea and making love to you, but we can't stay in bed all the time, Arthur. Besides, you've been wholly uninterested for a while now, it seems. That along with your callousness, and I—well—I just don't know what to think anymore."

"It's all to save you, Ava. Do you want to become a killer like I was all those years ago? Human blood makes it worse. As much as you suffer, my agony is worse, but you don't hear me complaining, now do you? Have some compassion, Avalon. Have some fucking courage. You're so weak, it's pathetic. Look at me, off human blood for as long as you, all along with an even stronger urge, more insatiable thirst, and I don't mewl about it."

That was rather convincing. I almost believed it myself.

Her face was streaked with lines of blood, tears that dripped from her lovely jaw and over her perfect lips. She dabbed her handkerchief under her nose and eyes, staining it with blood tears.

"I don't believe you," she said, looking up at me with her beautiful green eyes, rimmed in deep sanguine. She was perfection. She was mine. "The urge to kill grows stronger by the night. I don't believe that you haven't killed for your food. Not for a few centuries, you said. Not since the days of your brother's reign, since Catherine's death. You said her death made it all too real, and you couldn't do it anymore."

She actually believed that? How cute. Foolish girl.

"How did you manage? How could you resist this urge? You, Arthur? You who revel in your fineries and satiate your needs, carnal and otherwise. That's right. I've heard the stories, the rumors. You go out at all hours, leaving me here. You simply cannot be as good as you claim. "

"Are you accusing me of lying? Ingrate! I've given up everything for you. I saved you from death. Out of love for you, Avalon. I've given up my freedom, the life I had become accustomed to. All for you!"

She stood up from the bed and walked to the other side of the room. Facing the window, she wiped the tears from her face and took several deep breaths, calming herself. Framed by the daylight coming through the cracks of the drawn curtains, her silhouette stirred something in me. Her grating voice broke my lascivious thoughts about what I wanted to do to that body. "This is getting us nowhere, Arthur. Let's not fight anymore. We both have made sacrifices for each other, haven't we? We will adjust. Now, you wanted to talk about poor Nicholas."

"Yes. Let us go investigate the scene for ourselves. The paper said there was blood at the scene, and I want to see for myself."

"We have the Yule Ball in a few hours."

"Of course, we'll go tomorrow afternoon. Late afternoon."

"I'm sure the police will have had the place cleaned by now."

"We're vampires, Avalon. We'll be able to smell the blood, cleaned up or not. Now," I said, moving close to her. "Have your bath and wash away those tears." I kissed her cheeks, soft and sensual brushes with my lips along her jawline and cheekbone, allowing my tongue to trace along the tears' path, trying to recapture the desire. If she'd just keep her mouth shut.

She caught her breath and pressed against me. I had been neglecting her sexually, of that there was no doubt, but the same woman did get ever so boring. Truly, a man needed variety. Before I could turn her away toward the door, denying her again, she was kissing me with all that hunger for blood she had been trying to quell. Her passion was contagious. It had been quite a while, after all.

Her long, black hair fell in ringlets around her blood-streaked face, and suddenly I wanted to watch that hair bounce while I had her, as long as I didn't have to look at her. As long as she didn't say anything to spoil it. I spun her around and pressed her against me, grinding my hips into her derrière, nibbling down her neck while my hands caressed her breasts. Her breath coming faster, she tried to turn around to face me again, but I wouldn't let her. I bent her over the bed and hiked up her nightdress, kicking her feet apart.

"Wait, Arthur," she said, but I didn't listen. I didn't want to hear another word, so I held her head down pressed into the sheets, away from me, and had her then and there. Those curls did indeed bounce. They danced with vigor, matching her moans of ecstasy, or were they cries of pain? Hard to tell muffled in the blankets. She loved this. Of course she did. She loved me, and I her. I thrust harder and harder inside her.

This was.

Her place.

Beneath.

Me.

Surrounding.

Me.

Pleasing.

Me.

Before long, her moans turned to sobs, but I continued on, bearing down on her shoulders, driving her onto me. I was so close, so close.

Exploding inside her, I roared with her shriek.

We climaxed together.

That was what just happened.

That was why she screamed.

The day was already improving.

Avalon stood up with me still inside her and lay her head back on my shoulder. "Tell me you love me," she said. Fresh tears streamed down her face.

Great way to ruin a perfect moment, sweetheart.

"I not only love you, I absolutely adore you. Now, get in the bath." I withdrew from her, turned away, and left before she could say another word, covering myself with my dressing gown as I stepped out into the hallway. I'd had enough of her prattle for one day. Besides, I needed some real fucking blood. That along with that sweet release would certainly improve my mood. Perhaps a quick nibble while she was in the bath.

She need not know.

She never did.

CHAPTER 3

CONSTANCE

"I'm here to see Miss Sarah Ann Daughety, please. She's expecting me," I said to the peaked nurse dressed all in white. A long white skirt touched to tops of her white shoes, and a white apron protected the front of her white blouse. Even a white kerchief covered her hair.

After gathering some papers and snapping them under her board's clip, she came out from behind the desk and crossed in front of me. "This way," she said, without even looking at me and headed down the hall.

Of all the places I'd been in my life, Bethlem Hospital was one of the worst, especially for women. Although not quite as horrific as it was a century ago, it was still an unending nightmare for its inhabitants. As the nurse led me to Sarah Ann's room, the words of Thomas Tryon returned to me: "those that are more mad lock up those that are less." Sounds of chains, moans, screams, shouts, and weeping created a background din that struck the core of my soul. To even step onto these grounds, I had to go to great lengths to protect myself from the palpable misery within these walls, unmistakable to any with a heart capable of compassion, but to someone like me with supernatural powers of empathy, it was downright intolerable. For I felt into people, or perhaps more accurately, people projected themselves, unknowingly, into me. I felt their pain, tasted their misery. I saw their intentions. I touched their very soul and knew the truth of it, or in much of my work, the lack of it. Yes, I'd honed my skills well during my time. The danger of walking into a place like Bedlam was a necessary risk, but I prepared well. Still, the waves of grief emanated from the walls, permeated the air. With every breath I took, I swallowed more agony and fear until the despair filled my stomach and created a sickening nausea. The strength of the barriers, using every bit of my power, still could not completely block out these pitiable voices, demanding to be heard, to be seen, to be remembered.

Perhaps even worse than the background drone of vocal despondency was the silence behind it all. As I followed the nurse through the activity room, women sat rocking back and forth. A harrowing vacancy in their eyes stared at nothing. Others found a particular part of their dressing gown or spot on the wall and picked at it, an endless fingering and scratching and probing for some unknown purpose.

"She's in there." The nurse halted in front of a closed door and thrust her thumb toward its window. "Can't stay for long. She's got treatment at two."

With that, she turned and strode away, leaving me outside Sarah Ann's door. Through the window I saw Sarah Ann sitting on her bed, knees pulled up to her chest. Her wrists and ankles, shackled. Chains attached her to a metal pipe running up the wall behind her. Red rimmed her cold steel eyes, focused on nothing in particular. Surrounded in darkness, they sunk into her skull. Once healthy blonde hair hung in dingy strings about her sallow face. Patches of baldness peppered her skull. She rocked back and forth, a ghost who wasn't really there. Just a shadow of her former self.

I turned the knob and entered, but Sarah Ann didn't look over.

"Sarah Ann?" I said, keeping my voice gentle, as I had nothing but compassion and pity for this ill-used woman. Her life had been so promising, a young beautiful woman of London's High Society. It should've been a life of galas and balls and high teas, but instead, because that man chose her instead of another, she was now doomed to Bedlam and an existence worse than death.

Because of me, so was he.

Because she had had enough remaining fight and courage to summon me, he would never do this to anyone ever again. If only I had the power to take her suffering away, I would do so.

Alas, such things were not part of my repertoire.

I could reduce the suffering of the innocent by punishing the guilty, by keeping them from harming others. Although it took too much out of me to do it often, I could offer momentary relief, channeling the pain and transferring it where it belonged. The relief sometimes lasted long enough to allow the survivor to fall asleep. Sometimes, that was enough.

"Sarah Ann?" I said again, sitting down on the far edge of her narrow mattress.

Startled, her eyes widened and she flinched, backing up against the corner.

"It's all right. It's just me. Constance. Remember?"

Her agitation diminished slightly. I'd been doing this a long time, and all the survivors of such violence behaved in similar ways. After five centuries, I still did, too, at times. On bad days. Even five hundred years later, I still flashed back to that original attack, relived it, and it was like I was there all over again. The terror, immediate. The anguish, staggering.

Those were the bad days.

Easily frightened, jumping at the slightest sound. Reliving the event and subsequent cruelty through infinite loops in their minds. Sometimes they seemed to be in another world, as if they didn't know what was going on around them. Disconnected with time, lost. Conflicting emotions, a war in their hearts and minds tried to understand how "love" and "violation" could exist together. Feeling not of their body or even of this world, as if everything was an illusion. Heightened anxiety and severe depression, not to mention a propensity toward suicide, and who could blame them? They lived in a hell forced upon them by a selfish, barbaric act. Their reality forever altered. A reality without hope, without trust. A reality where love meant something altogether different. A reality in which the notions of love and sex were inseparable with exploitation and violation. Forever.

It was a life sentence, in or out of Bedlam.

This place just compounded the trauma, ensuring they never fully healed. Damning them to permanent duress. All because a man demanded a few moments of control, taking pleasure in his power over her. Treating her as an object rather than a human being.

Lives shattered. For mere moments. Over and over again.

Until I stopped it.

"It's done," I said. "He can't hurt anyone else."

Her chains rattled as she pulled her hands up to either side of her face, revealing red-raw wrists, and made a sort of squealing sound. Not in delight, but in mental turmoil.

"Shhhh. It's all right."

"I didn't deserve to be treated thus," she cried. "I loved him. I trusted him."

"I know you did. You did not deserve it, not in the least."

"My parents said I did. They said that was what I got for being alone with him. No one believed me. No one at all. I should've kept quiet, like a good girl. But I'm not a good girl, am I? This is why it's happened. I'm not a good girl at all! I did deserve it!"

"No, you did not deserve it, and it is not your fault. You had the great misfortune of falling in love with a monstrous man, a very convincing man in the ways of love, but monstrous in the end. You did not deserve it. It is not your fault." I repeated those two phrases as often as I could, as the entire world had told them the opposite with every action and word, with every glare and whisper. "You are so strong, Sarah Ann. Remember? You summoned me. You spoke out. You loved. There is no shame in that, my dear. No shame at all. The shame belongs to him, and he feels it fully now. Yes. Quite deeply, in fact, and he will for many decades to come."

"Really? He's been stopped? He can't hurt anyone else?"

"He cannot hurt anyone else, and that's because of you. Because of you and me together."

"Did he hurt you?" Tears filled her eyes, and she regarded me with such concern. Amazing how one who had been betrayed and violated by the cruelty of a lover, then discarded by society, still found compassion for a near stranger.

Her question brought up images of my attack last night, and I shuddered, remembering. My lasting pleasure in his fear and punishment helped me recover. I offered a sweet smile to soothe her as well. No need to share details with her, as it would only distress her further. "How kind of you, Sarah Ann, but don't you worry about me. I'm just fine."

"Oh good. I couldn't bear it if I was somehow responsible for him hurting you. No I just couldn't bear it! Were you scared?" Fresh tears wet her chapped cheeks, and her eyes searched me for relief. Even just a moment of relief, but there was none.

"Our fears empower us, like monsters to slay. Rest assured, this monster has indeed been slain. He can't hurt you, me, or anyone else ever again." Before I could say anything of further comfort, she buried her head beneath her arms, pulling her legs closer, and cried.

"I'm sorry," she whimpered. "I'm so sorry. I'm so sorry. I'm so sorry."

"It's all right. It's not your fault. It's all right." Her torment started to affect me as well, breaking down my barriers of self-protection. I had to leave soon or suffer along with her. My presence was not a comfort to her. No. Nothing could comfort this poor woman for long. Death would be her only release from this prison to which Lord Nicholas Stanton had sentenced her.

Lord Nicholas Stanton would not know such relief, not for centuries.

"I hate him," she groaned from her protective cave. "Yet, I love him still, even after everything he's done." Her face filled with an ethereal glow as she lifted her head. She smiled, revealing browning teeth from her neglect in this place. "Sometimes, I still think he'll come for me. That he'll walk through that door and smile, blue eyes shining, and tell me it was all a mistake. He'll take me by the hand and caress my cheek and say that he loves me and he's been trying to get to me for years. That it was all just a misunderstanding." She giggled, the sound innocent and harrowing at the same time. Then, her face fell.

"It's been two years, Constance. He's not coming, but sometimes I still dream he is. Sometimes it still feels so real, like he really did love me after all. Like I'm right back there, dancing with him. Laughing and planning our wedding. The way he'd look so deeply into my eyes when he'd kiss my wrist. Then, it fades, leaving only silence or the sound of my breathing, my weeping, my face against my wet sheets. A rattle of the chains that bind me, and I'm not talking about these." She shook her hands at me, jolting the chains into a clamor of sudden noise. "I'm talking about these!" she cried, pointing to either side of her head.

"I know, sweet Sarah Ann. I know. I must go now, my dear. My apologies. I've done what you've summoned me to do. Take some comfort in his demise, knowing he's not out dancing and laughing while you're trapped in here."

"Yes. That will be comforting, indeed. That was added torment, you see? Knowing he was wooing others, hurting others and enjoying it. Did I tell you of the pleasure I saw in his eyes as I cried? Did I? It was more frightening than anything I've seen before or since, to see how much he enjoyed my pain, my tears. Horrifying, Constance."

"Monstrous."

"Yes. Quite monstrous. Now I can rest easier, thanks to you."

"Thanks to you, Sarah Ann. Remember, your courage stopped him from hurting anyone else. Your voice. Always remember that, sweet lady. You are so strong, and I am in awe of you. You endure all this, and yet you have the clarity and courage to continue to fight. You are an inspiration to me."

"Thank you for that, dear Constance. Thank you so much. For the kindness you've shown in a world that is so cold, so devoid of hope, of love and tenderness. In a world such as this, genuine kindness is rather revolutionary."

"Take care of yourself. Take some comfort in this."

"I shall," she said, sitting up straight, head held high. "Now if I can just avoid the Rotating Chair, all will be well again. They say I ask too many questions and must be silenced. But I will not be silent. Never again."

"The Rotating Chair? They should've done away with such savage *treatments* fifty years ago."

"Yes, so they like everyone to think. They've kept them in the basement where no one goes, not the press, anyway. None of the private tours neither, and if you're not good enough, if you don't laugh and dance and paint and play the piano like a good girl—if you ask too many questions or don't take your medicine—you get the Rotating Chair, or worse. I have no need for frivolities like dancing anymore. It reminds me too much of what's lost, of what he took from me, but I would like to write. They won't let me write. Why is that, Constance? Why won't they let me write? What harm could come of it?"

"I shall ensure they let you write, Sarah Ann. Take this," I handed her a white feather from my reticule. "Keep it safe, beneath your mattress or pillow, and talk to it when you are in need of company. Then know, I can hear you, no matter where I am. Although I can't answer, I am there. Do you believe me, Constance?"

"Yes! Oh! Thank you, Constance. Thank you for being here for me. Thank you for just listening. Thank you most of all for believing me. You are the only one. Thank you."

"I shall also take care of the Rotating Chair business on my way out. If they ever use such wicked treatments on you or anyone again, you tell that feather, and I shall return to stop them. All right?"

"Yes! Thank you!"

"Can you sleep? Get some rest now."

"Not well." Her eyes drifted, unfocused again. "Too many thoughts over and over and over and over." The tears returned and she started to tremble. "'Round and 'round and 'round, grunting and sweating and laughing at me." Her chains rattled when she grabbed her head, as if she could push the thoughts out, or just stop thinking all together, if she squeezed hard enough.

"Shhhhhh," I said, bringing her back to the present with my touch, gently lowering her arms. "Look at this here, Sarah Ann. I brought something for you to see." I removed a crocheted poppet from of my reticule, and wiggled it in front of her, making her smile at its hand-stitched grin and floppy arms. "This is a magic poppet, my dear, and it can take away some of your pain, just for a while, I'm afraid. Would you like that?"

"Yes! Please! Oh! A magic poppet with a black heart!"

"Hold still, and I shall relieve your torment. Then, sleep. All right?"

"Yes! Oh, please." Tears anew. "Even for a moment. Yes, please."

Taking the poppet in one hand and laying my other on the side of her head, I focused my will on assuaging her distress, channeling it into the poppet, placing all that torment where it belonged.

If only for a few moments.

"Take care, sweet girl." I brushed the hair away from her temples as she curled up to sleep, pulling her shackled hands up to her face.

"Goodbye, Constance," she slurred as she began to doze. "Thank you so much. You've saved me, the small tiny part of me that's left. Bye-bye, now. Bye-bye." The last words formed more around whispers than voice as she drifted into a peaceful reprieve.

As I let myself out of the room, Sarah Ann was already fast sleep.

"Pardon me," I said to the same nurse who showed me back to Sarah Ann's room, now back at her station. "Might I please see the director? Immediately, please."

"I'm sorry, madam, but the superintendent physician is…" Her words faded away when she looked up into my eyes, blackened with the intent to convince.

My will. Always.

"Um—yes. Right away, madam."

Before too long, I was out in the beautiful winter day.

It didn't take too much to convince the good doctor to amend his medical regime. No, not too much at all, actually. I made it very clear that I knew his secrets and that his public image would reflect his darkest secrets all too soon if things didn't change. Additionally, the horrors that the patients experienced would be a carnival in comparison to his fate. A flash of my power impressed upon his innermost thoughts convinced him straight away. I found that a taste, a mere glimpse of eternal misery was usually enough to convince anyone of anything. Quite enough, in fact.

I also strongly suggested that Miss Daughety be allowed the implements with which to write and whatever else she needed to be as comfortable as possible. Warning him that I would know of any further mistreatment or neglect.

He obliged without hesitation.

The brisk air cleansed my mystical palate. One deep breath, and I felt revitalized. Now. Must prepare for the Yule Ball tonight. After all, there was much more work to be done.

 # CHAPTER 4

ARTHUR

Lord Pearson's home had been transformed into a magical Yuletide wonderland. He outdid himself every year. Of course, his wife, Lady Eliza Pearson had something to do with that. She would rather be publicly humiliated beyond repair than to be topped by anyone in society for parties, which would mean the same thing. This Yule Ball was just the start. The Pearsons had commissioned a dirigible for a Christmas cruise to Paris and back, inviting all their friends, and enemies, in the ton, including anyone of some repute whatsoever. It would no doubt surpass the singular evening airship gala held this past summer, the place I had met Avalon for the first time. She captivated me then as she did now.

Perhaps I had been cruel of late. She was a remarkable woman, after all.

"Lady Pearson must've been planning this for six months," I whispered to Avalon as we entered the great hall, holding her close to me.

"Indeed."

Still cross with me. Absurd. First she complained that we hadn't been sexual enough, and then when I let her have it, she was upset about that, too. I just couldn't win.

Visions and sounds of holiday merriment unfolded before us. Delight and laughter filled the air, mixing with the smooth notes of the string quartet. Down each side of the ballroom, giant Christmas trees lined the dark walnut walls. Reaching toward the ceiling, these glorious trees had been freshly cut and transported to London just for this gala. Draped with gold and maroon ribbon and adorned with fresh apples hanging from their branches, they were as fine as I'd ever seen in my long life. The top of each tree held a large star, glowing with gaslight. That couldn't have been easy, nor was it terribly safe.

"Look at all the splendor, sweetheart. Even with the gas-lights flickering all about us, it is you who light up this room. You look magnificent, tonight, my love. Even more so than usual. Positively stunning," I said, kissing her hand. I had been so busy trying to cover up my dalliances while Avalon prepared for the ball that I hadn't noticed her before now. She wore a strapless gown of scarlet velvet, trimmed with candlelight white lace across the bodice and draped across her hips, gathering in the back to make the most delicious bustle. The matching satin skirt gathered over each thigh revealed a candlelight white skirt beneath. To finish off this breathtaking ensemble, a matching flower brocade decorated the bodice and a scarlet velvet choker adorned her slender neck. The dark, blood-red gown made her cold flesh appear as fine porcelain. "Come. We must show you off properly. You are a vision."

That got me a smile. Finally.

"Your new haircut becomes you, Arthur, especially in that suit. You, too, look quite impressive this evening."

Truth, that. Majestic, more like. Paramount to my Tudor heritage, no doubt. I had my waistcoat made especially for this night, a deep red brocade to match Avalon's gown, decorated with black velvet designs. Then, I always looked smashing in black tie.

Extending her out to her scarlet-covered arms-length, for the gloves nearly reached her shoulder, I turned her around the center of the dance floor. All eyes landed on the beauty before me. Plain, indeed, as her aunt Emily Bainbridge would have all believe. No one would ever think of my Avalon as ordinary again. The couples waltzing around us stopped for a moment to watch Avalon spin under my arm and curtsy. Her sable curls fell softly about her face. Then we joined with the rest to the music of the string quartet.

"I hope it's all right I got a little rough before, my sweet. You just make me so hungry, and it had been too long. We simply must do that more often."

"It was rather rough." She said no more, tensing up in my arms.

"Yes, well. Bygones, and all that. I think your idea is a splendid one, by the by. A new mystery to solve will bridge the gap that has been growing between us. We shall visit Stanton's tomorrow afternoon."

"You seem all together unconcerned about your missing friend, Arthur."

"What? Nick? Ha! Good ol' Nick. If anyone can take care of himself, Avalon, he can. I'm sure the man is just fine. Probably in an opium den somewhere smothered in women."

The song ended and so did the conversation. I bowed to Avalon who in turn curtsied. As we made our way off the dance floor, the gaudiest gown I had ever seen assaulted my eyes. It, of course, covered no other than the willful Emily Bainbridge.

"Ah! There is your aunt."

"Yes. Rather hard to miss."

There's my girl.

As we approached, the gown became ever more revolting. It was red and green and white, with just the enough silver and gold to make it quite horrid, indeed. The back of the dress had no bustle, which, for once, I was glad. It had layers of red ruffles, each trimmed with a wide bright green ribbon. Every few inches sat another red sparkly puff of fabric, much like a large rose, bordered with gold on some and silver on others. Emily turned to greet us, and I had to use every ounce of self-control to keep my face arranged in a pleasant smile. A quick glance at Avalon showed she was doing the same. The front of the bodice was a stack of red bows with green tips against a white base, topped with a frilly red collar that stood stiff around her neck. A rather large white ruffle lined each side of the front panel.

"Avalon!" The feigned delight left her voice when she greeted me with a nod. "Lord York."

Yes. Still cross as well. Why did women stay cross with me for so long? Honestly, it was near half a year since our singular chartreuse indiscretion, yet this frilly woman was still annoyed with me for falling in love with Avalon. Although, I could understand how she would be vexed to lose me as a lover. I was rather skilled in the ways of passion, after all. No doubt the woman hadn't had an orgasm since. Poor lass.

"Good evening, Lady Bainbridge." Two could play the formality game. "My! Aren't you a sight this fine evening."

"Do you like it?" She spun around in place and posed with one leg stretched out to the side, to ensure that her ankles showed beneath the bottom ruffle. Scandalous.

Her husband, Baron Henry Bainbridge of Yorkshire, cleared his throat beside her in a rather disapproving way.

Avalon's uncle was the epitome of class and grace, dressed in a fine burgundy coat and brocade vest ensemble, topped with a black cravat. The waxed tips of his curled silver mustache bounced as he cleared his throat again. "Avalon, my dear. How lovely to see you. Good heavens, child. You are the picture of elegance. You remind me of your mother, and your eyes are the spitting image of my dear brother, may they both rest in peace."

Avalon dipped into a slight curtsy before embracing her uncle. She loved the man. He had given her the houses on Baker Street to tend after her father died. Lord Bainbridge, unlike his wife, was kind and generous and properly polite.

Emily hated to have attention stolen from her, especially by Avalon. "Yes. Quite," she snapped. "Although, you are looking a little pale, dear. Are you eating well?"

"I'm just fine, Aunt. Thank you for your concern."

"But you, Arthur,"—Emily turned to me—"There is a definite rosiness to your cheek this evening. You look well."

Avalon flashed a glare in my direction, imperceptible to all but me. Although she truly couldn't care less about society, she knew enough to pretend along with the rest of them. She, no doubt, suspected my afternoon snack. I would have to share sooner or later. Perhaps after the ball.

"Thank you, Lady Bainbridge. Avalon and I are quite well, considering."

"Considering?"

"Considering we have not had any wine. Where in all that's good and devilish are the servers? Ah! There! Over by Lady Pearson, to whom we must show our gratitude anyway. Would you please excuse us, dear lady? Baron."

"Of course," the Lord Bainbridge said, raising his glass to us before turning to another group of revelers.

Emily added, "Do what you will, as, of course, you will, Lord York. Avalon. Do return before you depart. I have a new lovely friend, and I'd like you both to make her acquaintance. Mrs. Chastity Rosengarten, but then, you know what they say about names. Might I suggest"—she lowered her voice and feigning a whisper behind her gold-gloved hand— "not all other roses by another would smell as sweet."

Intriguing!

Avalon's grip on my arm tightened as she inched me away toward Lady Pearson, our gracious hostess for this succulent gala. Lady Eliza Pearson spoke with a man around my height, but there was much more to him. His presence filled space, rather than his body. Stout, more with muscle than middle, and a kind look about him. His attire not quite to par with those of London's High Society, but he did look smart, albeit rather odd. The collar of his coat stood high about his ears, and his long dark hair fell loose about his face. A black cravat of sorts covered his neck, tied unlike that I have ever seen, and he wore it on the inside of an open collared shirt. Upon his head sat a large top hat strapped with brown leather goggles across the front.

"Lady Pearson," I said, bowing and kissing her proffered hand. "Your ball is magnificent. Utterly stupendous. I have never seen the like in all my years."

"In all your twenty or so years, Arthur?" she laughed. "Might I introduce you to Arron von Blackwolf, the captain of the Lone Star International Aerodrome?"

"How do you do, Mr. Blackwolf? Lord Arthur York, at your service, and this is my—" I wasn't sure what to call her—"Avalon. Avalon Bainbridge." I'd hear about that one later.

"Pleasure," she said, offering her hand.

Blackwolf kissed it, bowing, then spoke. "The pleasure is mine."

His accent was American, from the south, if I wasn't mistaken. The long drawl over the vowels gave that much away.

"An American," I said. "Lady Pearson, you never cease to amaze me. You commissioned an American for your Christmas cruise. How very interesting."

"Eliza, Arthur. I shan't tell you again." Her gown was of fine purple silk, adorned with black ribbon and lace. The black frills along the lace sleeves and neckline drew the eye to her bosoms. Although in her fifties, she was still young and delicious to me. Although, she would never, as much as I would like to sample that particular vintage.

"Of course, Eliza."

"Not terribly interesting, Arthur. Arron here is a veteran of that dreadful war over in the colonies, and now he has turned his ship into a passenger and commercial vessel. He had wanted to see the Old World, as the colonist's call it, and I was all too happy to oblige. He served with the journalist, W. D. MacFerret. You know, the one who wrote that dreadful piece about Lord Stanton's disappearance. I'm dear friends with MacFerret's wife, Gladys, although I still question her wisdom in marrying a colonist. One with Scottish heritage at that!"

"Yes. McFerret and I go way back, Lord York, but we've mostly fallen out of touch, as happens with those from our past. Don't it?"

There was a story there, no doubt. Otherwise, why mention it to someone he'd just met?

"Indeed," I said. "Excited about the cruise, Mr. Blackwolf?"

"I am. Yes sir. It'll be a first for me, but I'd like to see France before I head back across."

"How long will you be staying in London?" Avalon asked.

"Oh, not much after the new year, I'm afraid. I reckon I'd like to see more of Europe, and perhaps venture down into Africa before heading back. I met an odd chap before who was telling wild tales of adventure on the continent, as he called it. Doctor Nesbitt, I believe."

"Yes," Lady Pearson said, pulling her mouth into a bow as if she had just sucked on a lemon. "Doctor Nesbitt."

"Anyway," Blackwolf continued, "He got my curiosity up, and with Lady Pearson's generosity in hiring my boat for her gala, I might just be able to see it after all. Then back to Texas. I've got work waiting for me there, too."

"Doctor Nesbitt," Avalon said. "I'm not familiar with him."

Lady Pearson cleared her throat. "My, Arthur and Avalon, you don't have a glass of wine. We must remedy that at once. Garçon!" She got the attention of one of her servers, and motioned for him to come over. A tall, lanky gentleman, one that would even make Thomas look rather stout, accosted the waiter before he reached us. The spindly man sported a dark ensemble, styled to resemble an explorer who had just returned from the continent. Complete with a brown leather baldric, a utility belt full of items useless at a party, and knickers tucked into knee-high boots, he stood out from all the other men. Bushy black mutton chops covered his gaunt face. The tips of a waxed mustache stuck straight out either side and extended to his ears. Stumbling over other guests, nearly losing his wide-brimmed helmet, he slammed two empty wine glasses on the server's silver tray before picking up two more. "There's a good chap," he slurred, then disappeared back in the crowd.

"Speak of the devil," Lady Pearson said under her breath, frowning.

After Avalon took a moment to straighten the upset glass Doctor Nesbitt had left, she and I each took a glass of wine for ourselves. The comical man twirled on the dance floor, weaving in and out of the couples, waltzing with his wine. Every so often he would stop, feign a dip, and take a swig from one glass, holding the other stretched out, posing with his long limbs at odd angles as he did so. The couples around him laughed at his antics, clapping as he finished off each glass—for which he took a deep bow. His hat clanged as it hit the floor, leaving a black smudge on the wood.

He stood once again, stiff and straight, as if at attention in a military muster. Only his eyes moved, looking around wildly in mock nonchalance. Several couples had stopped dancing to watch this buffoon perform.

Lady Pearson's face shone crimson. Shame consumed her. "How I regret inviting that halfwit. I say! He came so highly recommended, as well. From Oxford. A doctor, not to mention professor of biology and astronomy. One would think some class was innate, wouldn't one? Too late to cancel his part in the cruise now, I'm afraid. Oh! How dreadful."

Nesbitt chose a few people from the crowd and pantomimed instructions. First, he enlisted the help of two gentlemen, one to hold each empty glass. Then, taking the younger of their two dance partners, waltzed her in a circle around his hat. Each time he passed it, he would make a dramatic bow to retrieve it, but instead, his long, pointed boot would just kick it someplace new.

"He is rather amusing," I said, laughing with the other onlookers.

"I am far from amused," Lady Pearson said, but she couldn't take her eyes off this clown either.

Finally, Nesbitt ended his antics with the song, lowering the lady in a very deep dip. Stringy strands of his long black hair fell from the sides of his face onto hers. She looked up at him with admiration. Once he had her back on her feet and in the arms of her original partner, Nesbitt bowed low again, scooping up his hat and rolling it up his arm onto his head. Applause exploded around him. As the next song began, he found the nearest server and helped himself to two more glasses of wine.

The room returned to as it was before the show. I toasted Lady Pearson: "To your Christmas Cruise, Eliza, and to this splendid Yule Ball!"

"Hear! Hear!" Blackwolf said, raising his glass with ours.

"Forgive us for interrupting your conversation," Avalon offered.

"Not at all, Avalon. Besides, you are a welcomed and elegant distraction from that buffoon. What were we talking about, Captain? Ah, yes! Nicholas's disappearance. Good riddance, I say. I hope he stays gone."

"Eliza is still cross about the short, torrid affair of Nick and her daughter, Fanny Mae."

"Arthur!" Avalon said, shocked at my blunt statement.

"It's fine, my dear. It's not as if it's a secret, certainly not in this society. Nothing remains secret for long, especially when the gossip is that of a tarnished woman. I hold that mongrel responsible. Like I said, I hope he stays gone."

"I have no patience for men who don't respect ladies," Blackwolf said. "If he don't stay gone, madam, you just let me know, and I'll take care of the wretch for ya."

"You are kind to offer, Arron, indeed. Fanny Mae recovered, well, as near as she could. Married a haberdasher, of all people, and a Scottish one at that," she spat. "But then, she didn't have much choice anymore, did she? No. It was all I and her father could do to not go down with her reputation, but I shan't pay for the foolish mistakes of a girl. Still, I know my daughter, and although she may have trusted the wrong man, it was his doing that ruined her. I shall never forgive him that."

"Nor should you, sweet lady."

"It's the way of the world, is it not?" This was all rather amusing to me. Eliza knew of my reputation, as well, and knew Nick and I were cockers.

"Quite," she said, clenching her jaw.

"There are many ways of the world that need changing, son," Blackwolf said.

How cute. He took me for his inferior because of my youthful appearance. Quaint, indeed.

"Rather," I said and sipped my wine. "Still, pleased or no, it is quite the mystery, isn't it? He just disappeared? Just like that?"

"That's what the article said." Eliza looked over my shoulder at the rest of the party, no doubt searching for an opening to excuse herself. "I suppose you'd have to ask Mr. McFerret for more details. The rest is only hearsay, and as long as I don't hear Lord Stanton is back, I'm perfectly satisfied. Here's Mr. McFerret to satisfy your curiosity."

"W. D. McFerret. How do ya'll do?" He said, vigorously shaking all our hands, one to the next.

McFerret was very similar to what the name would suggest, although shaped more like a walrus than a ferret, with a mustache to match, but there was something quite ferret-like in his mannerisms. The man had the most prominent jaw in the room, no doubt, on this side of The Atlantic. The large, bushy brown mutton chops that connected with his bushy brown mustache only served to accentuate his face's rather unfortunate shape. Quite a small man, too, about the size of Avalon, barely over five feet. His voice was of a heavy tenor and thick with a southern drawl, one that outdid even

Blackwolf's, yet somehow more refined. "There's a good chap! Listen to me sounding all English. Didn't we beat these blokes about a century ago?" He laughed a hearty laugh and slapped Blackwolf on the belly. "I've been here too long. And how are you, my old friend. How's 'The Iron Wolf' these days? Fancy meeting ya on this side of the pond, as they say. Yes. It's been something to live here in London."

"No one's called me that since the war, and I'd prefer to keep it that way. It's been a long time, William."

"Willie, please. It's Willie McFerret these days, unless it's a byline, of course. Then it's W. D. McFerret, and I've quite a few of those lately. Have you seen? Writing for *The Times* have you seen? Not to mention a novel or two in the works."

"Would you excuse me? I see Lady and Lord Hamilton over there, and I have yet to greet them." Eliza took her out.

"Of course," I said, bowing in tandem with Blackwolf. Willie, did not bow.

"Thank you for having us tonight," Avalon added, then Eliza was off.

I watched her go. The purple ruffles of her gown swayed as she crossed the floor with grace. She joined my Hazel. I had been so taken with Hazel Hamilton this summer, before Avalon made me forget interest in all other women. For a time, at least.

Hazel did look ravishing in red.

"I must take my leave as well," Blackwolf said, drawing my attention back, and, no doubt, trying to get away from Willie. "There is still a lot to do before the cruise. Lady Pearson is transforming my ship, and I don't doubt it will be as purty as this here hall when she's done. Lord York. Avalon," he said, kissing her hand again. "I'll see you aboard."

"Of course, Mr. Blackwolf. We are looking forward to it."

I was altogether terrified we would be left alone with this little ferret man, and though I wanted to learn more about Nicholas's supposed disappearance, I didn't believe I could bear a conversation with this weasel. Fortunately, he left us without so much as a by your leave, following Blackwolf across the room, prattling on about his stories.

"Arthur! Arthur! Over here!" Emily Bainbridge stood next to a gentleman I didn't know and a glorious creature, dressed all in copper and gold. Huge bustle. This must be her unchaste friend Chastity. How perfectly delightful.

"Arthur." Avalon's tone had a warning edge to it.

"Yes, quite the bore, my dear, but we mustn't be rude," I hissed back at her. The woman tried to control my every move. This must stop, and soon.

"Arthur, Avalon." She said the latter through clenched teeth. "May I present the Baron Vincent Von Rictus Baine and Mrs. Chastity Rosengarten? Baron, Chastity, may I introduced you to Lord Arthur York, and my niece, Miss Avalon Bainbridge?"

"Pleasure," Avalon said, offering the Baron her scarlet satin hand.

"The pleasure is mine, dear lady," he responded, kissing it.

"How do you do?" Chastity, in all her absolute loveliness, said. She appeared to be just slightly older than Avalon. Late thirties or early forties, I'd wager. Perfect age. Such a succulent mixture of experience and relative youthful vigor. Well, if she wasn't a spinster, and the Mrs. before her name told me she wasn't. I kissed her hand, and I took my time about it, too, locking eyes with hers. I wasn't sure who captivated the other more, but I was indeed taken by this portrait of elegance and beauty.

"We were just talking about the disappearance of Lord Stanton." Emily's voice was a little higher than normal, likely in delight at the cross expression on Avalon's face. She wasn't hiding that well. No, indeed. Avalon pulled back on my arm, forcing me away from the gaze with Chastity.

"It seems everyone is." Quite bored already. "Baron," I said, nodding a hello. He, as most of these here tonight, appeared well beneath me, despite the title, but one must be polite nonetheless. Lady and Lord Pearson might as well have invited all of London, no matter what their class. Actually, it seemed they had.

"Well, Baron, here, was saying his is not the first mysterious disappearance, and jolly old England isn't the first country, either."

"Is that so, Baron? And what is it you do, sir?"

"I'm a SteamMage, sir. Master and Principle of the Guilds of ChronoMages and PortalMages, as well as an inventor. I travel quite extensively."

"Is that so? What, exactly, is a SteamMage or ChronoMage, sir?"

"Well, sir, a ChronoMage is someone who travels in time and a PortalMage, between dimensions. A SteamMage does both. It's what I do, sir. I've built a Time Machine. One of my own invention."

"A time machine." I didn't hide the condescending, flat tone of my voice. That, coupled with the most pleasant smile, would surely make my point.

"Indeed, sir! A Time Machine!" Perhaps not. This SteamMage's eyes lit up as bright as any gaslamp when he spoke of such things. Madness, of course, but amusing to watch. His curly mustache spread wide with his smile. "But I did not need travel in time to discover these stories, sir. No, sir. There are stories of such bizarre disappearances all over Europe, sir. For decades, sir. Always a ladies' man, if you get my meaning. Always one who delights, perhaps too much, if

I do say so, sir, in the ladies. Not much of a loss. No, sir." He adjusted his spectacles, then exchanged his serious expression with a kind glance to each of the ladies among us.

"How perfectly delightful," Emily said, clapping her hands together, making her red and green bows bounce. "Perhaps you're next, Arthur." She giggled, enjoying this far too much.

"Not at all, Lady Bainbridge." I patted Avalon's hand, resting in the crook of my arm. "I have settled down, after all."

"Speaking of cads," Emily continued, "I understand Doctor Nesbitt is performing on the airship for Christmas Eve."

"Emily!" Avalon scolded.

"What, my dear? The man doesn't hide it, no. Not at all. Especially when he's had a few, which is, let's face it, always. In fact, if it were just a few, it wouldn't be so dreadfully pathetic."

"We saw him earlier. I think everyone did. How could they not? He's dressed in explorer gear, quite the odd thing to wear to a ball, don't you find?" I was continuously fascinated by fashion, how it came and went, ebbed and flowed. "I'm the first to be a little unconventional, as you well know, Lady Bainbridge."

"At least it wasn't the khaki one," she continued. "How very dull. Do you know he blackens that blasted pith helmet with shoe polish to wear to formal parties? And that cravat! Honestly! Red satin with a sprig of holly at its center. The man is a buffoon."

Ripe, coming from her. "Unlike you, my peach, who lights up the entire room with your grace and colorful ensemble." Painful to look at. Truly.

"He always wears that," Chastity said. "A friend of mine is in one of his classes at university, and she said he's always in explorer gear, even under his scholar robes. Always with that blasted helmet. Always talking about his adventures.

Sometimes, he even has binoculars around his neck, but I suppose they would get in the way of his dancing tonight."

"She?" Emily said with a scandalous lilt.

"Yes, she. It is uncommon, for certain, dear Emily, but there are a few women who attend university."

"And it's high time, too. Hear! Hear!" the SteamMage chimed in. "Women have strong, clear minds, sir! Indeed, sir! Much more so than men, I dare say. It is high time, too."

"Quite," Emily said in a terse tone. She didn't agree, but no surprise there.

"So, Mrs. Rosengarten, what brings you to London? Rosengarten, that's German, is it not?"

"It is, Lord York. My husband was German, but I actually live in Paris. I'm just visiting for the holidays. London is so beautiful this time of year, don't you find?"

"You don't sound French, or German, for that matter."

"No, I'm neither. I was raised in Yorkshire. Long story, widowed now, but I wouldn't want to bore you with all that history. The present is far more interesting." The coy, knowing look she shared with me didn't go unnoticed, not by Avalon nor Emily neither. Ah. Women. How I adored when they fought over me, even in silent polite ways. Yes, I was rather worth it, after all.

"Is what the good SteamMage here says true? Have you heard of these disappearances on your side of the channel?"

"We have. Whisperings here and there, is all. It will be delightful to see my Paris from aloft on Christmas Eve." Her eyes sparkled. "In all my years, I have yet to travel via dirigible. It is all rather new and frightening as well, to be up so high."

"It is sure to be a spectacular view, my dear. Even more so in another decade. Just wait until you see le Tour Eiffel. Magnifique! Vraiment!" The Baron Vincent Von Rictus Baine rocked forward on his toes, then back on his heels, quite pleased with himself.

This man spoke nonsense. "Indeed."

"But even now, sir. The view of Sacre Coeur et Notre Dame along The Seine, all gaslit for the holidays. It will be quite lovely, indeed. I understand we shall be landing on L'esplanade des Invalides for an overnight stay. Perhaps we could land on Champ de Mars while it's still possible."

"Oh, Baron. Do you think we will see Champs Elysees from the air?"

"No doubt, my dear. No doubt! Yes, Le Champs-Elysees, another sight to see in the future. Another beautiful sight. Not to mention the scandalous Moulin Rouge. All yet to be seen, my dears."

"Perhaps the good Mr. Blackwolf would make a special stop at Bedlum upon our return to London, Baron. Good evening, all. Please excuse us. Emily. Mrs. Rosengarten." My voice softened for the last, of course, and not by mistake. "We shall see you all over Paris."

"How rude." Avalon chided when we had left earshot.

"Please, Avalon, time travel? The man was quite obviously daft."

"There was still no need to be so impolite, Arthur. Really, what has gotten into you lately?"

The problem was the other way around, I hadn't gotten into enough ladies lately. That would change quite soon. "Apologies, my dear. I'm quite sure I don't know. Ah! Here is more wine, let us toast us. Always, my love. You and me together, forever."

In the meantime, I looked forward to cornering Mrs. Rosengarten in some dark shadows on the dirigible.

Yes, indeed.

CHAPTER 5

CONSTANCE

"Not here," he said, disguising the words as a harsh cough belched from the side of his mouth as I approached him standing near the sculpted marble fireplace, talking with a group of men. The great W. D. McFerret, too good, or too afraid, rather, to be seen with me at this opulent gala, turned from me and laughed heartily, clamping his black cigarette holder between his teeth, which only served to accentuate his unfortunate jaw. The great coward squeezed his eye around his monocle and said, "Excuse me, gentlemen," then joined in with a new group of revelers standing near the three tiered Christmas trees, each a perfect height to complement the other two, decorated with gold bows and red berries. Their opulence added to the overall splendor of the Pearson's parlour. Teal walls with golden trim framed frescoes of frolicking cherubs which, in turn, echoed the ornate carvings in the marble mantle, topped with poinsettias and winter foliage.

As I made pleasantries with a few people standing near the great grandfather clock set in an alcove, William Daniel McFerret shot a petty glare in my direction for the slightest moment for daring to be in the same room as he before masking his face again in revelry and charm.

Yes. Fear. Since his wife was amongst the partygoers, somewhere. Poor woman, likely had no idea.

They rarely did.

I held my head up high, excused myself from the conversation, and returned to the ballroom, curtsying to the first kind-looking gentleman I saw. He promptly asked me to dance, and I accepted. After all, this was a ball, and I was in such a pretty green gown. The beads of my black choker matched the handiwork down the front, and my supposed lover couldn't even look at me out of his cowardice. Nothing improper had happened with Willie yet, nothing like that, but he was certainly laying the groundwork with the intention of taking the title of lover soon enough. Absurd that he wouldn't speak to me here. It only made him look more guilty, but then, he wasn't as smart as he pretended to be.

They rarely were.

"Baron Vincent Von Rictus Baine," the man with whom I danced introduced himself as he turned me with the music. Beethoven, I believed. My favorite.

"Miss Charlotte Sopha," I said, introducing my current persona.

"Miss Sopha, thank you for doing me the honor of this dance."

"It is my pleasure, Baron." We spoke little as he spun me around the dance floor. A perfect gentleman. Not a single one of my internal warnings went off while dancing with him, for after so much experience, I could smell a scoundrel. Sense him deep inside. I had no doubt that this Baron was one of the very few good ones, as they say. And it was, indeed, a pleasure to dance with him. Once the song was over, the gentleman bowed and bid me a good night, just as a proper gentleman should.

On the other hand, there was that braggart.

William D. McFerret belched a boisterous laugh as he entered the ballroom, causing others to turn around and stare. Americans.

He had instructed me to meet him at a pub after the ball. A dark and dank one, no doubt. I was almost certain I knew what he would have to say. One could predict such things after all. There were types, and after so many centuries, I could tell with near certainty on the first meeting. In five hundred years, I'd only been mistaken once, as I said. It was in the early days, when I hadn't yet honed my empathic abilities, nor the supernatural gifts afforded me. No, I didn't make such mistakes anymore.

Willie was a coward, through and through, but one that was so very full of himself that he saw near nothing else besides his overly large head, or, in this one's case, jaw. He was broken inside, fractured into nothingness, which was likely what he feared the most: that others would see into this void. Still, it didn't excuse hurting others. None whatsoever.

Just as I was about to make my way into the library for a rest, a tall, lanky man tripped and spilled his wine all over the front of my gown. It was none other than Doctor Nesbitt.

"My dress!"

"So sorry," he slurred from beneath his black mustache, pointing straight out on either side. The amount of wax necessary for such a comical display had left flakes of yellow here and there from where it had cracked apart. His sunken black-rimmed, tea-colored eyes molested me as they took in every curve of my body and fold of my gown. He switched his pipe from one side of his mouth to the other. Grabbing the brim, he tipped his blackened helmet and nearly dropped it on the floor. Stringy black hair slipped from its single black ribbon and dangled in front of his sallow face, clinging to his bushy jaw. After fumbling with the hat for a few seconds, he plopped it back onto his head. "Do let me get that for you." Dragging his hands down the front of my dress, he wiped away the wine, more than grazing my breasts. He fondled me then and there, unapologetically, in front of all of London's elite.

"I beg your pardon, sir!" I tried to move away, but he held me in place with one hand and continued the pretense of wiping off my dress, slowly, with the other. Fortunately, my recent dance partner, the Baron, saved me by taking the offensive man away.

The doctor didn't go with grace. He spat and cursed and demanded to be left alone to attend to his most unfortunate blunder, but the soft-spoken and kind Baron whispered something about promising opium. The doctor's eyes lit up, and he said, "Well go get it, man! I'll wait over there. Chop! Chop!"

Such revolting behavior. Still, intrigued at these drunken public displays, I kept just outside of this bizarre man's peripheral view to see what I could. I was rather amazed to see the number of women who approached him, but none of them stayed too long.

Understandably.

§

"I so enjoyed your lecture the other night on big game hunting on the continent, Doctor. Such a delight, as usual," the first one said.

"It is you who are the delight, my lovely."

"Oh, my. Can we expect more tales from the continent this weekend?"

"And more dancing, too, Doctor? Perhaps you would dance with me?" the second asked.

"Yes. Yes, of course, my sweet dumpling. My, aren't you delicious." His salacious glare trailed from her head down to the bottom ruffle of her dress, and then back up again. He licked his lips and stroked his mustache on either side.

"Well. I'm about to join my husband for a cup of tea, so..."

"Yes! Murky delight! Deep and intense, just the way I like it. Deep. With sugar, so there is a touch of sweetness as well. It is rather grand. Yes, indeed! And I like you, madam. I do, I do. Would you fancy a romp, dear lady?"

"I beg your pardon?"

"Now. Don't act so surprised. I've seen the way you look at me. Besides, you wanted to dance," the doctor adjusted himself and licked his lips again, not even hiding the fact that his lustful eyes focused on the lady's bosom. "Let's not play charades, shall we? We could steal away for half an hour. Behind the bushes, perhaps? I'll be quick. Quick and deep. Deep!" He thrust his hips toward the woman in the most lewd and scandalous manner.

"Well!" She fanned herself wildly and turned away, walking quickly toward her husband, who gave a rather cross look back in the professor's direction.

Doctor Nesbitt downed a new drink with one hand while trading his empty glass for another full one as the waiter passed. "It's not the best wine, but it will do," he said to himself, then slammed that one back, too. His step faltered as he walked toward the next passing waiter, but a group of young women stopped him.

"Excuse me, Doctor. I found your lecture last evening simply brilliant. You, sir, are brilliant. A professor, doctor, and an explorer. How exciting! Not to mention your gift of laughter to us all. Impressive, sir. On top of your travels and scholarly work. Quite impressive, indeed."

"Thank you, dear ladies," he replied bowing to them, stumbling. "Have you come all on your own?"

"Are you suggesting impropriety?" The boldest one of the group crossed her arms ready for a fight but was presently hushed by the other two.

"Forgive my cousin, Doctor. She has had a rather unfortunate experience that has left her suspicious of all men. I assured her that you were nothing like that, so charming and witty. So intelligent and worldly."

"Yes, indeed! I am a gentleman, after all. I should never do anything to be considered improper. Certainly not! Never, my dear ladies."

"That is quite a relief, but I thought nothing else."

"So, are you ladies here all alone? There will be an exclusive gathering later this evening, and I'd like to invite you to join me there."

"Oh! Exclusive, sir! With you, sir? We should be honored to attend. Where is this gathering?"

"It is private and very hush-hush, you see. Mustn't step on any toes, as there are only room for so many. Only a very privileged few will be able to join me in the celebration, and I would be so very delighted to have you ladies join me. Certainly, you three must be the prettiest lovelies at this entire gathering." He moved off to the side out of earshot of those standing near, except for me, and motioned for the three young women to join him. Two of them giggled and bounced over near him, but the third remained wary. Still, she didn't lag far behind her cousins.

"Where is this celebration, sir? Do tell, and we shan't tell a soul."

"Shhhh," he whispered, looking around conspiratorially, "It's getting fuller by the second, ladies."

"Getting fuller, sir?"

"Yes, there will soon only be room for two of you."

His rank breath filled the air around them, not only for the sour looks on their faces as they tried to politely back away, but I could smell it from my position as well. He bent low, forcing the girls to bend over to hear him. Their mounding breasts peeked over their bodices, supple and sweet, ready for the picking, or the licking, as he'd have it.

"Come closer and give me your hand. I'll show you."

A look of disgust overcame the bolder cousin; she turned and strode away, but the other two eagerly put out their hands, no doubt thinking he would lead them to the festivities. Instead, he grabbed their proffered hands and placed them over the growing bulge in his trousers. They chirped a stifled scream and snatched their hands back before chasing after their wiser cousin.

He straightened up, nonchalant, as if they had all just finished with pleasantries and joined a group of people laughing and talking loudly.

I had heard such rumors of him, but now I was sure. Ripe for a lesson, this one was, but not tonight. Another venture for another time.

My dance card was getting rather full.

§

After the ball, I caught a hansom in Brompton and instructed the driver to take me to the address scribbled on the piece of paper Willie had slipped me in passing at the ball. He thought he was so clever and stealthy, but I found the entire thing ridiculous. Although, he did have it down, these surreptitious dalliances of his. No, this was not the first time he'd done this, but it shall be the last.

The Mitre Tavern, across town near Hatton Garden, turned out. It would take no less than half an hour to get there by carriage, but it was a nice evening after all, albeit cold. I sat back and let the clattering of the wheels over the cobblestones lull me into a kind of peace. It gave me time to think about Doctor Nesbitt. Truly a revolting specimen, was he not? I had heard tales of impropriety with his students and, well, obviously any other woman who admired him, or not. Really, any woman within his reach. He used his position of moderate celebrity and position in society to do what he would. He had a wife and three young children over in Oxford, but he spent much time away from the university, frequenting London for additional lectures and the like. He was reportedly here so much, he had set up a residence and laboratory for himself. It allowed him to keep things from his wife, and she none the wiser. I thought of the poor woman, at home alone with three youngsters while he was out doing what he did. She was much younger than he was, no doubt. They usually were. So young, and her life now set, trapped with this salacious man, unable to escape under the rules of society, not without being shunned and ridiculed and labeled a harlot. Women ended up in Bedlam for less. So, yes, she was a prisoner with no hope of escape.

Well, none before now.

I would set her free.

But how best to get close to the Doctor? Student, perhaps. Indeed, a student from abroad. Although that would take so much time for preparation. Plus, how tiresome to go through all the bureaucracy of university. A maid, perhaps. Hmmmm. I should think on it some more before committing to a plan. After all, there was still Mr. McFerret to attend to. Another who used his position and growing celebrity to exploit and destroy.

Not for long.

I had made it quite clear to him that I was not, or rather, Charlotte was not, in the least bit interested in impropriety. Our relationship was strictly professional. His pretense was that he wanted to help promising women writers break into journalism in an altogether male-dominated society. It was scandalous, and so, he had said, we must keep it under wraps for the time being. I would pass him articles written under a male pseudonym. When the editor loved my work, we would reveal my gender, in secret, so as not to cause an outrage. Then, only *The Times* would learn the truth.

However, soon thereafter, he began shunning me in public, like he did earlier this evening, and his intentions became quite clear to me, but Charlotte, as young and hopeful and idealistic as she was, wouldn't know any difference. She would believe this was the way things worked, as so many before her had believed.

He took their articles and added his own byline, passing them off as his work, after bedding them and blackmailing them into silence. Then, of course, he abandoned the poor girls, ruined and betrayed all while profiting off their work. He had done so she who had summoned me, and so many before, I had since learned.

Now it was my turn.

Then, his.

Yes. He was ripe for punishment, this one.

I looked out of the left side of the carriage as we turned onto Knightsbridge and passed Hyde Park, dark at such a late hour besides the gaslights along the streets. Still, it was lovely. From each gaslamp hung a Christmas wreath, above the reach of ne'er-do-wells. The warm golden glow fell on the evergreen boughs and continued onto the streets below, lighting those out for a late evening stroll after their holiday festivities. Perhaps heading back home to their families, preparing for Christmas in a few days.

The light of the waxing moon created a visible outline of the trees in the park, but before I could make out much more, the carriage had entered Mayfair with its tall, brick buildings, much like those in Brompton and along Knightsbridge. I imagined the families asleep behind those darkened windows, snuggled up from the cold London night air. It was quite nippy and, of course, wet this time of year, as it was every time of the year in London, which suited me just fine.

I nestled under my cloak, made of thick red wool and lined with a black velvet collar, protecting my cheeks from the night air, and let my mind drift from this to that until I felt the carriage slow and ultimately stop. The door remained closed until I slipped the fare up through the driver's hatch. He opened the doors and I climbed out onto the sidewalk.

"Where from here?" I asked up to the driver, standing beneath the light of a black iron gaslamp on the curb. Best to stay in the light, as a woman alone in London at night. It wasn't much, but it was some measure of safety.

"Just down there." He pointed to a white marble archway. Narrow. I wondered if my bustle would even fit through. Over the top of the arch between two white columns hung a sign that read *Ye Olde Mitre, Estd 1546*. I looked back up at the driver, and he nodded with determination. "Through there, Miss." He pointed through the archway, down a rather long, dark alley. "Not at all safe for a lady, especially at night. Are you quite sure, Miss?"

"I can take care of myself, sir, but I thank you for your concern. I'm headed to a business meeting."

"Strange place for a business meeting, mind. On Yule, as well. Strange business for a lady. Strange time a-night, too. What kind of business, miss, if ya don't mind me asking."

"Not any of yours, I'm afraid. Thank you for the ride."

The driver grumbled something under his breath before cracking his whip in the air above the horse, whose huff of breath at the sound caused a cloud of frozen breath around his big black nose. With a jolt, the carriage was off, and so was I. Toward the middle of the alley, which stretched through to the next street over, a singular gaslamp lit the entrance of the Mitre Tavern. Between me and the entrance, only one other gaslight stood, closer to the tavern than to me. Many nasties could be hiding in the shadows along the way. No, not a safe place for a lady at night. Not a safe place for anyone at night.

Moving down the alley, I focused on the light over the Mitre's door. The warm glow of the interior, where a welcoming fire awaited me, became closer with every step. The sounds from inside filled the dank alley with a hushed roar.

"Well. What 'ave we 'ere?" Foul, hot breath hit my face. As soon as he stepped out from against the wall, I could see his shape, just inches in front of me, backlit by the gaslamp. "Out for a stroll, are we, Miss?"

"I'm just heading to the tavern, please let me pass."

"Whatcha gonna give me in return, eh? 'Ows about a kiss?" He smacked his lips a few times and my stomach turned.

"No, sir, please. I'm meeting my husband, just inside there."

"And what kinda 'usband would let 'is pretty little wife walk all by 'er lonesome a'night? Eh? What kind? Just a little kiss and you'll be on your way."

"I don't have time for this. I'm already late."

"You'd rather 'ave a quick one against the wall, wouldn't ya, love? Yah. You're beggin' for it."

"They'll hear me scream. Just let me pass." I never raised my voice or showed an ounce of fear, for there was none there to show. Insects like this were far from frightening. More of an annoyance.

"They won't hear nothin', never do." He laughed once, then shoved me against the brick. His foul tongue licked up the side of my face while a hand hiked up my skirts.

"Good," I said. "Then they won't hear you, either."

He didn't have time to blink before I had him pinned by the throat against the opposite wall. The far glow illuminated half of his grotesque face, and his eyes were wide with horror.

Good.

"You're lucky I'm not hungry or properly prepared, or this would be much worse. You'll get off easy. Too easy, but I haven't the time."

His snaggletoothed mouth sputtered and spat, trying to say something. I didn't care what. After another moment, he lost consciousness. He fell to the ground in a heap of filth, and I spat on him, then wiped the side of my face dry. A few words and a finger snap later, his outer appearance mirrored that of the inside. With a pivot of my boot and a satisfying crunch, the cockroach would never again make a woman scream.

The tavern bustled with people, mostly men, of course, although there was a woman here and there, and a haggard barmaid, too. Most didn't notice my entry, as they were all too wrapped up in their own lives, but the few who did gaped. A lady of my standing, or how I, at least, appeared, was certainly a rarity in an establishment like this. Most definitely at this hour. One or two men elbowed his mate to draw their attention.

I absorbed the place. Walnut beams lined the ceiling. Dark wood covered the entire interior. Panels. Tables. Chairs. The bar and even the barstools all constructed from fine wood. Photographs and posters adorned the walls and mugs hung from the ceiling near the bar.

But, I didn't see McFerret.

The note had said *Ye Closet*, but surely he wasn't meeting me in a cupboard. A fire roared in the fireplace, and even after just a few moments. The chill of the night melted away. I took off my coat and draped it over one arm, which drew even more looks. Two gentleman, trying to get closer to the fire, moved away from an open doorway I hadn't seen before. A couple of leather upholstered chairs sat against the wall beside it. Over the doorway a small sign read: *Ye Closet*. That must be the place. I made my way through the crowd and looks, and although more than one hand brushed against my breast or bottom, I truly did not have time. Nor was this the place.

A quaint alcove lay just beyond the doorway where McFerret spoke with another man. He saw me, and his eyes lit up, almost surprised. His bristly mustache broadened with his smile. "Would you excuse us, sir? I have *urgent* business with this lady."

The other gentleman nodded and gave a slow, deliberate wink to McFerret, and then laughed when he looked at me. "Fanks for the autograph, sir," he said as he grabbed his pint and his signed copy of *The Times* as he scooted out of the alcove, chuckling again when he passed me.

"Charlotte. I must say, I'm quite impressed you got here." He motioned for me to sit beside him, so I did. He leaned in a little too close, and continued, "Your determination and bravery are astounding. That's good, because that's what you need, that and ambition, to make it in the newspaper business. To make it as a writer anywhere, especially with the hindrance of your gender, my darling. You must be shrewd and clever. Ambition! Perseverance! Courage! Yes, courage. You've got that in spades as well, don't you, my dear."

"What was that at the ball, William? You treated me like your mistress, and I was quite clear about this remaining professional. I shan't be reduced to a trollop, sir."

"Of course not! I'm offended that you would think such a thing, as that was exactly what I was protecting you from at the ball, Charlotte. Truly offended. I was thinking of your honor, and you accuse me of... My wife was there, as you know, as was all of her close friends who love to gossip and make trouble where there is none." He chuckled and swirled the Gin in his glass, then continued, "They excel at it. A young pretty lady talking to me as familiar as you have a tendency to do, and as frankly. It would be half across London by now had I indulged in any conversation with you at that party. Really,

Charlotte, I thought you were smarter than that. Perhaps this isn't such a good idea after all." He sipped his drink and looked away from me, face full of mock disappointment and offense.

The games had begun.

"I'm sorry, Mr. McFerret. I spoke out of turn, sir. You have been nothing but a complete gentleman and professional from the start, and I truly appreciate what you're doing for me sir. I truly do!" Determined to push me further into desperation, McFerret let the silence between us linger as the voices of men singing in the back courtyard wafted in through the thin paneled walls and thick, smoky window.

"I don't know. You're behaving like a child."

"I'm not a child, Mr. McFerret. You've read my work. You know I have talent."

"Of that there's no doubt, but—" He shook his head, looking down into his drink. I couldn't help but notice that the painting of a drunken, bloated monk held a striking resemblance to the drunken, bloated journalist who sat beneath it.

"Please, sir. Give me another chance."

"I can't talk work now. I'm too distressed and distracted by this nonsense." He finished off the amber liquid in the bottom of his glass. "I'm getting another Gin. Drink? I'll buy."

"I—I don't drink, sir. I mean, I wouldn't know what to get."

"Gin. Always Gin. It's the drink of writers. Get used to it." He held up two fingers, getting the attention of a passing barmaid. "Two. In fact, bring the bottle. We're not to be disturbed, understand?"

Although young, about twenty, the woman looked quite worn. Stray strands of dark hair fell about her face, and although she smiled, there was no delight in her eyes. Dead, killed, more like. Hollowed out by the pain that emanated from her in waves, making me nauseous. I focused on McFerret's bushy jawline, looking away from the barmaid, trying to put up a barrier between us.

"A-course, sir. Anyfink for you, gov. Two comin' up." Her voice was pleasant enough and she smiled with as much sweetness as she could muster. My nausea rose, but she left to get more liquor before I had to excuse myself.

So much pain, all over. Everywhere I went. There just wasn't enough time.

"You see, Charlotte, that's the kind of treatment you can look forward to. Once your name is known, people will be falling over themselves to serve you, to help you."

"Well, I don't care about that. I just want to write."

"Don't we all." He got a faraway look, then threw back his Gin. "Where's that damn barmaid?" he said, slamming his glass down on the table.

"What did you think of my article?"

"It could use some work, but it's a fine start. A fine start."

The barmaid arrived with two fresh glasses and a bottle of Gin. "Any fink else for you, sir?"

"Not at the moment. In fact, we are not to be disturbed. Understood?"

"Yes, sir. Fank you, sir." She took his dirty glass and left.

McFerret poured me two fingers of Gin and himself four. "To the written word," he said, holding his glass up. I picked up mine and clinked with his.

"The written word," I repeated. He swallowed his in one go. As he poured another for himself, he saw that I had not yet touched mine.

"Well, drink up. What are you waiting for? If you're going to be a working writer in this town, you had better learn to drink. Drink up!"

I sipped, grimacing as I did. Of course, this wasn't the first time I had Gin, but it was Charlotte's first time and so it was mine, too. Quite literally. It was this tongue's first time to taste the bitterness and bite, so the grimace was real. When I created a persona, I became that new person: body, mind, and soul. Although my thoughts were still in there and I knew what I was doing, hers were, too. It was like my mind was split with me in the background, guiding. Remaining grounded. Keeping reality in mind, but the innocence of the personas I played was real, too. It had to be for these kinds of men. They sensed prey, so I had to become prey.

McFerret laughed at me and clinked glasses again. "That's my girl," he said, eyes sparkling. "Now, onto business." He poured himself another and held the bottle over my glass until I forced down the Gin, enabling him to refill it.

My body shuddered as the drink burned my throat and sat heavy in my stomach.

McFerret laughed again.

"I've arranged a meeting with the editor on the Pearson's dirigible cruise this weekend. I've procured you a ticket again, and there's money in there for a new dress as well. You can't wear the same one you did tonight, not in this society, although you look stunning in it, my darling." He pulled an envelope out of his inner pocket and slid it in front of me. His eyes trailed down my neck, over my collar bones, and rested on my décolletage. I opened the envelope, and his eyes bore into my breasts, thinking, no doubt, that mine were on the envelope and didn't notice what he was doing, but they weren't.

They watched his every move.

He licked his lips, then sucked down another four fingers, never taking his eyes off the tops of my breasts.

"This is quite generous," I said. "Thank you for all your help, Mr. McFerret. I don't know how to repay you your kindness to me. Your belief in me."

"We'll think of something," he said, laying his hand over mine, raising his eyes to meet mine. After the worm patted my hand a few times in a way that made my insides squirm, he poured himself more Gin and indicated that I should finish mine again.

"I truly must be careful, sir. I'm not sure how much more of this I can take. It is my first time, after all. I'd rather not be sick. How humiliating that would be, indeed."

"Nonsense. We have to harden you up, my dear. It's a tough business, and you are still too soft. Although,"—he caught me with his wily eyes and flashed his sly smile, dragging a finger across my thumb—"soft is good, too."

I picked up my glass, pulling my hand out of his reach. "The meeting is set for Saturday night? That's Christmas Eve. Isn't that a strange time to meet? I'm sure Mr. Chenery doesn't wish to work on Christmas Eve."

"There you go questioning me again!" His voice wasn't in the least bit cross, though. He spoke with a huge grin and a twinkle in his eyes, amused if anything. "Are you going to trust me in this, Charlotte? This is how it must be done, at least for now. It can't be done during regular business hours, darling. This is altogether unconventional all around. It will be fine. It's just an introductory meeting, after all. But remember, it will have to be in private, as my wife, and his, will be on board, too. It is a party, after all, so discretion is imperative. This will be your first big break! I have no doubt Chenery will be as impressed with you as I am."

"I shall buy a smart dress, worthy of a journalist of *The Times*." I raised my glass and clinked with his, then forced it down, coughing afterward.

"That's my girl," he said again. "That's my good, good girl."

"Pardon me, but I must visit the powder room." Upon rising, I felt woozy and had to catch myself on the table or I would've fallen right back down.

McFerret laughed again. "Easy there, my darling. Maybe you have had enough for one night. We'll work on your ability to hold alcohol on the cruise."

"I feel rather ill, sir. Is this normal?"

"It is. It will pass. Let's get you some fresh air." As he stood, his walrus belly hit the edge of the table and knocked over the bottle of Gin, nearly empty anyway. The neck shattered when it hit my glass, which also broke. "Damn it all!"

"I'll get the barmaid," I said, feeling a little steadier.

"No need." He dug into his pocket and pulled out a handful of coins, tossing several onto the table before offering his hand to help me out of the alcove. He picked up my wrap and draped it over my back. His belly pressed against my bustle, and my stomach turned again. He was a handsome man, after all, and although shaped like a sea mammal, larger in the middle and tapering off on both ends, it didn't take away from his good looks. Even the strong jaw worked on him, especially adorned with those furry, dark sideburns.

Oh my, was this the Gin talking?

He led me out into the nippy air, and the cold sobered me up quite quickly. I turned back to McFerret, and he was looking down at his pocket watch.

"Damn it all," he said again. "It's later than I thought. I've got to get back to the missus, and I was so hoping for an evening stroll together, to talk writing, of course. I'm quite curious about your process. Your prose is inspired, Charlotte."

"Why, thank you, Mr. Ferret."

"As I've told you before, call me Willie, my darling." He leaned in for a kiss, and I let him peck my lips once before pushing him away. His mustache prickled my nose.

"Mr. Ferret—Willie—professional, remember? It's not that I find you repulsive, sir. Far from that, but it's just not proper. Besides, you're married. I couldn't do such a thing to another woman."

"Balderdash! My wife," he snuffed, then took both my hands and backed me up against the brick wall, pressing his walrus belly into me. "I only married her for her money." He leaned in for another kiss, pinning me against the wall, and this time I turned my head. His lips pressed against my cheek while the curled tips of his waxed mustache tickled my nose.

"Sir," I whispered. "Please."

Clearing his throat and backing away, he said, "Yes! Yes. You are right, Miss Sopha. Of course. It's the Gin, after all. Forgive me."

"Already forgotten, Willie."

"Excellent! Let's get you in a hansom straight away. I think we'll both sleep well tonight! Yes, indeed. That Gin's got a kick!"

He led me down the dark alleyway back to the curb and kept a respectable distance the entire way. After finding me a hansom, he kissed my hand and held it as I mounted the carriage. He paid the driver, instructing him to ensure I was safely inside before riding off while I snuggled within my wrap, preparing for the cold ride.

"Thank you again for arranging the meeting with Mr. Chenery. It will be such an honor to just meet the man, let alone entertain the thought of working with him. I'm all a flutter already!"

"It will prove to be a splendid evening all around," he said, tipping his hat. "Of that I have no doubt."

 # CHAPTER 6

ARTHUR

Christmas shoppers scampered from here to there. Thomas wound the brougham through the busy streets, stopping again and again for people with their arms' full of packages to cross the road. Other carriages blocked the street, trying to turn around or waiting for their occupants to return from the shop.

"We should've walked," I said to Avalon sitting beside me, but all I saw was her tiny black hat perched on her black curls. She looked out the window at the commotion around us. "It would've been faster."

"Perhaps," she said.

"It would've been faster."

"They all look so happy, rushing about, don't they? Places to go and getting goodies for their lovelies. We should get some gifts, Arthur. Don't you think?" She turned to me, her eyes lit with hope. "We could exchange them on the dirigible. Wouldn't that be fine?"

"If you'd like. One thing at a time, all right? We're here to see about Nick, remember? Let's get that done before we plan something else."

"Do you think the police will still be there? It's been several days, after all."

"I doubt it, but if they are, you can practice pressing your will upon them. Compelling them, as we sometimes call it. Coppers are notoriously easy to compel, Ava. If all else fails, we do still have the uniforms dear Victor procured for us after our last caper."

With the reminder of Victor, Avalon got quiet again, her smiled faded. "I miss Victor." The sadness in her voice was palpable and altogether disagreeable. How dull indeed, and how very careless for me to mention him.

"Yes, I'm well aware. It has been months, Ava. You must move on from that loss one day."

"It's been less than a year, Arthur. Barely half a year, and one doesn't have one's best friend and confidant brutally murdered before one's eyes all that often. And you're telling me to get over it already? What happened to you, Arthur? One minute you are my love, the man who I adore. The next, you are a monster. Unfeeling, uncaring. Cruel."

"Nonsense, Ava. I'm always the same." My calm voice, with the appropriate amount of concern, of course, suggested she settle down and listen to reason. No need to be so emotional. "It's no doubt your lady parts wreaking havoc on your mind, sweetheart. Perhaps you're suffering from hysteria. Yes, the symptoms are quite similar. Perhaps I should call the doctor. I am worried about you, Ava. For all I know, you contracted a venereal disease from another man. You say I was the first, but an unmarried woman having sexual relations? It is questionable to say the least. Well, the doctor and Bedlam, too, would be suspicious of that. They haven't yet repealed the Contagious Diseases Act, after all. Just a word from me, and you'd be required to submit to an exam, otherwise face imprisonment. The police do the exams, as you well know, and I understand they are far from pleasant. I would hate for you to be disgraced so, my darling girl. I just want you to be happy, Ava. To be well and genuinely happy. I'm just looking out for you, my love."

Avalon's eyes widened with horror. All of London knew what happened to women examined for venereal diseases. Humiliating exams. Unclean women were confined until perceived as cured. Many wound up in Bedlam.

The threat of such treatment served to keep them in line. Indeed.

Tears rimmed her eyes, jaw set. She spoke with determination. "I am not your property."

No. Nor any man's. Yet. With her new strength, she could rip any who tried to hurt her to shreds, but I'd done quite well to keep her ignorant of that fact.

"You have been dropping hints about marriage. Lady York, yes, I think that suits you well. I just love you so much, Ava. I want to ensure you are feeling your best. I miss my happy, loving lover, and I would like her back. Genuinely happy. Yes. I should very much like my cheery, cheeky Ava back. Ah! Here we are at Nicholas's. After you, my love."

Avalon took my proffered hand and stepped down onto the street. "Thank you, Thomas," she said with the most pleasant tone. Good girl. "It is such a pleasure to have you drive us. Will you wait for us here?"

"That is up to M'Lord, M'Lady."

"Yes, Thomas. Wait. We shan't be too long. Shall we, Ava? Looks like the coast is clear of coppers, so there should be no trouble whatsoever. No more trouble. Right, sweetheart?"

"No more trouble, my love." Her smile was not only bright and as genuine as could be, but she also leaned over and kissed me on the cheek. In public. Yes. This was much more like it. Just needed to put the foot down every so often, after all. Perhaps a wedding was just the thing. It had been ever so long since I was married. Over three centuries! Indeed! I had forgotten just how lovely marriage can be. Carnal pleasures whenever I wanted, no need to wait or search or put out the effort of seduction, but then…if I did find such pleasures elsewhere…well, it was to be expected! Especially by a man of my station. Yes! It was time to take a wife. Yes, indeed.

"Lord York! Miss Bainbridge! Funny seein' you here."

"Mr. Blackwolf, was it? Did you enjoy the gala last night?" His handshake was as strong as his husky appearance suggested. Dressed in much more comfortable attire than his relative finery of last night, he wore a standard-issue US Army shirt, braces, and wool trousers. Topped with a heavy wool coat and the same hat and goggles as at the gala. How very common.

Avalon stayed obedient and quiet. Good girl. Just a silent nod greeted our new friend.

"I did. I did. You do things up over here, don't ya?"

"We do, indeed. Well, it was lovely seeing you, and I suppose we shall see you again this weekend."

"I hope the weather is clear enough to see the moon over Paris. Ya almost forget there's a sun. Texas is very sunny and hot. It's always so gray here. "

"That it is. One gets used to it." Plus, we counted on it. Texas sounded like a miserable place.

"Although, you brighten up any day, Miss Bainbridge, if ya don't mind me saying."

"Oh, Mr. Blackwolf, how you flatter." She curtsied and offered her hand for him to kiss, and he did. Peeking out beneath her white lace cuff, she wore black lace fingerless gloves. His lips touched her skin. Something inside me roared, and I had to exert extra effort to keep my face pleasant. She was mine, after all. Yes, must marry and make that undeniable to any.

"I only speak the truth, dear lady."

Although Avalon smiled, her eyes held a sadness to them behind her round, purple-tinted spectacles. Her face showed nothing but pleasant calm, no sign of distress. Dressed in burgundy, fit for the season, Avalon's day dress suited her quite well. The snugness around the waist showed off her lovely shape. Brass buttons centered down the bodice accentuated her curves. The pocket watch chain affixed on one side of her bodice, then again on the other, creating the most fetching drape across her bosoms. I should pay more attention to this beauty. The remainder of the chain dangled down her side and attached to the time piece tucked into its little pocket.

I suddenly wanted her. Right here. In the carriage. Although her dress had no bustle, I wanted to be buried beneath her skirts. Now. Perhaps inside Nick's. There would be plenty of privacy there.

"We really must be going, Mr. Blackwolf," I said.

"Of course. This weekend then!"

"This weekend, indeed. Good day."

All three of us started to move at once, and all in the same direction: toward Nick's house. "Excuse me, sir," I said to him, indicating with my tone that I wished to know what the bloody hell he was doing.

"I've come to examine Lord Stanton's place, Lord York. I have some experience in these things, and, well, my curiosity just got the better of me. My ship is getting the holiday touch by Lady Pearson's decorators, and they needed me out of their way."

"Fascinating. Well, Lord Stanton is a dear friend of mine, so we've come to have a look ourselves. Shall we?" So much for a quick romp with Avalon inside. I chucked to myself, or a quick romp inside Avalon. I was ever so clever. Perhaps it was for the best. It would give my desires a chance to build, and then I would have her tonight.

"We were concerned the police would still be here," Avalon said as we approached Nick's door. "But there are none in sight. I'm not sure there will be much to see inside."

"It's locked," I said, trying the door. "Of course, it's locked. Did I think it would just be open for all of London to explore?

All his treasures would be gone by now. Never mind, we tried." I could, of course, easily open the door, but not with Mr. Blackwolf standing about.

"I've come prepared for that," he said, holding up a black leather pouch he had just produced from inside his coat. With a flick of his wrist, the thing unrolled, revealing a variety of tools. He chose a small contraption, similar to a turnscrew, only this had tiny gears where the tool met the shaft. Blackwolf flicked a switch, and the thing spread out and started to spin.

"Blimey! One didn't expect that."

"How very ingenious," Avalon said, eyes wide with wonder. She let go of my arm to get a closer look. My Avalon always found new technology so intriguing. My lovely love. "How does it work?"

"I'll show you." Blackwolf turned the thing off again, and it collapsed back into a regular turnscrew. He scrunched up the leather tool case with one hand and pocketed it while delighting in Avalon's curiosity.

"This is all quite captivating, but passersby are starting to stare at us huddled around the door. Perhaps you could show her another time, Mr. Blackwolf?"

"Eh. Call me Arron. Yer right. We're drawin' too much attention to ourselves. You two give me some cover, and I'll get this here door open."

Avalon and I turned around and faced the street. Thomas, just a ways up, sat on his driver's perch, lanky legs at comical angles. I pointed to some Christmas decorations across the street and leaned over to Avalon, making an ostensible show of describing them. Instead, I whispered, "You look simply scrumptious this afternoon, my love. I was so hoping to taste you once we were inside."

She remained composed at first, but as I continued whispering desires, her breath came faster.

Behind me, I heard a strange whirring sound followed by piercing squeals. I forced a bout of booming laughter, and invited Avalon to join me with a nudge. Even unnatural, her laugh was music to my ears. I nuzzled my nose against her cheek and whispered, "You're so delightful. I love you."

She turned to me, surprised with light in her eyes, which positively sparkled behind her colored spectacles. "Truly, Arthur?" she replied in hushed tones. "I love you, too."

"We're in, ya lovebirds," Arron said from behind us, now standing in Nicholas's foyer.

"Splendid," I said, squeezing Avalon's hand, which rested in the crook of my arm. "After you, my love." Once inside, we shut the door behind us and waited a moment to ensure there was no one else inside. I even called out a "Hello?" No one answered. "The paper said the blood was found in the parlour. Follow me."

There was blood here. I could smell it already, and Avalon could, too. She held a dainty hand up to her nose to help block the smell. The woman hadn't eaten properly in months, after all. Animal's blood only afforded so much strength. Must keep up the pretense that we didn't hurt anyone. Her need must be insatiable before I told her the truth of our existence. Well, my existence. Still, she would remain under my control, of course.

We all stood in the doorway and took in the room. "Nothing seems too out of sorts. The upset table and some blood here." I pointed just in front of our feet. A dark stain blemished the forest green rug. "It's substantial, but certainly not a fatal amount. The rest rather seems the same. It has been months since I've been here, of course, and there are some new items, but then Nick was always for keeping up with current trends. That red sofa is new, but the darker maroon one isn't. The chandelier, that's new. An electric one, too, but we're too far from Holborn Viaduct for electricity. He must've had this shipped from The Colonies. Optimistic of him."

"There's something off about that portrait of him, there." Avalon pointed to the gold framed painting over the fireplace. "He looks too... something."

"Indeed. It looks rather recent. That vest he's wearing he had commissioned shortly before we lost touch."

"Ugh! And that?" She pointed to a bizarre squatty statue, gargoyle like, but even more horrific than any gargoyle I'd seen. It squatted, legs spread wide, on Nick's writing desk by the front windows.

"That looks like an African fertility god, even though it's missin' the obvious appendage," Captain Blackwolf offered. "I've seen ones like that in the New Orleans Voodoo shops. It's said to give the bearer an insatiable appetite. Forgive me for saying so, ma'am."

"Nick had that without Voodoo."

"What difference does the decor make anyway?" Arron asked. "This room is odd all around, and that portrait is right creepy."

"It doesn't really make a difference, just working it out," I said, scanning the room again. "Getting a feel for the place. Something seems off, but I can't put my finger on it. He was entertaining, as I can smell a hint of perfume"—and that unmistakable scent of sex—"but that's not unusual for Nick."

"There's nothing here," Arron said. "The blood suggests foul play, but, as you pointed out, Lord York, there ain't enough for it to have been a fatal wound. Not much more than a bad cut, I'd say."

"It looks angry," Avalon said, moving closer to the gargoyle. "Like it's in a rage or terror."

"Agreed. There is nothing here," I said, ignoring Avalon. Her fascination with technology and history was tiresome. "This is a waste of time. I don't doubt good ol' Nick just went on holiday with his lady friend and forgot to tell his mum. Nothing more. You'll see. He'll be back in time for your cruise, no doubt, ready for new adventures."

"There's blood here," Avalon said. She had lifted the statue and beneath it was a ring of dried blood, shaped as the outline of the statue. Yet, it was darker than blood, even dried blood. It was black. "Murder weapon?"

"Perhaps, although I'd doubt it. Again, not enough blood. Head wounds tend to bleed a lot."

"The murderer could've caught the rest of the blood in something. Let's have a look in the kitchen," she suggested, setting the not-so-fertile god back down on the desk.

"I'm sure the police looked everywhere."

"They didn't find the blood beneath the statue, did they?"

"That's a good point, Miss Bainbridge. How could they have missed that?"

"Call me Avalon, please. Yes, rather odd that they would've missed it. Perhaps there wasn't this blood when they were here."

I scoffed. "Coppers are incompetent, of course, so it's not that much of a shock, now is it?"

We reached the kitchen, and everything seemed in place. I was becoming quite bored with this game.

"Indeed, Arthur, but are they quite that incompetent? There's something strange about that blood. It is rather too dark for blood, don't you think? Perhaps we should take the statue with us. Have a bit of it analyzed." Avalon gave the appearance of closely examining every surface, trying to find a trace of blood or of the black stuff, but I heard her sniffing, discovering the extent of her heightened senses. I could tell as soon as we entered there was no fresh blood here.

"I'm not so sure, Miss Ba—Avalon, if it turns out he was murdered, you don't want to be in possession of the murder weapon."

"Certainly not. Thank you, Arron. Nothing out of sorts here. I think we must speak with Mr. McFerret after all, and, if we can, the constable in charge of this investigation."

"Mr. McFerret will be on the cruise tomorrow night, so you'll have the chance to talk to him then."

Avalon and Arron faced each other, excited at the prospect of the mystery, and that same roar erupted in my gut, so I moved in between them, pulling Avalon close to my side. "Yes, indeed. That's exactly what we shall do."

§

"I think we'll walk for a bit, Thomas. Just take the carriage home."

"Yes, M'Lord." He bowed and climbed on the carriage as Avalon and I headed in the opposite direction toward the main street, parting ways with Mr. Blackwolf as well. A Compressed Air Tram rolled by, spewing black smoke into the air above it.

"We could take the CAT," Avalon said, "I've not been on one yet,"

"Another time? It is such a lovely afternoon, and it's already getting dark. We'll be quite safe, don't you think? Besides, it would be nice to have a stroll with your beauty on my arm."

She squeezed my arm and laid her head on my shoulder, breathing in the evening air. "Yes. I do like to be out for a change. Everything is so alive, and I'm so hungry, Arthur. Perhaps a stop at the butchers for some fresh blood?"

"Excellent idea, sweetheart. Excellent! You were quite impressive in there." She beamed up at me, thrilled at my approval, no doubt. But then, who wouldn't be? "Great find, the blood beneath the statue. That definitely adds to the mystery. We should discuss it more over dinner. How are you feeling?"

"Quite well, actually. The smell of the blood…as you well know. It is rather difficult to be among all these people. It's as if I can hear their blood flowing, their hearts beating, calling to me."

"You get used to it."

A group of women marched down the street chanting and holding placards that read such things as WE ARE NOT UNCLEAN and OUR UTERI DON'T WANDER and other Women's suffragette nonsense. The American movement had trickled across the pond, giving ladies here delusions of equality. Since I had so recently threatened Avalon with the very thing these women were protesting, I found it rather humorous, hoping Avalon wouldn't go on a tirade. It had been a long day.

To my great surprise and pleasure, she didn't say a word as they passed by us.

Good girl.

A newsboy called out the headlines just on the other side of the street. "Police stumped at Aristocrat's disappearance! Read all about it. Right here, right here, folks. Just two-p. Another ghastly murder in the East End—serial rapist and murderer on the move—third one this month! Hear ye! Hear ye! Only two-p. Right here, gents! Right here! Get all the gory details!"

"How dreadful," Avalon said. "Those poor women. How horrifying it must be for them to suffer such a fate, although, I suppose death after that horror would be a relief. I can't imagine surviving rape. I think I would go mad."

"Indeed," I said, then changed the subject, pointing. "What's going on over there?"

Just up ahead, a group of people gathered around a tall man in a bowler, standing atop overturned crates. On the wall behind him sat a wooden display case, the kind that could be closed up and carried from place to place. The man spoke over the chatterings of the crowd. American, from the sounds of it.

It was a bloody an invasion.

"Gather 'round. Gather 'round, folks. That's it. Plenty of room for everyone. Now I know I'm pretty ma'am, but give me some breathing room. That's it. That's it. Welcome! One and all! My name is Roderick A. Jeffries, and I'm here to make your day. Winter sniffles got you down? Can't keep those toes warm at night? Or are you just plain blue, feeling worn out? Well! This is your lucky day! One bottle of Doc Holliday's Snake Oil, and all your ailments will be a thing of the past. That's right! 100% pure rattlesnake oil from deep in the heart of Texas. Wrestled to the ground by our own cowboys, hired to ensure you have nothing but the best. Do you ail from headaches or toothaches? Melancholy? Hysteria? Sore chest-throat-joints-back-feet-hips? Doc Holliday's Snake Oil cures it all, instantly."

"Balderdash." A peep from inside the audience came. A single word, long drawn out in a southern drawl badly covered with a faux English accent, then silence.

"Do I hear doubt?" the salesman sang, grinning wide.

"I say it's nonsense." Same voice, same slow drawl. Several people in the crowd all looked down at something in the center of them. A haggard woman made her way to the front. Her creased face peeked through a long scarf draped over her head, and a wool shawl covered her short, hunched body. She hobbled with the use of a cane to the front of the crowd. "How can one thing cure everything? My son, he's fuzzy."

Murmurings from the crowd.

"That's right, he actually has grown fur all over his body, like a cat. Will it cure him?"

"It will indeed, old woman."

"Will it make me feel young again? Walk properly again? Cure my aching bones and my arthritis?" She held-up a claw-like hand. "Will it make me happy?"

"Yes and yes, good woman. You will be so happy, you will dance. I guarantee it. Here," the salesman said, opening a bottle. "Try it. On me. If you don't feel better instantly, I will pack up and no one will ever see me on the streets of London again."

"Well…." The woman regarded the man with a suspicious leer. "I guess I ain't got nuthin' to lose."

She took the dram of snake oil in her curled fingers, then sipped it, grimacing. After a few convulsions, for show, no doubt, the shill shrieked, and then threw off her shawl and scarf, revealing long, brown hair. Her ample-sized, scandalously-displayed bosoms outweighed the rest of her. With nimble leaps and turns, she danced near the Snake Oil Salesman. Although she couldn't have been much over thirty, her face was an odd mixture of leathery, sun-damaged skin and deep creases, making her appear quite older. A furry eyebrow stretched from one temple to the other. I wouldn't have recognized the gnome as female, maybe not even human, if it wasn't for her shapely curves.

Definitely a spinner, that one.

"There you have it, folks! Limited supply, please have your shillings at the ready. Only three crowns, folks! Hurry now, supplies won't last long."

"Three crowns!" Avalon exclaimed, ever the advocate for the people. "That's preposterous!"

The crowd didn't agree. Holding out his bowler, the salesman handed each a bottle after their coins clinked in the hat with the others. Before too long, he had sold all but one of his bottles. He stopped and held it up, all while the imp still danced, and said, "Last bottle folks, and I see there are many more here who want this, so who wants it most? Do I hear a quid?"

"One pound," a man shouted.

"I have one quid to the man in the top hat. Very nice hat, sir. Do I hear a guinea?"

"I've got a guinea," an older woman said, holding up her reticule.

"One guinea to the lovely lady in blue. Two? Two guineas?"

And so on, until he had raised an astronomical five pounds for the last bottle, and still the tiny troll danced. Twirling around in wide circles, she danced among the remaining people, bowing with a flourish to each new couple she'd dance near, who in turn appeared quite frightened at the spectacle and scuttled away. Each time she'd dance close to the salesman again, she'd look up at him with such adoration, one would think she worshipped him as god and savior.

I was not a tall man, I stood well under six feet, which this snake oil salesman was at least. Avalon was just a few inches over five, my petite love, but this harlot was even smaller than that. Well, shorter at least. Barely over four feet, I would say. Close to that of a proper dwarf, but proportionate and solid. If I didn't know better, I would've said she was a gypsy, but even gypsies had more class than this one. Quite bizarre. She tossed her long, mousy-brown curls to and fro as she danced, gyrating in the middle of the street, as if to music.

Suddenly, she belched forth the most offensive sound. It assaulted my ears. Cackling, loud and boisterous, much like a mixture between the braying of an ass and the sound of the hyena I had seen at the London Zoo. I was utterly appalled to realize it was this irritating creature's laughter.

I turned to Avalon in shock at such sights and sounds, which could only come from Americans, and she appeared as affronted as I, but always the lady, hid it better than I did.

Jeffries, with an air of being very pleased with himself indeed, tried to hide a smile as he regarded the sprite. His eyes sparkled in something between pride and condescension, much as one would look at a trained monkey or a prized show spaniel. Therefore, I soon deduced the cause of her madness. She looked up at him with complete adoration. Even though he was over two feet taller and at least fifteen years older, although much better preserved, she loved him. I knew it was rather rude to ask, but I couldn't help myself. Something inside me demanded an explanation for this freak show.

"Pardon my candor, but are you two..."

The eruption of new braying caused me to jump, and Avalon moved into my arms for protection from the offense.

"Us! No!" she said, but her eyes never left his. They stood locked in the most intense glare I had ever witnessed between two people. She was no doubt under his spell, bound to him, and he enjoyed every moment of her submission. He owned her.

"Heavens, no. Not since, well, we don't talk about that, do we, my poodle?"

Her expression changed to that of a dog who had just been caught piddling on the new carpet.

Mr. Jeffries smiled wider, not missing a tick. His pride swelled as he enjoyed her embarrassment.

"Rather a scandalous thing back in Boston, right my pet."

"Yes, Roddy," she said in a tiny voice, disgraced. "I am so sorry."

This salesman delighted in her discomfort, in her shame, even to the point where I couldn't bear it, and Avalon nudged me to do something, so I changed the subject.

"Lord Arthur York." Jeffries shook my proffered hand. "And this is Miss Avalon Bainbridge."

"How do you do?" Avalon said, tilting her head. She didn't offer her hand to the crook. Smart girl.

"Fine, ma'am, just fine. I'm Roderick A. Jeffries from Boston, Snake Oil Salesman, as you can see, and this is my assistant, Miss Polly Pooter."

"Howdy, ya'll!" Tail wagging once again.

"Roderick Jeffries? Any relation to Madame Jeffries, the notorious madame?"

"Yes, she's my cousin on my father's side."

"She's quite the businesswoman. I see it runs in the family."

"We all take business seriously, Mr. York." Mister? I looked into his eyes and saw he meant the slight. Other than that, nothing. Empty. His expression, too. Void. No affect whatsoever behind that false smile. "Unfortunate business, a few months back, at her establishment on Gray's Inn. She lost more than a few quid because of that. Half her clientele is gone."

He was testing me. Of course I remembered the unfortunate business quite well, as does Avalon. As does all of London, since there was nothing else in the papers for weeks, but this man was prying to see if I was a client. To see if Avalon would blush.

But my sweet love stood beside me, her face emitting the perfect amount of innocence. How I loved her.

"I read something about that. Rather gruesome murder, if I recall."

"Murders, Mr. York. Plural. Murders. Yes, her purse strings have been a bit tighter since then, but not for long. Men do have their needs, after all, and she does tend to their rather unique needs, don't you find?"

"I'm sure I don't know, Mr. Jeffries. Hearsay is all."

"Please, call me Roderick. All my friends do. Enough of this English propriety."

"I wanna be the puppy! I wanna be the puppy!" Polly screeched.

She had already succeeded.

Jeffries chuckled and sat upon one of the overturned crates with his arms spread wide. The mewling imp leapt on his lap and nuzzled her head in the crook of his neck.

I was quite surprised she didn't start licking his face.

Jeffries held an expression of complete satisfaction. "Isn't she delightful?"

Um. No.

Avalon's expression was that of complete shock, and no wonder. She tugged on my arm twice, indicating that she wished to leave at once. One couldn't blame her.

"Polly and Roderick, from Boston, you say?"

"I'm from Boston, yes. Polly here, Polly is from the south. Tennessee to be exact. Aren't you my poodle, my spaniel? Yes, you are! Oh, yes you are!" He rubbed his nose against the tip of hers. She cackled again, tossing her head back, belching laughter to the heavens.

Low class colonists. Well. That explained a lot.

Just as I was about to make my excuses and take leave of this ghastly couple, a ragged woman rushed up and started shouting. "It's you! It's you who done this to me!"

She pointed to her face full of pox. Disgusting, weeping sores around her mouth and nose, and, sticking out her tongue, revealed they were there as well. Avalon and I took a step back. Well, two. Thing was, beneath the sores, she could've been beautiful. Probably was until she got them.

"Pardon me, ma'am," Jeffries said with the most pleasant smile. "But I think you have me confused with someone else. What you're saying is slander."

The woman continued to make a scene, shouting about how he had forced himself into her mouth and given her the pox, demanding compensation for her suffering. Jeffries stood there, dumbfounded.

Polly was the first to react. She jumped up and stood much like a bulldog ready for a fight, shouting back at the woman, "You're a liar! You're a liar! He'd never do nuthin' like that. I've known him for years, and he'd not do that. Yer crazy, lady! Now git!"

Still, the woman kept shouting, and I would never forget the look on Jeffries' face. While everyone one else watched at the cat fight, I knew the truth lay with Jeffries, so I regarded him with a keen eye. His blank face didn't show an ounce of emotion or affect whatsoever, except when Polly had rushed to his defense. Then, ever so slight, nearly imperceptible, I saw it. Pride. Pleasure. Conquest.

What the woman said was true, and it was confirmed but moments later. The spectacle attracted several more people, and before long, others spoke on Jeffries' behalf.

"I've shared a pint with the man. He's a good one, ya wretch. Leave him be!"

"You're just trying to make an easy quid, you are."

"You need some of his Snake Oil!"

"Look at the likes of you, you harlot! He's a hardworking man, he is. Upstanding member of the community. See? He's got so much more class than you. He hasn't said a word against you. You should be ashamed of yourself."

Jeffries beamed, then spoke, "Now, now. This poor woman is obviously ill and deserves our pity, not our anger."

Mumblings around.

"He's a good bloke, he is."

"Bless 'im. Taking the moral high ground. Good for 'im."

"Such a handsome one, too, ain't he? Certain not to be cavorting with the likes of her."

"It's prolly just a case of love gone bad is all. Poor thing."

Jeffries walked up to the woman who at first stood tall, proud before him, but after a moment of looking into his eyes, cowered, as if she was afraid of being struck. Jeffries held a whole quid in the air, ensuring all could see, turning around and around with his chest thrust out and head held high to the point he had to look down his nose at everyone gathered. A smug smirk, not quite hidden, mocked the poor wretch as he turned back to her, and placed the money in the woman's palm, whispering something to her. It was too quiet for anyone else to hear, but Avalon and I heard it well.

He had said this through his devilish sneer: "Stuff your gob, woman, or I shall have to stuff it for you. Again."

CHAPTER 7

CONSTANCE

The yarn slipped through my fingers as I made the final stitches on the poppet. I loved to crochet. It was a meditation, of sorts, focusing with such intent on each stitch. Managing the tension. Keeping count of stitches. Feeling the roughness of the yarn against my soft hands, amazingly soft after so many centuries. That was one of the benefits of being an immortal succubus with transformative powers: young forever. I could, of course, appear as young or as old as I wished, but when I was at rest, I was as beautiful and supple as the day I died.

No. Not died, transcended.

"It's getting near time, Madam." Everett stood in the doorway. He started as a client, and became a friend. The ever-increasing love and trust between us made him more like a father every day. Over the years, he had aged while I had remained the same.

"Everett. You startled me. How long have you been standing there?"

His kind eyes regarded me through his square lenses. The magnifying loops were still attached to the wire frames, but rotated out of the way. He must've been working, tinkering with watches and clocks. He did that on the side to bring in a little extra income. We didn't need it, as I was well compensated when I could be. When I had a wealthy patron, like I had now. One of them was quite wealthy. Still, often I worked for nothing but gratitude and the knowledge that I was reducing evil in this world. Besides, I had good investments on top of all that, so it wasn't all that necessary. I figured he did it to keep busy more than anything else, to feel useful. It was very important to feel useful.

"Just a moment or two, mum. Is your trunk ready to go?" Everett had been with me a good fifty years now. Nearing seventy, he was as strong and devoted as ever. A horrific event had brought us together, and after I had helped him, he stayed, having nothing left after losing his Agnes, having been forever changed, as they all were.

"Almost, I'm finishing his poppet now."

"Is tonight the night for Mr. McFerret?"

"I believe so. At least sometime this weekend. I can't imagine he'll pass up the opportunity."

"Will you be all right, mum? I hate that you have to… endure."

"Don't you fret. It's fine, Everett. Just fine. I gather what will happen with Willie tonight will be more of the coercive nature. He is not the forcible type, not in the overtly violent sense of the word, I don't believe. Damaging nonetheless, of course. More so in a way, as it's so subtle. The woman, often left so deeply confused, blames herself."

"Indeed, mum. I've seen the results, as you well know."

"Indeed. Come in, Everett. Please, have a seat while we talk. I'm nearly finished. Yes, I'm rather certain this one uses emotional blackmail and just the right mixture of manipulation, fear, and intimidation to coerce these women, perhaps with a mixture of alcohol. I have been known to be taken unawares before, to be wrong about a man."

"Not since I've known you, mum. Not mistaken once." His jaw tensed, making his silver beard stand on end, as he remembered all those he'd seen me punish. He picked up a poppet out of the large cedar chest beneath the window. The same one as always. He squeezed it hard in his fist. A tear fell down his cheek.

"True, I am mistaken about the essence and method of a man so rarely, that it is safe to say virtually never. Yes. Virtually never." I had honed my skills over the years, and I could see into the black heart of a man in a matter of moments. Once I punished him and bound him with his poppet, then all was confirmed. "Still black, as you see. Still black as night, and it will be as long as you live. As long as they all live and still suffer."

"But this one, you say he's not violent?"

"I don't believe so. Not terribly anyway. He'll have another method so as not to get messy. This one likely gets a woman in a compromising position, one she can't explain without suspicion on her, and she knows it, too. He talks himself into her. Coerces her. Then, abandons her and denies anything ever happened. Leaving yet another ruined. Her career, her dreams, shattered. That's what happened to my patron, poor girl. At least she knew enough to summon me. Now he won't do that ever again."

"Poor girl," he repeated. "And all so that he could fulfill his lustful urges. All so that he can control her, manipulate her into doing what he wants. Into trusting him." Everett twisted the head of the poppet, his face contorted in a grimace of pain.

"Careful, my dear. Take the head off, and it's all over. He's not ready to be at peace, not for quite some time."

"No. Not for a very long time." He spat on the thing's face. "Then he has hell to look forward to as well."

"That or oblivion. Regardless, he's getting his, and rightly so."

"Yeah. He's getting his all right." Everett pulled a pin out of the cushion and thrust it in the poppet's gut and twisted it around.

"So. Power. It is about power, isn't it, Everett? Control. That's quite clear. Lust, sure, but the belief that one has a right to another's body, to their soul. I suppose it makes him feel powerful somehow, and a man that weak and scared likes to feel dominance over another. Cowards, all of them. Mice grasping at grandeur." I chuckled and turned to look out the window. It had begun to snow. "He hasn't seen true power, but he will tonight."

Succubi had a rather unfortunate reputation. Demons, those in the upper echelons of the church said. Those cowards sitting high on their thrones of gold. Demons, as if we worked for the devil himself. Of course they would consider us demons, as we were charged to avenge the women they harmed. Such were the ways of man. Those who did the devil's work hid behind pious robes and clever rhetoric. Their silver tongues convinced all around them of their innocence, sometimes even their victimization. Only behind closed doors did anyone see their true nature, and the relative few who were chosen as victims never stood a chance. Society looked for the stranger in the dark, the filthy man with no teeth, the overtly cruel. Although they, too, could have been abusers, and often were. Men who take pleasure in hurting others could be found at all levels of society. Still, they were not the most dangerous because one at least saw them coming, and they often left visible scars. No, by far the most dangerous and damaging were those one trusted. Those one admired. Those one loved.

Those were the worst.

The charmers. The politicians. The clergy. The professors. The leaders. The privileged. The elite.

Those who were educated and with affluent background were the most successful in keeping it hidden, thereby doing so much more damage. Lifetimes of damage for their dozens of victims.

Lifetimes.

That was how long they paid.

Lifetimes.

"Are you all right, mum? You stopped."

I looked down at the poppet and realized I had lost count. "Oh no. I lost my place, Everett. Give me a minute. One. Two. Three." I counted the stitches around the top of the poppet's head, and then finished the last few, counting out loud so as not to lose my place again. "Everett, would you hand me the wool, please? Just there on the other side of your chair." He sat in my normal sewing chair while I half lounged on the sofa, feet up. It would be a grueling weekend, so I needed all the rest I could muster. Taking a handful of batted wool, I stuffed the poppet's head before sewing it on its already-stuffed body. "Next, the eyes and mouth, and heart."

"I love to watch you do this part, mum. Especially the heart. It's quite remarkable." A crocheted white heart would adorn the top of the poppet's chest, but as soon as I infused it with the target's own heart, it would turn black and stay that way until he suffered as much fear, pain, and confusion as all his victims combined. I wove the thread in and out around the stitches at one side of the neck, I left a small hole that could be cinched tight and tied off after the spell had been cast.

It wasn't their essence I captured in these poppets. I hesitated to call it a soul, as these men were quite soulless, most of them. Their consciousness, perhaps. No. Not even that. It would be too dangerous to have had all those in such close proximity to me and to each other. Too dangerous for me, as all that blackness together would have created a palpable misery, even pain, for all those in miles around.

They were trapped elsewhere, nowhere and everywhere at once. These poppets enabled me to control their level of suffering from afar, and it worked quite well.

Everett spat on his pet poppet's face again before tossing it back into the cedar chest with the others, hundreds at the moment, all at different stages of atonement. Because of my compassionate nature, I sometimes sped up their sentence by inflicting pain directly into the poppet, and Everett helped with his personal poppet. Although it wasn't out of compassion from Everett. It was out of pure hatred and seething rage. Well-justified after what the monster had done to his wife, Agnes. It was more cathartic for Everett than anything, so I indulged him. One understood the depth of damage such trauma caused, and the length of time needed to heal. A lifetime, usually, for a few minutes of horror.

After finishing the heart and eyes, I tossed the finished poppet atop the packed clothes in my trunk. "Ready," I said. "This will be the first time I've been on airship cruise. How very exciting."

"They are rather rare, mum. Unnatural, too."

"Even so. Although I will be there to work, it doesn't mean I can't enjoy the view. Besides, I deserve a holiday."

"You do that, mum. No doubt. I've never in my long life known another so dedicated."

"Thank you, Everett. Nor have I known another so loyal. We shall leave London before long, and none too soon. I long for a change of scenery. Perhaps New York City next. With these Colonists I've met lately, it's time to return. Only four more to go here, at least four more planned. I do have the tendency to come across new scoundrels all the time, don't I, Everett? Causes one to believe that most men are thus, doesn't it?"

"Most men are, to one degree or another, Mum. Indeed they are."

"Pity. No mind. Plenty to do. This cruise will be the perfect opportunity to get information on at least two more of them here in London, in addition to Willie. He will likely make his move tonight, I believe. Indeed. A private meeting, no doubt. I'll get more on the doctor. Then the final two, well, I already have plenty of proof on both of them. Insidious. The one especially, his punishment will be of the most ruthless I have ever delivered."

"As well it should be, mum."

"I will take great delight in his demise."

"As will I, madam. Each one you stop heals those old wounds a little more."

"Now. Onto personas. Do I have time, Everett?"

"Not much, mum, but you have a few minutes."

"Two, at least, perhaps three for the cruise, I'd wager. Just to be safe."

Standing before the looking glass, I regarded myself in my natural state, more or less, the way I looked when I transcended, minus the bruises and fractured ribs. My body had been so broken and used after my husband and his three friends had finished with me, that I was hardly recognizable. They left me for dead, but I didn't die.

They did.

All of them did.

"Now. To practice." I said, shaking off the memory. Even after five hundred years, it sometimes felt as if it were moments ago. Such was the result of trauma. Sometimes I couldn't shake it off. Sometimes it consumed me as if it had just happened, but I was lucky today wasn't one of those days because now I had to get the feel of shifting from one to the next, as I wouldn't have a looking glass but in my cabin. I wanted to be prepared to shift on deck, if necessary, so I must learn the sensation of every curve, every color, every fold of the fabric.

"First, Charlotte Sopha, for Willie."

"The main course, as it were," Everett said.

"Quite," I said, smiling at him. It was nice to have company, after I had been without for so long. Everett had made a good companion, but he didn't have many years left. I would miss him terribly when he died but I couldn't mourn his passing too much, for he would finally be at peace. Finally reunited with Agnes.

Currently, I wore a black dress with lace sleeves, its bodice trimmed in gold piping at the bottom and decorated with a lovely piece of white lace that stretched up on either side of the neck. A golden brooch adorned the center of my black-satin covered throat. From it, as well as from various places within the lace, long strands of black pears draped across my décolletage in the most becoming way. My dark blonde hair was twisted up into a loose bun, but it would be so much more elegant tonight.

"Charlotte is an ambitious and talented girl from the other side of the city, given a grand sum to purchase a new gown for the gala. Hmmmm."

"She looked lovely for the Yule Ball. Green satin and adorned with black pearls. Elegant, for sure."

"Indeed, but it would be such a faux pas to wear the same dress, don't you know. Scandalous, indeed." With a flourish I took on the countenance of mock horror, making Everett laugh.

"We certainly couldn't have that, Madam. The sun might not rise after such a slight!"

"Tonight, I will stick with colors of the season, though. How about this one."

Drawing a long, slow breath, I pictured the gown and Charlotte's sable curls. Her wide, blue eyes, innocent and hopeful. Imperceptibly, I shifted into Charlotte. It took more control, more time, but in the event someone saw me out of the corner of their eye or in partial shadow, the change would be gradual enough that they wouldn't notice anything strange. Unaware of the atmosphere of an airship cruise ship, I had better be prepared. Before long, the white pearls had turned into red bows and the black gown into a deep shade of green, accented with a red overdress and bustle. Perfectly spiraled black ringlets fell from either side of my face.

"Beautiful, mum, and perfectly subtle. If I wasn't watching for it, I wouldn't have even seen the changes. Still, let's hope you have some privacy for your own sake. Best not to let onto the game too soon, lest one might get away."

"That will most certainly not happen. No one escapes my web. Now onto the professor's girl," I said, testing the timbre of Charlotte's voice. "Something a little more scandalous and stereotypical for the doctor, I think. Utterly pathetic, that man." The deep blue of my eyes lightened to nearly white and my hair went from black through all the shades of brown into a light blonde, pulled together loosely at the back. "Meet Claire Wiseheart, Everett. What do you think?"

"A chambermaid, mum? A young one at that."

"Barely seventeen," I said with Claire's new voice, which was higher and somehow a touch sweeter than Charlotte's. Childlike. Face a little more rounded, mouth pouty and full. Breasts larger, waist tighter. Perfect. "That'll do, indeed."

"Cuckoo! Cuckoo!" The tiny bird dashed out, then back in his door.

"Oh my! The time. I'll be late, I will," I said in Claire's sing-song voice. "Oooh! I do like this voice, govna. How perfectly delightful. But not for now." The timbre lowered as I shifted back into Charlotte. "Now you must get my trunk downstairs and find me a hansom." As I moved toward the door, I continued shifting until I was back to myself.

"Going out as yourself?"

"Yes. The gown must wait until I'm aboard and the gala begins anyway, and since I'm boarding alone, I shouldn't be concerned about anyone seeing me. Even if they did, no mind. Their eyes wouldn't stay on me for long. No one knows Constance Saggese, remember. Except for you, my dear, and my clients, of course."

"What a pleasure it's been, Madam."

"For me, too, Everett." I touched his frail hand as I passed him. Yes. I didn't have much longer with him, and it saddened me, but he was here now. That was all that mattered. Turning to the open trunk, I recounted the contents in my mind, ensuring I didn't forget anything. "Excellent, take that down. I must grab a little something from my room, and I'll meet you curbside."

"Very good, madam."

"Thank you, Everett." I left him to wrestle with the travel trunk while I grabbed a few peas from my chamber. I never indulged in the stuff, but the doctor certainly had the reputation as an addict, and after what I had seen at the ball, he would do just about anything for a pea, it seemed. Yes, addicted to many vices, that one. I descended the stairs and bundled up against the cold.

It was still snowing, and it made the streets quite slushy and muddy, but I didn't mind. Snow was always welcome, as it made this ugly world a little more beautiful, for a while. Then it, as everything, didn't last. It faded away as beauty always did.

Everett stood on the curb, my travel trunk by his side, teeth chattering against the cold. His bony arms wrapped around his weakening body.

"Get back inside, Everett. You're shivering."

"But your hansom, Madam." Hollow cheeks mottled with brownish spots and white whiskers trembled in the icy wind. Not so long ago, he was strong and full of rage. Young. Fit. Now his youth and physical strength had diminished as the time had passed. His kindness grew. His sense of peace grew. He knew he would be with Agnes soon, and that pleased him. It pleased me, too, in a very sad way.

"Not to worry. Send the doorman out. He'll hail one for me."

"Very good, mum. Take care of yourself tonight."

"Oh, I shall be fine. Make yourself a good cup of tea and warm up now. I'm not ready to lose you, Everett."

"Of course, mum." With that he was back inside. A moment later, the doorman emerged, greeted me, and then waited out by the curb to find a hansom.

In the meantime, I stood with my face turned skyward, catching snowflakes on my face, feeling them melt and leave a tiny cold spot behind. Moments like this, so few and far between, were what gave this life purpose. Fleeting moments of pure joy.

§

The driver dropped me at Hyde Park, where we were to board the great dirigible, and immense it most certainly was. No wonder we had to board in Hyde Park, as it wouldn't fit anywhere else in London.

My heart leapt at the sight of it. Before long, I would be snuggled in my cabin, out of the cold, looking out over London as we floated toward Paris. Amazing. Long life had few benefits, indeed, but watching technology progress was certainly one of them. I often wondered what wonders the future held.

Even still. Here. Now.

1882 London was a far cry from 1369 Romania.

1882 London was a far cry from 1882 Romania, come to think of it.

The ship alone filled a city block, and with its balloon overhead, it stretched at least as tall as the buildings therein. The dirigible astounded my Old World mind. Yet, there it was. They had a hanger or two on the outskirts of the city, down the east side, but the great elite of London's High Society would not be seen down the east side. Certainly not. It must've been where they had kept the colossal machine before tonight. I had never seen anything so big in all my existence, not even in the water. Although, I gathered half of a ship was below the surface, so it wouldn't have looked as big as this did all out in the open.

A line of passengers waited to board, so I wasn't too late after all. I paid the driver, plus a handsome tip, and he dragged my travel trunk across the road to where a porter took over with a curt nod. I presented my ticket to the porter, and he scribbled down something on a pocket pad before giving me a nod as well and loading my trunk on his wheeled cart along with the others.

The loading queue was starting to thin out as I approached the grand flying machine. I had never seen anything quite like it, certainly not from this close distance. The air held that fresh, crisp scent, like just after a cold rain or snow. Clean, pure somehow. I breathed in, allowing the frosty air to fill the entirety of my lungs, while taking in the splendor about me. Groups of people draped in fine coats and hats milled about heading toward the ramp along with me. Excited tones and a few unseemly squeals competed with the droning engines, which grew in volume as I got closer. A few familiar faces from the ball the other night caught my eye here and there, but not any of my targets yet. Perfect. I wanted to enjoy this moment free from the taint of those rogues.

A gentleman stood at the bottom of the ramp, checking tickets and saluting passengers. He saluted in the American way, I noticed, with the palm facing down. As part of the fun, no doubt, he had each group say "Permission to board, sir" before clicking his heels together and giving them a smart salute to allow them to pass. The groups giggled or made other sounds of delight, then began the long climb up the ramp to the open doors, about midship. Each time he would snap to attention and salute, the golden epaulettes jiggled in a most amusing way. Gold buttons lined the grey uniform in a double line down the front, and a gold braided belt cinched the waist.

"Good evening, Miss. Just one?"

"Yes, sir," I said, holding out my ticket. The whispers behind me spoke in scandalous tones about the woman traveling alone, but I kept my head up and smiled politely at the retired soldier.

"Very, good, ma'am." He handed my ticket back to me and waited patiently at parade rest.

"Permission to come aboard, sir."

"Granted." He snapped to attention and saluted me. Even though he had done it to every other passenger before me, it felt as though it was especially for me, like I was a proper lady, someone to be admired and respected. Which, of course, I was, but rarely did I get an outward show of it coming from anything but fear. I knew it was part of the experience, of course, but I let the glow of acceptance and honor warm my heart as I ascended to the ship.

Once on board, the comfortable atmosphere surprised me, since it had once been a war vessel. Although far from opulent like Lady Pearson's abode, the ship displayed fine craftsmanship at every turn without the frills. After spending some months penetrating London's sumptuous High Society, I found it quite refreshing.

As I awaited my turn to be welcomed aboard personally by Captain Blackwolf, I caught a glimpse of the chamber ahead, and it was fully decorated with all the finery one would expect from Lady Pearson. Boughs of garlands and holly draped across every doorway. A large Christmas tree, decorated with crimson and gold ribbons and hundreds of apples stood beside the staircase, which must have led to the upper decks.

Before being flooded with the light in the reception area, I took advantage of the relative darkness inside this vestibule to shift into Charlotte Sopha.

"Good evening, Captain," I said with a polite curtsey.

"Miss Sopha! How lovely to see you again," he said, eyes glowing. He kissed my proffered hand and smiled sweetly at me. If I didn't know better, I would think the attentive man fancied me, and he might just. He was an honorable man, through and through, so there was no reason for me to get close to him, however. Pity, that. It was one of the detriments to my work. I would never know the love of a truly good man.

"My crew is dressed in grey uniforms, and the servants are dressed in black and white. The gentleman over there," he explained, pointing to a man in grey by the stairway, "will hand you a map of the ship and an itinerary. He'll also inform you as to the location of your room and assign you a valet. Do enjoy your stay, Miss Sopha. Such a pleasure to see you again."

"Thank you, sir." As I made my way to the porter, I heard the captain greet the next guests with just as much warmth and care. It wasn't special for me after all. Just as well.

My cabin was small but comfy. I wondered how London's elite would react to the size of the lodgings. I slid past the narrow opening between the bunk beds and the desk to look out a small, round window that allowed me to see outside. The sun had already set, and Hyde Park was sheathed in darkness. It would be so lovely to watch the view change as we progressed. I only wished we were traveling during the day. On the way back Christmas morning, I didn't think I would leave the side of the ship. I'd watch the landscape change from France to The Channel to the white cliffs to farms and country towns, then finally back to the endless buildings of London. It would be my most memorable Christmas yet, no doubt.

I sat down at the small desk across from the single-width bunk beds and pulled out the itinerary. My skirt caught a rough edge of the bed's wooden frame, which tore the delicate fabric. I couldn't imagine what it would be like for two people to live here. Especially with bustles. There was hardly enough room for basic furnishings, let alone my skirts and travel trunk, which was already in my room when I arrived.

Turning to the schedule once again, I perused the events to take place over the next two evenings. Dinner at half past six, both nights. Tonight, a string quartet and a tour of the ship by Capt. Blackwolf or stargazing led by Doctor Nesbitt from eight until nine, then dancing until midnight. Tomorrow. Day in Paris, then at night, games at eight! Splendid! I did love games, and they would be playing Charades, Oranges and Lemons, and Pass the Slipper. How delightful.

As I was daydreamed about having a bit of time to myself for merriment, for a change, someone shoved a folded piece of paper beneath my cabin door, pulling me out of my fun fantasy of games, reminding me the purpose of my presence. It was, indeed, from Willie. Eight o'clock, tomorrow. His cabin. The rest of the note just said how I should keep out of sight tonight and destroy the note.

How stealthy of him. Did he expect me to swallow it?

The note also said how much he was looking forward to our meeting.

I just bet he was.

Eight o'clock, of course, during the one thing I wanted to do on this cruise. I was truly hoping to get in a game of charades. His wife would no doubt be playing games at that time.

Willie would be playing games, too.

Then again, so would I.

CHAPTER 8

ARTHUR

"I can barely move in here."

"Then we'll just have to be close, my love." Avalon sidled up to me, pressing herself against my chest, trying to kiss me, but I was not in the mood for frivolity. I pushed her away, a little too roughly perhaps, as she plopped down on the bottom bunk, hitting her head on the top one.

"Bunk beds! Honestly, Avalon!"

"It used to be a military vessel, remember?" She stayed sitting, rubbing her head, but she kept a smile on her face. Good girl.

"It's bad enough I will have to dress myself for the gala tonight, but we'll also have to dress in here together. There's barely enough room for the trunk, let alone your petticoats."

"We'll make do, my love. It's only two nights. We can get reacquainted." She reached out and touched me through my trousers, looking coyly up at me.

"Maybe later. I'm going for a walk." She moved as if she wanted to join me, but I wanted to be alone. I closed the door behind me and I wasn't but a few steps away before I heard her start crying. Glad she waited until I left. Her emotions weren't my responsibility, and I had grown weary of her using them to manipulate me. I made my way up to the top deck and watched the ship ascend over London. It reminded me of the first and only other time I was aboard an airship. It was the night I met Avalon. She was so beautiful and fascinated by it all. The wonder in her eyes was intoxicating. But now, she was different.

Take off wasn't as smooth as the first one had been back in the summer. Not used to having elite passengers on this vessel. Obviously.

"Catherine?" I said aloud. The woman standing down the rail from me was the spitting image. Deja vu. This was just how it happened with Avalon. She had displayed such a perfect likeness to Catherine, except for the black hair. Although, I swore the resemblance to my beloved Catherine had faded in my eyes over the months. But this beauty. Every curve of her body, up to the shape of the face and the color of the hair. Red. Beautiful coppery red, just like Catherine's. Could she be my destiny? Could this woman succeed where so many had failed?

I moved toward her, and when I got close she turned fully to me. It was Chastity, Lady Bainbridge's friend from the Yule Ball.

"Good evening, Lord York."

"Miss Rosengarten. How very lovely to see you again."

How had I not noticed the resemblance the other night? It was quite uncanny.

"Charmed, Lord York. I'm ever so looking forward to the gala tomorrow night. Did you see? They're having games at eight and tales of adventure by Doctor Nesbitt at nine. Then dancing and more dancing into the night. How splendid! I will surely not miss the tour of the ship tonight, or will it be star gazing for me? Such decisions! Then games tomorrow night. How I do love games/ Where is your lovely lady, Lord York. Did Miss Bainbridge join you on the cruise?"

Unfortunately.

"Yes. She's indisposed at the moment, poor girl. But no doubt she will be out later. She does enjoy games. Tomorrow night, you say? Perhaps we shall see you there." Sooner, if I had any say in the matter.

"Perhaps. I certainly love Charades, but I was sad to see they weren't playing 'You're Never Fully Dressed Without a Smile.' That's my personal motto anyway, but it is ever so much fun to watch the silly things people will do to try to get one to smile. Wouldn't it be grand if people tried so hard to make others smile all the time? It would be a much more pleasant world, would it not, Lord York?"

"Indeed, dear lady. It would, indeed." What a delightful woman. She seemed to think much like I did. Yes! No time for all this sadness and insecurity and emotional turmoil. We should all be happy, all the time. Genuinely happy. Especially women. I thought of Avalon puling in our cabin, and I grew wearier of her with each passing second in this goddess's company.

Still, Avalon was like me now. Vampires were a lonely lot, and it had been nice to have had company of late.

"I must take my leave, Lord York. Perhaps I shall see you later tonight? Stargazing, I think. Indeed."

"I sincerely hope so, my dove. Do save me a dance."

"Of course, Lord York. I'll save you two." She flashed a knowing look with her amber eyes.

How I adored older women. So experienced and not at all shy. Chastity had at least a decade on Avalon, being closer to Lady Bainbridge's age, and the experience to match, no doubt. Perhaps that was why I tired of Avalon. She just didn't have the experience to keep me satisfied, and a man had needs, after all. I especially had rather refined needs.

Must find a way to get Chastity alone later tonight and satiate some of those refined desires. After I watched, quite intently, Miss Rosengarten leave my presence, I took my time and explored the ship.

Lady Pearson rather outdid herself, yet again. True, it had been a military vessel, so it lacked the finery of a passenger ship, but Lady Pearson more than made up for the commonness of the ship with her lavish decor.

Every surface held a centerpiece of evergreen with a lit candle in its center. Holly and mistletoe hung over each doorway and arch. Oh, yes. Mistletoe. Must find a way to get Chastity beneath one later tonight. Or Hazel Hamilton. I bet she would squirm. I did love it when they squirmed.

As we reached our traveling altitude, I donned the goggles everyone was required to wear to enable us to see once up in the aether. Over the side of the ship, down in the darkness below, I saw the silvery Thames snake through the center of London. Far in the distance, a small yellow circle glowed in the darkness. Big Ben. Darkness cloaked most of the city, but the gaslights along the streets provided a magical view of hundreds of points of lights below. It was as if looking at the stars above, only below. This would be a splendid journey. Yes, indeed.

I had to stay out of that blasted cabin as much as possible. Only to sleep. It would be perfect for that, as it wasn't much larger than a coffin. Honestly, as absurd that it was for the mythos to claim we slept in coffins, I would rather, than sleep in that cramped cabin with Avalon. She was always around. A man needed his space, after all. So clingy and needy. I felt as if I was being smothered, slowly suffocating to death.

Once south of London, there wasn't much to see but blackness, so I explored the lower decks.

The ballroom, or rather the room converted to the ballroom, was even more gloriously decorated than the rest. A tree as high as the room, which must've been at least thirty feet tall, stood in the center of the dance floor. Already couples were swirling around it, dressed in their day wear. They danced to their own joy, as the musicians hadn't set up yet, and it was a lovely sight to see. I loved to watch people having fun, especially when they were in love. How had they found their perfect love, and I, after over three centuries, was still looking?

Of course, I knew the answer to that. I had had my perfect love with Catherine, and perhaps there was just no replacing her. Never replacing, but perhaps there was no matching her. Tried and tried as I might, every few decades or so, I would meet someone who was promising, but it always ended the same way. Disappointment. They were too human, too frail, too weak. I'd spit on love again and commence fucking for a while, and then another temptress would convince me, renew my hope, only to disappoint me again. Just like Avalon has done. It was always the same.

But not with Chastity. I had a feeling that it would be different with her. Finally.

Perhaps there was only one chance for true love in a life-time. Perhaps that time had passed for me with my Catherine.

Bah! I shan't accept that. Chastity would be the answer to my longing. She would be my perfect love.

Ascending the stairs, I slid my hand along the garland-trimmed the rail. The sensual prickly foliage of the evergreen delighted my fingers. On every fourth step, a brilliant red poinsettia adorned each end, its pot wrapped in a grand golden bow. The staircase led to the dining area where every table and chair was draped in white. Servants scampered about getting everything ready for dinner. Sprigs of evergreen and pinecones graced the center of red ribbons tied to the backs of each chair.

Finely dressed couples were already arriving and searching for their place card, so I must get dressed soon. I pulled out my pocket watch, and it had already gone six. Dinner started in thirty minutes, but if I hurried, perhaps I could have a quick romp with Avalon and a dash of blood to tide me over until I could find someone to eat later.

Upon arriving back to our cramped cabin, I was quite cross to see that Avalon was not there. Spoiling my fun again. The trunk was tucked neatly into the corner and her dressing gown was folded on the pillow of the top bunk. She had withdrawn my suit for tonight and hung it in the closet, along with my clothes for tomorrow.

Kind gestures, but what I needed right now was a quick poke. I had passed a chambermaid on my way up, perhaps her. Indeed. The help worked in a pinch, as they were quite good at keeping their mouths shut, unless I needed them open. Besides, she wouldn't remember a thing. So a giggle and a poke it was.

"Excuse me, Miss," I said, peeking my head out the door. The brunette woman dressed in a black and white uniform turned to me. She was plainly pretty and would do nicely. "Would you mind pressing my suit for dinner? It shan't take too long, as it has been hanging for a while."

"Yes, M'Lord," she said, abandoning her cart full of linens.

"Actually, bring a few towels please?"

"Of course, M'Lord." She grabbed three fresh towels and slid past me, keeping her head properly bowed in my presence, as she should. I shut the door behind her and shoved her against it, pinning her facing away from me. I caught one of the towels before it hit the floor and threw it over my shoulder. I'd be needing it shortly.

"Please, sir! Please! Don't hurt me! Just let me go. I won't tell no one, I won't. Promise, sir. Please!"

"You won't feel a thing," I said in calming tones. "Well, that's not quite true, you will feel me well enough, but you won't remember a thing. No screams, all right? No screams and I'll let you live. In fact, not a peep from you. Understand? I shan't be long."

Ah! Sweet variation.

She was quite well-behaved, as well, not a sound as I hammered into her. The scent of fresh blood sent me over the edge. She had broken skin while biting her lip to stay quiet, and I couldn't resist anymore.

Perfection.

The blood from her neck cascaded over my tongue, filling my mouth with her life, as I filled her cunt with my death.

Although she wept as I withdrew, she still didn't make a sound. Good girl. Except for the quiet mewling. Why must women cry so much? All for just a few moments of something that should be fun. She probably hadn't had a good jab for weeks, if ever. Certainly not by a viscount, indeed. She should be thanking me.

"Hold this," I said, indicating the towel I had pressed against her neck after I had enough blood. Well, at least enough without killing her. Don't want to have to dispose of a corpse, not with everyone heading to dinner.

Shaking, she held it against her neck, eyes wide. Lips quivering.

"Wipe your face. You look awful."

"I'm sorry, M'Lord," she whimpered. "I'm so sorry."

"Nonsense." As I moved toward her, she jumped, then cried anew. "Surely that wasn't your first time."

"Yes, M'Lord. I was a maid."

"You're welcome, then. You'll always be able to tell your friends that a viscount had you the first time. Not bad, either. Quite sweet. Still. You won't remember anything, no details anyway. Just a pleasant romp with a guest. Lucky girl."

"You bit me."

"That I did, but you shan't remember that either." Looking into her eyes, I compelled her. "You came in to press my shirt and seduced me into a quick romp, so excited at being on an airship. I, of course, couldn't help myself, but my sweetheart must never know. It's our secret. Tell your friends, if you must, but best just keep it to yourself. You don't remember which cabin it was. You don't remember what I look like."

Her eyes glazed over and her mouth hung open. She'd be all right in a moment, so I took the opportunity to check the bleeding. Nearly stopped. I pulled the towel away and licked the two tiny puncture wounds, sealing them, then reset her collar to cover them.

"Will that be all, M'Lord?" she said, smiling.

"Yes, my dear. Fine work on pressing my dinner wear. Look at the time," I said. "I must get dressed."

"Of course, M'Lord. I'll let myself out, sir. Thank you." She turned back to me just before she shut the door and smiled the sweetest smile I had ever seen.

Ah. It was quite lovely to be me.

§

I found Avalon already at dinner, seated with her aunt and uncle, as well as several people I didn't know.

"Good Evening, Lord Bainbridge, Lady Bainbridge. Miss Bainbridge. How are you all this fine evening?"

"Quite well, Arthur," Emily exclaimed, her outfit even louder than she. It did help me find them in this crowded dining room, however, so there was that. "Forgive us, we started without you. Cheers." She held up a glass of red wine as if to toast. Instead, she drank half the glass in one gulp.

"Yes, Arthur. We've missed you," Avalon said, looking as lovely as ever. She wore a deep green gown with full black skirts, trimmed in burgundy. She was the picture of grace, as I had no doubt she would be.

"Apologies all 'round. Got caught up in something and lost track of time." I sat next to Avalon, leaning over to give her a quick kiss on the cheek, but she didn't even smile. Rather, she kept her jaw set and eyes lowered.

Emily, on the other hand, was draped in a very light green, rather like the inside of a pea. It was accented in a much nicer color, the green of the surrounding evergreens adorning everything in sight. Then, in the style that was only Emily, it was also trimmed with the most hideous color, something between yellow and the pea green. Much like urine after eating asparagus.

And...perfect.

"Asparagus," I said as the waiters placed the first course in front of each of us: five tall asparagus stalks tied together with a red ribbon.

"Lord York," Lord Bainbridge began, "May I introduce Lord and Lady Ableson of Surrey and Lord and Lady McNairy of Crawley.

"How do you do?" Lady Ableson said. She was well past her prime. Around seventy, I would say. And Lady McNairy, who just nodded toward me, appeared even older than that. Oh, well. I had my fill for a few hours anyway.

"Quite well. It is such a pleasure to make your acquaintance. All of you. What do you make of this grand ship? It is the experience, is it not? Lord Ableson? Did you ever think you'd live to see such a sight?"

"No, sir. I daresay I almost wish I hadn't. It's unnatural being so high above life. Unnatural, I say!"

"Forgive my husband. He's an old fuddy duddy." Lord Abelson huffed and spurted at this, making his white, bushy mustache bounce. "It is positively splendid, my dear boy. Splendid. Yes, indeed. Did you see London down below? It rather puts much into perspective, don't you find?"

"Indeed," Avalon said. "Makes one feel rather small, no?"

"Exactly! When I think of all the people down there. That's all I could think of as I watched from the side, although I didn't get too close, mind, for fear of falling over. All those tiny people milling about on the streets below, all hustling about their business. Makes one feel rather insignificant."

Huh. Didn't make me feel insignificant at all.

"It did, rather, but at the same time, I felt so very privileged to experience such a thing."

"Quite right, Miss Bainbridge. Quite right."

"It's all rather old now, isn't it? I mean, we did have the gala over the summer," Emily said. "We have seen London from above before, haven't we?" She finished her wine and held up her glass until she attracted the attention of a waiter, who promptly came and refilled it, then topped off the rest of ours.

"It will never get old for me, Aunt. Not at all."

"Yes, well, Avalon, you have led a rather plain existence before cavorting with Lord York, here. If it wasn't for me, you two would never have even met. Remember, it was I who invited you on that summer dirigible gala. Me. It's your fault," she said, nudging her husband. "Talk about old fuddy duddies. My husband wouldn't come, and it just wouldn't do for me to go alone. How scandalous."

"That's right. Have some more wine, dear."

This banter entertained Lady McNairy, from the expression she held, being old enough to be outright weary of High Society pretense. I was with her on that one.

Lady Ableson, however, was not at all amused. "Quite," she snapped.

Emily did not take the hint from either her husband nor Lady Ableson.

"Speaking of being scandalously alone, did you see that woman boarding alone? She looked altogether common-place. Well, obviously. I wonder how she got invited to this. Honestly, Lady Pearson gets more altruistic with each passing year. First professors, then writers. The horror. And now country wenches, it appears."

"As Lady Ableson pointed out, dear aunt, we are all rather common in the larger view. Some of us are fortunate enough to have been born well, but there are others who are good people, even though they are not titled."

"If you say so, *Miss* Bainbridge. You are, after all, an expert on what's common."

Although Avalon likely just had a sip of pig's blood before she came to dinner, her cheeks flushed red in her anger. I thought she would leap across the table and devour Emily at once. Fortunately, she didn't, for that would've been rather inconvenient, but it was amusing just the same.

"Might I have everyone's attention, please?" The chattering of the crowd quieted down after Blackwolf repeated that a few times. "We will be reaching The Channel within the hour. The moon is overhead now, and the view is real purty. Remember to use your goggles when on the top deck to protect your eyes. If you forgot to bring some, you can check a pair out down at reception where you came in. It's between an eight to ten hour flight, depending on weather and wind and the like. But unless it's necessary, I'm not going to touch down until the morning to avoid waking y'all from your sleep, but if you feel a bump in the night, it's just that we've landed. No need to fret none. You will be free to spend the day in the city, but please be back on the boat by five in the afternoon. We'll be lifting off promptly at six, so we can watch the moon rise over Montmarte. Remember, take it easy tonight. Big day tomorrow, and an even bigger party tomorrow night. Well. I suppose that's all. All right, then," he said with an awkward movement of his arms, I gathered to indicate we could continue our dinner uninterrupted. I hoped. "Mercee, and, well, um—Bone appiteet!"

Incroyable.

CHAPTER 9

CONSTANCE

It was my complete pleasure to be seated next to the delightful Baron Vincent Von Rictus Baine. His sweet, yet proper flirtations throughout dinner caused me to lament my fate ever so slightly. Although as handsome as he was considerate, he dined alone. It always baffled me that the most warmhearted, genuine men were often the ones without companionship. If women only could see men for what they truly were, as I did, instead of only what they showed the world.

I promised him a dance later and said I hoped to be seated next to him again for dinner the next night.

"That is my wish, too, sweet lady," he said, kissing my hand. "Might I be so bold as to ask if you might accompany me in Paris tomorrow for some shopping?"

"You may, Vincent, but I'm afraid I must regretfully decline." Every single thing inside me wanted to spend the day in the company of this lovely man, but it would be cruel in the end, as I was unable to love for my own sake. It would be unfair and quite heartless to let him believe otherwise. For, unlike so many of my targets, I would never awaken love in a heart that I did not or could not love in return. I was charged with this duty, and I must fulfill my charge for the protection and safety of women now and in the future. Thousands, in the future, really, just as I had protected and avenged thousands in the past.

My heart sighed in disappointment, and I wished things could be different, especially when I saw the light in his eyes flicker and his sandy brown mustache quiver almost imperceptibly. Yet, he did not let his own disappointment show or his kind smile falter.

Besides, if he knew what I truly was…well, there was that as well.

"A dance later, though. Promise?" The last thing I wanted to do was to make this man feel rejected. If he only knew my heart and my duty. Alas, that couldn't be helped.

"Of course, my dear. It will be my greatest pleasure." With that, he kissed my hand and took his leave. He would not inquire romantically after me again. No. A true gentleman allowed a lady her choice, respected her boundaries. He did not push or coerce or manipulate. He would not ask again, and it was for the best.

Indeed, it was for the best. I must believe that.

As if for a perfect illustration of his opposite, Willie McFerret laughed alongside Mr. Thomas Chenery, his beautiful wife on his arm. I curtsied and smiled as they passed me on their way out of the dining hall. Willie's eyes fell on me but a moment and then whisked away. There was not the slightest indication that he knew me. Mr. Chenery, on the other hand, tipped his hat to me. A gentleman, that.

"I must have a pea!" a loud voice behind me demanded. I turned to see Doctor Nesbitt in a prolix appeal with one of the crew members who appeared to be the head butler for this gala. Forceful, although not at all in angry tones, the doctor spoke with pride and charm, every syllable.

"I'm sorry, sir, but we cannot distribute opium to our passengers," the butler, at least, had the decency to speak in hushed tones.

"I demand it, sir. It's been a long flight already, and I haven't been home in weeks, you see. Weeks! Away from my family and university. Forced to perform over the holidays! What-what? I must have a pea, sir, or I shall not lead the star-gazing tour tonight, and I shall not tell my tales of adventure and conquest tomorrow night. In fact, I daresay I shan't do a thing! A pea, sir! It was part of the arrangement. See to it!"

"If we could find a pea for you tonight, sir, would you be able to procure more once in Paris?"

"Nonsense! I'm not paying for my own pea, man! I'm here at the behest of the Pearson's. Lord Pearson and I are old friends, dear man. I should take this up with him and mention just how very incompetent his staff is. Pay for my own pea. Preposterous!"

While they were strapped in their conversation, I took the opportunity to slip behind the curtain and transform into my bait for the doctor. Claire, the chambermaid. I emerged young, innocent, and ever so perky. "Forgive me, sir. Beggin' yor pardon, sir," I said in Claire's high voice and curtsied.

Doctor Nesbitt doffed his helmet to greet me, and the goggles straddling it fell off. He scrambled to pick them up and dropped his pipe in the process, breaking it two.

"Drat!" he cursed, collecting those pieces and the fallen goggles. After pocketing the pipe pieces and putting the goggles back on his hat—all thumbs and lanky limbs, that man was—he turned back composed and proper like none of that had just happened.

The three of us, had all watched this show of grace, astounded. I, or rather Claire, continued, "I couldn't help but overhear, sir, but I might be of some assistance in this matter. M'lord brings opium with 'im, sir, and I'm sure I can get a pea from 'im, sir. 'E's a kind man, sir. A good man."

The crewman shrugged, and the butler cleared his throat. "I don't remember you in my staff, Miss. What is your name?"

"Weishart, sir. Claire Weishart. I'm a replacement, sir. Last minute, I'm afraid. M'lord offered me when he heard you was short one, sir." There was always someone who couldn't show up, and by offering an opening, they usually filled in the rest of the information. I was not disappointed.

"Ah, you must be replacing Miss Kennedy. Yes, very good." The butler turned to Doctor Nesbitt, who had his hands on his hips and commenced in tapping his toe, but the expression on his face was perfectly pleasant and patient. Eyebrows raised expectantly. "Follow her, Professor. She shall find something for you, sir. Please do let me know if you aren't satisfied, sir, and we will get you sorted."

"I should think so, dear man! Very good. Very good. Splendid, in fact. Yes. Oh, yes, indeed!" he said eyeing me as if I was a tasty strawberry tart or chocolate biscuit. "Lead on, dear girl! I'm right behind you. Ooooooh, and what a sweet—"

"Yes, sir," I said, interrupting him with a quick curtsey. "This way, sir." I led him down to the cabin level, and his eyes never left my bustle. He didn't speak on the trip down to my cabin, except to exclaim, "Oh! Oh! Oh!" during a short burst of rustling clothes.

I did not turn around.

Once outside my door, I said, "It's best if you wait down the hall, sir. It wouldn't be good for M'Lord to find us in his room togeva, sir. No, sir."

He twirled the edges of his straight black mustache, then pushed a stray, stringy strand of long, black hair off his face before laying a finger along his nose and winking at me, slow and deliberate, as if we shared a secret.

I already knew his secret, all right.

Once he was down the hall and around the corner, I slipped in my chamber and pulled a pea from my case. Perfectly prepared, as always, a reminder that research was always necessary.

After I rejoined Nesbitt, I dropped the pea in his palm.

"Thank you, sweet girl. You are quite young, aren't you? Nary eighteen, I'd wager."

"That's right, sir. I'm seventeen, sir. I was lucky to get this job, I was. Well, you've got yor pea now, sir. I got to get back to work."

"No. Please," he whined. "You've been so kind as to help me in this. Please, just come out on deck with me for a few minutes and smoke it with me. Just a few puffs is all. You'll have a much better time working if you do."

"No, sir. I really shouldn't, sir. It could be my job, sir."

"Nonsense. I'll talk to your employer if it comes to that, which I'm sure it won't. Go on then, you'll love it. Or is this a bit too grown up for you?" First clue, he didn't respect the word no.

"A'course not, sir!" Well played, inserting an insult that a young girl would try to disprove.

"Besides, you wouldn't leave me all alone now, would you?"

Playing on sympathy. "Well, sir. Just a few minutes, sir?"

"Of course, just a few. You can leave whenever you like. I promise."

Unsolicited promise. Always a sure sign manipulation was underway.

"Nofink improper, sir?"

"Improper? Blimey! No! I am a gentleman, dear lady. A gentleman, I say."

"Of course, sir. Forgive me, sir. I didn't mean no disrespect, sir."

"Come now. I bet we will see the moon over the water below. See how lucky we are to have met one another? You would be stuck below deck if it wasn't for me. That's right." Establishing debt. "I bet not many of those working the ship will get to see the sights. Stick with me, Miss, and I'll show you all sorts of wonders."

The moon shone bright over the water so far below. It made the channel a black void beneath us, but it was beautiful just the same. The light of the moon caught waves as they moved. A funnel of candlelight cast on the otherwise blackness of it all. A single sliver of iridescent magic reflected in the abyss.

Doctor Nesbitt dug in his trouser pockets, very deep and rather toward the center. "I know I have my pipe somewhere. Oh!" he said with a suggestive lilt. "No. That's not my pipe, but we might be needing that soon enough. Yes, indeed!"

Uncomfortable, I said, "Perhaps I had best just get back down below, sir."

"Nonsense! Here it is, see?" He pulled out a long, thin pipe about the length of his hand from his coat's pit. Its center was bamboo, and on either end was oxidized black metal, decorated with gold leaves. One end had the bowl and the other a golden mouthpiece. It was the finest opium pipe I had ever seen. "Got this in Japan last year. Great place, Japan. Loads of spinners there. Oh! Yes, indeed! Petit! Just like you, lovely. Just like you." He dropped the pea in the onyx bowl and lit it. After breathing in deep, coaxing the pea to life, he passed it to me.

"I'm not sure, sir. Not while I'm working."

"Go on, then. Just a puff. You'll love it."

"I really shouldn't, sir."

"Ah! Go on!" he insisted. Clear indication of a dangerous man, one that discounts a woman's comfort level and refuses to honor the word no, which this man had done at least four times in just the past few minutes alone. He used most people's, especially women's, fear of being rude against them. Coercion, it was called.

So, not to be rude and slight this important man, just as a good working-class chambermaid would be afraid to do, I took a quick puff and inhaled, then coughed.

"That's a girl," he laughed.

Handing the pipe back to him, I shivered. "It's right cold up here, it is, and I'm just in me uniform, sir. I had best get below before I catch my death."

"Just a few minutes more, my dear,"—five times—"then I must prepare for my lecture and tour tonight. Come here." He leaned against the wall, legs spread to match my height, and gathered me up in his arms, pulling me under his coat. "You're really quite fetching, you know. I'd like very much to see you again."

"Really, sir? A doctor and Oxford professor wants to make my acquaintance? You're putting me on, aren't ya? You just think I'm a tart, that's all! You're having a laugh at me expense."

He didn't try to hide his erection, rather he pressed it into my hip.

"Not at all, dear girl. Just the opposite. You're real. A hard worker, I can tell. You're loyal, too. All the girls I meet are just in admiration of my intellect or adventures, but you are just nice to me as a man. That's rare."

"I don't know, sir. You have a family and all. I heard you say as much down below. What would yor wife say, sir?"

He sighed. "Oh, my wife. Yes. Well. Unfortunate business, that. It was one of those arranged marriages, I'm afraid. Here I am, only thirty-two, and I'll never know love. Not real love. Cursed, I am. Doomed, even. She's never loved me, you see. I haven't felt the love of a woman in years."

I looked up at him and tears filled his eyes. He met my gaze and amplified the piteous look.

Brilliant performance, as always.

"That's terrible, sir. I don't have much of a chance either, sir. Being a house maid and all. Many of us end up childless and without husbands. It's a lonely life, I hear. But it's a good job, sir. I ain't like the fine ladies here on this ship, sir. I ain't got much to offer a man. No dowry to speak of. Nothin' like that."

"Nothing to offer a man? Oh, dear girl! That is nonsense, indeed. You have everything to offer a man! Your beauty and kindness and innocence." He kissed my forehead and then rested his cheek against it. "Might we just show ourselves enough kindness to give ourselves the chance of loving? Even if for tonight. Just let me love you tonight." With those last words, he pulled back to lock eyes with men, then bent down to kiss me, but I pulled back.

Surprisingly, he let me.

"Not tonight, sir. No. I'll lose me job, sir."

"Then meet me in London, after we're back."

"All right," I said, smiling up at him. "You mean it, sir? You think we could love each other?"

"If only for a few minutes, my dear. For everything is fleeting, isn't it? Nothing lasts in this cold world, but I know we can love, dear girl. Yet, I want more than a few moments with you. I desire a real love, the kind that lasts forever. A proper courtship. We could have that, couldn't we? Stranger things happen at sea, or in our case, over the sea. Isn't that right, my lovely?"

"Oh, sir! You can't be serious, sir! It would be so scandalous to take a maid for a wife, sir."

"We'll just see about that."

"Do ya really think I'm so special, sir?"

He didn't answer, just studied my face with the most serious expression, then tried to kiss me again. This time I let him. Yes, quite convincing for the lecher I'd seen in him. Charming when he wanted to be.

This young maid never had a chance.

"You're trembling," he said after he pulled away. "Let's get you inside. So, you'll meet me in London?"

"Yes, sir! I will, sir! Where? When? I can't believe this is 'appening to me, sir."

"We shall work out the details later. Come to my chamber tonight after you're off duty, and we'll figure something out then. All right?"

There it was.

"Yes, sir! All righ', sir!"

"Around midnight then?"

"Yes, sir. But not for long, sir. It'd be improper and all."

"We shan't do anything you do not wish, dear lady. I promise. Just to plan to meet back in London, that's all. Number 619."

"619. All righ', sir. Thank you, sir. Have a good night, sir!"

"See you in a few hours, my lovely."

"Yes, sir," I said, gazing back at him like a girl falling in love. "You will."

As I descended the stairs back into the belly of the ship, I was happy to transform back into Charlotte, if for no other reason than for the warmth of her clothing. It had been truly cold on the top deck, and Doctor Nesbitt showed he was capable of being likable, in a way. He was a master at coercion. That much was quite clear, so he would have had to be charming at some point. Perhaps his show of geniality was meant to be in stark contrast to the drunken lecher most see, increasing the feeling of specialness to the recipient of such warm behavior.

Well, tonight we would see what he was truly capable of.

My guess, violence.

CHAPTER 10

ARTHUR

"I've already seen around the ship, Ava. I have no need of a formal tour. Wouldn't you rather look at the stars? The doctor will be pointing out constellations and giving history and such. You like history."

"I find that doctor altogether unpleasant. I do not wish to be in his company at all. Not in the least. True, I'm quite fond of history and mythology, but I'm also fascinated with technology, Arthur. You know that. I want to see parts of the ship I haven't seen. I want to see the engines. Do you think they'll take us to the engines?"

"Well I'm going on the stargazing tour, my dear. Join me if you will or no. Your choice."

"Thank you, love. I'll be fine on my own, after all, it's how I've been most my life, and I got along just fine. We can meet again afterwards, no? For the dance."

"Of course." I kissed her on the cheek coldly and turned away, not sure how I felt about her spurt of renewed independence and determination.

"Have fun, love. Do tell me what you learned, won't you?"

But I didn't turn back. Fine with me after all, as I would get more time to talk with Chastity. Although that likely meant Emily would be there as well, but hopefully I would be spared from that bit of annoyance. It would be so nice to be free of all Bainbridges tonight. Indeed.

The schedule said to muster beneath the main mast. Muster. I loved that word. All these military sayings and such were quite entertaining. In the middle of the top deck, several pillars held up a cage, of sorts. Each pillar was the size of a tree trunk. This cage above didn't hold the great balloon aloft. Not at all, the gases inside did that, of course, as well as hold the ship up, but in case of a problem, it kept the ballon from falling onto the top deck. Long ropes extended from around the balloon down to these masts as well, tied off on each, as well as on the sides of the ship. Perhaps the tour of the ship would've been more interesting after all. As I approached the center mast, I didn't see Chastity, and the dullness of disappointment filled my chest. Neither was the doctor here. The group was a small one. Most stayed on the lower decks where it was warmer. Wise people.

The night air bit into my already cold skin. I wrapped a long scarf about my neck, although it would do no good. I had no body heat to keep in. Yet, appearances and all. Everyone looked quite comical in their goggles. Some of the ladies were complaining how the straps were mussing their coiffures and they would look affright for the ball.

"Good thing the main ball isn't until tomorrow night, when all the prior activities are inside," a woman's voice purred in my ear. I turned, delighted to find it was Chastity.

"Good evening, Mrs. Rosengarten, I'm sure you look lovely beneath all those layers." Her amber eyes shone out from behind her goggles and strands of that glorious red hair licked the side of her face from beneath the hood of her wrap.

"Thank you, Lord York. I do, indeed. And Miss Bainbridge? Shan't she be joining us?"

"She opted for the ship tour, I'm afraid, so you have me all to yourself."

"Wise woman, that. At least she'll be inside for most of it. It is very cold out here. Is it eight yet? I do hope we begin soon, or I might have to forego stargazing for the string quartet. Or, perhaps, just turn in for the evening." With the last, she slowed down the cadence of her speech and touched my arm. Yes. Ripe.

"Blimey! It's cold!" Doctor Nesbitt said as he approached the group. "Good thing I brought my own warmth. Yes, indeed!" He wiggled a leather flask between his fingers, and several of the ladies giggled. Chastity did not. "Let's get on with it, then. Shall we? Follow me!" After taking a giant swig that lasted several seconds, he led us all to the side of the ship.

"Do you mind?" Chastity said as she slipped her arm in the crook of mine. "It is so cold."

"Not at all, dear lady. I shouldn't have it any other way."

"Gather 'round! Gather 'round! See up there? Just over there." Nesbitt pointed up past the outside of the balloon, North Eastward. "There is Ursa Major, otherwise known as 'Great Bear.' It's made up of seventeen stars and can be seen anywhere in the Northern Hemisphere. If you follow its back to its derriere, you find that the Big Dipper, made up of the seven brightest stars in the whole constellation, makes up the great bear's hind quarters and tail. That's quite a bustle, isn't it, ladies. Yes!" He swigged from his flask again. "Pity it's so cold out tonight ladies. You are all so bundled up. How about a quick peek at all your bustles? Go on then. That's it!"

Several of the group turned around and flipped up their capes to show their bustles. A man after my own heart. For love of bustles. I'd drink to that.

"Very nice, ladies. Very nice, indeed! Now, give them a bit of a shake. Oh, yes."

To even my horror, he began rubbing himself through his trousers, and not even trying to hide it.

"Now see here!" one angry husband protested.

"Yes. Sorry. Got a bit carried away there." Swig. "Moving on!" Swig. He led us down the port side while husbands chided their wives in whispers that were lost in the aether.

Nesbitt stopped the group near the bow and continued, "The sky is so different here than it is in Africa. Oh yes. No view of the Great Bear there. No, sir. Well, not that great bear, anyway." Swig. "Just out there." His words started to slur. "See those two lines of stars there? Draw a line intersecting them toward the top, and you'll find their arms. That is Gemini, or the twins, although I like to think of them as the lovers." Swig. Adjust trousers. Swig. "They lie right between Taurus and Cancer. There and there. The two brightest stars in Gemini are Castor and Pollux, named after the twins in Greek Mythology. Those two stars make up the two heads of the twins. See? This was one of the forty-eight originally described by Ptolemy all the way back in the second century. Fascinating." Swig.

"Are you enjoying this, Lord York?" Chastity whispered.

"It's interesting. Mildly. Not near as interesting as you are, my dear. Would you care to sneak off for a more private chat?"

"I'd love to."

As the doctor crossed over to the starboard side, Chastity and I slipped away behind a building set in the middle near the bow of the ship. We waited in the shadows until we heard the doctor say something about the belt of Orion.

"Would you care to go back below?" I asked. "It's warmer."

"I was hoping for something a little more private. I'm sure we can find ways to warm up, Lord York. Let's see what's in here." How delightful! A sense of spontaneity and adventure in this one as well!

The door to the structure was serendipitously unlocked, so we ducked inside. It appeared to be some kind of navigation room. Maps spread out on a table. An astrolabe. Compasses and the like. A workspace desk with a journal.

"That's better already," she said, pulling off her goggles and pushing the hood of her cloak off. Her copper locks were a mess, but not nearly the mess they'd be soon. "Fortunate the moon is so bright, as we have some light in here. Made it rather difficult to see the stars though."

"Your eyes, my dear, outshine any star."

"Oh, Arthur. Please. That is not necessary with me. I'm not an innocent maid who needs to be wooed. We're both quite aware of where this is headed, now aren't we?"

"Quite," I said, and a moment later my mouth covered hers. Her hunger matched mine. I helped her off with her cloak, then took off mine as well. Tongues swirling. Lips gliding. Bodies pressed together. Lifting her up on the aforementioned desk, I raised her skirts, and she eagerly released me from my trousers. She grabbed me full on with both hands and stroked, kissing me ever more fervently. Guiding me toward her, she leaned back, allowing me to hover over her while I plunged inside.

We crashed together. Surrounded by the warmth of her along with her urging whispers in my ear, I failed to notice the lantern approaching outside the window.

The door opened, and there stood Avalon along with Captain Blackwolf and a few others. "This is our navigation room, not in use…Oh, my," he said.

Chastity giggled.

I withdrew and pulled up my trousers.

Avalon's face displayed utter betrayal. The kind of pain that fractured one's soul. Without a word, she turned, and in another moment, she was gone.

"Avalon!" I called, running after her, but she had used her supernatural speed and just disappeared. Everyone was so busy watching the spectacle of me and Chastity, that they obviously didn't notice the blur, but I couldn't be so careless.

I forced myself to move at human speed and went in search of her. I headed back to the cabin, but she wasn't there. Starting from the bow, I searched along each deck, hunting for any sign of her in every nook and cranny. Finally, on one of the lower decks, set for crew only, I smelled blood. Seems Avalon did some hunting of her own.

Good for her. Bad for me.

There, holding the side of his neck, a man stumbled around in a daze.

"Are you all right, man?" I asked.

"A ghost. A beautiful ghost came and she kissed me."

She had tried to compel him, but she wasn't very good at it yet. This man was just confused, and bleeding. Taking his head into my hands, I held him inches before me and engaged. "You were bit by a rat. That's all. Let me see." He took his hand away. I sucked some of the blood away, then with a generous amount of saliva, ensured it would coagulate soon.

"Keep this on it," I said. Putting the handkerchief I had just pulled from his pocket on the wound. "You'll be all right, son. Just watch out for those rats."

"Thank you, sir. I will, sir. Big rat, that. Big beautiful rat," he said as he wondered off rather dreamily. He'd be asleep soon, no doubt. She would have to go back to the cabin at some point, so I would just wait there for her.

I opened the cabin door and a shoe missed my head by about half an inch. "Ava! I was so worried about you." I had to duck to keep from being hit by the second shoe.

"You magsman! Villain! Go back to your mollisher, you fiend. I never want to see you again."

"Avalon, please. I can explain."

"You can explain? You can explain why you had your johnson inside another woman? Oh, Arthur. I'm done. You've been a beast lately, and now this! I won't stand for it. Now I remember why I chose to be a spinster. I was so much happier when I was myself, and I was certainly stronger-willed. You have made me altogether into something else! You forced me into this life, didn't you? I didn't have a choice, and it's by far the last time you forced me. What was that the other morning, Arthur? I felt violated, not loved, and I shan't make excuses for you or your treatment of me any longer. You've changed, and you made me change, too."

"I saved you, Avalon. You were dying!"

"Dying because of you. You deceived me and Victor for so long. Oh! Poor Victor!"—Great. Victor thrown in my face again—"He's dead because of you, too. Yes, I would've died without you, but now I am forever dead because of you!"

She sat down on the edge of the bunk and wept. I went to her, but she pushed me away, then paced to and for in the tiny cabin.

"You isolated me, you monster. You isolated me, trapped me, and convinced me you loved me, that I was somehow different. I believed you. My own ego allowed me to believe, but no more! You've shown your true self now, Arthur, and I am wholly disappointed to see that all those horrid rumors are true. That, mixed with the violence and cruelty. No more!"

"Avalon, please."

"You had me convinced it was my fault! That I was too needy or too talkative or too prudish or too randy or too… whatever. It wasn't me, Arthur. It's you. That's very clear now. You who hasn't made a commitment to anyone for over three centuries! It's you, and you dragged me into this, changed me. Tried to control me and intimidate me to your will, and then chided me for losing my independence. My independence." Her voice softened, and she sank into the chair, skirts spread wide. "That which I had taken so much social abuse for, gone. I believed in you, Arthur. I trusted you."

The anger had faded over that last tirade, but the sadness remained. When she spoke again, her voice was full of regret. "I love you, Arthur, but I cannot, shall not, live like this. I will reside back in Baker Street. I had decided to move home after your earlier cruelty, convinced we just needed more space between us. Now, however, you will stay away from me completely. Do whatever it is you are already doing without me. As soon as we're off this bloody dirigible, I'm off. You will get out of my life forever. I will find my own way, as I always have. It's so much better that way. Now. Go back to Chastity, and don't even think about coming back to our cabin tonight or tomorrow night. I'm sure you'll have no difficulty in securing other lodgings. I shan't leave the cabin, except to eat. I'm too ashamed now. So many saw you. It will be all about the ship by now. You've not only betrayed me, you've humiliated me, too."

Blood tears streaked her face, smeared across her cheeks each time she wiped the new ones away.

"You fed."

"I did, and now I see why you kept me from it. You did, didn't you? Keep it from me. Purposely. I see so clearly now, Arthur. You are quite good, aren't you? But I shan't be fooled by you any longer. I remember who I am now. I am not under your control, Arthur. Your threats and intimidation and manipulation won't work on me anymore. I know who I am. You are not worthy of me. I do love you, but I realize now that I don't truly know you. It's like you're two people. One who is kind and loving and affectionate. One who adores me."

"I do love you and adore you, Avalon. Please."

"The other who is cruel and controlling. Who ravished me."

"Ravished! Heavens, Avalon. I did no such thing!"

"Leave."

"But...Ava."

"Leave. Now. You owe me at least that much, at least privacy in my humiliation."

"I'll give you time to cool down, then I'll be back to check on you. All right?"

"No. Don't come back."

"You don't mean that. You'll feel better when you calm down." I opened the door, the same door I had that maid up against, although it seemed like years ago now. "I love you, Ava."

She made a sound that almost sounded like laughter.

"Goodbye, Arthur. You have hurt me for the last time."

§

Every time I passed a new group of people, whispers broke out anew. The entire ship was abuzz with this latest gossip, and I was the center of everyone's attention.

"How humiliating for her." I heard one woman say.

"Shame, such a lovely girl." Another added.

"She must've given him a reason." A gent spoke to others, all standing around in a circle sipping brandy. "Lucky chap, if you ask me."

"Yes. If only I had such luck, and stamina!" They all laughed together and toasted to men. Sometimes being able to hear every little peep, even from across the room or on different levels, was not all that much fun.

Someone slapped me on the shoulder and said, "Nice going, Ol' Boy!" A revolting mixture of Scotch and vomit, with a dash of opium, enveloped his words. "Tell me about it. Hm? Please? She was fiesty wasn't she. Nice and deep you gave it to her, right Ol' Boy? Nice and deep." With the last, Doctor Nesbitt thrust his hips forward.

"Pardon me," I said, slipping away from his heavy arm and rancid breath. Perhaps solitude for a few hours, and I would feel better. Then, Paris.

"Lord York," Captain Blackwolf stopped me as I headed out into the night again. Although his hands were folded behind him in a casual manner, his countenance was anything but. Terse, I'd say.

"Yes, Captain. What can I do for you."

"A word, please, sir."

"Of course."

"Follow me." He led me out of the ballroom, past the lovely decor. Sounds of chatter and Beethoven played by the quartet faded as we moved further away from the festivities. Taking a hidden staircase, he took me down into the bowels of the ship, lighting the way with a portable lantern.

The entire trip, he didn't say a single word.

The captain turned a brass knob then pushed the heavy oak door open. Inside was a lovely room, certainly much more posh that those we had been crammed into.

"My private quarters," he said.

"Very nice."

"Have a seat, Lord York." He indicated a long wooden bench along one of the walnut-paneled walls, then lit an oil lamp in the center of a claw-footed, round table centered on a deep red rug. Sitting, I watched him mill about his cabin for a few minutes. First he placed the lantern on his desk, illuminating a series of maps and a telescope. To the right, books and more rolled-up navigation charts cluttered a bookshelf.

He cleared his throat, and finally took a seat himself in a lovely velvet armchair near the center table and bench, where I sat.

"Look, Captain, about before…"

He put his hand up to silence me. "Please. No excuses, for what you did was inexcusable, Arthur. Now, I know I'm not your father and you are a grown man, capable of making his own decisions, but I intend on giving you some fatherly advice just the same. Yer young. Real young, and you think the world is at yer feet, and you'd be right about that. Titled and rich and all. You've got a good life."

The audacity of this man to speak to me as if he was my better, my superior!

"Now, look here, sir! You are too familiar!"

"I don't stand on no ceremony here. Not on my ship. I've seen too much already. Horrible things. War changes a man, I'll tell ya, and it ain't in a good way. The things I've seen, well a lad yer age couldn't understand."

"I am older than I look, sir. Save your condescending talk for a child." I stood, ready to leave, straightening my waistcoat.

"Please, sir. It weren't my intention to talk down to ya at all, and if I came across thata way, then I apologize. Really, I just want ta talk to ya, man to man, is all. Would ya give me a few minutes of yer time? I'm not the best with words, so I ask yer patience, sir."

That was more like it. Respect. I sat back down, chin raised in defiance. After all, I didn't have anything better to do. Still working it all out myself.

"I'll try again," Blackwolf started. "I cain't tell ya what to do, a'course, but…Miss Bainbridge, she's a good woman, she is. A fine woman, and she loves you. I can see it by the way she looks at ya. Yer too young to understand that the love of a good woman like her, well that's a rare thing. Someone to be devoted to ya and good to ya. Someone to keep ya warm and safe. Someone to spend the long days and nights with. That ain't nothing to take fer granted, son. Now, I know yer real rich and fancy an' all, and I'm sure you have yer choice of ladies bein' as handsome as ya are, but just know that not all of them will love you for you. Some might love yer money, others yer good looks, but I'll tell you something, son. Beauty fades an' a marriage based on money ain't one that's happy fer long."

My beauty would never fade. He had no idea to whom he spoke. The audacity.

"I guess what I'm sayin' is this: don't take a good woman's love fer granted, son. You earn that love every day. Every moment. That's what ya gotta do. Earn it, and return it in kind. Now what ya was doin' with that there other lady is all fun and pleasuresome and such, but it's a real small part of love. The sooner you get that, Arthur, the happier you'll be. Now, I don't know if you can mend things with Miss Bainbridge or no, but if I were you, I'd do everything in my power to mend things with that fine woman. She's more than a romp, son. She's a woman, through and through."

Unbelievable. I looked at him with complete disbelief, but I was sure to keep my face still, without emotion. This lonely man was lecturing me on love. Typical. I'd like to eat him, actually, here and now. Maybe blood was what I needed to feel better, but for some reason, as soon as I thought it, nausea spread through my belly, and I suddenly wanted nothing more than just to leave.

"Thank you for your advice, sir. It is well-received, I assure you. If you must know, Ava and I have not been well for a while now, but, yes, she is a remarkable woman, and I have every intention of making things right with her again. Every intention indeed." At least every intention of getting her back under my control. She was just a woman, after all. What was she without me? A landlady on Baker Street? Yes, she'd be back. No doubt.

"Well," Blackwolf said, "I hope I didn't overstep none. I just wish someone had said as much to me when I was yer age is all. I think my life would be altogether different." A sadness came over his features. Lost love, no doubt. How dreadfully common.

"I really must get back up, Captain. I've got a lot to work out still, but I thank you for your time."

"A'course." He didn't get up when I did, but rather just leaned his cheek on his hand. As I turned to leave, he tossed his top hat onto the table and ran his fingers through his hair.

I showed myself out and left him there with this thoughts.

Ha! I took Avalon for granted. How preposterous! I really didn't understand what all the fuss was about anyway. So I fucked someone else. It wasn't like Avalon expected me to be with her and only her forever! For eternity? Surely not! How absurd! Yes. Really, this was her mistake, wasn't it? These were her unreasonable demands. Indeed. I'd done nothing wrong, after all. Only what was natural, and a man can't be blamed for that.

CHAPTER 11

CONSTANCE

The McFerrets stayed indoors all evening, mostly listening to the string quartet and dancing or chatting with friends in the parlor. I didn't stick by his side all night, but I did stay around enough to make Willie a little nervous. I enjoyed seeing him tug at his collar when I walked past, forcing his eyes to stay off of me. The man already felt guilty for what he planned tomorrow night. No, that wasn't not quite right. Not guilty. Scared. It wasn't morality creeping up his thick neck, it was fear.

The fear of being caught.

The doctor and I crossed paths a few times during the evening, and he was full up to the knocker already. He, of course, didn't recognize me as Charlotte. His chambermaid would stay hidden until our clandestine meeting at midnight. I'd be surprised if he wasn't passed out by midnight. Such a lush and addict, too, no doubt, with the opium. Must be covering up some very deep pain. However, instead of facing it, coping with it, he ran from it. A sure way to ensure it would continue to chase him. The worst of it was he felt the need to spread it around, causing pain to others just to ease his own but for a minute or two. Selfish.

Pathetic.

Monstrous, even.

Cowardly, for sure.

There was never any excuse for victimizing an innocent, no matter how much pain one endured. Everyone had their ghosts, but not everyone transferred their hell to others for their own benefit. Those that did, like Nesbitt, would get that hell transferred back to them and then some.

"Good evening, sir," I said and curtsied to Baron Vincent Von Rictus Baine.

"Ah! Miss Sopha! Delighted to see you again! Are you enjoying the cruise thus far?"

"Oh, yes. I am indeed! Earlier I went on the stargazing tour, and that was very cold to be up there at night. I've stayed down here for the rest of the evening, but I do believe I shall be calling it a night soon enough. Big day, tomorrow. Although, I think I shall stay inside and get some writing done."

"Will you not see Paris at all?"

"Well, I'll tell you a secret, Vincent. I'm here for a very important business meeting that could very well start my career as a journalist. Oh, sir, it is my greatest dream!"

"I have no doubt you will inspire others with as much elegance and grace through your writing as you do through your company, my dear. How wonderful for you! Please, do let me know how it goes."

"Oh, I shall, Vincent! I shall, indeed."

"Would you care to dance once more before you retire, Charlotte?"

"I would be absolutely delighted, Baron!"

As we waltzed, we chatted about this and that as we'd done before. Just as I knew he would, he proved to be the perfect gentleman. Such a lovely man. With every word and action and genuine expression on his handsome face, he proved it. Not another word of romance or suggestion to pursue anything other than a friendly acquaintance, or perhaps even a friendship. No pouting or sardonic remarks about being in Paris alone tomorrow or my choice to write over his company. A true gentleman, indeed.

True gentlemen, I found, had no need to tell you that they were gentlemen.

They showed it with every breath.

As the dance ended, my few moments of grace with Vincent were ruined. Nesbitt stumbled through the ballroom, colliding with couples on his way to the staircase. He picked up one of the poinsettia plants and proceeded to vomit into it before placing it back on the corner of the stairs.

"Ugh! Why do they continue to invite that man?" I asked the Baron.

"Unfortunately, he is rather famous in these circles. Between the tales of his adventures and his position at Oxford, not to mention his silly antics, he has become a kind of celebrity, I'm afraid."

"That excuses his disgusting behavior?"

"Not in the least, my dear. People have a tendency to overlook certain things in celebrities, don't they? He makes people laugh with this pathetic buffoonery, plus he can be charming, not to mention quite brilliant. He's a doctor and professor of science at Oxford after all, but I quite agree with you. None of that excuses such behavior. I would not invite this man into my home or to any gathering. Not at all. I've seen how he treats ladies, and it is deplorable. I pity his wife and family, really. They deserve better than this pathetic debauchee. No amount of talent or brilliance or laughter can make that behavior acceptable in my opinion. I, however, am in the minority on this one, I'm afraid."

"I don't think I will ever understand High Society, then."

"Oh, sweet lady, it's not just High Society, sadly. I've traveled far and wide, even to other times, and it's always the same wherever or whenever. They believe lies because they want to, not because it's truth. People will look the other way unless if affects them directly. Then, they find, they're alone, because everyone around them is doing the same. Looking away. Pretending. Yes. Something I cannot do, my dear."

"No. You are far too genuine for that, and I respect you, sir, for that as well as for your kindness. It is all too rare, indeed."

The Baron blushed. "Well," he said, pulling out his pocket watch, "it's nearing midnight, my dear, so I believe I will retire for the night myself. It has been a pleasure, as always, to chat with you. Do tell me that your meeting goes as splendidly as I'm sure it will."

"Thank you, Baron. Good night."

"Good night," he said, bowing, then left, and I found myself watching him go with some longing to follow, a desire to love. If only my heart were my own. Best not dwell on that which one cannot change.

I turned to see the doctor stumble up the stairs. He looked at his own pocket watch, and realizing the time, straightened up and with his sleeve, wiped his mouth, then smoothed down his dark uniform. Throwing his chest out, he climbed the rest of the way up and headed, no doubt, to his chamber where I was to meet him minutes from now.

Best get changed.

I knocked on the doctor's cabin door, then smoothed down my white apron and ensured my now-blonde hair was tightly pulled back properly in a bun beneath the white kerchief.

The door opened with a swish, and the doctor stood there, poised as the perfect gentleman.

"Good, e'enin', sir." I curtsied.

"Sweet, Claire. I'm so pleased you came."

"I keep my word, sir, but I just came to tell you that I'd rather meet with you in public first, sir. Perhaps once we're back in London. This just don't seem righ', sir. I 'ope you'll forgive me, sir."

"Nonsense! You're perfectly safe, my girl. I am a gentleman, after all."

As I said…

"No, sir. I fink I should just—"

"Don't be silly, girl. You're here now." He grabbed my arm and started pulling me inside, but I resisted.

"Please, sir."

"It's fine. Like I told you before, I promise, we shan't do anything you don't wish to do. Don't you like me? You kissed me before didn't you? Were you just toying with me? Playing with the heart of a lonely man? You're not that cruel, are you Claire?" His eyebrows creased when he said this, and he let go of my arm and twisted each side of his mustache, arranging his face to an expression of one who has been slighted. Bravo.

"A'course not, sir!" My eyes were wide with fear of having offended such a noble man.

I could hardly even think those words without laughing.

"I like you, sir. I really do. It's just, well, sir, it's not propa, sir. Not propa at all, is it, sir? I mean, I jus' met ya an' all, and I don't want ya ta think I'm a trollop, sir."

He chuckled at this, his face softening. "Come here, you," he said with such sweetness. Gathering me up in his long arms, he embraced me and made a tsk tsk tsk noise. "Nonsense," he said again. "I think no such thing. I respect you, Claire. Utterly."

Mind you, while he spoke these words, he was grinding his erection into me again. Before I knew it, he had maneuvered me inside and shut the door.

"Now, let's get more comfortable, shall we?" He pushed me down on the bed and sat next to me. I scooted away from him, and he followed, until I was trapped between him and the wall. "It's all right," he said, putting his hand on my knee.

I tried to move it away, but he fought me until I gave up.

"Come now, silly girl, it's harmless. It's just a knee after all. No need to get huffy."

He began talking about how it would be once we were back in London, and every few minutes, he'd inch his hand further up my thigh. His other hand would sometimes go to his trousers and rub himself a few times and saying, "Oh! Oh! Oh!" as he did so. Then he'd continue talking as if nothing out of the ordinary had happened.

"How long have you been married?" I asked him and hoped talking about his family would dissuade him from progressing, yet knowing full well it wouldn't. It was always interesting to see how these libertines reacted to mention of their wives and responsibilities.

"Too long, I'm afraid. As I told you, arranged marriage. It's all rather unfortunate business, but I don't want to hurt them, you see. That's why we must meet in secret, just for a while. I have to let them down easy, you see. After the new baby is born, then perhaps a year afterward, so I just don't leave her in a state. You understand, don't you? Yes. It's for the best. Yes, indeed."

"New baby, sir?"

"Yes. My wife, she's pregnant with our fourth, you see. Then there is the matter of her dowry. Oh, yes. She has quite a sizable one, indeed. Yes, indeed. Can't have word getting back to her. No. Not yet anyway. You understand, don't you, Claire? But we can have a real courtship in London in the meantime. You're so young and…delicious. A few years is nothing to you, my dear. It will be perfect. Then we shall be together. Properly married." He licked his lips, tongue sticking far out and swirling around and around the outsides of his lips. "Could I have another kiss, please?" he asked. "The first one was so sweet."

"Well, all right. But just one kiss," I warned, and he kissed me with such tenderness, then pulled back and looked deeply into my eyes. His hand had reached all the way up to my privates, and he tickled my clitoris with his pinky finger while looking at me with a very serious look. With all Claire's might, I tried to push his hand away, but he resisted. Then, in another instant, he had me pinned back on the bed, kissing me and groping my breasts with one hand, pulling up my skirt with the other.

"No!" I cried. "Stop, sir. Please!"

"Shhhhhhh," he said. "It's all right. It's a proper courtship after all, so it's all right. I'm a gentleman."

"I don't want to, sir. Please. Not like this."

His hand had reached all the way up my skirts and into my bloomers. As his finger slid into me, I gasped.

He groaned, "Oh. Yes. So tight! So wet. You see, you love this. Let me please you, just tonight. Let me love you, just for tonight. All right? You will love this. I promise."

"Stop! Please, sir!"

"This feels good, doesn't it? Come on, now. It does feel good. Admit it! Admit it, and I'll stop."

"Yes. It does. Now please stop."

He kissed my mouth and cheeks and neck, then slipped another finger inside me and got more forceful with thrusting them in and out. Sitting up between my spread legs, he removed his fingers and licked between and all around them. His bulgy, black-rimmed, tea-colored eyes glared at me. The color reminded me of the mud on the banks of The Thames, filthy and rank. He started to remove my bloomers, and I grabbed both his hands, holding them steady for a moment. "No. I'm a maid, sir! Please, sir! I aim to stay one until I'm married as is proper, sir. Please let me go, sir."

"You shall stay a maid. I promise."

He ripped my bloomers down, then buried his head beneath my skirts and licked me, flicking his tongue around and around until I moaned. The entire time, I tried to struggle away, but he kept me held in place with his hands.

"Stop. Please. This isn't right. I'll scream, sir! I will!"

"Shhhhh," he said, popping his head up, mouth and chin wet. "It's all right. You don't have to do a thing. Just enjoy it. It feels good, right?" Sitting back up, he started to undo his belt. "This is a proper courtship after all."

"No! Please!" I said and squirmed out from under him, running to the door, tripping on my bloomers, but he got there before I did and held it shut, standing between me and the door.

"Shhhh," he said again. "Don't worry. I'm a gentleman. You said no, and I respect that. I shan't put it to you, girl. You will be a maid when you leave this room tonight. All right? You can trust me. You enjoyed that, didn't you? I heard you moan. Yes, indeed. You enjoyed it quite a bit."

"It was pleasurable sir, but I don't want this, sir. Please."

"See? You liked it. I can please you more."

"I just want to leave. We can meet in London. Right, sir? Do a courtship propa. Like ya said, sir."

"Foolish, girl. What do you think a courtship is? This is a real courtship. This. What we're doing tonight. Are you really so naive to think men and women just sit and have tea and chat for hours and hours? Ha! Now I promise I will leave you a maid, but you've had all the pleasure thus far. It's my turn. You care for me, don't you? You do, I know you do."

He pushed me down, and I tried to resist, but he was stronger than this young chambermaid was. He pushed down on my shoulders until I was on my knees, then released himself.

"No," I said, pushing against hips.

"It's all right. This is what people in love do, after all. This is a proper courtship, dear."

I tried to turn my head, but he held it straight and pushed himself into my mouth.

I wept.

"Shhhh. It's all right. I'll be gentle. Oh, yes. Oh! Oh! Oh!"

Enough proof. Since I didn't have a poppet ready for him, there wasn't too much I could do without it being too quick, and this one deserved a long punishment as well, so I endured. I pushed him away with all of Claire's might, which was just enough to get off my knees, since he was drunk.

"I don't like that, sir."

"I'm so close. You can't leave until I've finished. It's only fair, after all. If you leave me like this, I shall be right sick tomorrow. You know a man needs to finish? You do know that, right? Didn't your mum teach you anything about the ways of the world, child? Everyone else knows this. I thought you were wiser than this. Perhaps you really are a silly girl after all. Everyone knows if a man doesn't finish once a woman has gotten him all bothered that he will get sick. Really sick. You don't want that, do you?"

"Well, no, sir. I don't want you ill, sir." This man was even more disgusting than I had thought.

"I'd be no good to you dead, now would I? How will we marry if I'm dead?"

"No, sir. I don't want you dead, sir. But I don' like that, sir."

"All right. All right. Not in your mouth and I did promise to leave you a maid, and a gentleman keeps his word! Yes, indeed! Come. Lay back down."

I reached for the doorknob again, but he flattened his hand against the door, making it clear I wasn't going to leave. I turned away and cowered in the corner, crying.

"Shhhhh. It's all right. It's all right, sweet girl. You don't have to do anything. All right? I shan't even lift your skirts. All right? And look, I'll put him away." He shoved his penis back into his trousers. "See? He's gone now." Up until this moment, he had been stroking it while he pleaded with me. "Will you feel safer that way? It will be over soon. I'm so close. So so so close."

I nodded, and he led me back to bed.

"You'll keep your trousers on?"

"I will."

"And you won't put it back in my mouth?"

"No. I won't. I won't even take him back out, all right?"

"Well, all right. Will it hurt?"

"No, you silly girl. Just lay back." I did and crossed my legs, keeping my arms tucked in close over my breasts. To my horror, he started writhing against me, rubbing his erection against my hip bone, saying, "Oh! Oh! Oh! Oh! Oh!" over and over again until his face made the most comical, twisted expression and his eyes rolled up into his head.

He collapsed next to me and slept.

"Doctor Nesbitt?" I nudged him. "Doctor? I don't even know your name, sir."

"Hm?! Oh. Nimrod. But you can call me Rod, sweetheart. That was lovely. Splendid. Yes, indeed," he mumbled.

"Can we still meet in London, sir? For a proper courtship, sir?"

"Of course. Yes, my dear. Of course. But don't approach me on the ship tomorrow, remember." He forced his eyes open to see that I understood. "We must keep this secret for now."

"What if we don't get the chance to talk again, sir? How will I find you once in London, sir?"

With his closing, he slurred, "Boxing Day, behind St. Saviour's in Southwark. Tea time. All right? Satisfied? Can I sleep now?"

With that, he was out and there was no waking him.

Boxing Day? Looks like I'll be making a new poppet or two.

This would be a Merry Christmas indeed. Yes, indeed.

CHAPTER 12

ARTHUR

I must've wandered around for hours, weighing options and thinking about what the Captain had said, for when I looked again over the side of the ship, I could see Sacre Coeur in the distance. Paris at last.

This would be one lonely Christmas Eve.

"Balderdash!" I straightened up and smoothed down my labels. "I wanted to be done with her anyway. Bored. Truly. Chastity is my love. She's my true love. I can feel it," I said into the night, convincing myself.

The Captain was right. The love of a good woman was rare, indeed, but Avalon was the past now. Too much work to fix that. No doubt. Why not just start anew. Chastity. Yes. My sweet, perfect love. She would make me happy and fulfilled like no one ever had, and she would love me as Avalon did. Better. As Catherine did. True love, this time. For how could she not?

With a skip in my step, I danced around the top deck with Paris at my feet. Chastity and I would explore the city together, and I shouldn't have to worry about Avalon at all! She said she would stay out of sight. All the better. No need to cause more distress in our community. No need to ruin others' Christmas Eve. No. That would be quite rude, indeed. She should stay hidden away. She never quite belonged anyways, did she? I belonged here. This was my community, after all. I brought her into it, but it just wasn't meant to be. So Emily and her husband might not speak to me at the gala tonight, but they knew what was truly important in society. Before long, no one would remember this indiscretion anyway.

It wasn't even an indiscretion because it was love. Yes. Just a technicality that I hadn't broken things off with Avalon, yet. She was to blame, really. Not me. Never. She was cold and withdrawn. She was overemotional. Clingy and rather mad, too. Yes, perhaps the prospect of immortality weighed too heavy on her frail mind. That must've been it.

Besides. Even if the Bainbridges never spoke to me again. Well. Worse things had happened.

It would indeed be a splendid day!

Let's just hope for a cloudy one.

§

At breakfast, all those seated at tables murmured when I entered the room, but I walked in with my head held in pride. I joined the McNairys and the Ablesons, and the chattering stopped immediately. After shaking out the napkin and lying it on my lap, I signaled the waiter for a cup of tea.

"Good morning, M'Lord," he said.

"Earl Grey."

"Of course, M'Lord. And you've a choice of eggs, sausage, and tomatoes or an array of pastries."

"I'll have both."

"Very good, M'Lord."

"Exciting night, don't you find?" I had found so often in my existence that if one just pretended there was nothing amiss, most would join in the pretense, and these lovely folks did not disappoint. In fact, they didn't say a word. Although, Lady McNairy pursed her lips tightly together and looked down into her lap. "I particularly enjoyed the stargazing." The second option was to be very obvious indeed, making everyone else so uncomfortable they didn't know what to say. "Did any of you go on the ship tour or gaze at the stars?"

All four stayed silent for quite some time.

Lady McNairy finally spoke. "Where is the lovely Miss Bainbridge this morning, Lord York? Shan't she be joining you for breakfast?"

"I think not, Lady McNairy. No, but with some luck, Mrs. Rosengarten will be joining me for breakfast and for a lovely stroll in Paris. Did you see Montmartre this morning? It is rather lovely sitting on that hill in all its majesty. Don't you find?"

"Preposterous," Lord McNairy said. "Come, my dear, let's prepare for the day."

"Yes, let's. I do feel rather full at the moment. Positively unable to take any more."

"Indeed!" I said as the old couple hobbled away from the table.

Lord and Lady Ableson remained.

"That was rather rude of them," Lady Ableson whispered with a scandalous lilt. "What do you plan to see today in Paris, Lord York?"

"Oh, the usual sights, I suppose. It's been quite some time since I've been here. Must get a baguette, of course. What is Paris without a fresh baguette? Perhaps even some decadent pastry. Yes. By the by, have you heard of the weather? Will there be rain or sunshine?"

"I do believe they're predicting a beautiful sunny day!"

"That's a shame. Perhaps I shall stay in, then."

"Why on earth would you do that? There shan't be much to do on the ship, Arthur."

"I didn't sleep well last night, what with all the scandal and such, so I thought perhaps I'd have a kip." Plus, my manly parasol was locked in my former cabin with Avalon. I truly should find a way to get my clothes out of there and procure new lodgings. It would be scandalous to wear the same waistcoat to the gala tonight.

"Well, suit yourself. I, for one, wouldn't miss Paris on Christmas Eve!"

Lord Ableson cleared his throat and dabbed each side of his mouth with a napkin. Blood rushed up into his face, which meant he was either very angry or very embarrassed.

Lady Ableson said, "Oh, my."

All right. Shocked.

"Good morning, Lord York. Lovely day, no?" Chastity's voice sounded as sweet as the music of the spheres.

"Good morning! What a lovely surprise. Won't you join us?"

"I would be delighted," she said, leaning over and breathing the words into my ear.

Lord Ableson huffed and Lady Ableson gasped.

Chastity wore a sharp blue walking dress with a lovely bustle. The bright color complemented her auburn locks. A flower among all these dreary people. As she sat down, she kissed me on the cheek, and my lips spread out in a wide smile. I couldn't take my eyes off of her. She was a vision. The Ableson's said something about leaving, but I didn't notice, really, until they were already gone.

"Was it something I said?" Chastity asked, with as much admiration in her eyes as I felt for her.

"Not at all, my love. It's so much better for us to be alone anyway. I've had enough gossip for one cruise."

"I'm so sorry about last night, Arthur. That must've been quite difficult for you."

"It was rather uncomfortable. Avalon can be so unreasonable."

"You poor thing. How have you put up with her for so long?"

"Honestly, I couldn't tell you. Too nice, I suppose. She has been so clingy and smothering for so long, and I just didn't have the heart to break it off with her. She would be devastated, you see, and I couldn't bring myself to do that to her. I was only thinking of her."

"Such a selfless man. You deserve a partner who will be your equal. One who will allow you your freedom and breathing room."

"Yes, indeed." Her lips were a breath away from mine, and I so wanted to taste them again and to finish what we started last night. Blood rushed downward as I thought about being buried in her warmth again. "I'm so excited about this courtship, Chastity. I think I've finally found what I've been looking for for so long. So, so long. You have no idea."

"Courtship? So you think of me as more than just a quick poke, do you?"

"Heavens! Yes! Oh, my love. I think we have something real here, don't you?"

"I would love to find out."

Just as I was about to close those last few inches and slide my tongue across her bottom lip, a rather rude person stood just behind us and cleared her throat in a thunderous manner.

Emily Bainbridge.

"Have you no shame, Arthur? Are you even concerned about my niece and how she must be feeling right now? You scoundrel! And YOU!" she said, turning to Chastity.

"Why, Emily," I interrupted. "Don't you look fetching today! Ready for a day in Paris with all its romance and grace? You shall fit right in. I have no doubt with your style you will be mistaken for a Parisian at every turn."

"Really?" Softening. "You think so? This is from the latest Parisian fashion. I got it specifically for this trip. Do you really like it?" She spun around, seeming to have forgotten all about her feigned offense on Avalon's behalf. She cared nothing for her niece. She'd made that clear time and again. In fact, I would wager she found great delight in the rumors, especially since it involved her niece, she would be getting far more attention than usual. So, of course, she had to put on a show, at least for now.

"I have never seen you look more beautiful, Emily. Honestly, you get more lovely with each passing day."

It was, of course, the most hideous thing I'd seen since her last ensemble. Her hat was at least three times the width of her head, yet her puffy shoulders extended past even that. It served to make her cinched waist look ever so tiny. I'd give her that. And the bustle! Well, I did love large bustles, but this thing looked like the backend of a horse, which, come to think of it, was quite apropos for Emily Bainbridge.

"Thank you, Arthur!" As some others passed by, she regained her cross composure and shook her finger at me. "You watch yourself, Arthur York. I am not done with you."

With that, she was quite thankfully gone.

"Paris today, my love?" Chastity asked me, dragging the back of her hand down my cheek. Such a loving gesture. Ah, yes. How wonderful to feel adored again.

"Alas, I heard it was to be sunny, and I have a rather serious, albeit rare, allergy to the sun. It burns my skin on impact, so I must stay inside, I'm afraid."

"As fortune would have it, sir." Her finger traced my jaw-line, then over my lips. "I have a really large parasol, and I'm quite certain it would protect us both. There are lots of dark corners in the alleyways of Paris, my dear. Plenty of places for naughtiness."

On second thought, a day in the city was exactly what I needed.

CHAPTER 13

CONSTANCE

The crowd gathered inside the ballroom

Waiting until the hallway was clear, I dug through my reticule, ensuring I had all the tools I'd need for the Willie's sentence. Once all were gone and I was alone, I knocked on Willie's door, and he answered, peeking through the door first, then looking both ways down the hall, before he opened it for me to come in.

"Hurry," he said. "We don't want to be seen."

"Am I early?" I asked, commenting on the lack of Mr. Chenery's presence.

"No, my darling, you are right on time. Excellent! We have a full hour now."

"Where is Mr. Chenery?"

"Um. Running late. Yes. He said it wouldn't be until closer to nine, likely. But it's fine. Don't worry."

Flustered, I turned to leave.

"Wait. Don't panic. It will be fine. He just wants to meet you, after all. He's already been told all about you. He's already read your article and adored it, by the way. You're welcome. Meeting you won't take long. Besides." He said the word in a long, drawn out way, emphasizing his deep-south accent, not to mention his underlying intentions. "This will give us some time to ourselves. For practice, of course. You want to make a good impression, right? After all, you'd be the first woman writer at *The Times*, and that's a great achievement! Milestone, some would say. Tragedy, others."

"And which do you think, Mr. McFerret?" My behavior was properly miffed at being trapped in a small cabin with a man. I stood with my hands pulled in tight, but I stood proud, too.

"What? A milestone, of course. Why do you think I'm helping you, Charlotte? And what's with all this Mr. McFerret. Come on, we're colleagues. Call me Willie. You know better than that." He handed me a glass of Gin as a smile crawled across his face. "Bottoms up!"

He threw his back and I sipped mine.

"You're amazing," he said to me, eyes sparkling, then leaned in, putting his hand against the door, blocking me. "I'm going to be able to say I knew her when she was just a simple girl from the country. Now look at her, London's first woman journalist."

"How you flatter," I said, blushing, and I pushed him away. Gentle, so as not to cause offense. No, Charlotte wouldn't jeopardize her budding career. After all, she'd be telling herself everything was fine. I, however, knew better.

"See there. That's it. Smile! Drink up! Drink up!"

I polished off my Gin, and he promptly poured me and himself another, then sat down. "Sit. Come sit next to me. After all, we're not going to have the meeting standing up. Get comfortable. You'll do much better if you're not nervous. Drink up. It'll take the edge off, relax you. That's it."

I sat next to him on the bottom bunk, as there was no where else to sit in the room. Their travel trunk was, no doubt, intentionally on the desk chair which had been pushed under the porthole. He scooted closer to me, and I had flashes of the assault last night by the revolting Nimrod Nesbitt.

I looked forward to Boxing Day to take care of him.

Next thing I knew, Willie had poured me another drink, clinked my glass, and slid his arm around me.

"Willie, business, remember?"

"Just relax, please. You're so uptight! Drink." Clink. "Cheers." He downed the next, but I didn't even sip mine. Still my vision started to get rather blurred.

"Oh my," I said, reaching out to steady myself. "Something isn't right. I'm not feeling at all well."

"Oh, my. That's not good. Here, lay back. There you go. Just rest for now. It will be all right."

"But, Mr. Chenery," I slurred.

"We've got time, yet. Just take care of yourself. That's all that's important now. I'll wake you when Chenery gets here. Just rest."

Then, blackness.

I awoke to find Willie buttoning up his trousers and smoothing his hair back. A sharp pain along with a deeper ache below told me what had happened. "What did you do to me?"

My bloomers were in a heap of fabric in front of the desk, and my skirt was still above my knees.

"What did I do to you?" he laughed. "What did you do to me? You're amazing, Charlotte! You had me fooled with all that talk of business only, which would've been fine, of course, since this is what it's about. Writing. That's all that matters, after all, but then you wanted me to lick Gin off your thighs. It came out of nowhere, but I was already under your spell."

"I what?! No, I didn't! What did you do?"

"My darling, you seduced me." His face twisted in anger at the implied accusation. "I was completely at your mercy. I thought you were a maid."

"I am a maid."

Laughing, he said, "Well, you're not anymore. Quite a wild thing, too. Unlike anything I've ever had."

I pushed my skirts down past my knees and wept.

"Now don't be like that. It was fun. That's all, but, you know, no one can know about this. In fact, if anyone ever finds out about this, you won't ever see me again. I mean it. Then you can kiss that job goodbye, too. I have a reputation to uphold, and it won't be said I was consorting with a whore like yourself, now. I won't have it. Besides, no one would believe you. But,"—again with the long, drawn-out drawl—"as long as you want to fuck me in private like this. I'm game, darlin'. Anytime you want. A firecracker like you. Anytime you like."

He patted his walrus belly and stretched his braces out and back with his thumbs a few times, looking very pleased with himself.

"Yes. That was great, my darling, but you have to go now. It's nearly nine, and my wife might come straight back from her blasted games. Regardless, I'm supposed to meet her at the ball. Remember, if I see you out tonight, I'm going to make as if I don't know you, and you'd be wise to do the same. No one can know. But I'll meet you in some dark corner somewhere after midnight for round two." He leaned down and licked up the side of my face as I cringed, then nibbled on my ear. "Come on, then. Grab your knickers. You've got to go."

"What about Mr. Chenery?"

"Looks like we'll have to postpone that meeting until back in London. Busy man, Thomas."

"He never was coming, was he? Does he even know who I am? Has he even read my work?"

"Oh, he's read it all right. That last article you gave me, well, it's set to be published after Christmas."

"It is!"

"With my byline, of course. Do you really think the world is ready for a female journalist? If you do, you're even more foolish than you look. Harlot."

Now. Enough.

I flicked my eyes from him to the bed. His body flew onto the bottom bunk and landed about the way a wet walrus would. Each hand fought as I raised them above his head with nothing but my will.

My will. Always.

Then Charlotte melted away, revealing Constance before him. Calm, determined Constance. His fear was palatable, and I licked my lips this time, ready for my meal. A warmth spread.

No. That was just the bed sheets after he had lost control of certain functions.

Fear had the strangest effects sometimes.

"I—I'll do anything you want," he pleaded, eyes wide.

"That's true."

I picked up my reticule and removed my tools, laying them out one by one, reveling in his fear.

"My wife! She'll be back any minute now. I know she'll come back here first. Before she goes to the dance. I know my wife. She'll be here any minute!" Sweat dripped down his face, and the front of his shirt was now as wet as his trousers.

"That's all right. This won't take long."

"You'll get caught. They'll put you away, you manipulative bitch."

Back to aggression and intimidation. Nice.

"Seeing as how no one knows I'm here. No one even knows you know me, isn't that right? Even if they did, you knew Charlotte, but she's now served her purpose. No one will ever see her again." I leaned over him, putting my nose right up to his and looked into those dead blue eyes. "Don't worry, our secret is safe with me, *my darling*. No one will ever know about this, not to protect you, of course, and I can happily say I shall still never see you again."

He struggled against my restraints, trying to reach me, face twisted in an infernal scowl. "You'll be sorry! You cunt. How dare you? Do you know who I am?"

"Enough." With a twirling of my fingers, motioning around and around, I sewed his lips shut without ever touching him. His eyes widened even more, as if they'd pop out of his head at first, then turned into angry little slits. His nostrils flared in his indignation, but the fear returned as I raised the straight razor and flicked it open. Shaking his head side to side, willing this to stop, he shut his eyes tight.

"No. You'll watch this." Throwing my hand up inches from his sizable jaw, I made his head freeze in place and his eyes pop open. He wouldn't be able to close them again. Leaning forward, I steadied the blade and sawed off a lock of his hair, then stuffed it in the poppet's neck, cinching it shut.

Tears filled his eyes in his terror.

"Seems you don't like someone else controlling your body, Willie. Funny, really. As it's all right when you do it, isn't it? You think you have the right to control others, to use their body for your pleasure whether or not they agree? They don't get a say in the matter, do they? You drug them. Coerce them. Threaten them into doing what you want. Isn't that right, Willie? Well, *my darling*, it's time to pay for all that forced privilege."

My fingers traced along the top of his trousers, pulled halfway up his walrus belly, until they reached the button.

Undoing it, then the next and next, Willie's gaping eyes turned upward.

"No," I said with a flip of my fingers, and his eyes were forced down where I would work. "Watch." Pulling his pants down below his hips, I exposed his weapon.

"This thing that you make more important than women's will, this has to go. I think you know that, don't you, Willie?" I twirled the straight razor around in circles, extending the delectable moment. "You know you can't continue hurting others, right? Manipulating, violating, sexually exploiting, using emotional and psychological blackmail. It stops here, Willie. Right here," I positioned the razor over his shrunken weapon.

"Bon appetit, pour moi."

 # CHAPTER 14

ARTHUR

I never felt so proud as I did walking into the dining room with Chastity on my arm. Such a delight, so full of life. She made me feel alive again. Free! Through her, I could live again. Love again. Truly love once again, after so long.

We sat near the Starboard side, enabling us to look out the portholes as we pulled into London on this beautiful Christmas Morning. We had a delightful time in Paris, and I had had a delightful time in her. Over and over again. In Paris. Down an alley. In a church. Then, after a short reprieve—she wanted to play charades, but I couldn't be bothered—all night long. I was rather famished and looking quite forward to breakfast.

"Look, my love. The Thames. It will be good to get home, don't you think?"

"Yes, but remember, I'm only here for the holidays. Paris is my home."

"We shall see about that." Chastity's face went from prettily pink to white in an instant. She swallowed hard and looked down at her hands in her lap.

I turned to see Avalon standing behind me, her cheeks rosy from what I could only assume was another blood meal. "Ava, my love! What a pleasant surprise."

"Have you heard? Mr. McFerret has gone missing, just like Nicholas."

"Oh, my! No, I hadn't heard."

"I thought you would be interested to know. Also, if you would be so kind as to allow Thomas to bring me my things over in Baker Street later today. I shall be heading straight there. I don't have much, but if you wouldn't mind instructing him what should return with me, I would appreciate it."

Always the lady, my Avalon. I missed her already, and she looked so sweet this morning. That tiny "o" in the center of her lips beckoned me. As if she could read my mind, she pursed her lips tight, making my "o" disappear. Oh well, sometimes things just didn't work out. Such were the ways of life and love. Plenty of other women to be had, no doubt. I reached over and took Chastity's hand in mine, and giving it a little squeeze said, "Is that all, my dear?"

"Yes. That is all." Her chin started to quiver when I had reached for Chastity, but I couldn't understand why. Always with the tears, as if she didn't know Chastity and I were together now. She saw it for herself, obviously. What was there to be so upset about? Too emotional, that woman. Indeed.

"Well, then." Tilting my head, I locked Ava's eyes with mine, questioning why she was still here.

Blood rimmed her eyes as the tears welled up. She turned and was gone. Good girl. Best not make a scene, especially with bloody tears. Yes. That would certainly be difficult to explain.

"That was rather awkward," Chastity said.

"Was it? I didn't find it so. Where on earth is our bloody tea?" Searching the dining room, all the waiters were busy with other guests.

"What do you think of that? Another disappearance. I wonder what we can discover about that."

"Oh! My little cherry, do you have a mind for mystery?"

"I must admit, I do find it all rather fascinating. You knew Lord Stanton, did you not?"

"I did. Still not convinced of foul play, though. Well, not someone else's anyway. It's only been a week, hasn't it?"

"True, but the blood. I heard there was blood at the scene."

"Not much at all. No, I'm sure he's fine. Good ol' Nick."

"So what about Mr. McFerret? He was a writer, wasn't he?"

"One of the up-and-comers over at *The Times*, I understand. Strange for him to disappear while aloft, don't you find? I wonder if they've searched the entire ship for a body. I suppose he could've fallen overboard."

"I'd more expect that buffoon Doctor Nesbitt to fall overboard. Usually when I see him he can barely stand, let alone walk properly. Such a Lushington, that one."

"In my time, I don't think I've seen his equal in that regard, my love."

"He's quite crass, as well, don't you find? Rather rude with the ladies."

"Oh, my dear, rather rude all around, when he's knackered. When he's sober, though, he can be quite charming. That's what's important, isn't it? Ah! Finally."

"Sorry to have kept you waiting, M'Lord," he said. "What would you like this morning, sir? Madam?"

"Tea all 'round, I think, and some pastries as well. Pain au chocolate for the lady and a croissant for me. If you would, also bring some fruit and sausage."

"None for me, but I wouldn't say no to some eggs and tomatoes."

"Yes. Sounds lovely. Make it a whole plate. There's a good man. Sausage, eggs, baked beans, and tomatoes. Yes. Extra sausage for me as well. I'll have the lady's sausage for a change," I said, winking at my love. Certainly she had enough of my sausage last night.

"Very good, sir. Right away."

"The tea straight away," I said as he turned away, making him spin back around to face us.

"Yes, M'Lord. Of course, M'Lord."

Chastity savored every bite of the chocolate pastry, and I did love to watch her eat it. Every last morsel. Oh, this would be a fine New Year. Yes, indeed.

Just as we finished breakfast, Captain Blackwolf approached me.

"Excuse me," he said, looking rather disappointed when he saw Chastity sitting next to me, but, no mind.

"Yes! Captain. Lovely cruise. Truly, sir. You are to be commended."

"Thank you, Lord York, but I don't think Mrs. McFerret would agree with you. You see, her husband is missing."

"Yes. I heard. How very unfortunate."

"Don't you find it rather strange, just like Lord Stanton? There's something you have to see, Arthur. Would you mind accompanying me to his cabin?"

"Ohh! Can I come, too?" Chastity sang. "I do love a good mystery."

"Well, all right," I said, patting her hand. "Lead the way, sir. We shall follow."

Upon arriving in Mr. McFerret's cabin, the first thing I noticed was the smell of blood. Much fresher than at Nicholas's place, of course, as it had just happened. But there was something else, too.

"Ugh. That smell." Chastity covered her nose and moved closer to the door.

"Yes. Blood," I said, "and plenty of it, it would seem."

"More than at Stanton's," the Captain said. "Considerably more." He pulled the sheet off the bed, and the entire center of it was pooled with blood and a black sticky substance

"No body?" I thought of Avalon. Could he have been her meal last night? Her cheeks did look rather rosy this morning. Perhaps that was why she told me of the disappearance, as a sort of confession.

"We've searched the whole ship, and we ain't found nothin'. Nothin' at all. But there is that," he said pointing to a grotesque statue on the floor next to the bed.

I had been so captivated by the scent of blood, I hadn't even noticed it. It was as hideous as the bizarre one at Nick's, and it, too, was missing its johnson. "Blood there as well, I see," I said, noticing a thin line around the edge of its base.

"Yes. If you pick it up, it's sitting in a pool of blood along with some black substance. In fact, when I found it, it was here," he said, indicating the bed again. "Right smack in the center of that stain. Strange thing, I wiped off the bottom before placing it down there. Now, there's more blood. Fresh blood and ooze."

"Like it's bleeding? Why, that's impossible."

"I think I might be ill," Chastity said, swooning. I made it to her in time to catch her before she hit the floor.

"Let me just get her out of here, all right?"

"Of course."

I carried Chastity in my arms up to the top deck for some fresh air. Avalon was at the top of the stairs. "Ava." She frowned at the unconscious Chastity. "Fainted," I explained. "Sight of blood, I suppose. We just visited Mr. McFerret's chamber. You should see it."

"I've already seen it. Examined it with the captain this morning. Excuse me," she said as she tried to push past us.

"The statue is still bleeding."

"What?"

That got her attention.

"The statue. Still bleeding and seeping something else, too. This is supernatural, Ava. Like us. We're the best team to solve this, and I think you were right, Nicholas is gone, too. He's not just off on holiday."

"No, Lord York. I cannot work with you on this case."

"Why not?"

Her eyes widened and eyebrows went up. The tiny "o" in the center of her mouth got much larger as she gaped at me. "Honestly, Arthur!" she said with incredulity and stormed past me.

Shrugging, I continued out on the deck and set Chastity down gently, fanning her face. London lay out beneath us as we approached Hyde Park. We'd be landing soon, and I, for one, would be relieved to get home. Chastity came to after a few moments, her eyes fluttering open.

"Rest here, my love. Enjoy the view of landing. I'm heading back down to discuss this strange mystery with the Captain. I'll be back to check on you shortly."

"Thank you, love. So silly of me to faint."

"Nonsense. Just rest."

"I see ya didn't take my advice," Blackwolf said, when I returned to McFerret's room.

"On the contrary, good man. I most certainly did, just with a different woman. Do you really think I could make amends with Avalon? She perceives this as such a horrible slight, and she is far too proud. No. I think my efforts would be better spent creating something new and lasting, but I shan't take Chastity for granted. No, sir."

"Uh-huh. He didn't take my advice, neither," he said, nodding to the crimson and black stain.

"You knew him? Oh! That's right. Served together and all that. Charming. Really." Bored.

"I hated the way he treated Gladys. All women, really, but especially her. Mostly behind her back, mind, but it made it all the worst. Him makin' a fool of 'er and all. Such a fine woman, too."

"Gladys? It's Gladys? You're in love with Gladys, aren't you? Now you're blushing! How quaint," I teased. "Oh, this just became so much more interesting!"

"Enough," he growled. "Look at that statue, Arthur. Notice anything strange about it?"

"Other than the obvious?"

"Look closely."

"All right." It weighed heavy in my hand, heavier than the statue at Nick's. Quite. It was approximately the same size, perhaps a little squattier, and—"Oh! Blimey! The mutton chops. Blimey! The thing has mutton chops just like Ol' McFerret. Rather large jaw, too, and belly, I suppose. What do you think it means?"

"Maybe the statue is made in the likeness of the victim, then used to kill them. I'm not quite sure, but that is certainly worth noting. Don't ya think?"

"Yes, indeed."

§

After giving Thomas instruction to gather Avalon's things and deliver them to Baker Street, I had him drop me back off at Nick's. I didn't want to be there while he packed her things, not that I was sad to see her go. No. It wasn't that. I mean, I would miss her, of course. She was a part of my life for six months, give or take. So, of course, but one must move forward. Always onward.

Nick's was much as we left it, but I was quite curious to get a closer look at that statue. It still squatted on the desk where we left it. The dark ring beneath it had expanded and was now dried. So it had kept bleeding and oozing, too, just more slowly. Interesting. Picking it up, I studied every line of the gargoyle's face, looking for any resemblance of Nicholas, but I found none. From the scowling grimace to the angry eyes, it looked much more like a demon than Nick. Maybe the statues were made to resemble the victims, but this one didn't resemble Nick.

Although, artists. Their bloody license and all.

The blood, while bizarre to come from a statue, wasn't as curious as the black sticky substance. I had never seen anything like it in all my days. Even in its dried state, there was a faint fetid stench. Not quite sure how I hadn't picked up on anything but the blood the first time. Perhaps I had been denying myself too much the nourishment I needed to be at my best, so that was all I could smell.

In McFerret's cabin, the stuff was almost tar-like and putrid. Sticky with long strands extending from the pooled liquid to the statue after Blackwolf picked the thing up. Now dried, it was crusty.

I examined the black ring on Nick's desk more closely. From my vantage the last time, it looked black, but I assumed it was just dried blood. Now upon closer examination, along with what I had seen at McFerret's, I could see there was indeed both. I picked at the black and crimson swirled stain with my fingernail. The blood had seeped into the blotter and wood. A good scrubbing would be the only thing to get that out, but the black substance had more…substance. Thicker. It chipped and flaked as I picked at it.

"How odd." I turned to converse with Avalon, but remembered I was alone. No matter. I could figure it out myself, since I was rather clever.

Hmmmmm. Missing cock. Scowling angry or pained look. Blood on the carpet. Black sticky stuff.

Maybe…

Or, perhaps…

No. It was rubbish. I needed someone to bounce ideas off of. Someone to talk it through with.

Sadness came over me, clouding my eyes with a grey curtain. I missed Avalon so much. My gut felt heavy and empty at the same time, and I wished she were here more than anything. Perhaps I had acted too hastily on the ship with Chastity.

But, oh, Chastity!

Light, again. Light in my eyes. Light in my heart. Light in my life. Chastity.

Yes, I had made the right decision. I must follow my heart, after all. It was a shame Avalon took it so hard, truly, for I had not meant to hurt her. I loved her, of course. But it would be best if we didn't speak for awhile. I think that would be best. Perhaps we could be friends after some time had passed, after she accepted this. I hoped as much.

The weight of the statue brought me back to the present, and I decided if I couldn't discuss this with Avalon, for her own sake, poor girl, then I must discuss it with Blackwolf. He, too, had been privy to both scenes, and he was rather intelligent for a commoner.

Yes. I'd call on the captain for assistance.

Tomorrow, though. It was Christmas after all. Perhaps a fine dinner with Chastity tonight. That would keep my mind off of Avalon and other unpleasant things. This was a day of feasting and merriment and such. One should not be alone on Christmas if one could help it.

A man such as me always had options.

CHAPTER 15

CONSTANCE

I waited out in the cold, December afternoon behind St. Saviour's, just as Nimrod had instructed, but as the sun set and the temperature dropped, there was still no sign of the doctor.

"I really don't like being stood up," I said to the raven who had settled on the flint wall. "And after we had been so intimate. He was going to marry me, you see."

The raven cocked his head to one side trying to understand the sounds emerging from my mouth. It blinked twice, then took flight.

"Nevermore, indeed. Just as well." Now I wouldn't have to lure him back to his place. We could just begin and, he, anyway, could end there. It had been quite kind of me to allow him Christmas yesterday, after all, but now it was time to pay the doctor a visit.

When I arrived on his doorstep, I was taken aback by the horrid stench coming from within. After using my sleeve to cover my nose at an attempt to block out the offensive stench, if only for a moment, I knocked on the door.

"Lucas!" I heard the doctor shout. Then, silence.

I knocked again.

"Levi! Lester! Luther! Lafayette! Whatever your bloody name is, you old simian! Get the door!"

"It's Lionel, sir." I heard quietly behind the door, then it opened. An older gentleman with dark skin stood before me. A sadness about him tugged at my heart. He was likely taken from Africa during one of the Professor's many adventures. His features were kind and soft. If that display was any indication on how his employer treated him, I would be saving yet another person from his abuse on this day.

"Good day, ma'am."

"Good day, sir. I'm 'ere to see Doctor Nesbitt, sir."

"Please, come in from the cold, my dear. Who shall I say is calling?"

"Miss Claire Weisheart. Thank you." The inside of Nimrod's house was a cross between a laboratory and a museum. Upon each surface, in addition to being covered in thick dust, sat a taxidermied animal. All shapes and sizes and breeds, everywhere one looked. On the table in the foyer, for example, a gold cage tilted to one side, half on-half off a stack of books. Inside it, a brilliant red and yellow parrot was nailed to the perch, forever frozen in mid-squawk. Next to it a bobcat crouched, ready to pounce for all eternity.

Their glass eyes haunted me.

Some type of animal carcass or a glass jar with hideous things suspended in liquid filled every nook and cranny.

Explained the stench.

"What!" Nimrod exclaimed from the other room. "How did she find me?"

A moment later, he slid into the room and stiffened when he saw me, spindly legs locked at the knee. His preposterous mustache stuck straight out on either side. He squinted his muddy eyes, questioning me.

"I missed you at the church," I said, drawing a figure eight in the dust on the table

"Oh, yes. Well. That. You see. Well. I've realized. That"—he cleared his throat—"well, It's just, you see. It's just. I can't do this, Claire. I just can't. I mean, my children. Three girls, and another on the way. A boy, this time, I think. Yes. I just can't do this to them, you understand. Don't you? And my wife, she works so hard to raise them along with the few servants, only. Yes. Complicated business, this. You understand, don't you? I think it's best if you go. I—I just can't is all. There's a good girl. Off you go."

"Oh. I see, but, it can't be! I mean, I came here to—I'm ready to—I mean, I'm ready, Rod. I'm ready to give myself to you. Completely in love and desire. All for you. You already have my heart, my love. Right? After what we shared the other night. You said that was a proper courtship, right? Well it's time for the wedding night, then, even if there shall be no wedding. You still have my heart and I want to give you my body, too. Just grant me this one request, please. Then if you want me to go, I shall. I promise."

Upon hearing this, his eyes widened once again, then he commenced to rubbing his crotch and moaning, "Oh! Oh! Oh!" After a moment or two of that, he picked up the stuffed bobcat and began rubbing up against that as well, continuing, "Oh! Oh! Oh!"

"Yes, my love," I said, trying my damnedest not to laugh at this absurd display. "Yes! Let me please you. Could we go upstairs, perhaps? Oh, Nimrod, let me love you, just for today. Let us go and love one another, like in a proper courtship."

"Oh! Oh! Oh! Yes! Just this once. Yes! Real love, a proper courtship, even if just for a few moments. I am a gentleman—Oh! Oh! Oh!—after all. Must be proper. Yes, indeed! Oh! Oh!

Oh!—Luther!" he shouted, still writhing against the stuffed cat and groaning his delight. "Leonard! Oh! Oh! Oh!"

"It's Lionel, sir." The sadness in his voice, the humiliation, reinforced my resolve.

"Go and get some tea, will you? I believe we are out of tea. Yes. Must have enough tea. Go on, then, and be gone at least fifteen minutes." He licked his lips and gyrated against the cat even faster. "Oh! Oh! Oh! Better make that twenty."

"Yes, sir."

As Lionel closed the front door behind him, Nimrod put the stuffed bobcat down and bolted up the stairs, taking two at once, and I trotted up behind him, giggling. Once we arrived in his bedchamber, full of even more taxidermal animals, including a bear raised on his hind legs, he leapt on the bed and shed his clothes. "Come on then," he said. "Bring that tight fanny over here."

"Let me watch you first, my love. I want to see your entire body wanting me, aching for me. Then I shall change for you. You won't believe it, my love. You won't believe your eyes when you see all of me."

"Oh! Yes! Yes, indeed! Are you ready for all of this?" He ripped the ribbon out of his stringy hair, shaking it loose about his shoulders and then bucked his hips up in thrusting motions, erection bouncing quite comically. "Look at that there! Oh yes! Oh! Oh! Oh! Oh! Oh!"

"Sit back against the headboard now, and spread your arms and legs out wide. Yes, that's right. Oh, my! You are so very delicious."

Pathetic, I meant.

"Ready for me, love?"

"Oh, yes. Oh! Oh! Oh! Oh!"

Honestly. This man was beyond comical.

As I disrobed for him, I changed into Constance's countenance. He was so busy looking at my breasts and other parts that he didn't even notice until I spoke again, my voice altogether different. "Here I come."

I slinked toward the bed, reticule dangling from one wrist.

"Blimey! Who are you? How did you...Well, really doesn't matter. One minge is as good as the next. Come and get it, sweetheart. Sit on this. Oh! Oh! Oh!" he moaned, bucking his hips up and down, up and down, causing his erection to make a fap—fap—fap sound against his stomach.

"Oh, I am going to enjoy this so much, you revolting lush."

"What you got in there, love? A pea? Oh! Did you bring some opium? Yes, that would make this perfect. Perfect, I say! A bit of a pea then a bit of me!" He put extra emphasis on the word me, and thrust his hips toward me as I knelt between his spread legs.

"No, *love*, not a pea, but rather a few tools I'll need." I took out a large pair of scissors, my straight razor, and his personal poppet. "Did I ever tell you my favorite food?"

The smile from his face dropped, and horror filled his eyes as he realized he couldn't move. Muscles tense, trying to pull his hands away from the headboard, but there was no escape.

He was mine now.

"What have you done? What are you, woman? A witch? Help! Help!"

"No one can hear you. You sent your butler away, remember? How utterly appalling you refer to another human being as a simian because of his skin color. Atrocious, indeed. You don't even bother to remember his name, but then you don't respect other people, do you Nimrod? You certainly don't respect women, that's quite apparent. You don't respect your wife or your children, always betraying them with others. You don't respect the peace of others. In fact, the only thing that matters to you is this thing."

Throwing a leg over each hip, I straddled him and leaned in really close to his face, snipping my scissors in his ear.

"Stop! Please, don't."

"You remember poor Claire the other night on the ship? Isn't that what she said? Don't. No. Stop. But you didn't listen. You forced her. You forced me." I grabbed a fistful of long, greasy, black hair and cut it off with one snip of my loppers.

Now, tears streamed down his cheeks.

Satisfying tears.

Good.

"I didn't! You...she wanted it. She came to my room at midnight! What did she expect? Charades? Please. I'm a bloke! That's what blokes do?"

"No. That's what rapists do. What did she expect? She expected you to be a gentleman, as you so often claimed you were. She expected you to be decent. To be kind. She expected you to love her. After all, it's what you promised her." I had settled back down between his legs and picked up the poppet, stuffing the hair clippings inside.

"Don't be daft, woman. A doctor and a chambermaid? What-what? Besides, I have responsibilities, family. Surely she knew. What are you doing there?"

"She was seventeen. And before her, Nimrod. How many others? What about your students? Hmm? Miss Greenslade? Miss Dorton? Making them touch your John Thomas, while protected from prying eyes, or should I say, witnesses, tucked away in your office. Telling them how much you want to fuck them, telling them every time you look at them in class all you could think about was fucking them? Pinning them on the couch and writhing against them or worse."

With a quick flick of my wrist, the razor cut into his leg, drawing blood.

"Ow! Please! No, please!"

Holding the poppet just beneath the cut, I caught a few drops of blood in the opening beneath its neck, then continued, "As if women don't have a hard enough time in university, the few there are, and you make it infinitely worse. Then, how you make them earn their grade. Yes. I know about you, doctor. How many lives have you ruined, Nimrod? How many other women have you made promises of love, of kindness and friendship, and then discarded them once you had used them for your own pleasure? Hmm?"

After I had cinched the poppet's head shut and put it aside, I picked up my straight razor again. Looking down at his juicy erection, I licked my lips, then said, "Sausage, by the way. Sausage is my favorite food, if you were curious."

"I'm sorry! I'm sorry! I know I only have myself to blame, but I'm so lonely, you see. I haven't felt loved in years, and I just want to be loved. I just…please." He grimaced. The scraping sound of me flipping the razor opened and closed over and over grated his nerves, judging from the grimace on his face and his squinty eyes. That brightened my day. "Please don't hurt me! Please! I'll do anything you like. I'll leave my wife. I'll marry you. Is that what you want? You want all of this to yourself? You can have me. Please, just don't hurt me."

I threw my head back and laughed out loud. "You must be joking. You are pathetic."

"I'm a celebrated professor. Hunter and explorer," he said, thrusting his chest out.

"That's quite enough from you," I said, twirling my finger around and around in mid-air. A black cord whipped around his lips, in and out, sewing his mouth shut. "There." I wiggled the yellow poppet in front of his terrified eyes, bulged out of his head even more than usual. "More of a resemblance already."

Tears. Lots of tears and muffled whimpers, making his thin lips puff out between the stitching.

"Oh. Pity. Tears, now. The same tears you use to coerce your victims with pity. Yes, you do understand the power of pity used over a kind woman, don't you? Behind those tears this time is fear, Nimrod, much like the fear you instill in your prey. The fear you will feel from this minute forward until you have suffered as much as the women you've hurt have suffered. The women you've traumatized."

He shook his head violently, pleading with his eyes.

"But first, dinner." Remarkably, his erection was still as full and throbbing as before. "Mmmm. A juicy sausage tonight, I see. How very delicious, indeed."

The scream that came from the back of his throat and through his flared nostrils was music to my ears.

§

On my way home from the doctor's, my tools and his black-heart poppet tucked safely back inside my reticule, I came across a woman weeping in an alleyway. Not surprising, as every night there are more injured souls than the last, but most fall beneath my notice because either my focus is elsewhere, on a particular client, or their collective agony makes for a symphony of sorrow that permeates the air, making one individual indistiguishable from the next. However, my power heightened from my recent meal, I felt her immediately and almost became ill right on the street, not expecting such a fervent wave of misery. After composing myself, I turned down the alley to see if there was anything I could do. The sight of me made her jump and put her arms up in a defensive position.

I already knew what had happened.

"What is it, my dear? Is there anything I can do?"

"No one believes me," she cried. "The peelers, me friends. No one."

"Peelers? You mean the police?"

"No one. Them peelers, they—No. I learned to keep quiet now, I have. Just makin' it worse for meself. I know better now. Keep quiet. I know that. I know it. Good day, miss." A curt nod, then she tried to move past me.

"Wait, please. I will believe you." I rested a hand on her trembling shoulder. "I promise. You're safe with me."

"Well, me husband, ya see. He drinks too much sometimes and does finks to me, and I know he don' mean it. I know he loves me an' all, but this last time he went too far. It's not just me anymore, you see. It's our daughter now, too. An' I can't bear it, so I told the police. Just want my daughter safe, is all. Me is one fink, Miss. I'm his wife, after all. His property. But he won't do that to me daughter. But them peelers…they…"

Silent sobs screamed in my ears, and her sorrow filled my heart. I caught my balance on the brick wall, weak from her pain. "It's all right," I breathed, strengthening the protective walls around me. "You're safe now. It's all right. Please, just tell me. What did the police do?"

"They laughed at me and told me I had better keep quiet. Me 'usband's the butcher round 'ere, see? Respected, 'e is. They told me to keep quiet or they'd make sure I stayed quiet, them peelers did. I wouldn't stay quiet, though, Miss. I see how I was wrong now. I just need to do what I'm told is all. That's all. Then everyfink will be all right again. Me daughter will be all right. Right, Miss? She'll have to learn to take it, too. Just like all of us. We just have to take it, is all. Just take it and keep quiet. It's not so bad, really. Just take it and keep quiet. That's what I'll do, Miss. She'll learn to do it, too."

"What's your name?"

"Mary, Miss."

"Mary, what did the peelers do?"

Mary wept again, and when I moved to comfort her, the light of the gaslamp fell on her face. She had bruises, and her dress was torn. "I see. They just did this to you, did they?"

"They did. Both of them together, Miss. You believe me, right, Miss? Please say you believe me!" She grabbed a fistful of sleeve in each hand, shaking me in her desperation.

"Of course I believe you. I passed a couple of coppers on the way down the street. Would you be able to have a look around the corner and tell me if those are the ones who hurt you?"

"No! Miss. I mean, I don't want no more trouble. I've got to get 'ome, ya see. But 'e'll know, won't 'e? My 'usband, 'e'll know what they done, and then 'e'll punish me again. I'm scared, Miss! I don't know what to do."

"Look into my eyes," I said, stooping down and facing the light so she could see. "Believe me when I say I will take care of those coppers, all right? Your husband, too."

"Not my 'usband, Miss. 'e don't mean it, and we can't eat without 'im. We'd be on the streets. Don't hurt 'im! Please don't hurt 'im!"

"I promise I won't hurt him, Mary, but I will stop him from hurting you. All right? Those coppers, on the other hand, they're meant to protect you, and they just hurt you again. They won't get away so easily. Just have a look around the corner. They won't see you. I promise. Are they the ones?"

Hiding under my arm, she peeked down the street, and then she whipped back around, flattening herself against the brick wall, sheltered by the darkness of the alley. Her breath heavy and deep, gasping for breath. Eyes wide.

"It's all right, Mary. They can't hurt you again. Give me a few minutes, and they'll never hurt anyone again. All right?"

"All right."

"And your husband's butcher shop. Is it the one here in Southwark Street?"

"Yes, Miss. But don't 'urt 'im!"

"I shan't. I'll just scare him, all right? He'll be a kind as can be when he gets home. All right?"

"All right."

"Now, you go home now and care for your daughter. You did the right thing to protect her. He won't hurt either of you ever again, or he'll have me to answer to."

"Who are you, Miss?"

"I'm your protector, Mary. Yours, and all women's." As I spoke the words, I shifted form and visage right in front of her. She crossed herself, whispering to her god.

"Are you a witch?" she asked.

"No, Mary, I'm much more powerful than a witch, and much more dangerous. Go on home and care for yourself and your daughter. Be happy. I think you'll find your husband all too willing to put your happiness first now, yours and your daughter's, too. Take this," I said, removing a white feather from my reticule. "I can hear you through this. Keep it safe. This way I will know if your husband is behaving as a husband should, or if I need to return. Just speak to the feather like you're speaking to me. You're safe now."

"Thank you, Miss! Thank you!"

Mary went off behind me, and I stood in the street, shielding her from the police who smoked cigarettes and stood beneath a gaslamp on the corner, laughing. No doubt about their recent villainy.

"Help! Police!" I cried, gaining their attention. I had turned myself into a young barmaid, blonde hair a touch disheveled and rosy cheeks. I'd tell them of a true tale, something that happened all too recently, for even while spinning my web, I would never lie about something so important, so horrific and soul-destroying as rape.

The two men trotted down to where I stood, just on the edge of the alley, and I told them my tale.

"So, ya say, ya had relations with the bloke in question, did ya?" Constable Davis, judging from his name plate, said. The enjoyment in his eyes turned my stomach.

"No! Constable, no! I didn't. He forced me. In me mouth as well, and he enjoyed it, he did. I tried to push him away, but he just came at me harder, sir."

"Ah! So ya gave him oral pleasure." The constables exchanged knowing looks and winked before the first copper wrote in his notebook, speaking as he did so: "She remembers giving oral sex at one point to the suspect."

"No! No, I didn't *give* him anything, constable! Please, listen to me. Please. He was brutal, violent."

"Look, Miss. We wasn't there, alrigh'. We wasn't there, so we don' know wha'appened. You're talking about a very stand-up member of the community, whoever this bloke is. Y'understand this is a very serious accusation, Miss, don't ya?"

"It's a very serious offense, sir!"

"Yes, well that might be, if it's true. Who are you? And look what yer wearin'. Can't blame the bloke, really. No. I fink you prolly jus' regret it. Ya didn't tell him to stop, after all, did ya?"

"I—I couldn't speak. I was gagging on his—he was choking me!"

"Maybe he was tryin' to send you a message, Miss. Keep your bleedin' mouth shut, or he'll shut it for ya. Good lesson for a woman to learn, nice an' early, don't ya fink, 'owards?"

"Yes, indeed," Constable Howards replied.

"In fact, I fink that's a fine idea. Marvin," he indicated his partner with a nod, "help this fine lady learn that, would ya?" Marvin laughed as he grabbed me, and I shrieked as he pulled me down the alley. I put up a fight, and a few passersby looked momentarily, but didn't want to be involved in police business. After all, the police were there to protect the community. In the minds of passersby, I had obviously had done something wrong.

Marvin covered my mouth to ensure I didn't scream and bent me over some crates, holding my head flat against the hard crates. I heard his belt buckle jingle. Up the alley, Constable Davis snuffed, laughed, and unfastened his trousers as he headed toward us.

"Busy night," he said to himself, chuckling.

It certainly was, I mused.

This time I didn't even let them get started before I finished it, finished them.

It had been a long day, after all.

CHAPTER 16

ARTHUR

"M'Lord?" Thomas whispered through my chamber door. "Excuse me, M'Lord, but it's just gone four. The captain is set to arrive within the hour, M'Lord. I thought you might fancy a cup of tea before that."

"I'll be out presently, Thomas. Thank you."

"I could bring it in to you, M'Lord."

"Yes. Thank you, Thomas. Bring some up with the newspaper."

Still, I didn't budge. Curled up in a tight ball, I stared at Avalon's empty side. I had been like this for hours, unblinking. Couple of days, really. Since Christmas night. Alone after all. Just staring.

I had sent word to Blackwolf, but he couldn't meet on Boxing Day, and Chastity was unavailable as well. Seemed my options waned. Perhaps I should return to something simpler, like Hazel. Sweet Hazel Hamilton would be a challenge, and likely not all that experienced, but she would do as she was told, no doubt. Be available when I needed her, and be properly thankful for the attention.

Bah! Needed. I didn't need any woman.

I pulled Avalon's pillow to my face and inhaled her scent. It had been an empty Christmas without her, devoid of love and warmth. Lonely Boxing Day, too. I couldn't find the strength to sit up or to do anything, really. Tea would be good, indeed. Tea would help. Perhaps ten drops this morning, as I needed some sort of boost. I had company coming, after all. Must present myself properly, and all. Yes, a boost.

I could go back to keeping some living fruit in the cellar. Dangerous practice, that. For although they claimed to be willing at the beginning, they ended up wanting to leave. Then the shouts and screams did get ever so tiresome. No. Best to drink and run.

"C'mon, man!" I chided myself aloud, hoping hearing the words might stir me to action, and threw the pillow aside. "It's only been a few days. She'll be back. You know she will be back and she will bend to your will. They always do."

I would do as I pleased. No one would control me. I would fuck Avalon when I wanted and Chastity when I wanted and whomever else caught my fancy. Hazel, perhaps. Yes. It was time. Whomever caught my fancy. That was just how things were. I was a Tudor, after all. How dared she expect exclusivity. Of one like me? Honestly. Absurd. All of me for one woman? Preposterous.

A knock on the door pulled me from my thoughts again, but the indignation had done wonders already. Sitting up, I told Thomas to enter.

"Your tea, M'Lord," he said as he entered. "May I draw the curtains? The sun is well hidden, M'Lord."

"Very good, Thomas. I could use some light after all. Ten drops today."

"Yes, M'Lord." He raised his sleeve and administered the blood before going to open the curtains. The newspaper headlined the disappearance of McFerret, and now, it seemed,

Doctor Nesbitt as well. Blackwolf and I would be discussing the case and more, no doubt. Perhaps he had been right about Avalon. She was a fine woman, after all, but then so was Chastity.

"May I speak plainly, M'Lord?"

"Of course, Thomas. You've been with me quite some time now, always proper. Please, do."

"Thank you, M'Lord." Thomas stammered once or twice before he continued and looked away from me, then at me again, and then away once more. He wrung his hands then wiped them on his trousers. At last, with a slight tremor in his voice, he said, "I have served you a long while, and, if I may say so, I've noticed some patterns, M'Lord. You seemed quite happy with Miss Bainbridge. Well, at first, M'Lord. Always at first. Although you don't choose many women with whom to become so intricately involved, preferring to keep it casual. Well, M'Lord, perhaps that's best for you and for them. Miss Bainbridge is a fine woman, as fine as I've ever had the honor of knowing, and she doesn't deserve such treatment, M'Lord. No one does." He bowed in submission when he saw the angry scowl appear on my face. "Forgive me, M'Lord. I've overstepped, my apologies."

"That will be all, Thomas," I said through clenched teeth.

"M'Lord," he said, then turned on his heels and removed himself from my presence before I removed him from this earth. The insolence. So unlike Thomas, too. How dared he? First Blackwolf and now my own help. After placing my tea down, I collapsed back on the bed, reaching out to Avalon's empty side. She was indeed a good woman who was worthy of a man such as myself, and I worthy of her. For who wasn't worthy of a woman's love, but I would not accept being shackled so.

"No. That's that."

I stood, forcing myself to get ready for my imminent guest. Although, I was altogether miffed I had to dress myself. Again. Inconceivable, really. Especially now that Avalon was gone, I needed to find a new butler.

§

"Captain Arron von Blackwolf," Thomas announced the arrival of my guest, so I put the newspaper aside.

"Very good, Thomas. Show him in."

"Lord York," Blackwolf said as he entered my parlour, hat in hands.

"Good afternoon, Captain," I said, reaching out to shake his hand. "I was just reading about our little mystery. Did the police say anything else after we left McFerret's?" I motioned for him to join me, offering the seat closest to the fire, as I didn't need it, and moved to the tapestried chair opposite, settling in.

"They didn't. Baffled as you or me, I'm afraid. They took their samples and made their notes, but mostly they just stood around and scratched their heads."

"No surprise. They are rather worthless. I went back to Ol' Nick's and picked up this." I handed him the heavy statue, wrapped in a cloth to catch the blood and ooze still emanating from it. "Did you manage…?"

"No. That's one thing they did take, as it was so outta place. I suppose it went unnoticed at Lord Stanton's, but it was rather strange for it to be in the small cabin, especially when Gladys"—his voice faltered when he said her name—"didn't recognize it."

"Indeed."

"What do you think this black stuff is? Rather rancid."

"It is, and I'm sure I have no idea. Although, I no longer think Ol' Nick is off cavorting any more. No. Indeed, this was foul play. But a titled gentleman, a newspaper reporter, and an Oxford professor. What do they have in common, besides these bizarre statues? They found one at the professor's too, I read. Although the one there wasn't even human, really. More animal, from the sketch in the paper. He was quite the collector of animals, so they believe it was just part of his collection from his travels, but the other two? Too much of a coincidence for me, I'm afraid. What else do they have in common? I mean, what could possibly be the motive behind their disappearance?"

"I have a few theories. Do you think these men have been killed? Perhaps, bludgeoned with the statues?"

"My good man, I think these statues are the key to figuring out this mystery. Indeed. Perhaps there is something supernatural going on here. Perhaps these men have been turned into these statues."

The look on Blackwolf's face changed from curious to affronted, as if the suggestion of the supernatural offended him. "Don't be ridiculous." He dismissed the notion with a scoff, turning his attention once again to the statue in his hands.

"There are more things in heaven and earth..."

"That may be so, Arthur, but what you suggest is beyond ludicrous. How would such a thing even be possible? This is not one of McFerret's horrid novels, after all. This is real life."

"Do you have a better theory? Why are there no bodies? Why does the statue bleed and ooze as if it were alive? What do these men have in common? And why are they all missing their John Thomases?"

"Murdered, I think. No bodies because there are ways of disposing of such things. McFerret, likely over the side of the ship. He's somewhere at the bottom of the channel, if they was smart and weighted him. If not, he'll be a'washing up on the coast before long. Lord Stanton, maybe dumped in the Thames. Maybe buried somewhere. It's only been a few days, mind. Doctor, same."

"And motive? The statues? The missing piece?"

"Scorned woman'd be my guess, or angry father. Justified, I'd say, too. Scoundrels is too good a word to use for men like these. Hell, I'd have done it on my own for Gladys's sake, if I was that kind of man. I heard what Lord Stanton was like, what people say about him and the things he's done. Monstrous."

"Yes. Quite. Lady Bainbridge suggested the same, but I thought the idea absurd. Honestly. Because of a romp or two? How comical, indeed."

"A romp or two? Lord York, even as young as you are, you must understand the great significance of love, do ya not? The profound sacrilege of promising and behaving in love just to exploit a woman's affections? The staggering devastation of the broken heart and shattered soul that comes from betrayal."

"Don't be so dramatic, man. It's part of the game."

"Arthur. Hearts and souls are not toys to be trifled with. No, sir. They are sacred. They are gifts that are freely given, and to abuse and spit on such a gift is deserving of the greatest punishment. When abuse includes violence, sir, especially sexual in nature, then these men got what they deserved. Rather, they didn't suffer near enough."

"Are you speaking of the rumors that Nick ravished that girl now in Bedlam? Look here, Captain. I knew Nicholas Stanton, and he was many things, sir. A rapist, sir, he was not."

"How can you be so sure?"

With this investigation going on, I must keep my head about me. Although, what would one more disappearance do, indeed? No. I took a deep breath and changed the subject, or else Thomas would be scrubbing blood out of my carpet. "Beside the point, Captain. What of the statues? Can you explain those? Why do they ooze and bleed as if alive?"

"That I can't explain. A trick, maybe. Something inside the statue? Why someone would do such a thing is beyond me, sir. But I have seen men and women do inexplicable things for much less of a slight than these men were rumored to have done. Have you tried cracking the thing open to see what's inside?"

"I haven't. Good idea. Let's get to the heart of the matter, as it were. Follow me."

I led him down into my cellar, although I hadn't used it for nefarious purposes since the last mystery with Avalon. It had been rather splendid, hadn't it? Working together with that woman, and poor Victor. Down here was where I took Lady Haldenby, or what had become of her, for interrogation. What would Blackwolf think when he saw the table and shackles?

He was a man, after all. Certainly he understood the darker side of desire well enough. No mind. What did I care about his thoughts anyway? I didn't owe him or anyone an explanation.

"Interesting," he said, looking sideways at me.

"Yes. Well. Taboo tastes and all. My own little Chamber of Horrors. Surely you've heard of the place, haven't you?"

The Captain's hand went to his sidearm, and he took a step back from me. Of all the wicked men in this world, I had to team up with a good one. I most certainly did not desire to be judged by the likes of him, nor anyone.

"No. I have not. Who are you? What do you know of these men?"

"Captain," I said, smirking. "Don't be foolish. What reason do I have to hurt an unknown, or barely known, writer, a buffoon doctor, and certainly not my best friend?"

"You don't seem all that broken up that your best friend, as you call him, is missing and presumed dead."

"Well, I'm sure it's because we haven't been all that close of late, if you must know. Besides, it just seems all too preposterous somehow. I suppose I just don't accept it yet. I shall grieve when I know for sure."

"This looks like a torture chamber."

"Indeed it does"—and it rather is—"but it is not what you're thinking. The Chamber of Horrors. You know. The brothel? It's all perfectly acceptable, I assure you. It's…just a place for those with discerning tastes."

"Uh-huh," he grunted, disbelieving.

"Quite consensual, I assure you. Some ladies like it this way. What do you think of me? I am a gentleman, after all." Indignation often worked when reason did not, but he did not relent. Next, embrace him into the fold. Include him in the fun, as it were. "Madam Jeffries owns it over in Gray's Inn Road. It's all on the up and up. I'll take you there sometime," I said winking. "Matter of fact, I met Madam Jeffries' cousin the other day. Snake Oil Salesman seemed to be a man who understood such things. We'll make it a man's night out. What do you say?"

"Let's get on with examining that thing, but I'm keepin' an eye on ya, Arthur York. Know that. I ain't one to be trifled with, mind. Mark my word."

"Of course," I said, rolling my eyes. "Quite. Now, if you would be so kind as to hand me that hammer. That one there, the big one." On the wall hung implements of torture, all used for fun. Most of the time.

Blackwolf pulled his gun and aimed it at me. The thing, of course, wouldn't hurt me, but there was no time for any of it.

"Fine. I will get it myself. Honestly, Blackwolf, I thought you a more worldly man. Never heard of the Chamber of Horrors. How absurd." Mocking him, shaming him might get him to let down his guard, but no luck there. I placed the statue on the heavy table and, aiming the heavy hammer, came down on its head with greater strength than a man, but the thing didn't even crack. I did it again, with all my considerable strength, and this time when the hammer struck its head, a shock emerged from it, knocking both me and Blackwolf back to the wall. We each dropped our weapons in the blast and found ourselves on the floor.

"Still don't believe it's supernatural, Captain?" I rubbed my head as I looked over at him getting up, rather shaky. He reached around the back of his head and came back with blood on his hand. "Blimey! You're hurt!" My stomach rumbled.

"Just a bump is all. I've had worse." After pulling a handkerchief from his inner pocket, he held it to the back of his head. "You might be right about the supernatural, I suppose. Stranger things, and all. I'm convinced. So, now what?"

"We obviously can't crack it open to see what's inside. Ah ha!" I jumped to my feet and spun around to face the Captain. The sudden movement caused him to step back again, arms up in defense. "If it's supernatural, then to find out what's inside, what's making it ooze so, we must consult a witch or medium, perhaps. Yes. I think I know just the one."

§

Madame Nadine sat on a wooden stool outside her establishment, smoking a pipe. A fringed shawl covered her shoulders against the cold. From her ears hung great golden circles and multiple chains decorated her neck. Between draws on the pipe, she exhaled frozen breath, huffing with her lips in different shapes to see if the mist would change the way the exhaled smoke would. Then, taking another draw from her pipe, she puffed smoke circles in the air.

As we made our way through the crowd, that same cackling-hyena laugh pummeled my ears. Blackwolf said, "Good heavens! What on earth is that?"

"Miss Polly Pooter," I said to the little woman as she emerged through the people, right behind Jeffries. Always in tow. "And, Mr. Jeffries. How delightful to see you both again. May I introduce Captain Arron von Blackwolf? Captain, this is Mr. Roderick Jeffries and his assistant Miss Polly Pooter."

"How do you do?" the Captain said, offering his hand. Jeffries took it and stood up straight, looking down his nose at us, marinating in the fact that he was taller than us both.

"Exceptional," he said without returning the nicety. "As always."

"He sure is," Polly said, almost drooling.

"This is the chap I was telling you about, Blackwolf. His cousin owns the brothel with the Chamber of Horrors. Tell him, Jeffries. It's real."

"It's real all right, quite fun as well. I do like to have fun. What is the point of living if not to have fun, and my cousin, well, she caters to the less *propa* kind," he said, mocking the English accent on the word proper. Yes. I decided I didn't like him one bit.

"C'mon Rod! C'mon," Polly whined. "You said you'd buy me a biscuit. Please? You said."

"Isn't she adorable?" Jeffries said, beaming down at her as if she were...again, a prized spaniel came to mind. One who had been taught to do tricks for a treat.

Polly started dancing in the middle of the street, shaking her hips and flipping her hair and singing, "Please, Rod. Please. You said! You said! A biscuit! A BIIIIIISCUIIIIIIT!" People all around looked rather repulsed by the show, and I must admit, so was I. The expression on Blackwolf's face, although comical, told me he had never seen anything quite as peculiar as Miss Pooter. In all my centuries, neither had I. She was all together distinctive, and it inspired me to want her in quite a carnal way. But, I shook that though off, for even a trained spaniel was still but a spaniel. My tastes were taboo, but that that taboo.

"All right, my poodle. Come along. I'll get you that biscuit. C'mon! C'mon! That's a good girl." The captain and I watched in utter amazement as Jeffries patted her on the head when she danced back to him, smiling up in adulation at her god. "Gentleman," he said, tipping his bowler.

"And tomorrow," she whined. "Tomorrow you'll take me to the circus?"

To be in it or to watch it?

She spun around in circles beneath his hand. Around and around and around, never taking her eyes off the object of her worship. "Pleeeeease! Roddy! PLEEEEEASE!"

"You know that tomorrow I have a date with Cyndi, now don't you? After work, you shall have to go home without me."

Her face fell. All at once, as if her everything she lived for had just been ripped from her.

"Now, poodle. You know about our arrangement."

"I know," she said, kicking at a puddle in a dip of the cobblestones. "I know. Cyndi. I know. But a biscuit now. Right? Like you always say, Roddy, be here now. And now I'm with you. And now everything is wonderful because you're here with me. A biscuit, Roddy, please!"

Laughing, he squeezed her against him in a tight embrace, her nose hit right at his navel. Then, he spun her around, patted her on the head again, and pushed her forward. "A biscuit it is," he said. He started off, but turned to us at the last second and said, "Gotta keep them happy, but in their place, right gents? Good day!"

Madame Nadine spoke as we approached her. "He's next." Then, "I know why you're here. Come in."

I had heard rumors about Madame Nadine's skill. Rumors were often more true than not. Indeed. She cost rather more than other fortune tellers, but she was genuine, not a charlatan who would tell you what you wanted to hear. Madame Nadine told it like straight, and I liked my women like that. She revealed her delicious curves when she tossed the shawl over an old chair, its upholstery ripped and wood splintered. Her entire shop was similar. Things from the Old World hung in every free space, covering the walls in dusty memories. I followed those swaying hips to the back room, wishing Blackwolf had stayed behind. I'd be able to get more for my money that way.

"Have a seat, gentleman, and, no, Lord York, you wouldn't."

It was as if she read my mind, but her face was not that of a flattered woman. Why wouldn't a woman, any woman, be flattered someone as fine and titled as I wanting to fuck them? She regarded me with suspicion, and said, "You aren't far behind either."

"What are you talking about, woman?"

"Show me the statue."

"How did ya know?" Blackwolf said, stunned. "How could ya possibly know?"

"It's my job to know, Captain. Give me," she said, flicking her hand out. The numerous bangles on her wrist jangled.

I handed her the wrapped statue and warned, "It's rather messy. Careful of your dress."

As soon as she touched it, a grimace of agony tainted her handsome features, and she dropped it onto the small table between us. "I knew it. I felt it," she said. "For weeks now, but I couldn't let myself believe it until now." Her face brightened, and then she glowed, joy emanating from her.

"I don't understand, Madame Nadine," I said. "A moment ago, you appeared to be in great pain. What did you feel when you touched the statue?"

"Agony, unlike I've known in many years. It's the torment of a woman who has been ill-used, many times over. Horrible and harrowing, such anguish. Men do not understand. Until now," she said, a smile again spreading across her face. "I had heard stories, whisperings of a powerful woman who punished those who hurt women—but just stories. Now, I see they are true."

"This was found at my friend's home, Madame Nadine, and he's disappeared. Can you tell us what happened to him?"

"Exactly what he deserved," she sneered.

"How dare you! How do you know what he deserved? He was a good man, a fine gentleman," I scolded her. "What are you saying happened to him? Is he in there?"

"Parts of him. Parts, as you can see, are missing." Her smug expression mocked me and infuriated me. My fangs descended. A flash across her eyes told me she knew what I was capable of, but it wasn't fear that shone in that flash. No. Not that. It was defiance.

I controlled myself, not wanting to make a scene in front of Blackwolf, for I'd have to kill him, too. Yes, I really should've come alone. I'd have to return at some point to teach this bitch a lesson.

"You taunt me, Madame? You take pleasure in the pain of my friend?"

"I take pleasure in the punishment of rapists, Mr. York."

Mister? Insult!

She spoke as if she were my equal. This would not do, but even that wasn't what angered me the most.

"Rapist? Don't be absurd, woman. Nick was no rapist. He might have taken some liberties with his promises and all, but rape is a very serious accusation. I call slander, woman. Slander!"

"It's true. I feel it in him. I see it. I see it in you, too. I know. A woman, knows. A woman who has endured, knows."

"I'm so sorry," Blackwolf said. Her sweet smile assuaged him, judging from his blush.

"Nonsense! There was no trial. Are you suggesting, Madame Nadine, that a man be punished without a trial of his peers? By taking the word of a scorned woman? She lies. Everyone knows that. Women lie. If she was ravished, as you suggest, then why doesn't she go to the police? With evidence, they shall punish the scoundrel if he's guilty, which I assure you, Nicholas is not! Release him from his prison. This instant."

"No. Even if I had that power, I would not do it. He is enduring that which he has made so many endure, and it is justice. Finally." She put both hands on flat on the table and, leaning across, looked me square in the eyes. "Really, York. The police? You certainly jest to put your faith in their 'justice'."

"That's true," Blackwolf said. "You said so yourself. They're worthless."

My glare shot arrows at Blackwolf before turning back to the tramp before me, wanting so much to sink a few things into that sweet body, setting her mind right.

"Not in this lifetime, Mr. York," she said, reading my mind again. "Never again. You have no power over me. Now get out."

"You hate men, you harlot. Making such accusations and claims."

"Arthur!" Blackwolf chided, brow furrowed.

"I don't hate men, Mr. York. I don't trust them. My life has taught me thus, as every woman learns when she becomes wise, when she learns she must protect herself. Because men, those meant to protect us, are the ones who hurt us, almost exclusively."

"The lady is right, and good men know that. You best learn for yourself if you ever want to be a good man. One deserving of a woman like Miss Bainbridge. One deserving of any woman."

"You, sir," Madame Nadine said, reaching across the table to pat his hand, "are a wise man. A good man."

"Why, thank you, ma'am," he said, blushing again.

"Should I leave you two alone?" I scoffed, crossing my arms, quite pleased with myself. "Please, don't let me interrupt." This comment angered Madame Nadine even further, and Blackwolf, alike. Preposterous. Women were far too sensitive.

"Mr. York." She annunciated each word. Her contempt seethed from every syllable. "Women are not made for your pleasure, and there is worth far beyond their sexuality. Although you, at your age, should have learned this many times over. Indeed. You shall soon follow, and rightly so."

My age? She knew. She could tell by looking at me. She knew my nature. She knew my thoughts. She knew me. She saw me, the real me, and that was terrifying. I had never met a woman with such power and insight.

Me? Fearing a woman?

Never.

It mustn't be fear, then. No. Not fear.

Of course not.

Disgust. It was disgust. How dared she speak to me thus? "That will be all." I pulled the coins from my pocket and threw them at her.

She didn't flinch as the coins rained around her, but instead she sat tall, back straight and head held high.

"I apologize for my companion, Madame Nadine," Blackwolf said, tipping his hat. "We shall take our leave. Thank you for your kindness. Good day, and Happy New Year." He grabbed my arm and pushed me out the door in front of him. He didn't say another word until we were back onto the bustling street. "This is where we must part ways, *Mister* York. Although my mind draws me toward solving these crimes, my heart and my conscience tell me the only crime done here are what these men did. Madame Nadine's right. They have gotten what they deserve. And you, York, disgust me. I have no interest in knowing you or associating with you or any man like you. You are spoiled and entitled and altogether vile. That's the great thing about age, sir, one no longer cares about the niceties of society or how one should act for propriety's sake. One only cares about kindness. Through harsh lessons, I've learned the world sorely lacks kindness at every turn. Grow up, Arthur. Ya could be a great man, but I suspect you'll only ever be a petulant child. Good day."

With that, he disappeared into the crowd, and I stood there baffled, unable to speak or think or react in any way.

The rain came, and still I stood.

People milled around me, and still I stood.

For hours, I stood, drenched to the skin.

Then, surrounded by nothing but faint gaslight in the wee hours of the morning, I knew what I had to do.

 # CHAPTER 17

CONSTANCE

Roderick looked as handsome as ever, on the outside, at least, although I saw into the black void where his soul should be. To the careful observer, one would notice how his countenance would change from blank and emotionless to warm and loving in an instant. Every so often, that loving mask would slip, and one saw the truth. But, as everyone tended to do with that they did not understand, or with that they feared, they explained it away. Justified it.

That evening, I saw it. We were meeting at the pub after work, and I saw him pass by the window, face like stone. Not stoic, nothing like that. As if there was nothing inside. Empty. No anger or love, no thought or feeling. No affect whatsoever.

As soon as he saw me watching, the mask went on. His entire personality changed in an instant. To the untrained eye, this appeared to be a normal transition between a contemplative state to one of warmth upon seeing the object of his affection, but a sinister truth hid behind Mr. Jeffries' mask.

"Good evening, sweetheart," he said, leaning over to kiss me on the cheek.

Mr. Jeffries knew me as Cynthia Weismann, shop mistress.

"Roderick. How lovely to see you. The minutes pass like hours as I wait to catch a glimpse of you again, my love."

"Likewise." He sat opposite me and gathered my hands into his. Smiling, he imprisoned me with his intense gaze. "All day, I kept checking my pocket watch, wondering if it was seven o'clock yet. Then, on my way to see you tonight, my whole body filled with excitement. It was as if it sang into the night, buzzing and bursting with your song."

"Oh! Me, too!"

"Well, we're here together now. Wine?"

"Yes, please."

He signaled the barmaid and ordered some red wine before turning back to me. "Have you eaten?"

"I had a bite at the shop."

"Perfect." His eyes never left mine. His hands never let go of mine. The entire world around us disappeared. I was utterly captivated and charmed. True to the nature of his work, he could convince a woman of anything, subtly changing her reality to match his every thought or desire. All without her conscious knowledge or consent. Of all the predators I had the great pleasure of annihilating, this type was the most dangerous. Similar to that of Lord Stanton, Jeffries took his time priming his prey, shaping her into a food, of sorts. But unlike Lord Stanton, his end game wasn't just to have his way with her. No, his charms and social situation, not to mention his honed skills, were quite enough to have as many women in his bed as he chose. I have been there myself countless times. Unlike anything I'd known in five hundred years. Ecstasy on a level so rare, one might have thought it impossible or mere tales of grand exaggeration.

Not with Mr. Jeffries.

It all sounded so wonderful, but that was the cunning of it. One was so distracted by the heightened pleasure and overt attention and loving affection, feeling as if nothing and no one could ever come upset such a connection, that one was quite unaware of the underhanded damage done. So subtle, unless one was experienced in such matters, one was like a lamb who walked willingly into slaughter. Not all women, of course. Some he used for sex. Others he openly violated for power. But the really unfortunate ones—the ones he thought a challenge—he took his time with those, using love and ecstasy as his weapons.

Then he destroyed them.

"How was your day? Sell much product?"

"Of course. I'm very good at what I do." The level of arrogance never ceased to astound me. "I don't mean to sound vain, but I really am." Yes. Quite vain. "It doesn't hurt that it's the season for maladies of all sorts either. Even though Christmas has just passed, people are still in the holiday spirit. Jolly and generous, you see. I do very well this time of year."

"Splendid, my love. I'm so happy for you. So proud of you."

"I love that about you. Polly always complains she doesn't make as much as I do. She thinks she deserves a bigger cut for her performance, and I tell her she is welcome to find other employment if she's unhappy with our arrangement. That quiets her down pretty fast. Then she gets all pouty and sad, and I just have to laugh at the little spaniel. She's so cute when she gets huffed."

She was completely under his control, and he knew it. He thrived on it. Here was a woman that has been destroyed from the inside out, a woman who no longer had a shred of herself left, as he has taken it all from her over the years. His complete control made him feel powerful, invincible. As long as he had Polly at his heels, the others could be cast aside at will.

"Her part of the show is quite essential, I think. Don't you?"

"Of course, but it is my business. My product. My business plan and efforts. She just performs the words I wrote for her. A monkey could do it. What I do, on the other hand, takes skill. I'm worth ever farthing I make."

Polly knew what waited for her if she left at this point. Absolute annihilation. That was Mr. Jeffries' game, and he took complete delight in it. From initial pursuit, which was alone enough to convince a woman of his sincerity, to enjoying the high of a new lover. A drug so very addictive, neither opium nor cocaine could compare. All the while, he would feed from her. Shape her. Control her. Devour her until she mirrored him: an empty shell. Then, the moment she appeared anything less than adoring and willing to fulfill his every need and desire without question or comment, the mask came off. Then the woman would, in horror, see the monster that lay beneath.

Cold. Unfeeling. Incapable of love or tenderness or empathy. He would cast her aside without remorse or compassion. Reeling, she would try to understand what had happened. How something so perfect could have fallen apart so quickly. How anyone who had loved so much could in an instant become so cruel.

Then the withdrawals began, much like that of opium. Sickness follows. Confusion. Despair beyond description. Tears and panic and vomit-filled days of unending torment. As the endless weeks crept by in an agonizing haze of suffering, she would begin to see the abuse, the violation, the utter sadistic savagery with which he had taken the core of her very self.

That was why Polly stayed, fear of the withdrawal. No doubt she had had a taste of it a few times. She would take scraps forever rather than face that. Most women did not recover from that level of betrayal. For, like in the cases of men like Lord Stanton, Doctor Nesbitt, and even Mr. McFerret, one had no doubt a violation had occurred, a violent and heinous ravaging. Many women did not recover from those either. Rape was a life sentence for the victim, but in those cases there was at least no question the assault occurred.

Mr. Jeffries, on the other hand, violated so surreptitiously, one questioned if it even happened. When he was his most successful, as any rapist, the victim blamed herself for all of it, and society did as well.

For Roderick Jeffries, sexual defilement was not enough. He strove to violate every level of a woman, to destroy her from the inside out, and he had quite often succeeded.

But this time, he had me, and I had eyes to see the truth.

The most fortunate of those unfortunate enough to meet and fall prey to this man were the ones who did get away, perhaps even the ones who took their own life and ended their torment. The least fortunate didn't. Like Miss Polly Pooter. Forever tied to him, treated like a dog. Worse, in fact.

No more. I would be the last, then poor Miss Pooter would finally be free. He had kept the poor woman as a virtual slave, not overtly, of course. No, he was too smart for that. Like in everything he did, it was far more insidious in nature.

"Could we talk about something other than Polly anyway? You talk about her so much, Roderick. I'd rather just focus on us when we're together, if that's all right."

"Are you jealous?" The gleam of pleasure returned to his eyes. Invoking jealousy was one of the most entertaining ways to control someone. To play on that innate fear of abandonment gave him the ultimate feeling of sovereignty.

"Of Polly? Of course not. I'm just truly tired of hearing about her all the time. I mean, I know she's your business partner and a former lover, and I know she means a lot to you"—as food—"but I'd rather just focus on you and me, if that's all right. No matter what we do, it's always Polly and I did this, and then this time Polly and me we did that, and it gets rather old, is all. I mean, she's a bizarre little thing, but my relationship is with you, and I'd rather not feel like she's sitting here with us. You understand, don't you, love?"

He tensed, clenching his jaw. I knew this slightly veiled criticism would hit him hard, and if there was one thing such deeply-ingrained narcissism couldn't abide, it was criticism of any kind, especially from one considered beneath them, which in their eyes was everyone.

The barmaid brought the wine.

"To us," I said, my voice pitched higher in cheery excitement. "To our love, which in your own words, is unlike either has ever known. So deep, so quickly. A whirlwind of delight and ecstasy. Of intimacy and gratitude. So passionate." Then whispering, "I can't wait to get you alone tonight."

He put a smile back on his lips, and clinked glasses with me, regarding me over his glass as he drank. That predatory stare said: *you belong to me.*

Thus, we toasted to our love. A love, I had no doubt, that would be cast aside in a matter of days. He had already begun to slip more and more, allowing me to see behind the mask. My true form wasn't even as harrowing as looking into his inner abyss.

Leaning in close to me, his lips brushed against my ear as he whispered, "Let's move to someplace more private." My body quivered at his touch, at the suggestion of what I knew would follow. Of what I knew would end all too soon, and I was ready to strike when it did. Each time I met with him, I brought his poppet and my tools. With a man like Jeffries, one never knew when, but the merciless devalue and ultimate discard was as inevitable as death.

"Let's," I breathed. With my work, I didn't get to enjoy the pleasures of the flesh often, as it was mostly violation and violence, but sometimes I got to remember what it was like to be in love, even if it was just a façade. I delighted in the pretense now and again, for sentimentality of a more innocent time.

Never breaking contact. He had to feel in continuous control. To feel as if he owned me. In his mind, he did. Hand in hand, he led me out into the cold London night. Not able to wait until we got back to his flat, he teased me into an alleyway. Stealing a kiss, I melted into him. If I hadn't been me, I would've already lost myself in this man and his charms. I would've become another Polly Pooter.

Pity the thought.

He was the most effective predator known to humankind, therefore, the most dangerous.

Just as his hand slid up my corset to cup my breast, a taste of the hours of ecstasy to come, I was thrown to the ground, and when I looked up, another woman was at Jeffries' throat. Feeding.

"Stop," I shouted. "Please! Don't hurt him." That was for me to do. She would not take away my prey. The death she delivered would be too quick for this snake. He must suffer for centuries to make up for the harm he'd caused others.

Whipping her head around, she glared at me, blood dripping from her chin. It was none other than Avalon Bainbridge. We had met at the gala, briefly, and then again on the cruise. I was under a different guise, of course, so she wouldn't recognize me as Cyndi.

"Stay out of this," she said. "I won't hurt you, but this one deserves it."

He most certainly did.

"Please, don't kill him," I pled. "I love him."

Had to keep up the pretense for Jeffries' sake at the moment.

Roderick's mind hadn't yet processed what had happened, as she moved far faster than humans. He was kissing me one moment, and the next he just felt pain, and he didn't yet understand why. It was times like this one could see behind the mask, when he didn't know how to perform. There was no script for him to follow here. A situation he had not been able to study, to learn how to arrange his face or what to say. His face was again without affect. Blank.

He looked at me and saw the mock horror on my face, then he knew how to react.

"Get off me, bitch! What are you doing? Help! Stop!"

Avalon held him against the wall with one arm, and Roderick struggled beneath her, trying to shove her off. I wondered how many women had tried to shove him off. He was starting to get a taste, and I found I didn't want to stop Avalon from hurting him. I wanted to sit back and enjoy the show for a change.

But, I couldn't.

"Please. Please, Miss. Please don't hurt him. Please just let him be. Please." I knew better than to try to compel my will on a vampire. That, indeed, did not work, one supernatural to another.

"I'm not going to kill him, but I need to feed. Neither of you will remember a thing." She locked eyes with mine and tried to compel me. She didn't know I couldn't be manipulated thus, as she didn't know I was more like her, in many ways, it seemed, punishing the wicked.

Perhaps I'd found an ally after all this time, company.

Still, I had to lead her to believe I was thus malleable, so I relented. "All right," I said with a dreamy look in my eye, and I allowed her to continue.

"Cynthia!" Jeffries cried. "Cyndi! Get help. Please help me." The last word got lost in a muffle as Avalon clamped her hand tight over his mouth as she continued to feed. Slurping and gulping.

She must've been hungry.

Before long, Jeffries stopped pretending, and his face went blank, except for a hint of anger, contempt behind his darkened eyes.

No one controlled him, not even for a moment. It was he who was in control. Always.

He would be particularly angry tonight, and I, no doubt, would be punished for it. If he remembered. I knew how pushing one's will worked. It could erase conscious memories and the like, but it couldn't make the deeper mind forget. Somewhere, he would know. Viscerally, he would know, just as his many victims knew. Even when their conscious minds blamed themselves or denied the violence, deep down, their bodies and minds reacted to the violation as if it had been as overt as the physical attack before me.

Avalon finished and wiped her mouth with one sleeve while keeping him pinned against the wall with the other arm, but he didn't struggle anymore. He just looked at her through angry slits, as snakelike as he was on the inside. Still, a human's conscious mind would forget, and Avalon compelled him to do just that. She turned and apologized to me, then disappeared into the bustling street. While still in a daze, Roderick picked up the scarf Avalon had ripped off, and tied it tightly around his neck.

"Cold night," he said. "Better bundle up. Cyndi, are you all right?"

"Just cold."

"Well, why are we standing around out here? Let's get to my place. I've got a hearth ready for us." His voice held a forced tender tone, trying too hard to appear compassionate, which meant he felt anything but.

It would be a rough night.

§

I had been punished, all right, but he did so with great mastery. Gaining verbal consent for one thing, then taking it further, crossing boundaries we had set as lovers. Ignoring my reactions or indications to stop. Worse, mixed with the punishment and violation was joy and ecstasy. Proclamations of love and adoration. Explosive orgasms.

It was not true joy, however not genuine pleasure; like an opium high, it was manufactured.

The withdrawal proved it.

"Your tea, Constance." Everett's voice was kind, soft. He knew how drained I was when I returned from a night with Jeffries. "Please, end him soon. I can't bear to see you like this any more."

"Yes. The time has come. I almost did it last night, but after the attack in the alley...I had an idea."

"Is that what's stopping you? Be honest with yourself, Constance. Could it be you don't want to let this one go?"

"Everett, please. I'm a professional."

"My apologies, mum. But the way you speak of him..."

"True joy lay in its subtleties, Everett. Peace and true love might not be as passionate, but one would find that's a good thing because it was real. Passion, after all, means to suffer, from the Greek pathos. A few hours of ecstasy is not worth the months of agony to follow." Was I trying to convince myself? "A lifetime destroyed for a few moments of pleasure. Like poor, poor Polly, and another former lover, the patron who hired me. She'll never be the same either, but she'll heal, more or less, because she got away. Polly, on the other hand. She's doomed as long as she's tied to him. I aim to set that woman free."

Everett didn't say a word, but rather just sipped his tea and took up his pet poppet from the others again, jabbing a pin in its eye.

"Perhaps I have indulged for too long," I admitted. "Tomorrow night. I shall do it then. With some luck, I'll have some assistance."

"Heart is still as black as the day you made it," he said, jabbing the pin in the thing's heart. "As long as their heart remains black, or even when it turns red, they haven't yet suffered the sum of all their victims. It's not until the heart turns white, then, and only then, are they released from their prison, from their slice of purgatorial eternity. Is that right?"

"You know it to be true, Everett. He still has lifetimes to suffer. Worry not." Laughing to myself, I reflected on the image man had of succubi. Demon women who seduced men and devoured their sexuality.

Well, they were part right, but not in the manner they suggested.

Tomorrow it would be Jeffries' turn to be devoured.

"Men are altogether afraid of women's sexuality and innate power, aren't they, Everett? So frightened, in fact, too many men find it necessary to belittle and slander and control women. To hold them down. To force them to submit and remain downtrodden, if not physically then indeed emotionally and mentally. Do you think that's why? Everett? Could it all boil down to cowardice?"

"You know it does in most cases, mum. After centuries of proof, why do you ask for my validation every so often like this?"

"For precisely that. Validation. Support. Although I am supernatural, I am also a woman. Human, yet inhuman. Mortal, yet immortal. I'm a paradox, Everett, and it's maddening." My hand trembled, so I clutched the rocker's wooden arm to steady myself. It didn't help. "Sometimes, I feel too much like a woman, a human, and not enough like the destroyer. I'm confused. Yes. Jeffries is getting to me. You're right. I've waited too long, and I'm getting entangled like Miss Pooter. It brings it all back, Everett, and I need someone to pull me out of it." Tears welled, and it became difficult to catch my breath. Images pelted my mind.

Not now. Please.

Everett rushed to my side and put his arm around my shoulders, shushing me and rocking me as I cried. The original trauma rushed back as if it were yesterday. The span of five hundred years gone in a blink.

Hugging my knees close to my chest, I wept, as Everett held me tight. "I didn't deserve that, Everett!"

"No, my dear. You didn't deserve that."

"I didn't deserve to be treated thus. All I ever did was love him. How could he have done that to me?"

"He was a monstrous man, Constance. A horrible monster, and his friends, too."

"There wasn't enough openings for them to go all at once, so they created more," I cried, folding into Everett's embrace.

"Shhhh. It's over now. You're safe now. He did horrific things to you, and it wasn't your fault. Besides, he got his punishment. They all got what they deserved."

Yes they did. It was my wrath, the power and love for myself, that enabled me to exact my revenge, but they got off easy. Too easy. Yet, the past was the past. No going back now. It wasn't until a few decades after my transformation that I realized by killing them, and other rapists and abusers, I delivered them peace. Relief. Escape. While their victims had been destroyed, traumatized for life. Haunted by the memories and shattered by their actions.

So I had developed this new method.

"That's true!" I said, pulling out of the flashback, allowing rage to replace sorrow. Everett acted remarkably well, having to do this every so often. Sometimes those toxic memories came out of nowhere and brought horror and fear, pain and loss. I would never get over how it still felt so real.

"You're a powerful woman, Constance. It has been an honor to serve you these past decades."

"I am, indeed. All women are, Everett! If women had the slightest idea of their power...but centuries of misuse, rape, and bullying has broken the female spirit, for the most part."

"Yes, mum, but you do what you can to repair that. You save a lot of women from agony, and you deal out justice when justice fails them. That's what succubi do."

"Yes. That's what we do! We take on the pain and exploitation and violation for women. We sacrifice ourselves again and again to free women from their chains."

"It's noble work."

"It is! I have a purpose, Everett! My existence is necessary, and someone like Jeffries can't take that from me. A snake like Jeffries will pay dearly for this."

I turned to the looking glass and watched the last tear drop from my hazel eyes. The liner beneath my lower lids, trickled down my cheeks. After all this time, five hundred years, and the memory of my attack still triggered such profound sadness, regret, and fury. The mixture of conflicting emotions enveloped in such trauma was maddening in and of itself.

The attack was horrific enough, but sometimes I thought the worst trauma was what I endured afterward. The looks. The doubts. The gossip. Everything from what a harlot I was to take on five men at once to how I must've deserved it. Perhaps the worst was those who just didn't believe me.

Those who said I was saying so to get attention, to get even for my husband having an affair. After all, what should I expect being so outspoken, not staying in my place?

"Enough." I scolded myself.

The anger rose, and my eyes turned from hazel to black. The pink bow of my lips became a scowl. I breathed in, filled my lungs with air, held it for a moment, and then let it out with an audible whoosh. Again and again, until the rage subsided.

Five hundred years, and I remembered it, felt it, as if it were yesterday.

Yes. They got off far too easy with death. Death was, indeed, a relief.

"I can't do much, Heaven, and Hell, knows what a ubiquitous problem violence against women is, but I can do something, however small in the grand scheme, to balance the scales."

"That you do, mum. Quite a lot to balance the scales. All in all." The doorbell chimed, interrupting Everett's support and care of me.

"Answer the door, would you, Everett?"

"Of course, mum." I wiped the tears from under my eyes, smoothing out the smudged makeup, and waited at the top of the stairs for the announcement. Everett opened the door and addressed the caller, then turned and said, "Miss Avalon Bainbridge to see you."

Excellent, we had a lot to discuss.

CHAPTER 18

ARTHUR

The Wellington. I had taken Avalon on our first date here. Perhaps it wasn't the best idea to bring Chastity here tonight. I thought it might help me forget Avalon, or maybe it was to keep her closer.

I didn't know what to do or what to say. I wasn't sure how I felt.

Before this, it had always been so easy to move forward, forget the last, as they were all but placeholders for Catherine. Just warm bodies to please me. All falling short of the perfection that was Catherine all those centuries ago.

Avalon, too.

Chastity would be as well.

They all were.

Now Blackwolf and that harlot Nadine had shaken me to my core, making me question things I hadn't done before. Or, at least, not for some time. Self-examination and all that nonsense. So trite, so very dull and pointless. Such a waste of time and energy when there were far more interesting things like the sweetness seduction followed by betrayal. Indulging in lust and love, albeit short-lived. For me, it was enough. One fanny was as good as the next, after all.

Chastity chattered on and on across from me, but I wasn't listening. Just laughing when seemed appropriate and nodding my head. Time to focus on this beauty before me.

New memories, moving on, and all that. Forget Avalon and her need for control.

That was what I must do. It was what I always did, and I excelled at it, after all. Never let it be said that Arthur Tudor was tamed by a woman. Imprisoned, more like.

Yet, as I looked around at all the couples together, I missed Avalon all the more. Here before me sat this glorious creature, much more knowledgeable in the ways of love and lust and ecstasy than Avalon.

Yet, I longed to be with Avalon.

Yet, I felt empty without her and furious with her.

Yet, I loved her and hated her for making me feel vulnerable.

Might Thomas and Blackwolf and that blasted medium be right about me?

Balderdash.

Just push through it, man.

"You're distant tonight, Arthur. Is everything all right?" Chastity said touching my arm. Her amber eyes studied my face for any understanding of how I could be so distant tonight and so attentive the last time.

Women, I didn't know whether to pity them more for their stupidity or for the pain I caused them.

No, the pain they felt.

I had always been honest about my intentions.

Well, more or less.

"Forgive me, sweetheart, a lot on my mind, I suppose. With these disappearances and all." That should shut her up. I'd say anything to be free of the interrogation that would follow if I spoke of my doubts. Women said they wanted to know my thoughts, but then when I told them, I was punished. Always. With a thousand questions and those looks of judgment and disappointment and heartbreak. Why couldn't they just bend over and take it when I wanted it and shut up the rest of the time? Was that really too much to ask?

"I'll never forget that smell in McFerret's cabin. Ugh! Oh, it turns my stomach now to even think about it. Perhaps, it's best not to while we're eating."

"Of course. Forgive me." Such a delicate creature, wasn't she? We ate in peace for a moment or two, but then I couldn't get my mind off McFerret. "It is rather odd, though, is it not? The statue. The nasty black pus? Do you believe in witchcraft, Chastity?"

"Witchcraft!" Her eyes widened and her gloved hand flew up to her outburst. She lowered her voice, looking around to see if anyone had heard. She blinked at me once or twice, then shielding her lips from the rest of the restaurant—as if anyone was paying attention to anyone but themselves—said, "Are you mad? Speaking of such things in a public place? Of course I don't believe in such nonsense. Do you?"

"Nothing else makes sense."

She lifted her glass of wine, continuing the pretense for everyone else's sake, but the embarrassment rose in her cheeks. After a bout of nervous chuckling, she said through a plastered smile and clenched teeth, "Can we talk about this later, please?"

"I just can't get out of my head what that medium said today. She said Nicholas, wherever he was, was suffering. In a lot of pain, and, she said, he deserved it."

"What a dreadful thing to say!" Chastity pulled her napkin to her lips, shocked. That, at least, took her mind off her pretense. Yes. Women. So much empathy for complete strangers. Astounding. "Who said this? Avalon?"

Oh, Avalon. My heart ached at the sound of her name, and Chastity must've noticed for she stiffened. "No," I managed, bringing myself back to the conversation. "Madame Nadine. A medium, fortune teller."

"Are you truly going to believe a charlatan like that? Honestly, Arthur. You're not that young; surely you aren't that naive! It's for sport only. You can't take anything they say seriously, my love. Regardless, it was a dreadful thing to say. Pay her no mind."

"Dreadful, indeed. That's what I thought"—especially since I *knew* Nicholas—"She accused Nick of all sorts of heinous acts, and, come to think of it, I think she accused me as well. Preposterous."

"She sounds mad, of which I have no doubt, the fraud. How could she possibly know, even if it was true? Balderdash, all hocus pocus nonsense."

"That's what I said! How could she know? But she said she did know these things, and the way she looked at me. The things she knew, Chastity. There are certainly a lot of fakes out there, but this woman was genuine, I believe. No, I am not naive."—the nerve of calling me such had sealed her fate, my mind made up—"Not in the least. Give me some credit, woman, but this harlot Madame Nadine knew far too much to be a fake. It was unsettling, to say the least."

"Oh, Arthur," she said, reaching out across the table and touching my hand. "I'll be sure to get your mind off of it later. I promise." Her coy smile sent blood traveling downward, but I found myself pulling my hand from her touch. "What is it, Arthur? You're scaring me. Is everything all right?"

"Everything is just fine," I lied. "Finish your dinner."

"Arthur. Tell me. Please. If we're to be together, then we must be honest with one another. Know each other, intimately, and not just in body."

The very thought would have harrowed my very soul, if still had had one. "No, Chastity. Actually. Everything is not all right. I cannot do this anymore. With you." I sat back, stone-faced, daring her to defy me or argue.

"What?" she said, lips parted in surprise. "Whatever do you mean, Arthur?"

"Us. I mean, there can be no more us, Chastity. I'm in love with Avalon, and this is all just too wrong. There. I've said it." My flat voice pained her as much as my words, after having been so tender and loving.

No mind. She was a grown woman. Surely she understood it was a romp, after all. Nothing lasts forever.

"Is that so?" She pulled her lips in tight until there was nothing to them but a thin pink line. "All the business about a proper courtship? Was that all a lie, Arthur?"

"I meant it at the time."

"You meant it at the time," she said, her voice a broken whisper. Her eyes glistened with unshed tears. Looking down, she took a deep breath and composed herself. When she looked back up, there was no sign of hurt, which I found a little disappointing. I did like to see the pain on their faces, knowing how much losing me hurt them. How much I meant to them. Hardness, even hatred was the only thing behind this woman's eyes. That, and perhaps a touch of inexplicable joy. Strange. Twisting her napkin in her hands, she spoke, hostility dripping from each syllable, "You child. I truly should have known someone as handsome as you would be a complete dolt."

"Now see here." My whisper was harsh, but it was a whisper. Those at nearby tables stopped eating and looked over at me. The air became stale around me, making it distasteful to breathe. My throat clenched before I could say another word, but she had already started speaking again, interrupting me.

"Enough, Arthur. Go back and play with your toys, as that's all we are to you, isn't it? Well, I am not a toy, dear boy. Not in the least. A romp would've been just fine with me, but then you began making love to me, telling me I was so much more than that. How dare you awaken love for your selfish desires, when you are not prepared to follow through." She stood, facing me full on, hands on hips, not caring that people around stared at her defiant stance and raised voice. "Figure out what you want before involving another heart, Arthur. You are quite old enough to take responsibility for your actions, or perhaps you're not. You are a coward and a spoiled little boy."

Second time someone told me that today.

She threw her napkin down upon her half-eaten dinner. The entire restaurant had stopped eating and chatting. All eyes were on us. Now it was my face that burned in shame, something I didn't feel often. No. I didn't like it one bit.

"One day, quite soon, I suspect, you will learn a very harsh lesson, Arthur York. Hearts are not trifles to be toyed with. The price for doing so is higher than you will wish to pay. By then it shall be too late. Someone will hold you accountable, Arthur, and I suspect it is long overdue. Good night and goodbye."

Silence followed, and not only because Chastity had stormed away. Not only because the entire restaurant had frozen mid-meal to watch my humiliation, because they—one by one, two by two—went back to their dinners and conversations, with only a lingering glance or two in my direction.

Their lips moved again. Their cutlery hit their plates. Their glasses clinked over the candles.

Still, no sound reached my ears, not even the hiss of my own breath.

Nothing.

Chastity's gone. Avalon's gone.

I could start again. I always did start again.

Over and over and over.

Then I saw it. The pattern. The one Thomas had mentioned.

Over and over and over.

Each woman, a placeholder for the next, for the last. Dating back centuries to Catherine. What made Catherine so perfect?

Too inexperienced? Too pious? Too needy?

We were in love, yes, but we were barely adults. Frivolity. We had forever. King and Queen of England, that was our future.

Then I died.

She still became Queen, and I hated her for it. I longed for what we lost, such a short time together. Ever since, when I tried to love again, I looked for the perfection of an imperfect dead woman. Long dead. She represented some perfect love I fancied I once had. We were but children, weren't we? At least in the ways of love. It was new and exciting. We were rich and powerful. We had the world at our command.

Then I died, or was reborn into this death.

I hated her for it.

Yet, she was perfection, wasn't she? We had stayed up nights talking and laughing and fighting and loving together. I knew her better than she knew herself, and she knew me better than I knew myself. I respected her. We shared our thoughts. We shared everything, as equals.

I didn't control her, ever, nor she me.

We shared.

My eyes stared at nothing. The waiter came and spoke, but it didn't register.

We shared everything. That was the difference. I loved her because she was perfect. She was perfect in her imperfections. I loved her and cherished her because I knew her, I was invested in her. We were invested in each other.

Catherine was far from easy, but every ounce of effort was worth it.

I had never put forth such effort again, never invested myself in another person. I expected every new woman to be Catherine, but they weren't Catherine. No one was or would ever be.

I suddenly realized I didn't want Avalon to be Catherine. I wanted Avalon to be Avalon, and I wanted to know her imperfections, her thoughts, her dreams. I wanted to hear her opinions and share mine, without control.

Oh, Avalon!

"What have I done?" I said to the waiter, who was now shaking my shoulder. The Maitre'D came over and spoke in worried tones. "I have to fix this," I said to them, then stood and pushed past them.

"But sir," the Maitre'D said. "Your bill!"

I spun around and around in the middle of the restaurant, dancing with myself, laughing into the air. Pulling pound notes from my pockets, I tossed them up in the air and let them rain down on those around me. Gasps of delight and horror mixed with their laughter, my own hysterical laughter.

"I can fix this!" I exclaimed. "I know now. I understand now! Avalon, my love, I'm coming for you!"

CHAPTER 19

CONSTANCE

There was nothing more callous and ruthless than a privileged American man.

Well, except for me, of course.

"I think we should take a step back," Jeffries said, holding my hands and gazing into my eyes. Only this time, unlike the others, there was no affection. No love. Just callous emptiness.

"What? I mean, I'm sorry. This is so sudden. I thought everything was going well."

"It was, but I've realized you're not what I've been looking for after all, so we really need to slow things down. Perhaps see each other less."

"Is there someone else?"

"Not yet, but I've been getting to know someone a bit better over the last week or two, and I'd like to see where that goes, so…" Silence.

Then, snuffle. Two blinks. Head tilt. He raised his eyebrows, expecting me to say something, and waited.

"So? Just like that."

No affect. Two more blinks. Cold silence.

"But, just two nights ago," I continued. "You said you adored me, that you were basking in my love. You worshipped every pore, explored every inch of my body."

"Yes."

"And today you want to step back."

"That's right."

"But…I don't understand."

"What's there to understand, Cyndi? This has been lovely, true, but I know now it's not right. Not right for me. I have to be true to myself."—Derisive snuffle—"I know it's not forever with you, so I'm moving on. I mean, I'm not saying I never want to see you again. Nothing like that. I do love you, after all. For now, anyway. We can still get together now and again. You are delicious between the sheets, but I require my space. You're just too much, too needy."

"What about tonight? We were supposed to…" Tears burned the corners of my eyes as I looked toward the bedroom, and I watched his face as he watched my nose turn red and the first tear fall. There was a triumph there, behind those empty eyes. Pleasure.

"I still want to love you tonight. Honestly, Cyndi. I can't understand why you're so upset? You knew from the beginning I wouldn't be tied down by any woman. So, no surprise. It's not like I'm leaving you or anything. Not yet. You don't get this"—he said, hands sweeping down his body—"to yourself, no one does."

"This weekend. It's New Years, and we were going to bring in the New Year together. Kissing at midnight. What about that?"

"Let's not do that."

Blank stare. Cold Silence.

"What?"

"Let's not do that." Smirk. "I mean, if we're going to take a step back, Sunday feels like a good time to start, don't you think? No use putting off the inevitable."

"Are you going to be with her? This new woman?"

"Now, Cyndi." His chiding voice spoke as if I was a petulant child. Condescending. Cruel. Callous. He squeezed my hands and literally looked down his nose at me. "Situations change. Surely you know that. Don't take it so personally. You're a big girl. People change. Feelings change. Besides, you know how I feel about jealousy. What if I am to be with her? That's no concern of yours. Not now, not ever. You have no claim over me and my will."

Tears streamed fully now. I bowed my head and watched my tears make perfect little wet circles on my grey cotton skirt. Even with all my preparation. Even with knowing who he was. It still hurt. But nothing like it would to others who didn't see his true face.

For me, it stung.

For Cynthia, it was devastating.

"You're embarrassing yourself, Cyndi." He patted my head like I was his spaniel, like I was Polly. "Are we to love each other tonight or not? Will you be here in this moment with me or will you worry about the future? This moment is all we ever have, and we are here together. See? No reason to cry. We're here forever in this moment. Love me tonight. Your choice, Cynthia. Either way works for me."

"Yes, please." My voice managed those two words through the grief of being pushed aside so callously. Cynthia felt confusion around this sudden change mixed with a hope of somehow fixing it. Any woman in love would have looked for a way to fix it. Something, anything to take away the last hour and make it like it was.

He counted on it.

He counted on Cyndi's compassion, her fear, her determination to not lose love, so he led me into the bedroom, and laid me down on the bed.

And I cried.

He started undressing me.

And I cried.

He licked up my inner thighs and higher, moans of pleasure mixed with cries of torment. Tongue swirling, eyes locked with mine, until I had to look away in my despair, seeing his pleasure in my pain.

And I cried.

He climbed on top of me and entered, slithering inside me. Gliding. Thrusting. Mocking.

And I cried.

As he slid into me again and again, I knew it was the last time.

And I cried.

He knew Cynthia was terrified, that she would do anything not to lose him. To make everything all right again, and he exploited that, gaining double pleasure, first from the sexual sensation and second from witnessing his masterpiece: complete submission to his command. Complete fear, bending to his will, to his pleasure, to his every desire. Arrant, absolute pleasure emanated from his every pore, filling his void with my pain.

Complete destruction at his command.

He reveled in it.

He thought he had me. He thought he defeated me, broken me, in all his power. He thought he had just set up another lap dog, begging for scraps, glad to take any morsel tossed her way.

He thought wrong.

I flipped him over, removing him. Never again would he have the privilege of entering my, or any woman's, body. The motion was so quick, he didn't have time to respond before I had him pinned against the wall, unable to move.

Then, the slits. Jaw clenched. He didn't even try to move, at first.

"On second thought," he said. "I think I am rather done with you. Perhaps it's best."

"You're going to pay for the pain you've caused so many women, and you're going to suffer as they have, as deeply as they have, for as long as they have, until the amount of your suffering matches those you have destroyed."

"Please." It was not a supplication, but rather a snide reminder of his superiority. "I loved those women. Every one. I gave them untold pleasures. Ecstasy like they've never known. I was a gift to those ladies, showing them what was possible."

"A gift. These untold pleasures. This sexual ecstasy, which I've experienced firsthand, Mr. Jeffries, so I know you are quite skilled. I see how you use women, exploit and violate them with such skill, they don't even know what's happening. I see you, Mr. Jeffries, the real you."

"How could you...? We've only just met a few months back."

"Oh no, Mr. Jeffries. I have been the last four women you've bedded, or should I say used and discarded over the past year." As I spoke, I shifted from one to the next, reveling in his horror.

Now he tried to escape, tensing his muscles against the invisible restraints, and found he could not move. My will kept him still, always my will be done. My abilities far outmatched his. With a snap of my fingers, he could be a puddle of muck on the floor if I willed it, but annihilation was too good for this monster. His arms shuddered, trying with all his might, but a wave of my hand had him spread out, arms and legs stretched to each corner of the bed. I stood up and donned my skirt and blouse, leaving him naked and exposed. "I know you're quite skilled and you think—you lie to yourself—that you're truly connecting with these women, but you are well aware of the pain you cause, deep down. Aren't you, Jeffries? Didn't you say to me—women got hurt? Yes, I believe you did. In fact, you told me four separate times, just as you turned on the tears four separate times to gain my trust at the beginning of this 'relationship.' Oh, Mr. Jeffries, I know your kind all too well. I've been around for far too long, and I'm well aware of just how truly aware you are. The violence, I didn't expect from you, though, but it was so cunningly disguised, along with the continuous manipulation. Most, I fear, don't even recognize what you do to them. Their bodies know, and they suffer as if it was as overtly violent as a dockside ravishing in the dark, but they can't understand why. They blame themselves, and you help them do that, don't you Mr. Jeffries? Added agony on top of the assaults, in addition to the trauma."

"I took them—you—them to places they've never been, showed them ecstasy and spiritual awakening."

"Can you even hear yourself? The arrogance! Are you suggesting the orgasms you gave these women afforded you control over them? Enabled you to treat them and discard them as you will? Gave you the right to ravish them and destroy them? And love, sir? It is quite clear you do not know the meaning or the power of that word."

"I did love them! All of them."

"Love. Love to you is the fear in their eyes. Love to you is control. It's what makes it so easy for you, so delicious. I was wrong, actually, you quite obviously know the power of it, and you exploit that power just as you exploit all those women. They love and trust you. They are bound to you, body, heart, and soul. Your words and actions coupled with such ecstasy create such a profound bond with a woman. You understand the depth of that created bond all too well, don't you? Yes. I believe you do. Of course you do. You count on it. It is part of your game. It's why poor Polly trails after you like a spaniel, begging for scraps."

"I helped those women. I've done nothing wrong. They're adults and can make their own decisions. They are responsible for their own choices, their own emotions."

"But you also made them responsible for yours. For your actions, your choices, your emotions. If you are even capable of true emotion, of empathy or compassion. I rather think not, actually, else you couldn't have discarded those women so, used and ruined. Did you know Miss MacInyre killed herself? Took a dram of poison rather than end up in Bedlam like Miss Franklin. So distraught after you tired of them, after you tossed them aside after ruining them. One day, so loving and affectionate with your promises and such, the next so cruel and degrading. They suffered dearly, and there are plenty more. Shall I go through the names? Those now living on the streets, unable to feed the children you left them with. Some afflicted with the pox you gave to them. Unable to marry. Disowned by their families. Is this your gift to them, sir?"

"They knew what they were getting into. I needed my space, my independence. Always have. Told you the same thing. I will not be tied down. They knew from the start. I didn't lie."

"Yes, well, it seems you are rather tied down at the moment, aren't you, sir? We both know you lie with the truth, Mr. Jeffries. With those captivating green eyes and *your truth* spoken from the corner of your mouth, while your hands and your lips and your body and your breath tell them they are special, convincing them they are loved and cherished and adored." I paced in front of him, reveling in this moment. Finally, to be the woman to take this monster down was exhilarating. He would pay for everything he did to each of them. Every lie. Every manipulation. Every violation. "You made them feel unique and loved, didn't you? Telling them you love them. Telling them you've never felt like this before. Allowing them to believe it is forever. I know it is what you did to them, sir, because it is what you did to me. Four times. I did play my part well, though, didn't I? Yes. I am rather proud, as convincing as you. Remember when we last made love, as I do know you love to call it that. It does help with your mask, does it not? You were angry with me, as I remember, and you showed me who was in control. I saw it in your eyes. I felt it in every thrust of your hips as you rammed yourself down my throat. I was choking and pushing you away, but you paid me no mind. It was, after all, what *you* wanted, as usual. Always what you want, when you want, how you want. It was not about sharing. No. It was about power and control. That, sir, is called rape."

"Don't be ridiculous, woman. I didn't rape you or the others. You're daft. Just like Charlotte. She belongs in Bedlam, telling people such lies, and you do as well. You're mad."

"Then, after you violated me, you brushed it aside, telling me you loved me. It would've destroyed my soul, if it hadn't already been shattered beyond repair by men like you long ago. Shattered to the point of annihilation. Now I shatter men like you, and I certainly do not want for victims. I do take such delight in victimizing victimizers. In abusing abusers. In violating rapists on every level, as you do to all those women. For five hundred years I've taken such delight in exacting justice on men like you, those society ignores and even celebrates in their ignorance, blaming and punishing your victims again and again."

"Five hundred years? Now I know you are mad. Let me out of these restraints, this instant!" He didn't raise his voice, but rather his voice became low and calm. All affect washed from his face and it was stone. His eyes, void. Empty.

There he was.

The real Jeffries: a vacant, soulless monster, rearing his ugly face once again, but his cold rage didn't faze me.

Now I was in control.

"I shan't, actually. I have plans for you. We are going to set a few things right, you and I. Indeed. Before this is over, your women—you know, the ones who have a tendency to get hurt—will receive some peace of mind, some compensation."

"Over my dead body."

"If it comes to that, which it rarely does. Although, you will beg for death, before the end."

"Let me out of these restraints, this instant," he repeated, but this time there was a quiver to his voice.

"Do you not believe my age, sir? You call me mad, sir?"

"I do."

"Very well. I'll show you." Leaning over his bound arms and looking into those empty eyes, I showed him. For but a moment, my eyes turned from hazel to sable black and back again. I impressed upon him centuries of violation and fear and pain, the emotions he had forced upon others. My entire existence of pain, pushed into this man's black heart for just a moment, giving him a taste of his future.

He yelped, trying to scoot away from me, but my will held him in place. Nowhere to go, not anymore.

I twisted my hair up into a bun and emptied my reticule onto the bed between his legs. The poppet. The loppers. The razor.

His fear reached the breaking point, and he vomited on himself, entire body trembling in fear. Tears streamed down his face for a change. It was rather pleasurable to watch. "Please, I'll do whatever you want."

"Yes, that's quite true. Quite, quite true."

"Please," he begged. "Please, Cyndi. My sweet Cyndi, or whoever you are, you know I love you. Please. You don't want to do this. We can be together. I was wrong. It's you. It's always been you."

"It's over, Roderick." Jeffries turned his head to the door, looking toward the voice that spoke.

"Come in, Miss Bainbridge," I said. She was right on time. "Hungry?"

"Famished," she said, taunting him.

"Sorry for the mess," I said, indicating Jeffries' dinner covering his muscular chest.

"No worries, I can take it from elsewhere."

"Bon appetit, Ava. Then, my turn."

Vulnerable, spread wide across his own bed, on which he had ruined so many, Avalon descended. His eyes revealed abject fear, perhaps the only genuine emotion I'd ever seen on his face. He had been exposed, and nothing terrified a man like him more than exposure, except maybe annihilation. Horrifying for him to face the reality that he was just human after all. He would die and decay, just like any other person. He was not a god, not superior after all. He, in the end, was just a pathetic bully.

Helpless.

Avalon ripped open his inner thigh, and he shouted as she tore his flesh, which made the most satisfying sound. She fed, her power growing with every swallow. Her body filled with strength. I felt the energy of the room shift. "Careful, Ava. Remember, we're not going to kill him. That would be too easy for him. No. His fate will be much worse than death."

"You're not going to kill me? You had better kill me. I have very influential friends, and I will have you both destroyed. You will—"

"Do shut up, Jeffries." I clamped his mouth shut with a snap of my fingers. "Back to intimidation and threats again, Rod? Please. I have grown past weary of your squeaky voice, of your claims of grandeur and privilege and superiority. Enough. That's all over now. Embrace the present, Roderick. For this moment is all there is. This agonizing moment will last lifetimes. You will never know another moment of joy or pleasure or peace. For a thousand years you will suffer, unable to obtain a breath of relief. Then, and only then, will you understand what horrors you have created. Yes, justice after all. Tit for tat. For every woman you traumatized, for every woman you ruined, for every moment they spent crying or terrified or ashamed or in untold, silent agony, you will spend the same amount of time in the same amount of agony. Collectively. With the scores of women you've hurt in the past twenty-five years—multiply each of those with their lifetime of trauma, with their struggle and hatred of themselves—that's your future, Roderick. Pain. Anguish. Unlike them, however, you will not be able to take your own life to end the torment. You must endure, like you've made so many others endure."

I gathered the lock of hair needed for his poppet, then I settled between his legs, ready for my meal. Jeffries wept. Puling and coughing and sputtering.

"Admit it, Roderick. Admit the endless pain you've caused, and I shall be merciful. For a repentant man deserves some mercy. Admit the violations. The manipulations. The cruelty. Admit it, and your sentence will become lighter."

"Why are you doing this to me?" he cried. "I've done nothing wrong. I loved those women. Every one of them. It's not my fault they got hurt. It's not my fault they couldn't be responsible for themselves."

"Even facing an eternity of hell, you will not take responsibility for your part. So be it."

"You're pathetic," Avalon said, his blood dripping down her chin. "I heard you, you know. In the street that day when that poor woman came up for any sign of kindness from you. Any sign of humanity, but you shamed her further. Then you whispered something to her, and I heard it. I know of your guilt as well, Jeffries. You deserve everything coming to you, just for her alone. Then, to hear about all the others. Beyond shameful. Beyond evil."

I settled between his legs, ready for my supper. "It's barely an appetizer, really," I said looking down, "Let alone a meal. Diseased as it is and all as well. Yes, so underwhelming. Quite amazing you caused so much pain and suffering, let alone pleasure, with such a small thing. How violent you had to be to get me to choke on such a tiny morsel. Now it's your turn to choke on it, Jeffries. Watch in horror and say goodbye to your precious pet, forever."

"No! Please!"

I took as much pleasure in his fear as he had taken in mine. More so, knowing his fear was quite justified. Whereas I normally made this part of the ritual rather quick, with this one, I would take my time.

"Please. No," he whimpered.

"Enough talk." I sewed his mouth shut, as I had done the others whipping my fingers through the air, taking from him even the ability to express his agony. He wouldn't even have that much relief from his pain. With the suffering this one had caused, he would suffer a millennium. At least.

Holding my hands above the flaccid phallus, hovering over it, I channeled my will and absorbed its power—his power—

consuming him. As his prowess and skill and desire flowed from his body to mine, it shrunk even more, shriveling up into a dry, twisted twig before crumbling into nothing, leaving just black, oozing puss behind. Simultaneously, as I absorbed the energy, the black bile from below filled his throat.

"Choke on it, the way you made me choke, Roderick. The way you made so many others. And now," I said, after he swallowed to avoid suffocation, "the real punishment begins."

As I fed off the sexual energy I drained from him, gathering enough strength to finish the ritual and move on to the next, he wailed and screamed through his sealed lips, eyes bulging at the horror of his shriveled member and the muck filling his throat. Yes, horror. Pain. Fear. Exactly what he deserved. He coughed and sputtered, bile oozed from between the stitches, loosening them. "Kill me," he managed through the stitching. "Please, just kill me."

"Yes. Beg for your life, you demon. Beg. I want to hear you beg the way you've made so many others beg for kindness, for mercy."

"Please," he whimpered.

"No." With a flourish of my arms, I tightened the stitches once again, altogether weary of his squeaky voice. "Now your heart," I said, and in a motion that would be too quick for a human to register, I thrust my hand into his chest, pulling out his still-beating heart. Then, it shrunk in my hand until it was compact and black, its true form. Positioning my free hand over the hole in his chest, I initiated his final transformation, turning the inside into the outside. In cries of such deep despair, of such pure agony as if the sounds came from the very empty core of his being, he transformed, shrinking into a hideous creature. An angry grimace frozen forever on its odious face, mouth open just enough to see the hollow interior. A forked tongue curled over its lips, lapping at nothing. Angry slits for eyes and legs spread to allow for the mighty erection, but, of course, that vital part was now missing. His weapon of choice forever disabled.

"Well, that's done," I said, turning to Avalon while I affixed the black heart onto the poppet, fusing it with the white yarn one already sewn in place.

"He'll remain thus? Forever?"

"Well, until his heart turns white again. In this one's case, I estimate about a millennium, like I said. He has done much damage."

Avalon took the poppet and examined it. "He's in here?"

"No, he's in there, as much as he's anywhere," I said, pointing to the grotesque statue. "The hair and blood inside the doll, not to mention the heart, keeps it attached to the consciousness inside the statue, enabling me control of his pain or mercy wherever I go. The statue stays here or goes wherever. Doesn't matter. Just an outward representation of what his true self on the inside. So often their handsome exterior hides just a repulsive interior. I think they hide it from themselves as well."

"So, he was a demon?"

"Not at all, Ava. That would explain so much, though, wouldn't it? He was human, all right. Remember, humans, not monsters, have perfected the ability to deceive and destroy. Monsters can't help but be monsters. Humans have a choice. His actions, his choices, made him the monster. The way he used his gifts and free will to betray and manipulate and shatter lives, that's what made him monstrous. He had the choice to change and repent at any time. I even gave him the chance again, at the very end. They rarely take it. Even facing torture, they won't take responsibility for what they've done. Few ever do, and it would take decades off their sentence, at least, if they but just admitted it. More if they apologized and meant it, if they took responsibility."

A sad expression crossed Avalon's face. "So much pain. They do deserve it—I can see that—but so very much pain. Now at least his pain will be contained to just him. He'll hurt no one else." A tear slid down her cheek.

"Indeed. I have one more to go, then I shall be leaving London for a while. Work calls me elsewhere. I never want for work, unfortunately."

"One more? Can I come, too?" she said, wiping the tear away. "This was fascinating, albeit gruesome."

"You can come with me wherever you wish, Avalon, my beauty. We would make quite the team, and we would only use men as they use us, never trust them again. Feed from them, punish them, protect others from ending up like us."

"Who is this last one? Is he as vile as this one was?"

"More so. Every bit as bad, only he's had centuries to perfect his ruse, as you well know." The light brown hair assembled on top of my head brightened to a brilliant red, and the recognition dawned on Avalon's face.

"Oh my," she said.

"You know it must be done," I said. "Tomorrow night, just as the clock chimes midnight, I think. You are quite welcome to watch, my dear. I have no doubt it will be most cathartic for you."

A bizarre sound came from the bed, a groaning of sorts. Then, laughter, causing us both to turn around to see what made the noise.

"Is that supposed to happen?" Avalon asked, pointing to the statue which had started to squirm. Arms flapping and forked tongue thrashing to and fro.

"No. It's not."

Before I could even get back to the bed, the thing began to grow, laughing and thrusting its forked tongue about. The sound of skin stretching, ripping, morphing, along with the putrid smell of hell filled the room.

Avalon grabbed my hand, and I was all too happy to take it for comfort myself. With disgust, we watched, unable to move out of fear, as the thing grew back into the form of Roderick Jeffries, except for its face, which remained heinous. Instead of hair, long phallic snakes twisted their mushroom heads around the demon's head. Its hollowed cheeks, still cracked like stone. Its laughter thumped in my ears, chilling my spine. Forked tongue slithering, it looked down at its chest and closed the hole over the demon's own black heart which had filled the empty cavity. Next, with a roar of triumph, it regrew its penis, but the atrocious thing that emerged from between the monster's legs was huge and scaly and blue, barbs poking out from the bottom ridge. Erect, it curved halfway up the fiend's torso.

"All right," I whispered. "Maybe this one is a demon after all."

"Thank you for getting rid of that pathetic little thing, by the way," it hissed. "It did the job well enough, after all, but this will do so much more damage. How delicious." It stroked the length of its enormous blue shaft and moaned, sending chills throughout my body

I took a protective stance in front of Avalon, but the thing just laughed again, its face becoming more human by the second. Before long, I was looking at Roderick Jeffries' handsome features again. Except for the blue erection, he looked human.

"But—how?" I sputtered. "You're not human?"

"I'm very human, of course, you wretched bitch, and I've taken my delights with women for the past fifteen years. Fucking and raping and devouring them as I chose, honing my skills in pleasure and in manipulation and pain. I suppose my choices in life attracted my little friend inside. Since I wasn't burdened with a soul, I had plenty of room. He found my lifestyle so irresistible, he had to join in the fun, and we have had so much fun together, too. So very much. He's shown me wickedness and pleasure I couldn't have dreamt of before. He had his suspicions about you, and he was right. You won the bet, old friend. You get to choose the next one. How about one of these lovely ladies here, or, both? Do you think they can handle all of this?" He grabbed the blue monstrosity with both hands and stroked it up and down with long lascivious motions, twisting his hands back and forth. Tongue, still forked, licked his lips around and around.

"Leave her out of this, Jeffries. Just let her go. Take me," I said, knowing I could endure any sort of atrocity the thing could inflict upon me without further damage. Well, lasting damage anyway. Although the assault itself, however long it lasted, and I suspect he'd make it last, would be as harrowing for me as for any woman, after it was over, I'd suffer no further trauma. Any memory of it would just be a memory, without emotional attachment.

It was one of the gifts of my power.

"No?" Jeffries said, but I got the impression he wasn't talking to us. "Her? Are you sure? Well, all right. Like I said, dear boy, it's your choice. It'll split her little body in two, but no matter. I've had my fill of her anyway. Rather bored with her cackling and whimpering." He bowed a brief goodbye. "Ladies." Ripping the sheet off the bed, he wrapped himself in it and jumped out the window to the alley below, hooting and crowing like a madman as he ran down the darkened alley out of sight.

"We've got a problem," I said to Avalon.

CHAPTER 20

ARTHUR

Deja-vu.

Again.

Wasn't I just here not so long ago? Standing outside Avalon's, hoping she'd speak to me. Seems so.

I had sent message after message to Avalon all day today, but Thomas always came back empty handed. He said she hadn't been home. I came here myself, determined to wait, and I was delighted, and then terrified, to discover she was home now.

The wood of Avalon's door felt somehow too hard, knowing behind its protection my love felt a hardness toward me that was all too well deserved. I knew that now. Every bit of this heartache I had brought on myself. Tilting my head up to the second story, I whispered, "Avalon? Please, Ava. Talk to me." She could hear me even if I whispered.

No answer, but she was in there. As I had approached the house, I could hear her crying up in the library, the place where she and Victor used to work together, and she wasn't alone. Another woman whose voice I didn't recognize was with her. A friend, perhaps, comforting her and her broken heart. Her life had changed so much since she met me, and

I'm not sure I could say for the better. Avalon stopped weeping and became very quiet. Two sets of footsteps came down the stairs and stopped just on the other side of the door. I didn't care who else heard me or if I looked weak, I only wanted to fix things between us.

"Ava," I whispered this time, my head leaning against the door. "I know you're there. Please just hear me out. Please. Perhaps I acted rashly. It was quite callous of me to behave so on the airship. Things just hadn't been right with us for some time, and I just fell into old patterns, is all. I see that now. I love you, Avalon. I love you so much, and I just don't know what to do to make it better. Please help me."

The tears stung my eyes, and I couldn't risk crying blood tears here in the street for all to see. I truly did miss her.

She opened the door, and she looked beautiful, despite the red streaks down her face. The woman standing behind her was breathtaking, and she regarded me with none too friendly a stare.

"Come in, Arthur," Avalon said, and I did, stepping past her and her curious friend. "I'm glad you're here." My heart leapt with joy. Avalon turned the key and took us into the parlour. Her house had been empty since Victor's death, as he was her only tenant, and even more so since she had been living with me. The place had a stale air to it, and this woman with Avalon, beautiful though she was, made me feel all the more uneasy.

"Aren't you going to introduce me to your friend, Ava?"

"This is Constance. She's a succubus. Constance, Arthur. Vampire."

"Pleasure," she said, although her tone told me it was anything but.

"Succubus? A Demon? Really, Avalon, you're consorting with a demon?

"She's not a demon, Arthur, but there is one in town we have to deal with, and fast."

"Avalon, sweetheart." I tried to ensure my tone wasn't condescending, but it was ever so hard. How foolish could she be? Of course a succubus was a demon. A demon who devours men after sexually engulfing them, a man's worse nightmare. Right up there with vagina dentata. Dreadful stuff.

"No, Arthur," the demon said. "I am older than you in life and in death, so you will listen to me, boy." Disgust and hostility dripped from her words, and I was aghast, wondering what I had done to deserve such treatment by anyone, let alone a she-demon. "Succubi are vengeance spirits, of sorts. We're corporeal, part human shape-shifters, and we do have supernatural power, but it is far from evil, and neither it, nor we, originate in hell. In most cases, as in mine, our power springs from hell being delivered upon us. Brutal acts, too ghastly to endure as a human, so instead of being destroyed, something inside us rises up. Our strength and rage fuels us to avenge the wronged, starting with ourselves. Then, others.

"An incubi, on the other hand, is, indeed, a demon. It comes from the deepest bowels of hell, and it has particularly lascivious tastes. It possesses and violates humans. Kills."

"Ah! The serial rapist, right? The one who's been murdering those women, in the papers."

"Looks that way, although, one need not be a demon to be a serial rapist. I've known thousands in my time, and this is the first demon I've come across. His...style...is rather brutal, no doubt, but I've seen as bad and even worse from humans. Experienced it. Endured it. The difference is, I can punish a human. They can be forced into accountability, living out the suffering they cause until their heart and souls, if they have one, have been purified, then they're released. Demons. I don't know how to stop a demon, and they can't be punished. They can't be trapped, which is where you come in."

"Me? How on earth can I help?"

"Your books, Arthur. Your library. You have centuries of mythology and lore on your shelves, and we need to come up with a plan." Avalon spoke to me, hands folded politely in her lap, and she kept her face rather blank, but there was a slight quiver to her voice. "We need you, Arthur. Victor's books fall short, and we have to stop this thing. He's going after Polly, we think."

"Polly? Polly Pooter? The spaniel?"

"Don't call her that," Avalon said, offense filled her voice and form.

"Why not? He calls her that, and that's how she acts."

"She acts that way because of a lifetime of abuse, by many men, most recently and atrociously, Roderick Jeffries. The demon possessing him wants to rip her in two, quite literally, from the inside out. We have to stop him. That woman has suffered enough for one lifetime, and once we get that demon out of him, Jeffries will get his."

"Jeffries? The American snake-oil salesman is an incubus? Don't be absurd."

Preposterous!

I was doing my utmost not to be cruel or condescending. I came here to make up, after all. To invest in the relationship with Avalon. To be kind.

They made it very hard.

"I saw it with my own two eyes, Arthur, or has it come to where you don't even believe what I say anymore. Has it come to that?"

"Besides," the succubus said. "He's not a demon. No. He's very human, but he has a demon possessing him and he will do so much more damage now that I tried to punish him, and failed. I took his heart and his weapon, but the demon grew another one. It's huge, Arthur. He will skewer women with it and laugh while he does it. If we don't stop him, there will be much more bloodshed before New Year's alone. No woman will be safe."

"You cut off his—You bitch! You're the one who got Ol' Nick, aren't you? The journalist and that daft doctor, too. You cut off —Ugh! I can't even say it."

"I don't cut anything off. Don't be barbaric, Arthur. But I do indeed absorb their power, and that does have unfortunate side effects. Well, unfortunate for them. Rest assured, if I punish someone, they deserve it. Your good friend Nick was also a serial rapist, as was the professor and reporter, as you call them. As are so many entitled, selfish men"—she glared at me with her insinuation—"but they're just not as overt about it, not as sensational and gruesome. They don't do it so it's splashed all over the front page of the paper. They do it behind closed doors with no evidence but the traumatized woman's word. They do it to people they know, women who trust them or believe they love them. They do it in such a way their victims remain silent or where no one will believe them if they find the voice to speak. After all, women are unstable and emotional and prone to exaggeration. Right? Hysteria? Jeffries did it that way as well, but the demon preferred to supplement his activity with the spectacle, with severe brutality. Even though society doesn't care about the woman's silent weeping as she endures, those are by far the most common assaults. It takes unimaginable violence, grisly tales of gang rapes that last for hours or are particularly brutal, to gain anyone's attention, and those happen so rarely. Then the public can shake their heads and breathe a little easier when that man or those few men are caught, and turn their backs on the hundreds—yes hundreds—of women who are raped every day in this kingdom, let alone around the world."

Daggers flew from her eyes and poison from her tongue, and I felt sick just listening to her. Rage boiled up inside me, and it took all the strength I had not to rip her throat out. I opened my mouth to speak, but now Avalon had the audacity to stop me.

"Not now, Arthur," she said, raising her palm to me. "There will be time for understanding and explanation later, but now, we have to do something. Please. Can we just go to your library? I'll gather the books I can from upstairs, but then, we must find a way to stop this man tonight. Tomorrow, I fear, Miss Pooter, and who knows who else, will be in great danger."

CHAPTER 21

CONSTANCE

Arthur started, his countenance of one affronted. Yes. How dare a woman speak to him thus?

"And weapons, dear Ava?" he questioned. "What about weapons? You know I have none, save a stake or two, ironically. Perhaps we should peruse Victor's inventions before we trek across town. Hmmm?" My stomach turned at his tone. He spoke down to her, each word full of malice at being forced to be polite in mixed company, squeezing his fists to keep calm at her defiance.

Not much longer, Arthur York. Not much longer.

Avalon turned from the powerful woman who had been by my side just hours ago as we punished Jeffries into a broken woman. Just a few muscles of her face told of the change, imperceptible to most, no doubt, but not to me. The intent behind her eyes turned from the brightness of righteous anger, the feeling that one deserves better and was prepared to fight for it, to the darkness of defeat. This man had quite the hold over her, as they usually did once the woman had fallen in love. That was when they made their great change, that was when their abusive nature became more overt.

Arthur York was no different, not that I ever suspected he was. Now, however, was not the time. More pressing matters.

"Fine," Avalon said in a broken whisper. "You're right, of course. This way."

I didn't say a word at this juncture, just followed as Ava led us back up to Victor's study. Avalon had told me a little about Victor when we were up there before. She had admired him, deeply, and he had been a good man. Lamenting his fate, not to mention how she felt, how her trust in Arthur was at least in part responsible for Victor's death, how she had cried in my arms, and how I had comforted her best I could. She was alone. With Victor, her best friend and confidant gone, with Arthur behaving so monstrously of late, and with her losing her life and becoming something altogether otherworldly, it was too much to bear over a short few months. With my support, however, she had begun to remember who she was, she had begun to break that deep bond one makes with their abuser. That inexplicable, ironic, near-unbreakable bond.

Her insistence to turn to Arthur in this time of need was rather against my better judgment, but we didn't have much time and so many more lives were at stake. We had to take the chance.

Victor's study glowed in dim gaslight, soft shadows danced across the room and bookshelves from light filtering in from outside. Avalon lit the two candles on the center table, brightening the dark room.

"Get what you like," she said to Arthur. "Of course, we don't have any idea what we'll need yet, since the research is at yours, but get what you like."

Cheekiness. Good for her.

She sat on the white window seat, looking down at Baker Street, her face calm, somber.

"We might not know exactly, *sweetheart*, but we do know we're dealing with something evil, do we not? Crucifixes at the very least." Arthur spoke in the most delightful tone possible, edged with condescension, before collecting a bag from beneath Victor's desk. He took three crosses from the top drawer and held them up to me, impressed with himself. He leaned in close to me and whispered, "They don't really burn us, that's just one of the many false myths around vampires."

Yes. I knew that, of course, but more importantly, he was trying to impress me. Get a rise out of Avalon, more like. She didn't take the bait. Good for her.

Such childish games men played.

Arthur thrust the crosses in the bag and picked up a long brass gauntlet adorned with vials and gauges. "Remember this, Ava?" he asked as he strapped it to his arm. Since jealousy didn't work, he moved to nostalgia. "Right here," he said pointing to the floor in front of the desk, "Right here Victor showed me how this worked. Remember, sweetheart?"

"I remember Victor quite well." She spoke in a cold tone and didn't look away from whatever held her attention below. Likely nothing, certainly not as interesting as the show up here.

Arthur stiffened and shoved the contraption into the bag along with the crosses. He grabbed a handful of extra vials from the second drawer and shoved them one at a time into leather loops protruding from a belt piece. "Holy water," he explained for my benefit. "Again, pointless for vampires, but it might have an effect on a demon."

"I would imagine so," I said. "Great thinking, Arthur. How does the thing work?"

"There is a trigger release that goes around the finger like a ring, and with a flick of the wrist, it shoots a stream of holy water. It came in handy a few months back when Avalon,

Victor, and I battled some vampire-hybrids. Long story, you see—"

"There isn't time, Arthur. Please." Avalon stood up and strode to the bookshelf.

"Fine."

"You can tell me on the way to yours, Arthur."—trying to keep the peace, at least until we'd stopped Jeffries—"She's right. We best get going. Anything else?"

"This." Avalon held up a thick revolver and pointed it at Arthur's heart.

"Ah. The Slayer. Yes. I suppose you're particularly keen on that one at the moment."

"Indeed, I am." If the glare she shot Arthur had been full of whatever ammunition that revolver held, I would be sweeping up dust at the moment.

"We're not hunting a vampire, Avalon. This is a demon. Remember?" He didn't even try to hide the condescending tone anymore.

After a jerk to the right, she pulled the trigger, and the straw-stuffed dummy in the corner right behind Arthur had a new hole in the center of its painted heart. "I think a wooden bullet through the heart of most creatures would do some damage, don't you, Constance?"

"She's got a point." Glad to see she'd found her strength against this brute again.

"Take it," she said, tossing the gun to Arthur who caught it and shoved it in the bag along with the rest. "Extra bullets as well."

"Of course, sweetheart." He was not amused.

"Is that all? Can we go to yours now? We have a lot of work to do and not much time," she said, her voice softened. "Arthur, can we just put the rest of this aside for now. Please?"

"My preference."

CHAPTER TWENTY-ONE

"Thank you."

"All right," I interjected, standing between them, breaking this lovers' dance. "I'll find a cab."

Avalon walked out of the room first, and I followed. We didn't wait for Arthur, but his footfalls followed soon enough.

The street was rather quiet, deserted. "What was I thinking?" I chided myself. "It's too late for a cab."

"We don't need a cab, of course. We can move much faster than a cab can carry us anyway. Can you?" His eyes scanned me from my dark curls down to the tips of my buttoned up boots.

"Lead the way."

"Up," he said to Avalon, "Just in case."

She nodded, and they were off at human speed until they came to the first alley. As soon as they turned, the next thing I knew Arthur called down from the rooftop. "Are you coming, or not?"

Something came over both Arthur and Avalon, a sense of energy and excitement. Avalon glowed. She lifted up her skirt and the sound of ripping fabric followed as she tore it clean off, revealing her bloomers below. "Only a hindrance, really," she said with a smile, tossing the torn skirt off the building. It floated down next to me, landing in a pool of fabric at my feet.

This would be fun, a quick run and romp before work on this exhilarating winter night. As Avalon shed her bulky overcoat, dropping it, too, down to me, I transformed into some more moveable clothes myself.

"How convenient for you," she said when I reached the rooftop, commenting on my dungarees and fisherman sweater. "That was my favorite coat."

"One of the perks," I mused.

"Fine for the two of you. Women's suffrage and all that nonsense. Can we go now, or would you ladies like to continue exchanging fashion tips?" His tone was light, although his words weren't.

Not the time.

"What are you waiting for, vampire?"

"Follow me she-demon."

He took off in a blur, Avalon following, but it was only a moment before I was right behind them. We laughed as we jumped from building to building, dashing through the cold December air. I really must do this more often. I hadn't felt so alive in years, decades, even. The wind through my hair. The sting of the cold in my ears and the tip of my nose. I must be a sight, red tipped nose, appled cheeks, and what felt like icicles forming around my ears.

Still, I laughed.

Little was more exhilarating than running. It was what the body was built for, methinks. As I hit my stride, my hips led the way and my feet barely touched the surface. I was flying. Coming down on the ball of each foot, again and again, feeling the muscles in my feet and calves and thighs propelling me forward, buildings whipping by, and the sound of laughter.

More laughter.

More joy.

More momentary, fleeting bliss.

Yes, moments like these, indeed. It was what made existence bearable.

Yet, as everything, good or bad, euphoric or devastating—before long, it was over.

Time to work.

Arthur's home was beyond ornate. The finest of everything from wood to decor to rugs furnished this fine abode. But, of course, nothing but the best for this viscount. This once and forgotten heir apparent. He was, after all, a Tudor.

"Thomas," Arthur addressed his butler. "Tea in the Library. Then, we shan't be disturbed."

"Very good, M'Lord." Thomas had been roused from sleep, his hair a little on end, but he showed nothing but loyalty and grace, even in his disheveled state. With a click of his heels and a quick spin, he strode out of the foyer.

"Upstairs," Arthur said, pointing. He removed his gloves, hat, and overcoat, leaving them all lying on the table near the front door.

Avalon had started to shiver.

"Cold?" I asked, wishing I could manifest more clothes for her as I did for myself.

"Yes, now that I'm cooling down from the run, my body is remembering that it's, in fact, quite freezing out there." Her teeth chattered, but Arthur turned from her, as cold as he was dead.

"Pity you moved out, then." He didn't look at her, but rather set his jaw and puffed out his chest in his arrogance. "Library. Now."

He took the steps two at a time and Avalon and I followed. "Just through there," she said, pointing. "I'll be right back down." She continued up to the third story and I went into Arthur's Library.

He plopped the bag full of weapons on the edge of a burgundy chaise before moving to the far side of his impressive library. Avalon had not exaggerated. Sumptuous like the rest of his house, the room was full of bookshelves made from dark, fine wood. Books overflowed from each shelf, some sitting on the tops of others in many places, but it was far from chaos. There was an order to it all. The shelves reached to the ceiling, lined the walls, and there was even self-standing bookshelves in the middle of the room. Arthur climbed up to the third step of a wooden ladder set on a track and pulled himself along the shelves, taking a book from here and there before tossing them down onto the nearest leather sofa or chair.

"Collect those, would you? We'll work over there," he said, pointing to a table set in the center of two leather sofas as a sort of conversation area. "Get the bag of weapons, too."

"I got them," Avalon said, entering, dressed in what I assumed was Arthur's clothes. Fine black trousers, a white, high-collared shirt, and a brocade waistcoat. A black cravat and her sable curls framed her heart-shaped face.

Arthur chuckled, shaking his head from side to side. "That's my Ava," he said.

He leapt down from the fourth step and swept Avalon up into his arms, kissing her. Her hands changed from defensive, against his chest trying to push him away, to wrapped around his neck halfway through the kiss.

"Now," he said, pulling back from her. "To work." He jumped over the back of one of the sofa's and landed in the corner, arms and legs crossed.

"To work," she repeated, breathless, then walked around and sat near him.

"I'm surprised the cold affects you, Avalon," I said. "As a vampire. Arthur didn't seem affected by it." No. Little affect at all, actually.

"I'm still young in this new life, but over time it shall cease to do so." Her rosy cheeks held a glow about them, no doubt from the kiss. Poor girl.

"These are quite old, Arthur. Impressive collection." I gathered the books he had strewn about and placed them neatly in the middle of the table. "Although, I wouldn't toss them about like that. They are rather fragile at this age, unlike us."

"Books, Connie. They're books. I once had a deep reverence for books, too, but, then I figured, they're just books. There were so many other things more important than books."

"Like what?" I challenged.

"This is not a game of wits and I have no interest in entering this debate with you. Of course the information therein is quite valuable, but why would it matter if a spine is cracked or no? The information remains the same. Besides, they're unharmed."

"Yes. Finely made, as is everything in your home, Arthur." I took the top book that looked as old as me. I ran my hand over the cloth cover, even the leather corners had worn through. Barely readable, the title had little of its original gold leaf in the letters. It read: DAEMONS.

"I like my luxury. Will you chide me for that, too, she-beast? Are we here to prattle or to work?"

"Demons," Avalon interrupted. "What do we know about Demons?"

"Um. They come from hell?" Arthur's tone had returned to complete condescension toward Avalon again. Loving one moment, patronizing the next. Affectionate one moment, withdrawn the next. How maddening, indeed.

"Yes. They come from hell," she said, then moved to the chair adjacent to both couches, alone. Likely, how she felt safe at the moment, and I couldn't blame her there. She sunk back between the arms and curled her legs beneath her. "What else do we know?" she asked, directing her question at me.

"Many of these books look like religious doctrine and history, and I know from personal experience their information can be suspect at best and utterly self-serving, incorrect at worst. I don't think an exorcism is the answer, but I just don't know what is. As I said, I've never come across a demon before."

"Connie's right there," Arthur said. "Not a reliable resource, the church, but it's a start. There is so much false information about vampires as well, even from those who have studied and experimented on them. Facts get diluted with belief and dogma and mythology. I'm sure it's no different here."

"True," Avalon said, "But remember, even though Victor's research had many things wrong about vampirism, they did help us in the end with the hybrids. It is a start, as you said. Bear with me here. Demon. Hell. Which is the opposite of heaven, right?"

"Yes, but those concepts are oversimplified, you understand," I explained. "These are but other dimensions, not necessary what dogma dictates."

"Of course. Still, the holy water is worth a shot, as are the bullets," Arthur said. "I agree that a priest and exorcism won't do much good here. Certainly not alone, perhaps as a distraction or ally."

"That's risky," I said. "Putting an innocent in danger like that for something we're not even sure about. Still, I agree, it will be best to take a multi-tiered approach, as we don't know what will or won't work."

"Agreed." Arthur said, then leaned forward and grabbed a book. "So, crosses and holy water—"

"—And wooden bullets!"

"Yes, sweetheart, and wooden bullets, that much without reading, we've decided."

Thomas entered with a silver platter, a porcelain teapot and three cups with saucers. "Forgive me for the wait, M'Lord." He was fully dressed and hair combed. Presentable and proud.

"Not at all, Thomas. Just set it there," Arthur said, distracted. "That will be all."

"Thank you, M'Lord.

"So," Arthur continued, "that much we've decided as a place to start, and those books won't likely tell us anything else, but my darling insisted. She must have her way, after all."

"Please, Arthur."

Before they could start up again, I interrupted, "We have about four hours until dawn, so how about we read for a little and see if any other ideas come to mind, shall we?"

"Yes, but—forgive me—" Avalon said. "What about Polly? I mean, there are two issues here, correct? Stopping the demon, of course. But also protecting Polly—and everyone, of course—but we know she's his next target. He might be headed there right now."

"Unlikely," I said. "He's going to want to draw this out, especially with someone as besotted as Polly. I've known many like him in my time, but this monster has a true demon working with him. They will thrive off her pain, but her broken heart–broken soul–will be their icing. He's regrouping and planning for now. Going to her in the middle of the night would be too suspect. I'd say we have until sunrise."

"All right, but what then? How can we protect her?"

"Kidnap her." Arthur said. "Next?"

"I'd rather not cause any more fear or horror, if necessary, Arthur. There is just too much already," Avalon said.

"Have you got a better idea?"

"I do," I said. "You've seen what I can do for yourself. I'll just appear to her as Jeffries. She trusts him. We can convince her to go with us if he's there, too."

"Splendid idea!" Avalon said.

"If it works. Won't she know the difference?"

"I'm very good at what I do."

"And then what?" Arthur asked. "Wouldn't she be the bait? If we take her out of the equation, then how will we know when and where to find Jeffries? Besides, if she's missing, he'll know the game is afoot, and we don't want him anymore aware of trouble than he already is."

"True. We want him to think he's so much more powerful and intelligent than we are. Which, shouldn't pose a problem. He already thinks he's more powerful and intelligent than anyone else. After all, he's the smartest, most perfect and interesting fellow that has ever existed! In his demented eyes, at least, so that's easy enough."

"He is rather arrogant, isn't he?" Avalon said. "I mean, I've known some creeps in my time, but this salesman tops them all. Indeed."

"Indeed," I said. "You don't know the half of it. I've been tracking him for months. Astounding. More so that I didn't sense something off, sense the evil behind the evil. Or, that it didn't sense me. Its power, too, not an issue until the castration and breakdown of form, then it emerged. That must mean the demon is both protected and hindered by Jeffries' flesh, by his form."

"There's a part of him not protected by form anymore," Avalon said. Her hands slid between her trousered legs, protecting herself from idea of the revolting blue phallus.

"Yes. I suspect that is our first attack, his most vulnerable and prized part. The holy water. It's worth a shot, quite literally, but you'll have to be precise, Arthur. It's huge, in one aspect, but still a narrow target, relative to his overall form."

"His cock, you mean? Yes, you had mentioned. Leave it to me."

"Hopefully that will weaken him enough for the second wave of attack, which we may have to improvise unless we find something very useful in the next few hours."

"How will we get him...exposed, as it were? And you still haven't answered my question. What to do once we have

Polly? Where do we bring her? Here? That braying ass! I don't want her to know where I live or anywhere near this finery."

"Arthur, please." Avalon's shame was quite apparent and understandable.

"What?"

"We'll think of something, Connie." Avalon's kind tone made me quite sad for her. I looked forward to freeing her tomorrow night, if I survived the incubus. "A hotel, perhaps. Please, continue."

"Thank you," I said to Avalon, giving Arthur an altogether unpleasant glance. "To answer your other question, your highness, isn't it obvious? I will impersonate Polly. Remember, he can't sense me behind Jeffries' skin. Exposing his vulnerability won't be an issue, as we already know what he's planning. We just don't know when or where."

"We'll stay close," Avalon said, seeing the worry on my brow. "In fact, there is an apparatus I've used before where we can hear what's happening, even from a distance."

"Yes!" Arthur said, "But it's back at yours. Didn't think of that."

"How can you do that?" I asked.

"Another device Victor invented. He was a genius, after all," Avalon said.

"Yes. Yes. He was perfect. Continuing…" Arthur spat.

"You wear one part over your ear, the other down your sleeve. That's the part where you can talk back to us," Avalon said in an excited tone, eyes lighting up.

"This new technology is quite astounding, Avalon. The problem is that when it matters most, I shan't have a sleeve nor another stitch covering me."

"Too true."

Arthur perked up at this. "Nothing? You'll be wearing nothing?"

"How else do you think I'll be able to expose him, Arthur? We will be likely in the middle of things, as it were, and knowing Jeffries, he'll want to make it last. He finds the buildup quite important, after all. Otherwise, it sounds like a remarkable bit of technology, but I'm afraid you will have to stay even closer. I don't know where he'll take me or when, but my guess would be his home. He does like to be in control, after all. This is his masterpiece, not just one of the others he's violated, mutilated, and discarded in the past weeks. This is his pet, and he will want to savor it along with his new weapon of mutilation. How he must be salivating at the thought of it."

My lip curled into a scowl of disgust. The sooner we destroyed this man and the demon within, the better.

"Now, read," I ordered. "Just in case there is anything that could help when we're in the thick of it, but I fear we are in unchartered territory here. It will take all our supernatural strength combined to destroy him. Once the demon is gone, Jeffries is mine."

I was taking a holiday after this.

CHAPTER 22

ARTHUR

"Are you sure you can pull this off?" This plan seemed altogether too far-fetched to work. "These two know each other too well, even someone as vapid as Polly Pooter will be able to tell the difference."

"I told you, I can take any form, although it's usually female. This will work. Trust me," the she-demon said.

"I'll never trust a demon," I said, scoffing.

"I told you, vampire, between us, I'm not the demon."

I raised a finger to scold her, put the woman in her place, but then I remembered what she did to protruding body parts and retracted it.

Avalon came between us, "Enough. Both of you."—Then, pointing.—"It's just around here."

"How do you know where she lives, Ava?"

"I followed them home from their show one night. The night we met, Constance. Remember? I fed off him, Arthur." She confessed, then added. "Now, don't chide me for it. I will take care of myself, thank you very much. I have done so most of my life. You are not my keeper. Nor shall you ever be, Arthur Tudor. You did this to me, and I need blood to survive and to thrive, so I figured I'd take it from someone deserving, just in case I couldn't wipe their memory properly. Turns out, I did it quite well on my own. Didn't I, Constance?"

"I was very impressed."

Great. They'd teamed up against me. I just couldn't win. Women.

"Jeffries brought Polly home first before going off to meet with you, Constance," Avalon continued. "She hung on him as if her very life depended on his presence, but he rather coldly pushed her away and patted her on the head. You're right about one thing, Arthur. The man treats her like a pet dog, not like a friend and certainly not like a former lover."

She lowered her voice as we approached the imp's window.

In her one-room flat, Polly's tiny body slept curled around a photograph of her and Jeffries. No kitchen or indoor plumbing. It just had a wash basin on a dresser. He did keep her in poverty, and by the looks of his clothes, he made decent money. Scoundrel.

She looked even older as she slept, nearly as old as the crone she played in the street show. Her long brown curls fanned out over the pillow and her face sagged, a crumpling of skin and more skin. She had no doubt had a rough life, and if anything this she-demon said was true, then part of it had to do with this chap Jeffries. Listening to the witch talk for hours about the abuses of men on the gentler sex and what these abuses did to them over time really started to get me thinking about how I'd treated women.

It had been a week of self-reflection. How exhausting.

I, of course, was beyond reproach, I had decided. I mean, I loved every woman I wooed and bedded. In my own way, anyway. They knew what they were getting into, after all. Plus, I wiped their memories, or killed them. No traumatic after effects there.

Could Avalon be feeling this kind of pain? What about Emily Bainbridge? Certainly not Emily. She knew she was a just a romp. She seduced me after all, didn't she? No. Not her. What about Chastity? Surely things were all too new with her for her to be truly hurt. No. I was just fine.

Beyond reproach.

I reached for the knob, ready to break in, but the she-demon stopped me. "Wait," she said. "Let me go to her first. We don't want her to scream."

I was about to tell her that, whether she or I went in, it would frighten the woman, but there were ways to muffle screams. I was, after all, rather an expert at it, but before I could say any of that, her body started stretching before me. Her jaw changed shape. Her nose elongated. Her hair short-ened. Her clothes changed. Aghast, I watched the she-demon turn into Roderick Jeffries.

She really could do it. I didn't believe she could until now. If I hadn't seen the transformation myself, I would've sworn on my long damned life that it was the snake-oil salesman standing before me.

"What—how—?" I stammered.

"She does that," Avalon said with a smile in her voice. "Remarkable woman, don't you find?"

"Now," the she-demon-Jeffries said, and even her voice was his. Not deep. No, his voice was quite weaselly, and now, so was hers. "What are you waiting for?"

I shook myself out of my stunned stupor and turned the door handle, breaking the lock with ease. By the time the door was open, Polly had been stirred awake and she looked up at Jeffries half-conscious then over to us, but she didn't care we were there. Her world was there. Her eyes went back to Jeffries. "Rod! Oh, my love! You've come back to me, haven't you? After all this time. I knew if I was patient enough, you'd return to my bed. I love you, Roddy. I love you with all my heart." She jumped up into his arms, wrapping her arms and legs around him.

"That was easy," Avalon whispered to me.

I felt nothing but pity for this little spaniel. Her entire world was that man. He was her sun, her moon, the air she breathed, and he just kept her around for the adoration, never intending to offer any true love back to her. It was beyond cruel. Even by my standards.

"Polly," the she-devil-Jeffries said. "I want you to go with these people, all right? I'll be along presently."

"Then we can be together again, Roddy? Then you will take me to heaven again? Oh, how I've missed you, Roddy. Oh! Roddy!" She kissed him all over the face, not allowing him to push her away, and the she-demon-Jeffries tried. "My body aches for you. Every night. Empty without you. Fill me up, again, Roddy! Oh, please! Say you'll come back to my bed! Please, Roddy! Oh, please!"

"Go with them, Polly. We'll be together soon." Constance pushed her away, and I gathered her up into my arms. She turned and wrapped herself around me, rubbing her eyes as if she was a sleepy toddler being passed from parent to parent to be put to bed.

"You know what to do," Constance said through Jeffries's lips. I just couldn't get over how it was Jeffries before me, yet it was Constance. I had never in all my time seen such a thing.

Constance pulled up a blanket from Polly's bed and wrapped it around her.

"I love you, Roddy."

"I love you, too, sweetheart. I'll see you soon." Constance mouthed the word "go" to me and Avalon.

I nodded, and Avalon led me, holding Polly, back out into the cold night. Before we were all the way out her door, Polly's heavy head on my shoulder and steady breathing told me she slept again. I looked back through the window, and saw the new Polly sitting on her bed.

Constance had shifted again. That fast.

She looked terrified.

"I hope this works," I said, walking back to where Thomas waited with the brougham.

"It will," Avalon said. "It has to."

"Why is Constance putting herself in such danger? If she's right about what he intends to do, then she could be killed." We kept our voices in a whisper, so as not to wake the sleeping imp.

"I'm not so sure she can be, Arthur. She's immortal, like us."

"Yes, Ava. There is immortal, then there is immortal. We can be killed, as you know, and I bet she can be, too. That would be an atrocious way to die, split in half from the inside out by a demon's cock. No. This has to work, like you said. This has to work."

"We know the plan. We'll just get this one home and safe, then we'll follow the plan."

CHAPTER 23

CONSTANCE

Jeffries arrived just after sunrise, mistletoe on his head. Under the guise of Polly Pooter, I hopped up and flipped my curly brown hair to and fro and acted as silly as I could muster, remembering how childlike the nymph was. "Roddy!" I cried. "Mistletoe! Do I get a kiss, Roddy? Please! Please can I have a kiss? It's mistletoe after all! Even if it's after Christmas! I WANNA KIIIIIISSSSSSSS!"

I hopped up on the bed and jumped up and down. My, I felt ridiculous behaving so, but I had to give the performance of my existence today. That demon inside him couldn't feel me before, but he sensed something was off. I had to put up extra barriers to block that sense from him, and I had to be flawless as Miss Pooter. So I would dance around and beg for scraps like a good little poodle. The alternative, I didn't know if I could survive it. I did know that I wouldn't want to.

Jeffries slithered up to the bed, slimy smile on his smug face. With the height of the bed, I was eye to eye with him. "Ready for this, Polly?" he said, sliding his arms around my tiny body. "It's been awhile. Can you stop at a kiss? You know we have to stop at a kiss, don't you?"

"I know, Roddy. I know." I pouted. "Just one, pleeeeeaaaaaase!"

"Just one?" With a condescending lilt, he mocked Polly with the power he held over her, humiliating her further, as if making her plead with him for affection wasn't embarrassing enough. Being inside Polly—being Polly—was horrible. Worse than Bedlam, imprisoned by a toxic love that forced her to perform like a circus dog for her very survival. I felt it. The noxious bond with Jeffries had become her life line. If he shunned her, discarded her, she would die from a broken heart, and her demise wouldn't be quick. It would linger as her mind left her, piece by piece. Until she was insane. Well, more insane.

I couldn't wait to get out of this body.

"Just one. I know. Just one!" I stuck Polly's bottom lip out and pouted, rocking side to side, as childlike as I could stomach.

He came in for a kiss, and her eager lips parted to meet him in joy. Mmmmm. So very tender and sweet, full of love. His tongue swept across mine, then went deeper. His lips lingered, sliding the bottom one over mine, causing me to catch my breath.

It was no act.

As he pulled back, I teetered, weak from such a powerful kiss. His hands were still around my waist, and once my eyes regained focus, his smug smile reminded me what was happening once again.

That was a kiss a man gives to his lover, and not just any lover, a serious this-is-real-and-forever lover. The bastard was going to manipulate her feelings for him even further, as if she wasn't already completely his slave. She had accepted their new arrangement, but now he was going to lead her to believe they would be together. Then destroy her, because somehow, that extra little bit of betrayal would be delicious to him.

A few moments of triumph to shatter another forever.

"Oh," I whispered through Polly's lips, still moist with him. "You haven't kissed me like that since…"

"I've been thinking." The intensity of his stare unsettled me, shook me to my core. He looked into my soul and I into his, but I saw no demon crouching there. Even though I knew this man was soulless, he had such skill as to make even me believe it. Insidious. "We've been so close these past months, and I know it's been hard on you to watch me with others, still wanting me for yourself. Still yearning for all of this." He swept his hand down his body to indicate all that Polly had been missing. "Yesterday, I realized something. As I watched you perform and dance—how I love to watch you dance—my heart felt such an overwhelming sadness. I watched you and saw my future, my life. Without you, Polly, I—I just couldn't survive." Tears formed in those grass green eyes, his face somber—yet so full of love. Along with the weight of his words, I was almost convinced. With all my experience and wisdom, such words spoken with such tenderness, coupled with the sexual ecstasy this man had mastered, would've swayed any woman's heart.

And he knew it.

It worked for him time and again, not often satisfied with quick romps or commonplace exploitation. No. Like Nicholas Stanton, he had to make them fall in love. The betrayal must taste like ambrosia to their blackened hearts.

Polly was his masterpiece, and now, at the will of the demon inside, he would get to relish her demise, savoring every second of this day, for a betrayal of this magnitude would keep him fed for months, perhaps even years.

I reacted as Polly would. Elation washed over me, and the entire room brightened around him. Not because of the dawn, for he was her only sun. "Oh, Roddy! Is it true? Can we be together again?"

"Yes," he whispered the word with such profound weight, emphasizing its significance. That one beautiful word carried the entire universe within it when it came to love. A tear slithered down his cheek. In another moment, his face filled with the bliss Polly felt, and he said it again, this time through a smile. "Yes," he whispered into my lips and kissed me again, lifting me off the bed and twirling me around.

I kissed him frantically, over and over, devouring his lips then placing tiny kisses all over his face before settling on his lips again. He laughed with me, and then we fell back on the bed together.

"I want you inside me, Roddy. Please. It has been so long!" It was a risk to say this, but it was also abundantly clear that he was in control. It would happen when he wanted it to, whether it was now or later. I held my breath as I waited for his response, looking up at him looming over me. Hoping beyond hope he wanted to milk this all day, otherwise, it might be the last words I ever spoke.

The skin on his face, normally so smooth, albeit deeply lined, fell forward in folds of flesh. Only his eyes, so full of love and desire, feigned yet convincing, made him recognizable in this position. My legs wrapped around him, inviting him, and I could already feel him growing against me.

Maybe it would be now. I swallowed hard.

Maybe this was the end, as Arthur and Avalon weren't set to come until after the Snake Oil Show.

It would be a relief, after all these centuries. Death was always a relief.

Perhaps I even hoped it would be now. Then, peace. At last. Time for someone else to protect.

Please, give me my respite.

He sat up and moved back, leaving me cold on the bed alone. Hands on hips. Face devoid of affect. Derisive snuffle. Then, after all that love and longing magically reappeared and glowed from every pore, he said, "I want to feel this longing for you all day. Let it charge me from the inside, and then tonight, devour you. For hours. Tonight will be all about you. Your desires. Your pleasure. All for you, my love."

"But—but—Roddy!   I   want   you   now! NNNOOOWWWW" I whined in my best impression of petulant child, extending every vowel in the most annoying way imaginable.

"Now, Polly," he said, getting that parental scolding gleam in his eye. "You know we have work to do today. You do know that, right? I mean, you do know we have things to do?"

"All right." I pouted, crossing my legs and arms at the same time.

"Get dressed," he said, patting my thigh. "Then tonight: wine, candlelight, you." As his lips brushed mine again with such tenderness, that spark of femininity deep inside me hoped it was all a misunderstanding. Hoped this was real. Not the demon inside. Not the cruelty. Not what all the evidence shows. Not what I'd seen with my own eyes. But this. This kiss. This love. This desire.

The cold air stung my lips, moist with his, as he withdrew. Before I could even open my eyes, he was at the door, arrogant stance and a taunting expression. "Right ho, Polly! Get dressed! I'll buy you a sticky bun…"

"Ooooh! Really? Really, Roddy? Splendid! Yes, a sticky bun is a great start. But—but then, later? You and me together again. Like it should be. You promise? You promise, Roddy?" I felt ridiculous speaking in the inflections of a child, but since

I had been watching and testing Jeffries these past months, I got a clear impression of Polly's mannerisms and her intense attachment and agony. This was what she would do, and although I had to fight back the nausea with every word and absurd action and farcical flip of her long mousy brown hair, it was essential to stop this monster from not only destroying me and Polly, but dozens or hundreds of others. In the mean time, I must appear to play his game. If he suspects I'm not Polly, Arthur and Avalon won't have time to get her to safety and I'll be annihilated, even with my considerable power. I had better not try to defeat him alone. We only have one chance to get it right, and if he gets away, he might never be stopped.

"Of course, I promise. Didn't I already tell you? In fact, how about dinner first. Just me and you at the patisserie down on Fleet Street?"

"Oh! Yes! Yes! Yes!" I said, now jumping up and down on the bed. Dinner, too? He's going to draw this out all day as part of his game. It would make his betrayal and violation all that more succulent for him.

"Wear a nice dress today, Polly. I'm taking you out, doing this properly." He stood and thrust out his chest, grabbing his lapels, mocking the English with his fake, over-annunciated accent. "Don't you know, Polly. We must all be *propa* and sort it out. Perhaps after a cup of tea. Yes. Splendid, indeed." He tipped his bowler and smiled. So charming. Even though I knew what was underneath, I still laughed along with his antics.

§

I performed Polly's part during the Snake Oil Show flawlessly, but then I had mastered the craft of impersonation long ago and had plenty of practice over the years. Arthur and Avalon had strolled by, precisely on time, as planned, and nodded to me while Jeffries was taking the money from those he had conned. I nodded back, then barked that horrendous braying of a laugh and twirled and danced some more.

Now I felt safe. They'd be just on the outside, looking in. They'd be there, unseen by Jeffries, until the time came, and then, goodbye Roddy. Forever.

Once all the people cleared away, Jeffries came over to me and slid his hand into mine, interlocking fingers. The softness of his hands revealed a man who had never done a day's hard labor in his privileged life. I obediently looked up at him with all the adoration I could muster, imagining starlight gleaming from my eyes upon all his glory and perfection.

I might be sick.

He danced with me in the street, and our eyes never left the other's. We spun around and showed the entire world just how much we were in love, just how very fortunate we were to have found each other.

Repulsive.

Then he took my hand and placed it in the crook of his arm. In all these months, I didn't think I had ever seen Jeffries look quite this smug. He was salivating in anticipation of ripping this little body in two with his big blue scepter, and he was going to milk this evening with everything he had, convincing Polly of the love and the desire he felt for her. Convincing her that he wanted her and only her. Then, destroy her.

How delicious that would be for him. His pièce de résistance, demolished. Built up and then shattered by the almighty him.

"Don't I look pretty today, Roddy? You haven't said anything about my dress." I held the bright blue skirt out from under the tattered overcoat and curtsied like a proper lady, then brayed again.

"Quite lovely, sweetheart. You are a vision. You're right, I had been so busy with work I hadn't really looked. You look stunning, sweetheart! Simply stunning."

I cupped and bounced the brown ringlets hanging down from my coiffed hair, braying anew.

So glad this night would be over soon. This act was ever so tiresome.

The patisserie of Fleet Street, a place called Mrs. Mooney's Pie Shop, was full of people, savoring the different flavors of pastries, pies, and cakes. Although meat pies were Mrs. Mooney's specialty, it had the reputation of containing unsavory sorts of meat. Having stopped eating animals long ago, I didn't understand the difference people saw in one dead animal from another. Another one of those cultural anomalies. Why was it all right to slaughter and eat a pig but not a dog or cat? It was all abominable.

For me, I did what I could to protect innocent life, regardless of species. Although it wasn't much, as my focus was elsewhere, I did not partake in the flesh of tortured and slaughtered animals, socially accepted cuisine or not. I had taken quite a bit of pleasure, more than usual, in setting that blasted butcher straight. Perhaps it would be him hanging from a meat hook before long.

I smiled at the thought.

Blokes like him rarely changed their behavior for long.

When he violated his wife or his daughter again, I'd be there.

We took a seat near the center where it was warm, as it was situated near the hearth and stoves. A large stone encasement had been built up in the center of the shop, and fires roared within the stone walls, beneath the iron grate on top where copper pots filled with savory foods. Four different chefs, dressed in white aprons and puffy white hats simmered and boiled and sautéd, each taking a section of the iron grate. More copper pots hung overhead along with bundles of drying herbs, all around the center pit. Just to one side, against the back wall, an archway of brick outlined the bread and pie oven. Cooks thrust in flat wooden paddles on the ends of long wooden poles, removing the bubbling pies and pastries.

Arthur and Avalon passed by the window, strolling by outside. Glad to see them still here. It wouldn't be long now, and I was a little nervous. It had to work. It just had to.

"I think I'll have the meat pie and some red wine," Jeffries said. "You? What do you fancy tonight, sweetheart. Other than me, of course. Remember, tonight is all about you. Whatever you want."

"Could I get an apple tart for dessert?"

"Of course, but you can't start with dessert." He tilted his head and gave me that condescending tone, paternal discipline in his eyes. The sides of his mouth turned up ever so slightly. Contempt. Then, wicked. Now sweet, loving. All imperceptible changes others wouldn't see. Their mind would register the changes. They'd feel off somehow, but they would explain it away, reminding themselves of just how funny and charming and handsome Jeffries was. They would push down that instinct that recognizes the predator, his particular form of insidious danger.

"All right," I said, pouting. "Here's a shepherd's pie, but will all vegetables. I'll try that. And yes, please, some wine. Can I have a kiss with wine? Please, Roddy, Please? I want a wine-flavored kiss, all right? Pleeeeeaaaase? Then an apple tart."

I clapped my hands together and vibrated with excitement.

"And a chocolate one, too?" I added.

"A chocolate one, too, my little spaniel. Yes, a chocolate one, too."

Jeffries stopped the wandering fiddler, and flipped him a shilling. "Play us something. This is a special night, a very special night." His sly eyes slipped back to me for a moment. Lips, smirking.

"Oh my, sir. Thank ya, sir. A ditty fer ya and the lady, sir? A ditty and a jig for this. Wha'eva ya like, sir." The dirty fiddler doffed his dirty hat and bowed with a flourish. A dirty dust cloud wafted after he hit his cap against his trousers before donning it again. Then pulling the bow across the strings, the fiddle whined once or twice, then burst into song.

Jeffries reached across the table and squeezed my hand, then flashed his duplicitous sneer. As the fiddler played and danced, Jeffries pulled out a long cigar and slid it under his nose, slowly. Inhaling. Savoring. His predatory stare fixed on me.

Quite unsettling.

After the fiddle had stopped and moved away, our meal was served. Jeffries even bought me a pansy from the flower girl's basket. He went all out.

Arthur and Avalon passed by the window again. This time Arthur looked at his pocket watch. It was getting rather late. With that small gesture, he told me they were ready to set this in motion. I wasn't sure I was. Rather afraid it wouldn't work. It would be horrible way to die, but it would be over soon enough.

Then, peace. Finally.

I extended my foot beneath the wooden table, having to crouch down in my seat because of Polly's height, and rubbed Jeffries' leg.

"Eager, are you, poodle? Can't wait to have me again?"

"You know all too well, Roddy," I said in a husky, breathy voice, dropping the childish act for a moment, if only to remind myself I was an adult. "Can we go to your place now? I don't think I can wait another moment."

Keeping up Polly's folly was rather exhausting.

That self-satisfying gleam sparkled in his eyes. Then, he nodded, smiling. He stood and reached for my hand. I took it and let him lead me out with an air of giddiness of the pleasures to come. Polly wouldn't know what was truly in store, she would expect the ecstasy and skill from before, of course. She would feel lucky to be beneath his touch again, feeling his tongue teasing her to climax again and again. Feeling him filling her, becoming one with her in the way only a con artist can. Intense eye contact while moving inside, feigning intimacy.

I had known other men like him in my long existence. Never one was genuine.

Trotting alongside of him, I chattered away, a little tipsy from the wine, all the way back to his. Happy we were heading there, as Polly's was too small and dingy. The neighbors too close. Jeffries' cousin, the notorious Madame Jeffries, set him up in a rather posh abode during his time in London. One of her "safe houses," a place she used to train, that is, break, the young girls she stole for sex slavery.

Perhaps a visit to Madame Jeffries next. Indeed.

§

He lowered me onto the bed, kissing me with such tenderness and love. Adoration. The promise of euphoria. The promise of forever. As he unbuttoned my dress, I, in turn, tried to relieve him of his jacket, but he guided my hands away.

"You are not allowed to move unless I say," he said with a seductive lilt. "That's the game. Remember, this is all for you. Your pleasure. Polly, my love, it's all for you."

I could almost see the demon crouching behind this monstrous man's eyes, both of them feasting on Polly's love, on her desire for him.

Jeffries relieved me from the satin gown and the petticoat beneath, and I lay naked before him, my body open wide, inviting. His deft lips and gifted tongue explored my body while his hands manipulated the lower parts, and I gave into the blissful waves of orgasm after orgasm, drenching his hand and the bed with each explosion.

"What do you want?" he taunted me.

"You. Please. Now." Breathless. Depleted.

"Not yet. You can't make a sound. No more screaming or moaning, just silence. Otherwise, I'll have to punish you."

I nodded and pursed my lips tight. I knew Arthur and Avalon were right outside, waiting for their moment, but I couldn't give into embarrassment and spoil the Polly illusion. The demon had to expose part of himself before they could begin, and there was only one part the demon would expose, at first.

His eyes never strayed from mine as he took off his jacket and loosened his cravat. Next, he removed his waistcoat and shirt beneath, revealing his well-defined torso. I grappled at his trousers, but he pushed my hands away, making a "tsk tsk tsk" sound and shook his finger at me for misbehaving.

"Don't make me punish you, Polly. I'll take you over my knee. Now, keep still." He slowly sunk between my spread legs, never breaking that predatory stare, and licked me. Slow circles, gradually increasing, bringing my body to the edge, which responded with a will of its own, despite other parts of me having to suppress the urge to be sick, knowing what he was. I bit my lip and grabbed the pillows, anything to keep me from crying out in so much disgust. I could barely contain it, and I'd known ecstasy in my time—the pain and the pleasure of it. That was what these men did: used pleasure for pain, ecstasy and love and sex as their weapons. Effective weapons, that. The best way to destroy a woman was to love her, then betray and abandon her, changing in an instant. No explanation. No remorse. No apology. Just leave. Sexual violence and violation—just the icing for these monsters, if they wanted to ensure the damage was irrevocable.

Try as I might to remain quiet, a tiny squeak emerged from my pursed lips as he tongue brought me again.

"That's it," he said, coyly, his chin wet with my pleasure. "Time for your punishment." He sat up, away from me so I might have a full view of what he'd unleash. His fingers fondled the buttons on his trousers, and the bulge beneath grew. Already much bigger than Jeffries had been before—he had been so much smaller than average—this demon's blue, scaly phallus would do much damage. Still, without dropping eye contact, it was almost as if he didn't blink, such was the intensity of his stare, he undid his buttons one at a time. "Are you ready for this?" he asked.

"Yes. Oh, yes! Yes, please!"

He laughed, then turned aside, and slipped his trousers off his hips, displaying his delicious derriere. Keeping his back to me, he looked back over his shoulder at me. I could see his hand making long, slow strokes along the length of the thing. How I hoped Arthur and Avalon were ready to break in, because once Jeffries made the big reveal, I wouldn't have much time.

"Are you sure you're ready for all of this?" he said, still turned over his shoulder.

"Yes! Yes, please," I repeated.

"Then, it's yours," he said through the biggest smile I had ever seen on his smug face. When he turned, I screamed. Polly screamed for sure, but even I screamed. The thing was even viler than I recalled. Easily three feet long. The underside had barbs curved back from the tip, even if the length of it didn't do damage—which it would in any sized body, but especially in one this small—the barbs would rip apart my insides with each thrust and withdraw.

Jeffries' devious grin turned into a barking laughter of his own at my screams.

Polly's little body scrambled in fear against the wall, trying to get away from him.

"But you said yes, my spaniel. Surely, you won't tease me, not after everything I've done for you. You said yes, so no turning back now."

"Get away from me! Roddy! What? Please! I—I don't understand. Please, don't hurt me," I whimpered.

"You can't get away from me. I think you've known that for quite some time. I own you, and tonight you are completely mine to do with as I will. Don't make me chase you, Polly. It will be all the worse for you."

My breath came faster and I wondered what was taking Arthur and Avalon so long. They should've burst inside by now. The demon was exposed enough to start the exorcism.

But I was alone.

Jeffries walked slowly toward me cowered in the corner, stroking his big blue erection and taking such delight in my fear. He would be upon me in a moment, and this body would never survive this.

I did the only thing I could do, to at least distract him for a minute.

I shifted.

Fast.

My breasts shrunk, legs lengthened, hair darkened. In an instant, I was Constance again.

Jeffries didn't even blink, but something almost impercep-tible flashed in his eyes.

Rage.

I had taken his triumph away, and now, if Arthur and Avalon would get in here, I would take away his life and damn the demon back to hell.

"You." A slimy smile slithered across his face. "Good. I was regretting not finishing you off last night. In fact, you were my priority after little Polly, but, no matter. I'll get her next."

"You won't, Jeffries. You will never hurt another woman."

The burst of laughter came out of his mouth with such force, it threw his head back. "Hurt? No, you're right. I'll never hurt another woman again. I will utterly destroy them. Every one of you bitches. I'll use you for the only thing you're good for, then discard you. Well, as I've always done, but now with such sharp end." He thrust his hips toward me and stroked his blue cock with both hands, slowly walking toward me. "Ready for all of this? No? Tough."

"Wait," I said, holding out my hands in defense. Where was Arthur and Avalon?

"Whatever for? I've spent the last hour pleasing you, mak-ing you orgasm repeatedly to the point of exhaustion, having to taste you and smell you. It's revolting. It was all meant for Polly, also disgusting, of course, but the betrayal would be so much sweeter with her. That's what it's all for, you see, to get them hooked on the pleasure, on all of this. Oh yes, it is so much more fun when they are in love, and, let's be honest, they always fall in love. How could they not? If you think I'm going to have done all of that for you, stomaching your stench, you whore, and not get what I want, you are sorely mistaken. You owe me. It's my turn now." He reached out for my throat, but I ducked under his arm and ran toward the door.

Then, he was there. In a blink, with his hand around my throat.

"But—how?" I squeaked.

"This is so much fun. You are so much fun." Turning, he flung me across the room back onto the bed. My head hit the wall, and I must've blacked out for a moment, because I came to with the horrid thing pinning me down and forcing my legs apart.

"No!" With every bit of power I could muster, I forced him off me, which should've hurled him back across the room and broken several bones when he hit, but he didn't go farther than the edge of the bed. Then he laughed, and I curled up in a protective ball, my ankles crossed and knees pulled in tight.

"Give up, sweetheart. This is happening. I'm so much stronger than you are now, imbued with power now that part of the demon is part of me. We're fused now, thanks to your little trick yesterday, and his power is my power, no longer trapped inside, as you can see." He sat on his knees across the mattress from me, his huge erection curling toward his torso, and his face went blank. That same terrifying lack of any affect whatsoever. It was more frightening than any scowl, any display of anger. Just nothing. Empty eyes. No expression.

Then that blasted, arrogant snuffle.

"Polly has done nothing but love you, Jeffries. Me, I understand. Destroy me, but Polly? How could you do that to her?"

"It's what he wants," he said, indicating the demon within. "And what he wants, I want. And I get what I want, when I want it. Period."

A noise outside the window made us both take a moment. It had to be Arthur and Avalon, finally. A tiny wave of relief washed over my trembling body. Jeffries saw it.

"Expecting someone?" he asked, smirking. "That luscious cunt from the other night, I hope."

"Her, and her beau as well. You will be stopped, Jeffries, and that demon inside you sent back to hell." Not a great plan to divulge this, but right now I just needed to stall.

"I took measures to ensure we were—alone, as I thought I'd be with Polly, and she's a screamer. Didn't want to be interrupted."

"Whatever you think you did, Jeffries, won't keep out a vampire, especially not two of them."

"Really? Then where are they? I'm getting rather bored with this conversation. One of the many intolerable things about women, they want to talk all the time. Talk. Talk. Talk. Talk. Talk. Talk."—I was on my back again with my legs spread before I even knew what had hit me.—"I'm a man of action."

With that, he plunged his huge blue demon inside of me, and I felt it rip through, up to my heart. I coughed, blood spurting out of my mouth, but Jeffries didn't move. He lay on top of me, looking down at me with adoration and love, and even now, it was so convincing. Even now, as I lay bleeding to death, I would've sworn he was true.

"Oh, yes. You feel so good, sweetheart. So very good. Your warmth and wetness surrounding me. I don't know if I'll be able to control myself. Just that put me on the verge, and I want this to last, a long, long time. Just, give me a minute." His voice was soft, loving.

Foul.

Time stopped.

Everything became a blur. Unreal, somehow. I knew I would die, as I should've died from that first violation centuries ago, but I wasn't afraid. I was glad. Finally, rest.

The door opened, and I heard someone say "Get off of her."

Then, Jeffries laughed.

Then, blackness crept in the sides of my vision and all became surreal, as if I was no longer there.

CHAPTER 24

ARTHUR

"Get off of her," I said, positioning the copper thing strapped to my arm at the ready. With just one flick of my wrist, one of the vacuum-packed vials of holy water would activate, shooting it across the room. Ten feet, Victor had said, and he was modest with that estimate. I had seen it in action, and although it was useless for vampire slaying, it would do some damage to a proper demon.

I hoped.

"Oh no!" Avalon said, likely commenting on the state of Constance, pinned beneath this beast, blood dripping from the corners of her mouth and splattered in tiny red spots all over her face, the wall next to her, and even on Jeffries, himself. Her eyes, unfocused, as if she was already gone, but she wasn't dead. Not yet.

"Focus, Ava," I said out of the side of my mouth, hoping she could keep it together enough to finish this. She raised The Slayer gun again, having let it droop in her shock.

That was my girl.

The Slayer had also been designed and built by Avalon's late friend, Victor. He had been a good man, and a good vampire hunter. Although these tools were built for fighting vampires, with a little modification, we were optimistic they would work on a demon. At least initially, enough to distract it in order to strike the final blow.

Constance had told us to hit the demon itself. Jeffries' body acted as a protective sheath, both for the demon and the world. Now that part of the demon protruded from him, they were more powerful, but also more vulnerable.

Jeffries turned his head to us, his face changing from pure love to amusement. He laughed. Then with the most dreadful ripping sound and the smell of fresh blood permeating the air, he withdrew from Constance. When I saw the thing, I felt at once a mixture of intense envy at the sheer size and horror at the rest. Seeing the barbs along the underneath side of it, I suddenly understood what the ripping had been. It looked rather purple, covered in blood and bits of Constance's flesh.

Avalon gasped, and I protectively stepped in front of her.

"Oh good. Fresh meat. A variety, too. Splendid. A man needs variety, after all. Maybe we could take turns being on top," he said to me.

Then with the speed of, well, me, he came at us. Luckily, we were as fast, and although any human watching would've seen but a blur, Ava and I were able to react in time.

He lunged at me, meaning to knock me out of the way to get to Ava, but we each ducked to either side of him, making Jeffries hit the oak door with all his forward momentum, splintering it with a loud crack. Another supernatural moment later, after shaking off the daze, he was on his feet. I lowered my aim and flicked my wrist, propelling holy water toward the giant phallus, but I missed, hitting his stomach. Human flesh. No reaction.

Jeffries smirked and turned toward my Avalon as I reloaded the gun with the next vial, ready to shoot again.

He would not rip apart my Avalon.

Avalon shot three rounds into Jeffries' chest, wooden bullets launched with compressed air from the copper revolver. Wood into the heart of a vampire would turn him to dust in an instant, and it would do quite a bit of damage to a human as well, likely killing him instantly, but a demon. Unknown.

It slowed him for but a moment, but then came taunting laughter again, followed by a hiss. Like the snake he was, he hissed. I took the opportunity to sprint next to Avalon, stepping in front of her, another vial at the ready. Just as I aimed, a howling erupted from Jeffries' tainted lips unlike I had ever heard. The smell of burning flesh mixed with the pervading coppery scent of blood. His eyes and hands jumped to the base of his monstrous blue erection, which started to soften, his lust fading away as the holy water dripping down from his stomach singed the base. He howled again.

I shot again, not missing this time. The vial burst on the engorged shaft this time.

Horrible wails. Smoke. Burning flesh.

Jeffries fell to his knees, glancing up momentarily with utter horror in his eyes before looking back down at disintegrating demon phallus. It melted as the holy water burned through it, before long, it detached into Jeffries' desperate hands.

"Bring it to me," a small voice from the bed said.

"Constance!" Avalon exclaimed, starting to go to her, but I stopped her. Jeffries wasn't dead yet. She understood, aiming The Slayer at his howling head.

"I don't really see how that's important at the moment, Connie. Just rest, we'll care for you when we're done here."

"No," she managed. "He can't get off so easily. He must be stopped. I need it—need it to shift, to heal. Its power. Quick. Please."

"I'm not touching that odious thing. Just wait, woman."

"She's right, Arthur," Avalon said, defying me. She pushed me aside, knocking the wooden stock of The Slayer gun against Jeffries' jaw.

She grabbed the withering phallus, as he raised one hand to cradle his bruised jaw, and tossed it to Constance on the bed. Jeffries and the demon inside had recovered their wits enough to retaliate, slapping Avalon to the ground and raring back from another blow, mouth wide, screaming in rage.

I shot another vial directly into the back of his throat.

Flesh ripping. Gurgle. Two blinks.

Then Jeffries' visage altered, the demon within pressing through. His nose morphed into a snake-like snout, teeth protruded, eyes black. Long mushroom-tipped snakes emerged from his head, writhing and squirming.

Avalon scooted back against me, and I took The Slayer from her and pushed her behind me once again.

Constance gasped, causing me to glance over at her shredded body. She had the severed, deplorable thing in her hand, and it dissolved into a black, oily ooze. Its power rippled visibly through her body, a new energy slid over her.

Jeffries hands split open as the demon's blue scaly fingers pushed through, and I knew I had but a moment to act before the demon was upon me, and a few drops of holy water wouldn't work fast enough before he ripped my head off. Improvising, I took some of the vials from my arm apparatus and loaded them into The Slayer. They were about the same size and shape of the wooden bullets, so hopefully it wouldn't jam the gun. Thrusting The Slayer forward until I felt the barrel against the morphing thing's chest. Just as its horrid claw clamped around my throat and started squeezing, I pulled the trigger.

I couldn't tell if The Slayer had misfired or not at first. Avalon was tugging on the demon's arm, trying to get him to let me loose, but then revelation came over the demon's face. Realization of what had just happened. The holy water had pierced the demon's heart and was dissolving it from the inside out.

It released me, and Avalon came to my aid as my knees faltered.

"Not yet," Constance said, standing behind him, arm outstretched to the half-demon-half-Jeffries head. The dual creature wailed anew as Constance pulled Jeffries and the demon apart. Channeling Jeffries and his consciousness through her body and into the poppet in her other hand.

I held Avalon close and massaged my throat, unable to process what I saw. The weakened incubus dripped black bile from the heart and groin wound. Even the snakes on its head slowed, slumped into lethargy.

Constance cinched the head of the poppet and tossed it onto the bed, unceremoniously.

"Now," she said. Blood caked around her lips and down her naked thighs, she stepped up behind the dying body of the demon and placed a hand on either side of its head.

But the demon was not yet ready to die. It spun around and faltered in its weakness, but not before knocking Constance's legs out from under her. She hit the floor with a thud, but in a moment had sprung into a readied stance.

Then, she shifted.

Not into Polly Pooter.

Not into anything remotely human.

She shifted.

Long leathery wings burst from her back, spreading the width of the room. Her ears elongated into sharp points, and her flesh cracked, still the same hue, only as if her entire body had been shattered into a million pieces, like broken porcelain. Talons emerged from the tip of each finger, and her eyes turned completely black. Bony protrusions extended from each shoulder and at the end of each wing. Her lips, full and blood red, turned up into a smile, and said, "Let's try this again, shall we?"

The incubus hissed, as he lay weakened, and Avalon held me tightly against her.

Constance, in what I could only assume to be her true form, stepped up to the demon again and placed her clawed, shattered hands on either side of his head.

"Wait," it said. "Don't."

"No," she said.

Nothing more.

Then twisted his head clear off.

"Arthur," she shouted. "Finish it."

I scrambled to my feet and out of Avalon's grasp, who didn't want me to be away from her, nor I from her, readied the holy water apparatus, and shot a stream into its gaping neck. It sizzled and dissolved. The creature's head, which Constance held by the now-limp mushroom-tipped snakes, screamed in agony as its body melted into Jeffries' fine rug. Soon to follow, his head disintegrated in a pile of ooze, like sand dripping through an hourglass, until Constance's hand was empty. She spun around, and when she faced us again, she looked human. Like Constance again, fully clothed. Blood gone. Standing strong.

She folded her hands properly on top of one another and said, "That's done. Thank you, Arthur, Avalon, for your help. Demon sausage."—soft chuckle—"who knew it was so potent?"

"Is it dead?" I asked, although that seemed rather evident.

"This manifestation is, for now. Evil cannot be destroyed, sadly, but it has been cast back to hell. It will take some time to work its way back to this plane. If ever. Likely not even in our long lives."

"Good work," I said.

"What about Polly?" Constance asked.

"I instructed Thomas to secure her transport back to the Colonies."

"Perfect. She'll need the support of family to get through the next year."

"Thank goodness it's all over." Avalon's soft lips pressed against my temple. I was so grateful she was here, unharmed, at least not permanently harmed. I loved her so much. Closing my eyes, I savored this moment in time, embraced in Avalon's love. Safe.

"Ahem," Constance cleared her throat, and when I opened my eyes, in my horror, Chastity stood in her place. "Your turn," she said.

CHAPTER 25

CONSTANCE

Still charged from the demon meal, such power, I held Avalon against the wall with one extended hand, and with the other, I made a sharp movement that pulled Arthur away from her and cast him onto the bloody bed, which had so recently almost become my tomb.

"No!" Avalon cried, but I didn't listen, just kept her held to the wall with my right hand extended out toward her. My left motioned through the air, imposing my will on Arthur. I stripped him bare and pinned him onto the bed, legs and arms spread wide.

Always. My will.

"Please," Avalon pleaded. "He just saved you! Without him you would be dead. Without him, I'd be dead. Please! Constance, please. I beg you. Spare him."

Whipping my head around to her, I reasoned, "Look at him! He was barely a man when he died. He's a perpetual child in the body of a man with supernatural power. Do you know how dangerous that combination is? He wants what he wants when he wants it, and he cares nothing about anything or anyone else. People are just a means to an end. They're food, or tools for ejaculation and pleasure. They're entertainment, like watching a play. If he doesn't like the show anymore, he finds another theatre, burning the last. You've experienced this, Avalon. You know this."

"I do, and I was hurt and angry, and I'm still hurt and angry. And. I don't know. He does deserve something, but not this. I—I love him."

"You are bonded to him, through his cruelty. Ironic, indeed, but it creates a very deep, almost unbreakable link. Once you're free of him, you will thank me. Just as Polly will thank us for freeing her. Jeffries got what he deserved, and now Arthur will, too."

"He's not like Jeffries. He's not possessed with a demon. He's not a rapist."

"Tsk—tsk—tsk." I shook my head in disappointment, but with understanding. Denial. A durable force. "You told me how he treated you that day. That was rape. You even said so yourself, Avalon."

"It was just that once. Maybe he just got carried away."

"He is a rapist, Avalon, and trust me, it wasn't just that once. He's not possessed with a demon, no. He, like Jeffries, chooses to violate, to hurt. Jeffries' choices attracted that demon. We've been over this, and although the severity might not match Jeffries, Arthur has been doing this far, far longer. That's the thing about rape, one only needs to commit it once to be labeled a rapist. That never goes away. Even if you were the first, which you weren't, and even if you were the last, which you weren't—isn't that right Arthur. The chambermaid on the airship? Yes. At least her in the past week, isn't that right?"

"Let me go, you ungrateful bitch," Arthur spat, but I sewed his mouth shut so he couldn't say any more.

"That's not true. Arthur, is that true?"

"Careful, Arthur, your response will determine whether I will show mercy or not. You've already earned some for saving me, but you have hundreds of years and thousands of women to atone for. Answer her carefully."

"Arthur? My love?"

Arthur, much to my great surprise, admitted it. He nodded, slowly, with shame.

Avalon's horror erupted from her soul, and as I released my hold on her, she fell to her knees in grief. Weeping. Gasping for breath. "It can't be. It can't be. I gave myself to you. Trusted you. Loved you. And this? How can you be this? Has everything been a lie? All of it?"

Again, shocked, Arthur nodded. At first, but then his eyes widened and he shook his head from side to side.

"Don't you see? To him, you are not a person with feelings, with a heart and soul. He took those from you. Arthur did one worse than these other men. He not only destroyed your soul through insidious manipulation and eventual betrayal, he quite literally stole your soul. He took your humanity, dehumanized you because it's what he wanted. Now you, too, are damned, and you never had a choice.

"You but fell in love."

"I did fall in love," she said so softly, broken. "So deeply in love. Never before. I had sworn off love because of this, but he convinced me. He broke down my protective barriers and made me love him. All…for nothing."

Arthur shook his head, more violently than before. Fixing his eyes on me, he pleaded with me, jutting his chin out at me, wanting to speak.

"Do you want to hear what this man has to say, Avalon?"

"It will only be more lies."

"Likely."

"I don't care. Let him speak."

I loosened the cords around his mouth, allowing him to speak.

"I'm so sorry, Ava," he said. "I am a horrible monster, and I have been for centuries. She's right, but I've changed. Your love, my dear. I've only realized how much in just the last few days, and seeing how Jeffries' lust for power and sex consumed him, destroyed him. I've learned. I see my pattern now. I see what I've done to you, to others. Always expecting perfection, expecting Catherine. But even she wasn't perfect, but she was perfect because I knew her. I took the time to know her, to love her, to respect her. I don't want a replacement for Catherine any more. I want you. I want to invest in this with you. Just in that moment before she turned to Chastity, I knew. I felt it with every fiber of my being. I love you, Ava. I'm safe with you, and I shan't treat you so roughly ever again."

Tears fell from Avalon's eyes one after the next, but I just rolled mine. I had heard it all before, although, they didn't usually admit to rape, no matter what, and this one did. He turned to me and said, "Please. I've changed. Please show me mercy."

"What of the *thousands* of women you destroyed over the years? Thousands! Do they get no vengeance? And the ones you killed, they are the lucky ones, save poor Lady Haldenby, of course. The others you cast aside, alone, ruined, devastated insane. What of them, Arthur? You say you've changed? I've been looking for you for a hundred years, Arthur Tudor. Oh yes, I know who you are."

"I have changed, and I don't blame you for not believing me. You're right. I do deserve to be punished for what I've done. I have destroyed thousands. Every word you say is true, and I am completely at your mercy."

This was new.

"Please," Avalon whispered, and began crawling over to Arthur spread out on the bed. When she got to the edge, she reached out and placed a hand on his foot, looking up at him with love.

"Ava, his love for you wasn't real. He's even admitted as such. Astounding, really, but there it is. He says he loves you now, but how can you trust it? Everything has been a lie, and after the way he's treated you, violated you, cast you aside. Remember, just days ago, he threw you over for me. You know full well just how intimate we were. He didn't love you. It was an illusion, a fantasy, Avalon."

"My love was real. My love is real, and I ask for your mercy, too. Please, Constance. Please. Spare him."

"You are foolish to believe he will be different with you, Avalon. Do you think your love cured him? This monster who has destroyed thousands. It is our own arrogance to think we can love the monster out of the man. More often than not, the woman who tries damns herself to a lifetime of abuse-but, your choice, my dear.

"When the newness wears off, again, and he becomes bored, again—*and he will*—you will see his true face. You already have, remember, when he was fucking me. When he was forcing you, enjoying your tears. Your sorrow and fear feeding his lust. But this time, I'll be there, waiting."

"Thank you!" Avalon said, throwing herself onto Arthur's body, kissing him all over. "Thank you! Thank you!"

"I'm not finished," I said. "He will be punished for the thousands he destroyed."

"But—you just said."

"I'll make a compromise, as I'm not an unreasonable woman. Besides, he admitted it, seeming to repent without provocation." I moved to the opposite edge of the bed and sat down, transforming into the visage of Constance once again. "You have so much faith in him, Ava, and I believe it is quite unwarranted, but this is a new situation for me. First, he's repentant. Never in five centuries has a man admitted to it. Well, not with the intention of accepting his punishment. Repentance does not go unnoticed. No. So, he's repentant. Next, he's apologized, which is often empty words, but mixed with his willingness to take what punishment I deliver, he might be sincere."

"I am!"

"Shut up, Arthur. I'm not finished. Plus, he did just save my life, which is also worth some mercy, as I've already said, and finally, you're requesting it. My friend. Although I know well his kind, and as soon as he's out of this entanglement and threat of eternal torment, give it a week or two—a few months at the outset—he'll be back to his old tricks."

"I won't! I promise!"

"Enough from you." I tightened the cord around his lips again. "The ladies are talking. You are no longer in control, Arthur. Not even a little bit. Your fate is completely up to us. Your freedom, gone. Your entire existence is in our hands. What do you think we should do with you?"

Again, surprise. He didn't fight or rail. No anger appeared in his eyes, just a tear.

With a nod, with complete acceptance of his fate, he relented.

"Here is what I shall do, and I'm afraid, this is not up for negotiation. You believe in him, Avalon, so I will allow it. But if you are mistaken, if he, but for a moment falters, the punishment will take hold. Now and forever. Stand back, and let me do my work."

"Don't hurt him," Avalon cried.

"Ava. Let me do my work, or this compromise is void. Stand back or I shall force you back, and I really don't want to do that. This must be done."

Avalon nodded, caressed the side of Arthur's face, and kissed his sewn lips, then stepped away, hands pulled in tight, fearful of what I would do. Removing the poppet I had prepared from my reticule, I laid it on the bed, and Avalon gasped. I shot her a warning glance, then removed the scissors and blade as well. After taking a clipping of his auburn hair and a sample of blood, I closed the poppet's head and placed it back into my reticule.

"Here is your deal, Arthur. Normally, I take the heart, so I can see when to release the suffering consciousness, when it turned white, I knew to release the soul from its torment. Now, I'm letting you keep your heart, so you may love."

"Oh! Thank you, Constance," Avalon cried. "Thank you."

"I'm not finished. There is a catch. Because I don't have your heart, I cannot release you from your torment, so there will never be a release. Ever. Unless Avalon or someone on your behalf finds me again and pleads your case. Again. I have no doubt you have a millennia of atonement ahead of you if you falter. Which, I have no doubt you will. You're lucky, Arthur, to have this woman who believes in you as she does. But, as so many things that seem good at first, it might just be your damnation."

"What do you mean, Constance? What torment? I thought you were going to spare him."

"For now, but as I said, if he falters, he's mine. Forever."

I whispered the words and cast the spell, weaving a new one, a special one for this special case. Avalon watched, eyes wide. Their respect for my position and power did not go unnoticed, so I showed them another kindness.

"Avalon, your love is as pure as any I've seen, so I will do one more thing for you. Here," I said, removing a white feather from my reticule, "through this, you may contact me. At any time, if you wish to change his fate and give him over to the standard punishment, give me his already dead heart. His torment will end when he pays his debt. Or for any other reason, call me, and I will come." Turning to Arthur, I was surprised to see a kind of peace in his eyes. A release. Resolve.

"Forsake her, even in thought, and the spell will be broken. You will forever be trapped, impotent, tormented. In her sight—in her love—you shall be spared. As long as you love her and she loves you, you will have a reprieve, but, every day while she sleeps, you will atone. If she dies, you will atone. Unless you are within her conscious presence, you will atone. As far as that's concerned." I indicated that which he had used to hurt so many. "It will work for Avalon, only in love. Only through her love. Otherwise, you will be impotent. In fact, for the first year, you will be impotent regardless. You will learn to love without sex."

"You're taking away his free will."

"I'm not, really. I'm giving him a reprieve for your love. I'm counting on your judgment and your love for him to save him, although, in the end, I know it won't. It never does. He is not true, Avalon, but you believe he can be. For your sake, not his, I hope you are right. For your sake," I continued, turning back to Arthur, "you will be true or you will be in the most horrific agony imaginable. Only what you have inflicted on so many thousands. No more, no less. Although, in your case, unless your atonement continues unfaltering, it will be unending. Forever and ever. Amen."

As soon as I released him from his invisible restraints, he ran into the arms of his love, and she welcomed him with a heartfelt embrace and kisses.

"How touching," I said.

CHAPTER 26

ARTHUR

I wasn't sure what had just happened, but I was in the arms of my Avalon again. All would be all right in the end. The succubus had spared me.

"Thank you," I said to her, and I meant it. Truly meant it with all that I was.

She did not smile.

"You're not free, Arthur. You will pay for the suffering you've caused. You will pay for every second of it."

"I know. I accept that fate. I will atone, properly."

"You cannot escape it, not even like this."

Her hand clasped the headboard's spindle and with a loud crack she broke it off. She whipped around, faster than even I could move, and when she stood back, she smiled. Avalon held a look of horror. A pain in my chest consumed every other thought. The wooden stake struck right through my heart, but it didn't kill me. It should've killed me.

"Perfect," she said. "As you see, you cannot be killed now, Arthur. Even a stake will not release you. Your body is now your prison, forever. Allow Avalon here to teach you the true meaning of love."

Avalon's hand hovered over the stake, afraid to touch it or move it. Blood tears flowed from her eyes, and from mine. Was this the torment the succubus spoke of? Watching my love in pain over me? The torture of having my freedom taken away, at being at the whim and control of a woman?

Perhaps it was what I deserved.

Perhaps death would be welcomed.

"Not even death?" I whispered.

"No. Not even like that. Death is a release, Arthur. A relief, and you will never know relief. Not until you pay for what you've done. Not until you suffer the sum of all the suffering you've caused for over three centuries. Thousands of women. Men, too. Families. Rape. Murder. Exploitation. Each one of their lives were forever altered because of you, Arthur. Now, you will take responsibility for that pain. You will accept responsibility for every moment of pain from every single soul you damaged. You will pay it back in kind."

"Is there no reprieve? But I said I'd repent? What can I do to repent?"

"You can start by admitting it all and apologizing for it. Genuine, remember. Not just words. Not just out of fear, but from your blackened heart. You will repent or you will beg for the true death. For centuries you'll beg for release, and during all that time, you will be unable to hurt anyone else."

"I do admit it. I did already and I will do so again. I have done horrible things, and I deserve this punishment. I am sorry for all of it. The weight of the truth suffocates me. I've hidden behind denial for so long, justification and power and privilege, but now, I can't run anymore. I'll face it now, and it is horrible. The guilt, the sorrow. Oh God!" I thought I'd be sick. As I fully, truly admitted what I had done, without justification, every scream, every plea for mercy came rushing back, threatening to stifle the undead life from me.

It would be welcome. It would be a release.

"Just to be very clear, if you, even in thought, think yourself above Avalon, try to control her, behave or think you own her, or lie to her, you will be thrust into your punishment. Forever. You will learn what it means to love. You will take your atonement seriously. You will get a taste of your punishment every day while Avalon sleeps. Do you accept this?"

"I do. Completely." After all, I didn't have much of a choice. How bad could it be anyway? If I had Avalon by my side, I could endure anything. I kissed her then.

"If you so much as look at another woman in lust, this is what will happen," she said. In an instant I was enveloped in darkness. Nausea overcame me, unlike I'd ever known. If the worst sickness I had known in all my time was nausea, this was something altogether worse. Gorge rose, not from my stomach, but from my tainted soul. I felt a panic. My breath came fast and horrific images of every woman I had ever had, ever taken by force, pelted my brain. Not just their images, but what they felt. Their fear. Oh, God. No. This couldn't be what it had been like for them. I leaned over to vomit, but I had no body, no mouth. Just pain. Just fear. Just darkness. Just agony.

Every scream. Every plea. Like before, but tenfold. A hundred fold. Not just some distant memory now, but as if I was living it. As if I was them experiencing the violation. The murder. The humiliation. It was a kind of agony that surpassed all physical pain, for I have endured physical pain, and there was a realness to it. Horrible, yes, but always satiable. Not this. Somehow because it was intangible it made it all the more horrific, all the more unbearable. It was bottomless. Timeless.

It was forever.

Every moment lasted a lifetime, and I knew I had been abandoned here. Alone in this despair and darkness. Forever. Years passed in every moment. Each second stretched out for an eternity. No relief. No breath. Nothing but fear. Pain. Unspeakable agony.

Then, as quickly as it had started, it was gone. Constance and Avalon stood before me once again.

"That's what is waiting for you, Arthur. The moment you slip up. The moment she is no longer happy or loved or absolutely adored, genuinely, this is what awaits you. If she dies, this is what awaits you. When you die, this is what awaits you, but you will not die. You cannot die, not unless this woman wills it. Not unless you have atoned for all, and this woman wills it."

I gasped for breath, then leaned over and vomited blood.

"This is mercy?" Avalon cried. "This is hell!"

"What did you expect, my dear? It is hell, the same hell he has inflicted on countless women, men, families, children. It is hell, but the mercy is in the reprieve. Jeffries here," she said, shaking his poppet at us, "he will know no relief, not even a moment of it for, I would guess, a few centuries. Likely a millennium. Arthur will feel relief every night in your arms, through your love.

"That's mercy, Avalon. That is the only mercy I can offer. Or," she said, pointing to my dead heart, "I could take his heart and consciousness now, and he will start his own millennia-long atonement, uninterrupted like the rest."

"No!" Avalon and I said together. Then Ava continued, "No. Thank you, Constance. You are merciful in allowing us this time. He will change. He has changed. You'll see. He will be genuine. May I ask for one thing?"

"You may."

"Allow him choice. Allow him his thoughts." Avalon's eyes pleaded with Constance, begged her for mercy on my pathetic behalf.

"Ava. That's where betrayal starts." Constance remained cold, detached. Even her tone was flat.

"True, and I'm not asking you let up on your sentence, but I don't want to control him. I don't want him to fear me or be forced to love me. That's not love."

"Too true, my dear. Too true." With this, Constance raised an eyebrow, in curiosity, perhaps.

"Allow him his choice. If he is unhappy, let him think it, as long as he talks to me. If he desires another woman, let him desire her. As long as he is open and honest with me about that and everything. As long as he is willing to be vulnerable. As long as he is genuine. That's all I or anyone can ask. Allow us to build true intimacy. Allow him to learn genuine love. Allow him his choice. I only require him to be respectful and loving, open and honest. I don't want him imprisoned."

Constance crossed her arms and set her jaw. Her eyes became misty, but then hardened again when she fixed them on me. "That is love, Arthur. Do you see? She is already teaching you the true meaning." She softened again when she turned her attention back to my beloved Avalon. I didn't deserve this fine woman's love, and Constance knew it. "I will allow him his thoughts and what you ask, but if he chooses to leave you, or you choose to leave him, if he is cruel or condescending or disrespectful or violent in any way, I'm afraid what I said holds. You need not be lovers. You need not force anything. Do be genuine, be real. But he will learn commitment. He will learn the true meaning of love, and there are many forms of love, not just erotic. He will learn, and when you sleep, he will be reminded of what he's done. If this is an act, I have no doubt he will soften for real, quite quickly. People who've known suffering, they're kinder. I think even this taste of what he's caused has already made him kinder."

"Indeed. It has. I had no idea. Truly. It was as you said, like they weren't real. Like they were puppets or like your poppet, there for my enjoyment, but now I can feel it. Now I can feel them, and I am so sorry. Ava, my sweet love, I am so ..."

"It's called empathy, Arthur. Welcome to humanity," Constance said, then turned to leave. "Remember the feather, Avalon. Call me if you ever need me on this or any matter." She turned to me with eyes of stone one last time before she left. "Arthur, behave."

"You know I will," I called out after her, and I felt a wave of peace flow through my heart, and it wasn't just because I removed the wooden splint from it. There was truth in her words, and I felt it. As sure as I felt Avalon's lips all over my cheeks and eyelids and forehead, and, finally, lips. No stirring below, even as she kissed me deeper.

Impotent for a year, she said. I thought that would be horrifying, but it actually felt like freedom.

CHAPTER 27

CONSTANCE

It wouldn't be too sad to leave this place. Although I loved London, this had been a trying time. Back home, Everett packed for the journey back to Paris. We'd start there for a bit of a holiday, then on to New York. Still, something kept nagging me from my time in London, something I couldn't shake.

I had given Arthur a reprieve, of sorts, showed him mercy. Being so close to my own end got me thinking perhaps I could love for myself.

Although my stomach fluttered like a young girl's, having her first dance with that handsome stranger, not knowing what horrors were possible, I rapped my knuckles on the door and held my breath.

A midsize, rather roundish butler answered the door. "Yes?"

"Miss Charlotte Sopha calling. Is the baron available?"

"I shall check, ma'am. Do come in from the cold and wait in the parlour."

"Thank you," I said, stepping into the warm house. His home was as he was: comforting and inviting, and somehow kind. Although I knew he was a man of some means, titled and the like, not to mention his inventions, but his home was far from lavish. Basic necessities with an elegance and just a hint of whimsy. "I rather think I'm in love," I said to the empty parlour.

"Miss Sopha!" Vincent's voice delighted my ears. I turned to see him smiling at me. "To what do I owe this very pleasant surprise?"

"I'm leaving London, I'm afraid, and I couldn't bear to do so without saying goodbye."

"Oh, I'm so sorry to hear that. I am ever so pleased to have made your acquaintance, Charlotte. So, did the interview not go well? Forgive me," he said as soon as the words left his lips. "How rude of me to pry."

"Nonsense, Vincent. I had promised to tell you, and I'd like to tell you much more. Might we speak in private?"

"My dear, I wouldn't want you to feel unsafe. I have heard tales, after all."

"I am quite sure you are the perfect gentleman, Baron. I feel perfectly safe with you."

"Very well." He turned and shut the doors to the parlour, and moved across the room to a bizarre contraption. It looked like a big horn protruding from a wooden box. A black disc sat beneath an arm attached to the horn. He cranked the handle and tilted the brass end of the arm until it rested on the black disc, which was now turning.

Music came from it!

"Whatever is that?"

"It's something called a Victrola, my dear. Yes. Not invented for several years yet, so must keep it quiet for now. It is rather remarkable, though, isn't it?"

"It is indeed!"

"Yes, this will keep us protected from prying ears. What would you like to tell me, Miss Sopha?"

"Please, call me Charlotte."

He nodded and sat on a chair adjacent to the sofa on which I sat. Perfect gentleman.

"This will all be rather difficult to say, I'm afraid, and even more difficult to believe."

"Nonsense, I've seen more than most, and there is nothing too bizarre for me anymore. No, not anymore."

"Well, you see, Vincent, to be quite frank, I'm rather in love with you."

"Oh! My! Well, my dear, of all the things I thought you would say, I must admit that was the last. You had been quite clear of your level of interest on the airship. Why this change of heart?"

"It's not a change of heart, but rather a change of mind. Allow me to explain. First, I'll show you my preferred visage."

His brows furrowed, not knowing what I meant by this, but then arched high on his forehead as I shifted to Constance before him.

"Oh. Well. That is indeed something I haven't come across before. Are you human, my dear?"

"I was. I still am in some ways. I'm a succubus." I braced myself for the cringe and questions about being a demon and the like, but none came. So I offered, "I'm not a demon."

"I'm well aware of what a succubus is, my dear. Vengeance mostly, isn't that right? Well, that explains why you were keeping company with McFerret. I suppose you were the cause behind his disappearance? The Professor's, too, no doubt."

There wasn't a trace of judgment or disapproval in his voice. It was as if we were discussing the weather over tea. "I was. Well deserved, both."

"Of that I have no doubt. But I am curious as to why you are here. Why have you revealed your true self to me? Am I to be punished?"

Again, no fear. No accusatory tone. This man wasn't jumping to defense because there was no defense needed. How refreshing to be in the presence of true courage.

"No. My heart is not my own, you see. My existence is to punish men and protect women, but I started to wonder, after having a rather rough week, if there wasn't some room for both. Perhaps I could love again. I have many faces, as you see. I can be whomever you want. Fulfill your every fantasy."

"Sweet Charlotte, is that your name?"

"Constance."

"Yes, Constance. It suites you. I think you know well my affection for you, but I'm afraid I have no need of fantasy. I desire a genuine woman, real love, which, I suppose, is why I am a bachelor. There aren't many genuine people, are there, Constance?"

"No, Vincent, not in either gender, although your odds are better than women's, I'm afraid."

"No doubt. No doubt. I'm not suggesting you are disingenuous, my dear, not in the least! Your courage to reveal yourself to a virtual stranger is testament to your integrity. Indeed. Although I would be honored to call you my own, with your work, you could never be, could you?"

"Not completely, and I know that's not fair to you."

"I couldn't bear to think of what you must endure, time and again. Oh, Constance, would you leave it behind? Not for me, of course—I would never ask a woman to alter her life to suit me—but for your own safety? Your own happiness?"

"It is who I am now."

"Understood."

There wasn't much else to say. I pulled a white feather from my reticule, the last one I had brought on this trip, and handed it to him. "If you should ever change your mind, Vincent, or even want a traveling companion now and again, for I would love to see the future—only the future, I've had enough of the past—just whisper into this feather, and I will hear."

"Perhaps out of time will be our time, my dear. Somewhere out of time."

THANK YOU SO MUCH FOR READING.

I HOPE YOU ENJOYED
THE ADVENTURES OF ARTHUR,
AVALON, & CONSTANCE.

PLEASE CONSIDER WRITING A REVIEW ON
AMAZON.COM AND GOODREADS. JUST A
FEW SENTENCES IS SO VERY APPRECIATED.

PLEASE SHARE IT ON YOUR NETWORKS &
RECOMMEND IT TO YOUR FRIENDS!

PEACE.

Acknowledgements

Special Thanks to...

My amazing husband, Ethan, for your unending support and for standing by me through the toughest and most wondrous times. I love you.

My awesome beta readers who gave me invaluable feedback and confidence to move forward:
>James Conrad Agin
>Bekah June
>Adrian Hutchens
>C. L. Stegall
>James & Deborah Kent

Susan Greene & LaMon Perales. Your care and concern helped me find my voice again. Thank you for all that you do for survivors of sexualized and domestic violence.

 A special remembrance for my buddy, buddy boy, Oreo. Beloved son and companion for well over a decade. He died an untimely death during the same month I wrote this book: January 2013.

You will never be forgotten, my love. You are now with Brontë and Star. I'll be joining you all shortly.

OTHER BLUE MOOSE PRESS TITLES

Rowan of the Wood

Winner of the 2009 Indie Excellence Award

978-0-9819949-2-5 $12.95 trade paperback

After a millennium of imprisonment in his magic wand, an ancient wizard possesses the young boy who released him. Plus, somehow the wizard's bride from the ancient past has survived and become something evil.

http://www.rowanofthewood.com

Witch on the Water

Rowan of the Wood: Book Two

978-0-9819949-2-5 $12.95 trade paperback

Rowan's wife, the sadistic vampire Fiana, comes back seeking revenge, Cullen and his band of misfits must do what they can to stop her.

Fire of the Fey

Rowan of the Wood: Book Three

978-0-9819949-6-3 $12.95 trade paperback

Still possessed by the wizard Rowan, Cullen settles into his new home with his fire elemental sister, Aidan, and their fey uncle, Moody Marlin. But all is not well. A series of fires raging through the redwoods puts Aidan in the hot seat, as the group looks to her for an explanation.

Power of the Zephyr

Rowan of the Wood: Book Four

978-1-936960-94-1 $12.95 trade paperback

The Freak Squad, as Trudy takes to calling them, confront Fiana in the desert of Northern Nevada. she has developed a cult of mesmerized zombies in an intricate plot to capture Rowan and his wand for herself, once and for all.

ABOUT THE AUTHOR

Nestled in the mountains of Northern California, Olivia M. Grey lives in the cobwebbed corners of her mind writing Gothic stories and controversial nonfiction. Olivia focuses both her poetry and prose on alternative relationship lifestyles and deliciously dark matters of the heart and soul. Her work has won various awards, been on Amazon's Gothic Romance bestseller list, and has been published in various anthologies and magazines like *Stories in the Ether, Steampunk Adventures, SNM Horror Magazine* and *How The West Was Wicked.* Visit her blog for a list of her complete published works: http:// omgrey.wordpress.com

Under the name Christine Rose, Ms. Grey also writes the award-winning YA fantasy series *Rowan of the Wood* with her husband, Ethan. Find articles on publishing, writing, marketing, and meet emerging authors on Christine's blog: http:// christinerose.wordpress.com

Connect with her on Twitter: @omgrey
On Facebook: http://facebook.com/OMGREY